The Ascension
Book Two

The Mists of Faeron

Cover Illustration by Henning Ludvigsen.
Interior Illustrations by Henning Ludvigsen.

Brick Cave Books
brickcavebooks.com
2012

In loving memory of
Kasim Amyx
Feb 28, 1976 to Feb 7, 2007

By J.A. Giunta

THE ASCENSION
Book One: *The Last Incarnation*
Book Two: *The Mists of Faeron*
Book Three: *Out of the Dark* *

  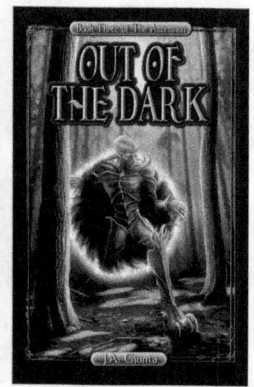

THE GUARDIANS
Book One: *Knights of Virtue*

* Forthcoming

The Mists of Faeron

J.A. Giunta

Acknowledgements

I'd like to thank my wife Lori for all her help, support and understanding. Writers aren't the easiest people to live with. I'm probably worse than others.

My daughter Ada often reminds me, through actions and words, that I'm a father first. She's five at the time of this writing, and I think she inherited my addiction to video games. Sorry honey!

My good friend Melissa Clazie, who teaches English to a great bunch of kids at La Sierra High School, was a big help in getting me away from World of Warcraft and finishing this book. She then helped me with editing and proofreading. Thanks again, Melissa!

Thanks to my beta readers and proofreaders: Nelson Sperling, Deb Bozek, Karen Miller, Scott Macy, Heather Baldwin and Greg Highberger.

It's difficult, to say the least, to find every typo and grammatical error in such a large body of work. I need all the help I can get.

Thanks to my family, friends and fans (hey, I have a couple) who continue to support my work. It would be much more difficult to write without knowing you're out there frantically waiting to read my lengthy outbursts of imaginative indulgence.

And lastly, a *big* thank you to Henning Ludvigsen! More than his incredible talent as an artist, I consider myself lucky to have him as a friend. I am also eternally grateful that he's worked on my books. His cover art and illustrations have made a world of difference.

Foreword

I thought I'd explain why it took so long to finish this book or even why a rewrite was necessary. I say rewrite because I used almost nothing but ideas from the first version. There were so many changes when I revised the first book of the trilogy that I had no choice but to revisit the second. I went at the project with the same vision in mind as the first. I changed the point of view, reduced the number of storylines, really focused the book to two main storylines that merged in a cohesive manner at the end.

It was difficult but worth it.

Unfortunately, there are so many changes to this version that the manuscript I have written for the third book cannot be salvaged. Aside from very basic ideas, the entire book has to be redone. It will be some time for this to happen. I have decided to take a little break from the trilogy and write a new novel, one I can submit to agents and publishers. It may be a few months before I start work on book three.

As for why this book took so long to finish, I expect it had *something* to do with the year and half long hiatus that occurred after chapter nine. My absolute best friend came to me with the news he was dying from stage IV renal carcinoma. He thought it would help him if we re-subscribed to World of Warcraft. Those of you familiar with my gaming addiction can already see where this is going.

Kasim died, and it hit me harder than I expected. Even now, I still think about him every day. We were roommates for years, played online games together on a daily basis, spoke on the phone or emailed or instant messaged every day. If you've never lost someone who is a part of your everyday life... Well, let's just hope that doesn't happen to you any time soon.

I continued to play games, immersing myself yet again into online worlds. It was just easier to play than to think about the loss. When you're trying not to think, writing is the last thing you should do. For me, writing is flat out hard. It drains me. It forces me to think, to see life from multiple perspectives. I wasn't ready for that. Not for a long time.

I'm back to writing now, with games mostly behind me. Hopefully I can keep at it for much longer than last time.

Enjoy the story everyone. I did my best to make it one worth waiting for.

J.A. Giunta

– 1 –

he pain was fully gone, carried off in the swirls of cloying mist and ripples of dark water all about. It still lapped up against him, head to toe, like the intimate warmth and touch of a body, but the water had finally loosened its hold and allowed him to come awake. Stars glittered in the nighttime shroud overhead, but their light offered little to see by. At the edge of vision, where darkness reigned, mist stirred and came alive with the movement of furtive shadows.

"Who's there?" Barr called out and rolled into a crouch, straining to see through the gloom. Mist roiled about and clung to his skin, sent a shiver down his back that conquered all warmth. "Hello?"

He saw them scatter and fade, as a whisper of magic touched his ears. His mother appeared from nowhere, stepping through the mists as if she too were a shadow given substance. Seeing her again brought back all the uncertainty he had tried to deal with the first time they met. He wasn't sure how to react, how he was supposed to feel. All those years before his father Daroth was killed, then with Tuvrin and the elves, Barr had no idea what it was like to have a mother of his own.

At least not in this lifetime.

Aren and Idelle were both silent in his mind, and the exceptional quiet unsettled him more than any shadows or strange news. Everything came rushing back to him in vivid detail, the twelve Guardians that had attacked and Ealdan's treachery. He had watched his companions fall to both blade and dark magic, and he feared for the worst when he couldn't hear them in his thoughts.

Can either of you hear me? Barr asked, his calm giving way. *Are you two alright?*

Daesidaoli looked as if she could see the growing concern in his eyes and dropped to both knees beside him. She was shorter than he was, a full-blooded faeron, and had the same unusual contrast of eyes as the forest spirit that had given him Aislin – the sentient bracer Ealdan had betrayed him for. Barr rubbed his chest at the bitter memory, where the thief's knife had pierced clean through his heart, but felt neither pain nor scar beneath his fingers.

Your friends await you, Daesi said in his thoughts.

Her eyes were the deep blue of an ocean at sunrise, ringed with an impenetrable black that reflected the starlight overhead. With hair down to her waist, neatly tied and interwoven in a web of silver filigree, the ebon ringlets that wrapped about tapered ears and a slender neck offset the pale shimmer of her skin. She looked out into the distance, then back down to Barr's hand.

Are you well? she pressed.

"I think so." Barr deliberately answered her out loud, unused to hearing any voice in his mind but Aren, Idelle or his own. "I need to see my friends right away. I... can't hear them."

With a nod, she helped him to stand. *Another reason why I have come. With Aislin gone from the mists, my strength is not what it once was and has been steadily waning. I am not sure how much longer I can hold still this moment.*

Barr then remembered what she had told him when he woke the first time, near dead from his wounds and frantic at the absence of his friends. She had rescued them after the attack, brought them to this place and froze a moment in time. There was no way of knowing how long he had slept, but he knew the waters would only heal the blood of a faeron. He had to get to the others as soon as he could.

He stood and gently pulled her up with him. "Would you take me to them? Please."

Daesi glanced out into the darkness once more, as if seeing something he could not, then closed her eyes in concentration. Mist coalesced and quickly gathered, like the ghostly tendrils of a sun-strewn wraith. It wrapped about them both in a shimmering embrace that tingled his skin. To Barr, it felt not so much like moving, as it did the world all around him had shifted and changed. He looked down and saw his friends, wounded and still.

Seeing what had become of Aren brought a tear to Barr's eyes. The giant war hound could have easily been confused for a bear, so large was his muscled frame. He was the strongest animal Barr had ever known, could carry a man in his jaws at a full run and not miss a step. Yet sprawled out in the dark water, with torn flesh and burned mane, Aren seemed weak as a newborn pup, bordering on death.

Slumped over beside the hound, Dar-Paj was nearly unrecognizable. There was a knife handle protruding from his chest, expertly struck through both robes and heart, and a frilly kerchief tossed over his face. Barr knew the stink of its perfume all too well. Commingled with the coppery scent of blood, it would have made him gag but for the anger boiling up deep inside him. He knelt and snatched the cloth away, clenched it in a fist, then swallowed hard at the frozen grimace staring back at him. Dar-Paj's frosted gold skin was flecked with his own blood, and normally white hair was matted black about his neck and shoulders.

Idelle was far larger than Aren, with a wingspan the length of two wagons, and she looked the worst off of all three. Her wings were broken and pointed at odd angles, where bones came free and showed through the skin. She had feathers smashed and torn away, where her fragile body had been pummeled, and a black morass of dried blood pooled over an open wound from neck to leg. Her eyes were closed to the devastation, and Barr feared they would never again open.

Barr, please hurry, Daesi pleaded.

Putting aside his grief and anger, Barr summoned *furie* from within and brought his will to bear. Both hands out before him, he let the magic flow outward from his palms and encompass all three. An iridescent blue glow surrounded their bodies, brightening at the point of each wound. He let them take what they needed, allowing their bodies to heal themselves, offering his life force to fuel the repairs. Bones knitted together of their own volition, as muscle and sinew were fully restored. Blood cleansed itself of poisons and earth, while burns faded away and were gone. With a dying of the light, wounds slowly closed over and left no trace of a scar. The knife in Dar-Paj's chest fell over and disappeared into the water beside him.

Daesi dropped to her knees, as time was set loose. Barr came to her side and steadied her.

I am fine, she assured him. *I just need a moment.*

"Betrayed!" Dar-Paj shot up and cried out, revealing rows of sharp pointed teeth. He looked about, expecting to see something that was not there. He felt at his chest, where the knife had been, then looked at Barr and the others. "What happened? Barr, it was Ealdan!"

"I know. We'll deal with him."

Where are we? Aren asked, lifting his head from both paws. *Idelle?*

I'm here, she answered and pushed herself up. She spread her wings, as if testing their strength. *I felt myself fall, and I tumbled...*

Barr rushed over to the giant hawk and hugged her tight. She nestled her head against his and closed both wings around him.

I thought I lost you, he said, choking on the words. *I saw it all in a dream, and still I let you come with me to Lumintor. I'm sorry.*

It's alright, she reassured. *We're all fine now. You saved us.*

Barr leaned in closer, took a deep breath of her scent and let the comfort of her feathers encompass him fully. Grateful that his friends were alive and well, he was still plagued by thoughts of their loss. Overcome with sudden weariness, it was all he could do to keep standing. It felt as if sorrow and guilt had finally taken their toll. With the exhaustion from healing their bodies, it was simply more than he could bear. His breath became labored, as if stolen away, and darkness loomed up to claim him. He fell, reeling back through memory and time, through a collage of vision not wholly his own...

Laerna knelt upon the ground, rocking back and forth, as she held her baby girl tight. If only she'd been paying attention! Tears burned her cheeks, as she continued to rock the lifeless child, cursing herself for a fool and that damned wagon...

...that sped past, nearly crushing him beneath its wheels. Yaeri didn't care. The world could end in a fiery blaze, and it wouldn't matter in the least. The loss he felt tugging at his gut, tearing his heart to bits, was like a feral creature fighting to get out, desperate...

...to break free and save her son! Try as she may, Adelay couldn't pull her leg from the fallen beams. Her son lay unconscious just a few feet away, as the fire drew ever closer. Though her broken leg sent waves of pain with each tug, she would not give up...

...trying to reach them. If but a single one made it past, the village was doomed, would be put to the torch. Screaming out a challenge, Karyd charged into the fray with pitchfork in hand. He punched one soldier on his left while spearing another to the right. Though it cost him his life, it was worth protecting...

...her husband if she could. There were just too many! Drunken fools, the lot of them. Tawen cradled him in her arms, crying as she berated. Though she held a hand to his neck, frantically trying to stem the flow, the blood would not stop...

...crying. His body had a mind of its own, and grief had come to lay claim. Was there ever a man so wretched as he? His wife and two children taken by the plague, leaving him to watch them wither and fade like so much

dust on a breeze. He wanted to be angry, but the pain left room for naught...

...but pounding little fists and an ear-shattering cry. Faren shook his mother for the tenth time in as many breaths, but still she would not wake. Her eyes were open, but she couldn't see. Her hands were cold to the touch, their nails rimmed with blue, and no amount of squeezing would force her awake...

When the visions faded and reality took hold, Barr gasped and clutched his stomach at the overwhelming grief. He rolled onto all fours in the water, fighting for air and wrestling with the emotions of past lives. In a losing battle, he fell over to his back, succumbing to the dark all around.

*   *   *

It tugged at his middle, tearing through long unused innards with a claw that gripped his spine and pulled him forward. Its voice rang in his ears, a distant whisper cooing promise of power and a desire for freedom. It beckoned him onward, coiled about his decaying frame like the odor of a lightning strike, and where Solastin's cursed feet touched the ground, only withered flora and deadened earth were left in their wake.

The revenant roared at the skies.

His once vibrant flesh had long ago given way to rot, leaving behind hardened remnants of muscle and sinew. His skeleton was yellowed and jagged, where armor and black cloak did not conceal. Engraved into each bone were runes of great power, etched wards filled with the blood of a god. They protected his body more surely than any armor and fueled the bond with his lord.

Having ridden his horse lame, Solastin took the last of its *furie*. In a malevolent tendril of black energy, it spiraled about his fist like an obsidian snake. He kicked the drained corpse, splintering its remains with a steel boot, and turned his attention to the sun on the horizon. As always, time was running short and working against him.

Dropping to all fours, the revenant summoned up *furie* in a swirling ball of brackish green light. It swelled from his spacious middle and encompassed his frame. Bones twisted and popped, shimmering in the foul glow, and reshaped themselves into another form. Long barbs sprouted from the back of his new legs, with claws that elongated at each end. His torso stretched into a massive chamber of intertwined bone and web-like sinew. A pronged tail emerged from behind, as a saurian head jutted outward to fore. Rows of long, serrated teeth sprouted from his maw, beneath glowing narrowed eyes. Like two bloody suns, they set alight the ground ahead in a ghastly crimson shade.

Transformation complete, Solastin tore at the earth with all his strength, propelling himself forward with incredible speed. Tufts of rotted soil flew into the air at every stride. Ambient magic radiated off the revenant, sending coruscating waves of heat all around him. For those with an eye to see enchantment, his trail lit up the darkness behind for miles.

How close are you to Faelsha? Markus asked, his voice a painful echo in the revenant's mind.

Very close, my lord.

Markus had ordered all of them to find and claim the remaining artifacts. Eleven in all, it would take some doing. Some were buried in distant lands, hidden long ago by the father god. Others were not so far away at all. So long as one of the Brood possessed an Emblem, finding the rest would be a matter of time.

The twelve swords were different now. Solastin could feel it, the spark of sentience in their whispers, the cunning in each image. The Emblems had become alive over the millennia, born of the very magic that gave them shape.

He sensed Faelsha nearby, prickling the air with its presence, like the scent of thunder before a storm. His skeletal body fairly crackled with dark energy, at the prospect of seizing new power. He slowed his gait and surveyed the rocky expanse ahead. Its whispers grew stronger, a feminine voice muffled by the oppressive wind and a billowy fog that seeped up from the ground. Something about the voice had changed since last it spoke. It was taunting now, daring him to approach. Solastin reverted to his human form, as he rounded a corner of rock, where he knew the Emblem awaited.

He instead found a small boy glaring back.

Wild-eyed and bloodied, the human child held the visage of one possessed by a great anger, brimming with rage and longing to release it. Blood flecked his cracked lips, as white froth erupted with each volatile breath. His simple clothing was torn and burned, frayed at the ends and swelling outward as if buffeted by a wind rising up beneath him. A crimson trail led back to a pile of sharp rocks, where the ground was clearly upended. In the boy's hands was Faelsha, alight with a cerulean fire.

And he leveled the blade at Solastin.

"You're too late," the boy said in a ghostly voice. The same blue glow of the sword emanated from his mouth as he spoke, frosting the air with each word.

Solastin had no need of words. He came only for the sword, regardless of where it was hidden or who was unfortunate enough to claim it before him. This human child was but an obstacle, a nuisance to be dealt with.

Reaching out a claw, the revenant stomped at the ground and sent a tendril of midnight outwards. It coiled about the boy's chest and neck, tightening its hold, and tore the *furie* from him. He cried out in pain but held tight to the Emblem. His small body rose up, flailing in the air, as the life was wrenched from his flesh. To Solastin's surprise, the human swung Faelsha across the inky light and severed the connection between them. He then dropped to one knee and regained his feet, with what could only be considered a grim determination.

With his right hand gripping Faelsha and the other held to fore, the child pushed his palm outward in a roar of gathered *furie*. The amount of sheer force he let loose tore rock and dead earth from the ground a foot deep, and it blasted a path toward the revenant.

It struck Solastin full on and sent him sprawling.

"I warned you," the boy told him in that frosty breath, lifting Solastin into the air by will alone. "Now learn what it is to fear."

The revenant's body crashed against a man-sized rock, impaled by a jagged edge that passed between enchanted bone.

"Learn what it is to bend."

He was lifted once more, surrounded by an unseen force, and felt the crushing weight of its strength push inward. Armor crumpled under the strain and began to bubble from the heat. Higher he went, as armor melted and scorched its way down his limbs, until the force drove him downward into unforgiving earth. A cloud of rock and debris spewed outward.

"Learn what it is to break."

Solastin was pulled toward the boy, plowing torn earth with his skeletal remains. Faelsha loomed over him, taunting with its whispers, caring only to serve who was stronger. He struggled to rise on one knee, but a palpable force continued to press inward, straining the divine runes etched into his bones.

Finish him! Markus roared, lending him strength.

Rasping out a feral growl, the revenant lurched his body forward and dug his teeth into soft flesh. Blow after terrible blow landed across his back, but Solastin would not relent and kept firm his hold on the leg. The sigils across his bones flared to life with a beryl sheen, as he drank deep of the boy's *furie* and began to heal. Short moments passed before the child was fully drained.

Faelsha slipped to the ground from lifeless fingers.

*   *   *

Barr opened his eyes to the brightness of afternoon shining in from all around. Directly above him, painted onto a ceiling of crystal interspersed with blue veins, was the image of faeron men and women dancing beneath a canopy of night. He blinked to clear his vision, as the image began to move. The people danced and sang out their soundless revelry beneath the stars, moving across the panorama in an endless display.

He found himself lying on a couch full of pillows and silken blankets, in a room fully open to the sun. Or at least that was how it seemed at first. A closer inspection showed the walls were transparent, made up of runic patterns floating in midair and spinning in the rhythm of an azure glow. Leaves were piled at the base of one wall, where a gentle wind swept through the room but left the foliage behind. Crystal pillars stretched up from an array of opalescent tiles a mirror-smooth sheen, touched upon the ceiling and extended outward in a swirl of fanciful artistry. Vines grew freely about each column and were tipped with blooms of pink and white. The webwork of veins that ran all throughout the crystal, up the length of each column and the expanse overhead, was like the semblance of nature in its coursing of vibrant light. It left Barr with the sense that the stronghold was alive.

The sound of others could be heard, conversation and bright laughter. Barr caught sight of a few women tending flowers in another room. They were dressed in colorful linens, both light and revealing, and had hair neatly tied down their backs. Men with bows thrown over a shoulder passed by one transparent wall, but they paid Barr no attention.

You're awake! Idelle said happily. Barr could feel her in the sky above him. *I was worried.*

I told you he'd be fine, Aren said, clearly gorging on something wonderful. The sense of it was making Barr hungry. *Want me to bring you some?*

Yes, I'm fine. And no, I can get my own food, thanks.

What, I'd use a basket. Aren seemed offended. *Suit yourself, but everything is outside. I don't know if they eat like this all the time, but this is the biggest feast I've ever seen. They're a lot more hospitable than the elves.*

Idelle laughed. *Be nice.*

"I see you are awake," Daesi said from the vaulted opening between rooms. She cleared her throat and added, somewhat apologetically, "I know our way of speaking is unsettling for you, so I will talk aloud until you are more at ease."

"Thank you," Barr said, feeling a bit sheepish. Out of anyone, he thought he should be the last to feel uneasy at hearing voices in his head.

Stop brooding and come outside. Idelle swooped past Aren, ruffling his thick coat of hair. *We're having fun out here.*

Aren growled. *Cut that out. Can't I have a moment of peace to finish my lunch?*

You haven't stopped eating since we got here!

"Would you like to come outside? You can refresh yourself with food and drink while we talk." She waved a hand toward the runic walls, and they filled with an ivory mist until completely opaque. She then offered her hand and smiled. "There is much to discuss."

"Are we on Faeron?"

"Yes. I brought us here through the mists when you fell from exhaustion. This is my home." She squeezed his hand. "You are welcome to make it yours." They passed through an arched trellis of flowers in the front doorway. She stopped and asked, "Is your friend Dar-Paj well?"

Barr considered a moment. "As well as can be, I suppose. Do you mean his appearance?"

It was then Daesi's turn to ponder the question, but she chose not to answer. "His thoughts are troubled, haunted. I cannot easily explain it."

"He has no memory of who he is or where he comes from. My uncle found him starving in the streets and took him in. He's only with me because he wants to find others like himself." Barr looked out at the long wooden table, where Dar-Paj and many faeron were eating. "He helped me avenge my father's murder. I owe him for that. I also promised I would help find his people."

"That might not be wise. What he seeks, he must find on his own." Daesi stepped out into the sun and pulled Barr along with her. "There is something I must ask of you, before you start making plans."

"Barr!" Dar-Paj reached across the table and clasped his arm in a crushing grip. Frail as the gold-skinned apprentice looked, he could easily bend iron with his bare hands. "It is good to see you up and about. I have been thinking."

"Not yet," Daesi admonished and motioned for all to sit. Everyone had risen at their approach. "Please, take your seats and enjoy."

Aren licked his chops. *Why are they all looking at you like that?*

He didn't notice right away, but all of the faeron did seem overly intrigued. Despite the glances and giggling, and the not so quiet whispers in his mind, they did look happy to have him there. Barr began filling his plate with fruit and warm bread.

Maybe they've never seen a human before.

But they don't have a problem with golden skin? Or animals three times their size?

Hmm, good point. "Is there a special occasion, or are all your meals like this?" Barr poured himself a glass of wine, admiring the silver metalwork on each piece. "The only thing that would make this absolutely perfect," he said and watched his wine become iced milk, "is if... How did you do that?"

Daesi replied, "I did nothing. All that you see is a gift from the land. Your thoughts and desires can give shape to many things."

That caught Aren's attention. *Does that mean I can make boar –*

"No, it does not," she said to the hound. "There is game to be found on Faeronthalsos, but it cannot be made from thought alone."

She can hear us? Aren stopped eating.

"Amazing," Dar-Paj said, turning a second piece of bread into a fig the size of his palm. "Your uncle would be astounded by this place."

Barr agreed between mouthfuls. "We should let him know we're alright. I won't stay in Alixhir, but we did –"

Daesi cleared her throat. "Everyone, please excuse us. I must speak with my son." To Dar-Paj, she added, "You may stay, of course."

That doesn't bode well, Idelle said from her vantage far above.

Glancing upward, Daesi said, "I fear your winged friend is correct. First off, I must apologize. Things did not go at all as I had planned. When my mother took Aislin, we had no idea what effect it would have on the mists."

With a hard swallow, Barr said, "Your mother? Do you mean I have a grandmother? Do I have any other family?"

"Not anymore. I should have mentioned it sooner, but this matter is more pressing."

She looked as if struck by a terrible headache. Her brow furrowed in pain, and her hands began to shake as she rubbed at her temples. Barr put down his glass and stood, but she motioned for him to stay.

"I will be fine." A few deep breaths, and her hands became steady, her brow once more smooth. "The mists are a gift from Saernol – the Goddess of Magic. It is a place between realms, a source of great magic and a part of who we are. It allows us to travel to any place we can think of or talk with one another over great distances." She let out a sigh but did not seem in any pain. "Such a wondrous gift, however, is not without cost. As in all things magical, there is a balance to maintain. There are dark creatures within the mists that feed on its power. We call them umbrals."

"I think I've seen them," Barr said, recalling shadows at the edge of vision when he had woken in the mists. "They didn't do much, though, or respond when I called out."

"As Matron of the Guiding Mists, my spirit is bonded to that realm. It is my will alone that keeps the umbrals at bay. If not for me, and the presence of Aislin lending its strength, they would break free and overrun Faeron, feeding on the magic of every living thing."

"And now Ealdan has Aislin." Barr's jaw clenched at the memory of the thief's betrayal. "I planned on hunting him down anyway. I'll get it back."

Dar-Paj said, "Hold on a minute. What exactly are we talking about? I have no qualms about finding Ealdan and breaking him in two, but what is this Aislin?"

"It's what he took after stabbing me in the heart."

"Aislin is a very old artifact," Daesi explained, "first found within the mists, cradled in the arms of a statue of Saernol. In truth, I did not know until recently just how important it was. We have never before been without it. I am afraid, in its absence, I will eventually falter."

"You were carrying this artifact?" Dar-Paj asked.

"I didn't know it at the time. To me, it was just a bracer." Barr shook his head. "I shouldn't have trusted him. I knew what he was, a thief – or worse. All I could think of was killing that shapeling."

Stop blaming yourself, Idelle said. *Trying to see the good in others is not a shortcoming.*

It is if you're blinded to everything else.

"I am to blame," Daesi said. "I was watching over you and planned to intervene should anything happen to you or Aislin. The ones who attacked... I stood no chance against them. I let them take Aislin, so that I could save you. No matter what happens now, I –"

A trickle of blood ran from her nose.

"Are you alright?" Barr came to her side. She tried to staunch the bleeding with a napkin, but the flow would not stop. He could see the fear in her eyes, in the tremble of her body. "Hold still. It's alright, I can help."

With both hands to her cheeks, Barr summoned up the *furie* to heal and opened himself to her. The amount her body took with the first tug of desire nearly floored him with the strength of its need. Like a vast chasm of darkness, it longed to be filled. It dug into his spirit and pulled without relent, flailing against the barrier of his resolve. All around him was a growing blackness, a miasma full of shadow, and at the edge of that murk were scrabbling black claws and gnashing teeth.

"Enough!" Barr shouted, severing their connection with all the will he could muster. He fell to the ground, breathing heavy and exhausted. There was an emptiness in his middle, as if all his strength had been consumed. "What *was* that? I've never seen anything like it."

Did she attack you? Aren was genuinely concerned. *It felt like you were fighting for your life.*

I think I was.

"I am not sure what just happened." Daesi looked light-headed and about to faint. "I do feel better, though. I thank you for that."

Whatever it was, Idelle put in, *it didn't feel like her. It was something else.*

Dar-Paj helped Barr to his feet. "At least the bleeding has stopped. Here, take a seat. You look a little pale."

It was the umbrals. They're killing her. "I have to get that sword back."

Daesi said, "Before you may leave, there is another matter to discuss. Your return to Faeron was not entirely unexpected. You will need to make an appearance at Starshrine."

Barr raised a brow. "Do we have time for that? I don't think we do. If I don't get Aislin back soon –"

"The prince must make an appearance at Court," she said firmly. "To do otherwise would be a grave insult, to both the Queen and our people."

Sounding dubious, Barr asked, "And what prince would that be?"

Getting to her feet, Daesi took hold of him by the shoulders. She smiled then, and despite the strangeness of her eyes, it warmed his heart to see it.

"That would be you."

– 2 –

s they left through the courtyard of Daesi's estate, past an array of sculpted shrubbery and a veritable palette of flowerbeds, she pointed out a new gazebo being formed. Coaxed from the rich soil and given shape by skillful artisans, it was solely comprised of the lively blue crystal from which all faeron structures were made. Though still incomplete, veins within its parts already thrummed and pulsed with a soft glow, as if coursing with the lifeblood of a growing creature.

The faeron, she told them, were not alone but shared their world with a number of other races. Homes were all about, dotting the verdant landscape. Many would have gone by unnoticed without her calling attention to each one. Massive hollowed trees were the abodes of playful sprites, a winged faeron-like people that could fit in the palm of any man. Sylphs, on the other hand, were only half the size of a faeron, and adored sunlight across a field more than honeyed milk or a good rain. They dug comfortable dwellings beneath wide, grassy hills and encouraged flowers to grow all around.

Many others lived there as well, from moss-farming pixies and their great cozy logs to bird-taming nymphs and their leafy cottages in the trees. It was a beautiful place, alive with magic in every crevice and a surprise at each turn. In all his time with the sylvannis, Barr had seen much of magic, but not even the elven tree city could compare to this splendor.

You still miss it, Aren noted.

Barr scratched under the hound's jaw as they left the estate and stepped onto a road of smoothed earth. His mother was talking of dryads, a once serene people who were forced to move far to the south to avoid war.

How could I not? My father and Seltruin are there. He scuffed his boot in the road, kicking up an eddy of dust. *I spent over half my life in Geilon-Rai. I won't be forgetting it any time soon.*

Idelle said, *We haven't been gone all that long, you know. It's been barely a week since you were...*

The word hung in the air, unspoken but stinging. Exiled. No matter that he was innocent of Harduen's murder, the council had punished him all the same for disobeying their traditions. Barr could never again see his elven father nor the mentor who had trained him to be a sage.

I know. It feels longer, though.

How are we going to find Ealdan? Aren asked, with a growl at the edge of his thoughts. He made it clear there was a debt to settle between them. *Even if he doesn't have the sword anymore, I still want to track him down.*

Yes, Idelle agreed. *I would very much like to see him again.*

Barr nodded, drawing a glance from Dar-Paj. *I'm not sure just yet, but hopefully my mother can help us. After all, she's the one who brought us here.* He looked up at the foreign sky, where two suns were still rising at either end of a cloudless green vista that turned blue as it stretched down toward the land. *I still can't believe that my grandmother is the Queen of Faeronthalsos.*

Hmm, Aren said.

What's wrong?

This Starshrine place we're going to. Do you think they'll have a feast like the one we just had?

We just *finished eating...*

With as sour a face a giant hound could muster, *I was just curious, is all.*

Daesi laughed, then caught herself and stopped. "My apologies," she said to Aren. "I should not have been listening."

"I will never get used to that," Dar-Paj said, "the way you can communicate by thought alone. The notion of hearing any voice in my head but my own is disturbing, to say the least."

"I don't know." Barr gave the hound a pat on his broad chest. "I can't imagine being without Aren and Idelle. Their voices in my thoughts are as natural as my own. It's hearing other people," he added, with a glance to his mother, "that sometimes can feel a bit odd. It's too open. I feel like I don't have the option of choosing my words. You just get whatever unfiltered thought I have at the time."

Daesi said, "It is true that we have our differences, and faeron are not as... guarded as you are. You can in

21

time, however, control what thoughts others may hear, just as you learned to use your voice. I can also assure you that none would be so rude as to listen to your thoughts, when it so clearly makes you uncomfortable."

"But they could if they wanted to," Dar-Paj pressed, "like what you just did. That is what makes it so unsettling." He seemed struck by a thought, and a glimmer of hope passed over his gold visage. "I wonder. Could it be possible –"

"It cannot. I know you have lost your memories, but I am afraid only you can restore them."

"Oh. I see."

As they walked on in silence, the grass to either side of the road began to yellow and dry, as brambles sprang up between the shoots. Wind grew from a cool breeze and turned bitter with its grasp, harassing clothing and hair in its wake. The road ahead grew less smooth, gradually scored by rock and a brackish mud that gave root to dark weeds.

What's happening? Idelle asked, her voice edged with concern.

Barr looked to his uncle's apprentice. *I think it's Dar-Paj. Do you remember what my mother said at the table?*

"None of that now." Daesi stopped and turned, put a gentle hand to Dar-Paj's shoulder. "I may not be able to restore your memories, but neither will brooding."

She closed her eyes and took in a deep breath, then let it out with great calm and concentration. The ground began to change back, once more bristling with life, and the wind settled into a tranquil breeze. When she opened her eyes, the road was again smooth, and not a single blade of grass was less than a brilliant shade of green.

"My apologies." Dar-Paj bowed his head and reached back to draw up his hood.

"No hiding, either," she said and stopped him. "Be at ease with who you are. It just may lead to unlocking your past."

Off in the distance, Barr noticed two figures walking toward them from down the road. By their slender limbs and small stature, he guessed they were sylphs. Though child-like in size, there was no mistaking these women for young faeron. With short hair that barely hid the length of tapered ears or silken cloth the shape of leaves doing little to appease modesty, there was a wild freedom to their stride and the smiles that accompanied girlish laughter in his mind. The silver runes glittering across their pale skin, from decorative swirls at each cheek to long wards down each leg, did more to conceal than the gauzy cloth ever could.

Barr nodded a greeting as the two passed. Though their eyes were white about the iris, there was no pupil to speak of, just a blackless pane of color. One a vibrant purple hue, the other yellow like a sunrise, both sets of eyes were aglow with a strange radiance born of magic and surveyed him with unspoken desire.

He was still blushing long after they were gone.

Well, they seemed like fun, Aren said in the face of an uncomfortable silence.

Idelle chuckled. *They had a much different kind of fun in mind.*

What do you mean?

Never mind, Barr said. "Maybe someone here has come across others like you, Dar. This just seems like the sort of place you might come from."

The apprentice considered a moment. "I suppose my eyes are somewhat similar." There was no indication of hope in his tone, only the cynical resignation of one

23

long used to disappointment. "If there were others here like me, though, would your mother not have met one?"

"Perhaps," Daesi replied, "but Faeronthalsos is a big world, even larger than Taellus. No one can claim to have seen it all."

A handful of yellow lights sprang up from seemingly thin air and encircled Dar-Paj in a flickering dance. They buzzed about him in greeting, as if delighted to see him, then dashed ahead down the road to Starshrine.

Aren snorted a laugh. *What were those?*

Daesi explained, "Those were fey, what humans will often think of as fairies. They are very intelligent but so playful as to sometimes be a nuisance. They did seem quite taken with you, however. Such a warm welcome is considered good luck."

Barr offered, "They could have recognized you."

"They looked like glow bugs." Dar-Paj shook his head, as if disregarding a notion. "There was something familiar about them, but I have no idea where I could have seen any while living with your uncle."

"Something to ponder, in any case," Daesi said, as the road dipped into a valley. "For now, let us put aside any unpleasant thoughts and prepare ourselves for a celebration."

Just ahead, the faeron city came into view.

* * *

The Guardian stronghold outside Noria might have once been known as a place of refuge, a sanctuary from turners and deserving of its name, but Haven was now a collection of cold stones, with a demeanor as gray and somber as those housed within. Overlooking the city from its walled vantage on a hill, it was immense by any standard and daunting to behold. Jutting masonry along the battlements of all four towers were shaped in the many guises of Herne, from horned hunter with a stag's head to baleful grimace of a warrior, painted warden of the forest to venerable father of mankind. Heavy banners dropped beneath each bust, stretching down toward the crenellated outer wall. Each one a swath of midnight, they hung from the parapets with an emblazoned orange sun, as if the light of creation forever shone upon the Guardians.

Markus noted the bowmen pacing the wall and atop the main gate. The portcullis was raised, and two guards stood without. In long capes and steel mail, tower shield held to fore, they appeared capable but most likely had never been to war. The Guardians, in his opinion, were infected with nobles, men who would sooner shed gold than blood.

Both are useful, Revyn said in his mind. The god must have been in a good mood, since his words caused no pain.

We can gather the Emblems without help. Feraesk was beside him, leading their mounts, as they got closer to the main gate. The acrid stench of death and decay about the revenant was overpowering, but their illusion masked even that. *There is nothing that can stand in our way.*

Do not question my desires, child.

Markus sighed and stood before the guards. *Must you call me that?*

Would you prefer Ealdan?

He knew better than to answer the jibe.

"Good morn to you, brothers," one guard said, while the second eyed them with disinterest. "What business does Garand have here this day?"

"None of your concern." Markus leveled a gaze at the man until he looked away. "Have our horses seen to. We may be here a while."

He walked into the inner passage without another word, eyeing murder holes to either side before passing through the second portcullis. Feraesk handed over the reins to a guard and lingered a moment. In the pit of his stomach, Markus could feel the revenant's desire to drain the life from the man.

Soon, he promised.

Feraesk came up from behind, as the inner gate was unbarred and opened. They entered the courtyard, and the main keep loomed before them. It was overgrown with ivy and begging to be put to the torch. Putting aside his disdain, Markus strode past the guardhouse and toward the main hall. Numerous peasants were tending gardens to either side, filthy and afraid, while Guardians went about their own business. He could hear the forge on the eastern edge of the compound, right beside the stables, which put the soldiers quarters on his left. More guards on the wall and standing firm by the keep's doors.

How easy it would be to leave it all in utter ruin.

"May I be of assistance?" a man asked, as they came into the main hall. He was older than most and dressed as a steward, but he spoke in a manner that pleased Markus.

"We are here to see the Lord High Hunter." He gave a nod to Feraesk, who held out a fist. Though nothing was clutched in that skeletal grasp, the illusory papers must have seemed in order. "As you can see, we have been sent by Marshal Hunter Naero."

Be ready to use Aislin, Markus warned. *If our guises do not hold, we will be forced to fight our way out.*

They will hold, my lord. Feraesk's voice in his mind was like a wintry echo, a rasp that chilled the nape of his neck. *But I am prepared, nonetheless.*

"If you gentlemen would please follow me. I'll just need a moment to announce you."

The stone floor was covered with thick red decorative rugs, both to ward off cold and the drab of gray stone. Sconces lit up the hall in flickering shades of yellow, while tapestries hung between the flames. Depicting scenes of a dark past, when turners had brought to bear all the magic at their disposal, it was shown that the power of Herne had flowed through each Guardian. It had made them an extension of his will, bearers of a divine providence. No turner had stood a chance, and all were brought low by the combined might of the Order.

Two guards were posted outside heavy double doors at the end of the corridor. The steward motioned toward empty cushioned chairs along both walls. Neither of them sat.

"I'll just be a moment." He was allowed to enter and closed the doors behind him. After a brief time, he called them both in. "The Lord High Hunter will see you now."

"My thanks, Claremont," a gruff voice said. When the steward didn't leave, "You're dismissed."

"Then I shall take my leave. If you need anything, I'll be just outside the door."

The steward left them alone, in the dark of a large office, where light through a glass window strained to brighten the room. Even a hearth in the far wall seemed to wilt beneath the shadows. Despite bear rugs and the fire, it still felt as if winter had taken root in the stones.

A shield and crossed swords hung over the hearth, beneath a portrait of the man before them. He sat on the other side of a wide oaken desk, where maps and iron markers were strewn about. The High Hunter studied one map in particular and mumbled to himself while placing metal discs across its surface. He glanced up at the two beneath a thick brow but refused to take his mind from the task.

Markus was one of the first immortal children born onto Taellus, the illuminaire, and Saernol had blessed them with a pleasing shape. Though he had freely given up his long life in a bargain with Revyn, he maintained the incredible beauty he was born with. Human women threw their bodies on his mercy, begged for his touch, and counted themselves lucky to receive but a smile.

In comparison, the hulking bear of a High Hunter was a monster of bristly hair and unwashed muscle. His hair was long and unkempt, the hue of mud in a heavy rain, and there was no telling what insects made a home of it. His eyes were sunken beneath a brow more suited to scowling than surprise, and by the look of his crooked nose it had been broken many times. Soiled with the lingering remnants of a meal, his beard fell over oiled mail and nearly reached his middle. Undoubtedly fit, a soldier born to the sword, his bestial visage left much to be desired.

"Alright then," Grailyn said, getting up to his feet. "What's this about?"

"We were sent by Marshal Naero," Markus explained, trying to distract the man's mind while Feraesk went to work. Binding the High Hunter would not be easy. "He has asked that we assist with the coming troubles, act as advisors to you alone. It has been a long time since we have faced true turners, and the omens do not bode well."

As Markus slowly spoke each word, the High Hunter tried to listen but appeared to be straining, as if the words came from a great distance, through a tunnel in the dark. Squinting turned to pain, and a hand went up to his temple. As if stricken by a sudden headache, he grunted and fell forward, barely holding himself up with a shaky grasp on the desk. Markus and Feraesk moved cautiously to either side, as the whispers echoed in the corners of the man's mind. Throwing themselves against the barrier of his resolve, worming through the cracks and widening each fissure, they sought out weakness in the depths of subconscious, turning hope into darkness and light into despair.

Biting his lip until it bled, the High Hunter let loose a growl and pulled a dagger from his waist. He drove it into Feraesk, through illusion and bone, but managed only to shatter the fine blade.

"Just take him," Markus said.

The revenant grabbed hold and dug his teeth into the man, biting through armor and flesh. Grailyn fell to his knees, unable to stand, as a magical disease worked its way into and through his body. Fueled by his own *furie*, weaving itself into every pore, the lycanthropy took hold and gave rise to a new voice in his mind.

Feraesk let go and backed away, with a wary hand to the hilt of Aislin. The High Hunter pulled himself up and looked about the room with new eyes, as if he had died in the shadows and was reborn into the light. A beryl sheen flashed across his gaze, reflecting fire from the hearth. He seemed to be listening to something only he could hear.

"Yes, Lord Revyn," Grailyn said. "Your will be done."

*   *   *

Their arrival at the faeron city was not unexpected, as evidenced by the happy throng at either side. Six or more deep, of all ages and size, the citizens of Aranadir cheered at the long-awaited return of their prince. From children who strained to see past the crowd and catch a glimpse, to adults that clapped and whistled out their salutation, all surprised Barr with their enthusiasm and sincerity. There were sprites gathering overhead, like a swarm of butterflies, and the telltale wisp of feys darting through the air with a buzzing glow. Pixies squeezed their way forward and watched from between faeron legs, while nymphs and sylphs called out for his attention. It was disconcerting at first, all those voices clamoring in his mind, but he was able to get control by focusing his will. He could still hear them mixed in with vocal shouts and wild cries of joy, but the volume was no longer so intrusive.

Barr did his best to wave and smile at each one. *I had no idea there'd be so many.* It was very different from his life as a sage with the elves, where his efforts went mostly unappreciated. *None of them have ever even seen me before, but they all seem so happy that I'm here.*

What's a prince, anyway? Aren asked. *Is that like a sage?*

It's more like an Eneir. If the sylvannis had a king, Landrin would be their prince.

Idelle watched on from above. *I think it's wonderful, but it does make me wonder at their expectations.*

The road had changed from smooth earth to cobbled white stones, rounded and polished to perfection. The grass lanes that rimmed its edge were a lively green and neatly trimmed, as if each blade had been tended to by hand. Crystal structures dotted the landscape, but they offered little shade, so trees with wide boughs were as plentiful as wild flowers. Daesi led them down a twisting path, past fountains whose stonework came alive. The statuary danced in time to the cadence of rising droplets, as the water swirled ever higher and rained back down in a cool mist. More and more people could be found at each turn, edging closer but not impeding their prince.

They arrived at the steps of Starshrine, where two long rows of faeron guards led up to the top. In blue livery and silver armor, they stood firm and at attention. With ebon shields that ran the length from pointed boot to plumed helm and crystal spears that caught the sun in a cerulean glow, each soldier tapped out a salute against the ground and grunted a military welcome.

Starshrine was a circular collection of white marble pillars and transparent runic walls, topped by a crystal dome that opened wide at its center. The floors were polished black tile, and clouds were mirrored in its sheen. It was far less crowded inside, but there were easily hundreds of people waiting on his arrival. They were dressed in highly decorative silken clothes, from wraps interwoven with gold filigree to flowing gowns alive with crystal dust and the petals of a thousand flowers. Hued fires danced about the neck or wrist of some women, while droplets of water adorned others in the semblance of a coursing stream. There were many blends of precious gem and fanciful enchantment, but none came close to the grandeur of the Queen's living crown.

Blue fire burned within each fist-sized clear gem, as they floated freely about her raven hair in a twisting dance. Light spilled off every turn, like a waterfall of *furie*, and splashed her shoulders in a shower of azure glow. It stressed the deep richness of her eyes and set them alight with a vibrant luster, like the brilliance of a cloudless sky at midday.

Barr recognized her immediately as the forest spirit that had given him Aislin. Standing before a silver-runed throne, atop a carpeted dais on the other side of the room, she smiled and beckoned them over. The gathered faeron all bowed, with fingertips to forehead in a show of respect, and a hush fell over the chamber.

"Welcome," the Queen said, as they came to stand before her. To Barr, she added, "We have waited a very long time for you to find your way home."

The gathered faeron clapped, and at a nod from the Queen, music began to play. Everyone returned to their soundless conversation, though it seemed to Barr as if their combined thoughts buzzed in his mind. The pitch rose and fell, focusing on one voice at a time, then faded back into the mix to be replaced by another.

Arianaolis was wearing an opalescent gown, mixed with enchanted feathers that seemed to move on their own and tied with cords of brushed platinum about the waist. She straightened a glittering fold and drew closer to her daughter.

With a warm embrace, she said "It is good to have you home safely." She let go and added, "I know there is much to discuss."

Daesi gave a somber nod.

Aren said, *I hope it's not more bad news.*

"And you," the Queen said to the giant hound and arched her neck to meet his gaze, "I have already met once before. You are still a magnificent creature."

He bowed his head, allowing her to scratch behind an ear. *I like it here. Everyone's so small and pretty.* He glanced about the room. *I don't see a banquet, though.*

Idelle laughed. *Don't take that as an invitation to go out and find one of your own. You never know just whose friend you might eat.*

The Queen raised a brow but made no comment at the notion. She moved to stand before Dar-Paj, and a puzzled look crossed her features. She reached out and touched a lock of his hair, then let the snowy length fall back into place. All the while, he seemed unable to meet her gaze. Barr was expecting the apprentice to pull up his hood at any moment.

"Be at ease," she said. "We are honored to have you here among us. I know all of your deeds in aiding my grandson. We owe you much. If there is anything you desire, you need only ask."

Dar-Paj looked to Barr, then bowed his head to the Queen. "I wish only to find others like myself, in the hopes of regaining my lost memories. Have you ever met anyone like me?"

The Queen shared a glance with her daughter.

"No," she considered a moment, touching a glossy nail to her chin, "not quite like you. While it is true, that we cannot restore your memories, I do know of a place that might help reveal why it is you lost them to begin with. Are you familiar with the Mirror Pool?"

I feel like a bug in a jar, Aren said, glancing back at all the quiet faeron watching on. *They're just looking at us. They aren't even saying a word to each other.*

None that you can hear, anyway, Barr returned. *Trust me, they're talking... and mostly about you.*

He grinned at the hound's narrowed eyes.

"I have not left Alixhir," Dar-Paj said, "since Barr's uncle Therol had found me in the streets. This is my first time out of the city."

"I see. Well, the Mirror Pool was formed when Taellus was created, fashioned as a conduit between our realms and the astral. Through it, the gods work their will." She indicated Starshrine with a hand. "As with all things magical, it gradually took on a life of its own, growing sentient over time. Though it has no voice with which to speak, it can communicate quite well. Its name aptly comes from the visions it grants, laying bear the soul of those who gaze into its surface. Those who pilgrimage to its waters hope to gain insight into themselves, peering into the recesses of their inner being, without barriers or constraints. It is considered a source of divine blessing, by the mothers who bring their children to its edge and the soldiers who dip both sword and shield within its depths." She put a hand to his shoulder. "Perhaps there you might find the past that so eludes you."

"Thank you," he said, his tone heartfelt. Though he smiled, the rows of sharp teeth remained hidden behind his lips. "I will seek out this Mirror Pool, as time permits. For now, we have a more pressing matter to contend with."

Barr turned and looked out over the faeron, unable to disregard their voices completely. Whether dancing or politely chatting with one another, their eyes fell upon him with a heaviness he could feel in his middle, and a voice accompanied each face. Their words in his mind grew louder, as his eyes passed over them, then faded again to the backdrop of murmurs. Out of all those he saw, only one remained quiet, making no sound in his thoughts at all.

To say she was attractive would be akin to noting how bright the sun could be at times. Her beauty was the sort that blotted out those around her, laying claim to all eyes in the room. In a terrible moment of silence that caught breath in his throat, her eyes met his and held fast. So clear and luminescent was the cast of each blue orb, that he imagined himself falling within. Spilling about her shoulders in waves of lustrous curls, her hair was a deep crimson that offset the porcelain cast of her freckled cheeks. She had the pert nose and full lips often associated with pixies, and the smile that crept upon her lit his heart with its perfect brilliance. In a gossamer summer blouse the soft hue of polished jade, she wore a single piece of animated crystal that wove about her waist and up across either shoulder. Her attire left little to the imagination, and a troubling warmth began to stir within Barr.

He was aware of his mother and grandmother beside him, talking of the dark creatures in the mists, but all other voices in his mind seemed to dim and fall away. It was as if they hung on his every move, eager to gauge his reaction to the young woman, and then he realized she too was waiting. He raised a hand in weak greeting, wondering if he should go over and talk with her, when he heard Daesi in his mind.

That is Fluoralandylae, she said with an odd hint of satisfaction or pride. *Daughter of the Grand Seeress, her hand is already spoken for.*

She's to be married?

"Yes," Daesi whispered in his ear with a chuckle. "To the Prince of Faeronthalsos."

"Regarding Aislin," the Queen said, as the heavy hand of realization dropped upon Barr, "the oracles will do all they can to find it. When they do, one will carry you through the mists, so you can take back what rightfully belongs to us."

Idelle sighed. *I don't think I can take any more of these surprises.*

Barr swallowed hard, fighting to get control of his emotions. He wasn't sure what to think. There was no doubting the girl was attractive, but marriage? And an arranged one, no less.

You could do a lot worse, Aren noted. *I don't think I've ever seen a prettier girl. She looks about your age, too.*

"I'll be ready," Barr told his grandmother. "I know what's at stake." He glanced at Daesi, aware of how little time she had left before the umbrals completely drained her. "I wasn't prepared for Ealdan's attack, but this time I will be. I'll have Aislin back in no time."

"Good," Daesi said, then leaned in for a whisper, "and she is exactly your age. You were both born on the same day. It is the main reason for your arrangement, though not the only one."

"Pardon me," a feminine voice said from behind.

It was Fluoralandylae. When Barr turned to face her, he was stricken once more with a dumbfounded sense of being overwhelmed by her beauty. He remembered to draw breath, though barely, but no words found their way out of his mouth.

"Always a pleasure," Daesi said, smoothly covering Barr's poor attempt at speech. "You two have not yet been formally introduced. Please, allow me. Fluora, this is Aoleontril, my first and only son, also called Barr, and the Prince of Faeronthalsos." The girl gave a slight bow of red curls in respect. "And Barr, this is Fluoralandylae, only daughter to the Grand Seeress Elaedraoni, and an Oracle of Saernol."

Unsure what to do, Barr held out a hand in greeting. "It's a pleasure to meet you." She seemed perplexed by the proffered hand and hesitated. He asked Daesi, "Do faeron not shake hands? I don't mean to insult –"

"No," Fluora said, "there is no insult. It is just that, as an oracle..." She looked to Barr's mother, seemingly for support but found none. With a wan smile, she said, "It is also my pleasure to finally meet you."

She took hold of his hand.

Barr's heart began to race at her touch, the soft skin beneath his, like shimmering porcelain, delicate in its shape but firm in its resolve. He thought she too was affected, growing shallow of breath, as her grip tightened all the more. His smile, however, slowly faded away, as he realized she was looking past him, her eyes seeing through to some vision that took hold. She breathed even faster, clutching his hand, as if he alone kept her anchored to the present. Her body began to shake, all the while unblinking, staring ahead in growing horror, until the tears began to flow.

Barr caught her, as she collapsed, and brought her gently to the floor. He saw nothing physically wrong with her, but something dire had clearly happened. He was left with the sense she had been overcome with a terrible grief, and the intensity of what she saw was just too much for her to bear.

Others tried to get close, to see what ill had befallen her, but the tone of Daesi's voice ordered them all back, with an air of authority not even the Queen would dare question.

"She will be fine," Daesi said, her voice carrying across the chamber with the weight of her station, as Matron of the Guiding Mists. "This was to be expected, after all."

Two faeron women in white robes appeared from outside and scooped up the fallen girl. They carried Fluora away, through a passage in the back.

I don't understand, Barr said. *What did she see?*

Whatever it was, Idelle said, perched on the dome above them and looking down with dark eyes, *it doesn't seem like you two are off to a very good start.*

37

– 3 –

oth suns dipped low at either end of the horizon, blending sky and land in a fiery glow. With night fast approaching, emerald skies gave way to violet in a darkening sheen, as the light of day struggled on to keep hazy stars from gaining focus. Heat rose in the distance as visible waves, distorting grasslands and dense forest beyond the field of snowy dandelion.

With Aren beside him, Barr sat in the low grass and tried to sort out his thoughts. Twirling one of the fragile flowers in his fingers, he let the wind carry its seeds off in a feathery trail. Idelle was overhead, a shadow edged by silvery white, and came to land on the wide branch of a tree that wasn't there before. Still wearing the fur-lined leathers of an elven hunter and sitting beneath the heat of two suns, Barr thought it odd he felt no warmer than he had in the bitter winter on Taellus.

It's definitely a strange place, Aren said, mirroring the thought. Lying with his head in both paws, he let loose a snort that sent a flurry of dandelion shooting outward. *As thick as my coat is, I'm not the least bit hot.*

The air is warm enough, Idelle noted.

Neither one of them had mentioned what was really troubling Barr but waited for him to broach the subject. To the Ballar, the elven beastmasters, the bond with a companion was an incredible gift. It brought them closer to the hound, bear or hawk they were pledged to and melded their emotions into a single, stronger vessel. That unbreakable bond was even greater with Barr. It allowed him to speak with his companions in a manner like no Ballar had ever done. They shared feelings and thoughts without conscious effort and more often than not felt three parts of a whole.

This business of an arranged marriage, he said after a long moment of silence, *has me a little worried, but not nearly as much as Ealdan.*

We weren't ready, Aren argued.

They killed us. All of us, including Dar-Paj. Barr shook his head. *Without my mother intervening, we'd all be dead. I don't even know what those creatures were.*

Idelle ruffled her feathers. *They certainly weren't Guardians.*

They weren't even alive! All twelve of them were just animated corpses. Barr tossed away the flower. *They wove furie like nothing I've ever seen before, and now Ealdan has Aislin. That sword... it's more than just a weapon. It was able to store the furie I stole from those shapelings.* He looked over at Aren, into the hound's pale blue eyes. *How are we supposed to defeat them all?*

We don't, Aren replied simply. *We just wait 'til he's alone with Aislin and take it from him.*

Idelle said, *That's actually a good plan.* Ignoring the hound's snort at the implication that his plans weren't always good ones, she added, *Assuming one of these oracles can take us wherever we want, we should arrive near Ealdan and hide. I can watch from the skies until he's alone. Then we'll strike.*

That might work, Barr agreed. *We'll just have to wait and see if they can even find him, or if he still has the sword. In the meantime,* he reached out and ran his fingers over the runes on Aren's ironwood collar. *Can I see that? You too, Idelle.*

"Enear il ashan," he said in elven.

Runes along the collar flared with a sapphire light, offsetting the dark hue and emerald veins of the heavy wood. The collar then expanded in diameter, until it slipped easily from Aren's head. Barr did the same for Idelle and returned to sitting in the grass. Both collars resumed their normal size, solid rings about the width of three fingers. Light faded from the elven markings, until they were again an ashen black.

Studying the complex joining of each rune into wards, Barr looked for ways to improve upon their design without compromising flow or integrity. Some runes had to remain a particular size to accommodate an influx of *furie*, while others could be reduced or even gotten rid of. It was a difficult task, going over so many possibilities in his mind, while faced with the realization that a mistake could render the collars useless or worse – explode when called upon.

Umm, Aren said in a nervous tone. *I sort of like mine the way it is.*

Trust me, Barr said and winked.

He focused his will and brought it to bear on each collar. Like midnight quicksilver, the runes trembled and collapsed in on themselves. They slipped across the dark surface until most of what remained was condensed to but a fraction of their previous size. Just as he had done with his kyan, the dual ironwood blades of a Maurdon at his waist, he made room on both collars for additional enchantments.

While Aren's allowed the hound to become invisible for short periods and removed all trace of his passing, it had done little to protect him from the onslaught of dark magic that Ealdan's Guardians had thrown about. Much the same with Idelle, hers granted speed beyond the limit of her unusual size and the ability to survive on the thin air far overhead, but it hadn't kept her safe from Ealdan's blade or the incessant pummeling that nearly ended her life.

Barr looked around for a rock or small branch to score new runes into each collar, when a branch lowered itself from the tree above.

"Thanks," he said and snapped off a twig.

You know it can't hear you, Aren said and stifled a chuckle.

Shush!

Whispering words of power as he wrote, drawing *furie* from inward and letting it flow through his fingers, Barr scrawled new runes into the ironwood. Though the twig barely grazed the glossy resin that encased each collar, the elaborate lettering settled in and burned its way deep inside. As each rune wove together to form a separate ward, it flared briefly in a tinge of sapphire. The wards linked one by one, into a pattern never intended for an item so small. The complex joining of a glyph took shape and became whole.

By the time Barr was finished inscribing, weariness came upon him with the setting of both suns. All that remained was to empower the glyphs, but exhaustion fought against him.

Let's finish tomorrow, Idelle said tiredly, as if she too felt the effects of the endeavor.

I'm almost done.

With eyes closed, Barr strained at the effort. It ached his middle and set his hands to shaking, as the *furie* left each palm in a growing nimbus of golden light. The glow encompassed both collars and filled each engraved rune with a watery fire. It seeped ever slowly into each etching and lilting scrawl, but mounting pain at the exertion was overcoming his resolve.

Just when Barr thought it would be too much to withstand, the overwhelming ache in his body lessened. A rush of raw power filled him like the bursting of a dam into the confines of a ceramic cup. It washed over and through him, screaming in his ears like banshees on a rampage. The world around him was drowned out in its raging sounds and blinding radiance. He struggled against the intense flood, fought to push the magic back and shield himself from the burning recoil. Only once before had he felt such a surge of pure *furie*, and that incident paled in comparison. While the other was a brisk rainstorm, this was a torrential downpour.

Through great effort and greater restraint, the influx began to dissipate. White faded to vision, and the roar all about him subsided to a whisper. Though his body still shook, it was but a quiet vibration and not the tremors of a struggle. The magic pulsed a final time and left his body in an exhalation of chilled air. When finally he opened his eyes, what he saw left him breathless. Panic gripped his heart.

For as far as he could see, the land was decimated.

Oh no, he thought, fighting for the strength to stand on shaky legs. *Not again. I didn't mean to.*

Aren lay on his side a few feet away, breathing but unmoving, and Idelle had fallen over as well. Usually black and shining with oil, her feathers were dulled and had a gray tinge to their lackluster sheen. The earth all around them was devoid of any life, a drained miasma of brown and lilting debris that stretched outward in a ring of destruction. The air itself seemed affected, now dry and without a whisper of a breeze. What ashen remnants floated about, drifting through the air in a semblance of black snowflakes, threatened to choke Barr with every breath.

Tears welled in his eyes with the rising fear of a not so distant memory, when his need for a reprieve had drained Seltruin's garden of all its *furie.* No matter how he tried to reason it out, the results were the same. He hadn't tried to wrest magic from the land or even ask for its assistance, though of the latter he couldn't be entirely sure. It was simply offered up for him to use, like a storm through a windmill.

He ran to Aren and checked the hound's thick neck for a pulse. The flow of blood was still strong, but his breath was ragged and unsteady. Idelle was much the same, alive but trembling as her body struggled for air. Both were quiet in his mind, despite calling out their names, and true fear took hold in his middle. The mere thought that he had somehow injured his friends made him suddenly nauseous. Leaning against the blackened husk of a tree, he slipped down to his knees and spilled the contents of his stomach.

When there was nothing left inside him but hollow guilt, he wiped his mouth on a sleeve and crawled over to Idelle. Even if it meant his own life, he planned to do all he could to save theirs.

I'm sorry, he said and called up his remaining *furie.*

Before he could expend even the slightest energy, a verdant wave came rolling in from all around. It restored vitality to the land, with thick grass and bright flowers sprouting up from renewed soil. Floating at the forward edge of this incoming growth was a lambent mist of shining emerald. It shot upward and out, like froth on an ocean tide, seeking out ash and debris with its splash of glowing life. When the mist rolled up and passed over them, Aren opened his eyes and sneezed. Idelle pushed back to her feet and shook out vibrant feathers. Even Barr felt refreshed, though mostly from the relief of seeing his friends whole again.

Are you two alright? He hugged Idelle, gripping his arms about her chest. Aren was subjected to the same affection. *I'm so sorry. I don't know how it happened.*

I think I'm okay. Aren's stomach grumbled so loudly that nearby villages might have heard it. *Yep, I'm fine. Just need some dinner is all.*

Me too, Idelle reassured Barr. *Being fine, that is, not needing another dinner.*

We haven't even had a first yet!

Barr laughed and wiped away his tears. *No fighting, you two. I'm sure we'll have plenty to eat when we get back. I'm just glad you're both fine, and the land seems to have righted itself. This time was even worse than Seltruin's garden.*

That's what happened? Idelle asked. *I just sort of blacked out for a moment. Our collars seem none the worse, though I don't recall them glowing like that.*

The collars were both a good distance away, as if they had been tossed through the air by the outpour of magic. They seemed fine by all appearance, with no trace of fracture or burns, but their runes were all aglow with a silvery light and outlined in cerulean.

Warm to the touch, they felt heavier than before, and their ironwood thrummed with power.

The glyphs are holding, Barr said. *I really don't see how these weren't destroyed.*

He slipped the appropriate one over Aren's head and was surprised when the collar shrank to fit of its own accord. Its runes then lost their glow and faded to black, but its power still tickled Barr's ears. The other formed itself to Idelle's neck as well, and the light within each rune shimmered away and was gone.

Do they work? Barr asked tentatively, worried he might have ruined the enchantments. *If not, I can –*

Aren disappeared, and Idelle thrust herself skyward with enough force to send Barr down to his back. Night engulfed her in a matter of seconds.

I'd say that's a yes. Aren came into view again. *So how about we head to your mother's estate, eat some dinner for a while and then get some sleep?*

Getting to his feet, Barr wholeheartedly agreed.

After nearly an hour of walking, they caught sight of the main gates, where three soldiers on horseback spoke to Daesi's guards. Each carried a crystal spear more than two feet longer than they were tall, and two of them appeared to have been wounded. There were gashes in their silken wraps, stained with dark blood around the edges, where something sharp had pierced through the scale armor beneath. Neither faeron looked pained, nor did they move stiffly or with trouble. Barr guessed they had already been healed, though the bloodstains were fresh.

"Trouble?" Barr asked and indicated the wound.

All three turned and bowed their heads, while the two guards gave a salute of fist to chest.

"None that we could not handle, my Prince," the middle soldier replied in a stilted tongue, as if unused to speaking aloud. "The central glyph... faltered for a brief moment, but it was enough time for a demon to squeeze through."

"The central glyph?" Mention of a demon caused a tingle in Barr's middle, a flutter he could not yet explain. "I'm not familiar with that."

"There are five glyphs that protect the rift between Faeronthalsos and Danarriden, the demon plane. For reasons we are not yet sure of, one of the outer glyphs was weakened, which caused the central one to fail. A single demon crossed the portal and was summarily dealt with."

Barr glanced down at the bloodstains and wondered just how summarily it had really been.

The faeron continued, "More soldiers have been sent to watch over the rift, and able enchanters are looking for any fault in the glyph structure. Two seers have also been dispatched to forewarn of any danger."

A sudden weakening? Idelle prompted.

I know. Barr inwardly kicked himself. *It had to have been me.*

The soldiers gave him an odd look.

"Thank you for the report," he told them and hurried past the gate. *What if I've done something to damage that glyph?*

Idelle swooped past. *He said it was momentary.*

Really, Aren agreed, *I don't see any point in worrying about it. They killed the demon that got through, and the glyph is back to normal.*

Barr shook his head as he entered the stronghold. *You didn't see the ruin I caused. For all we know, one of those glyphs could be permanently damaged. If that rift opens again and can't be closed...*

Both Aren and Idelle went silent.

*   *   *

Markus leaned on the parapet, tapping his fingers against stone, while Feraesk stood motionless beside him. The revenant remained equally silent, concealed within the illusory guise of a Guardian. There were more pressing matters to contend with, as far as Markus was concerned, but as usual Revyn disagreed. With little else to be done for it, they waited for nightfall.

Perched much higher than Noria, the stronghold looked down over the city from its hill and ever rising embankments, a bird of prey prepared to swoop. Despite walls of heavy stone, Markus could see all four quarters clearly from his vantage. Black smoke rose up in thick plumes, melding with the gray of winter skies, as a lesser haze from a thousand hearths crept along the tops of thatched roofs. The cobbled streets, slick with rain, seemed to weave a maze through the city, with no rhyme or reason as to their path. Unmindful of the cold, those who went about their daily schedule passed by wagons and playful children without so much as a second glance. It left Markus with the impression of industry, of busy people with busy lives.

If only they knew what awaited, he thought.

What purpose would that serve. It wasn't a question. By the dull ache left in his skull, stamped out by each word, he knew Revyn was not in a good mood. *Panic and chaos is not to our advantage. I want them turned in an orderly fashion.*

Unable to reply with anything that would satisfy or even placate the god, Markus chose instead to ignore the grating in his mind. It was one thing to be irritated by incessant delays and another to give cause for a bloodied nose or fractured jaw. As it often went with the chain of command, his mounting frustration found an outlet in Feraesk.

"Has that damnable Guardian fully turned?" Markus gritted his teeth, waiting for the throbbing to subside. He knew the headache to follow would linger for hours. "I cannot abide this waiting."

"He has not."

Sometimes the hollow ring of that voice annoyed him to no end. No more than an animated skeleton, a bony cage for Feraesk's soul, the corpse lacked the capacity for speech. What seemed to be spoken words was merely an illusion, one among many, and one of the revenant's choosing.

Markus took a deep breath and let it out, shedding frustration like clothes or a persona. There was no point in being angry with the revenant, nor could much be done about it if he were. Feraesk was but an instrument, a weapon to be used. Though his presence was a painful reminder of mortality, the two were inextricably bound.

"It will be time soon." Markus glanced at the setting sun and guessed half an hour before dusk. "Go to him. Let no one else enter until I arrive."

Feraesk bowed his head slightly and left.

It took him little time to find Claremont down in the kitchen eating supper. Markus stood outside in the hall and nodded the old steward over, away from prying ears. A scullery maid hurried past, head low and eyes averted. Serving boys rushed about, dropping off used plates and picking up new ones from the cook. Claremont wiped his mouth on a dirty napkin and came over to join him.

"It is urgent," Markus whispered, before the other could speak a word. "Follow, but do not look alarmed."

They arrived outside the High Hunter's door to the muffled sounds of groaning beyond the heavy wood. Few candles lit up the empty corridor.

"Where are the guards?" Claremont asked, his eyes betraying concern. "Something's not right."

I'm coming in. Markus opened the door. "Step inside, and I will explain everything." He waited for Claremont to enter and struck him from behind as he passed. The steward collapsed into a heap. Markus closed the door. "I assume he is ready to feed?"

Two guards lay sprawled to one side of the room, no sign of binding or blood to be found. Curled at Feraesk's feet was the Lord High Hunter, snarling and clawing at invisible restraints. His clothes were torn apart, his hair disheveled and matted with sweat, but he had not yet begun to turn.

"Any minute now," Feraesk answered.

Markus nodded. "I have a matter to tend to in the city. Be sure to clean up when he is finished." He looked down at the two guards. "So it begins."

He turned and left as Grailyn began to change.

* * *

Early the next day, Barr skipped morning meal and made his way out into the courtyard. He chose to sit within a fold of a clover-shaped fountain, its outer ring of black marble and its center a crystal aviary. Water shot up and outward in a spray like summer rain and struck against a runic cover overhead. Each drop lit off a soft glow of random color then trickled back into the basin. It lent a measure of calm, the sound of gentle showers all about, but the guilt that gnawed his middle would not allow him to relax.

You worry too much, Idelle said. She and Aren were off hunting breakfast in a dense forest to the west. *Your mother said it wasn't your fault.*

No, she said I couldn't have taken enough from the land to cause a glyph to fail. Barr clearly disagreed. *If she saw what I'd done, she'd probably ask me to leave.*

Nonsense.

Aren grumbled. *Focus. I want to eat and get back before noon. Besides,* he added, *it's pointless to worry about something that may or may not happen.*

Hello? Fluora called in his mind from outside the fountain's spray. She cleared her throat and said aloud. "Is it alright if I join you?"

Well, look who it is. Aren chuckled.

Shush. Barr replied, "Of course, please have a seat."

Oh, now *he wants quiet.*

Idelle laughed but didn't comment. While his heart raced at the sight of Fluora, he also felt Idelle dive and give chase after a stag. The surge in his veins brought a flush to his cheeks that made it difficult to meet Fluora's gaze. Unease soured his stomach with a flutter of wings, and he was suddenly glad for missing breakfast. With a deep breath, he steadied his nerves and looked upon her.

She wore a teal summer dress so light and airy that the freckles on her pale skin could be seen through the material. In the warmth of morning light, the deep red of her hair had a golden cast to each curl, and her eyes seemed to sparkle all the more. Her feet were bare and stained by the lush grass. She walked over with a smile and sat beside him on the fountain's edge, then curled her legs up beneath her. Closer than expected, Barr nearly jumped at the touch of her knee against his arm.

"Sorry," Barr said, embarrassed. In an attempt to hide his anxiety, he turned away and looked anywhere but directly at her. Fear of her hearing his thoughts only served to make matters worse. "I'm just a little bit jumpy this morning."

"No apology is necessary. In fact, I came to apologize myself." She took a lily from the basin and turned it over in her fingers. "I did not mean to leave your celebration so abruptly."

"What exactly happened?"

Whatever terrible premonition had caused her to faint, it had been sparked by his touch. He couldn't help but feel responsible and fought down the desire to reach out and hold her hand.

She was quiet for a while, as if searching for the right words, when he remembered faeron didn't normally speak aloud. That she did so was only to accommodate him and his unease at sharing thoughts with a stranger. Fluora looked at him with a puzzled expression, and an idea seemed to light up her eyes.

"Care to go for a walk?" She got up and held out a hand. "We could get to know each other a little better, maybe even talk about this arrangement of ours."

Arrangement? Aren asked. *More like a sentence.*

Fluora laughed, then covered her mouth with her other hand, somewhat apologetic for having listened but giggling all the same.

"You can hear Aren?"

Barr stood and accepted her hand. The strength of her grip belied its delicate appearance, a gentle firmness surprising from one so small. Her skin was soft to the touch and much warmer than he expected, like liquid fire running freely through her veins.

A squeeze pulled him from his reverie.

"Not directly," she explained. "I can hear his voice in your mind, which you are openly sharing."

"I am?" Barr considered a moment. "I'm really not doing anything that I'm aware of. Aren, Idelle and I just hear each other. I don't try to share those thoughts with anyone else."

"No, you would have to conceal them for others not to hear." She led him away from the fountain and down a path toward the main road. "Our minds are naturally open. The way you and your friends converse, without fear or reservation, is how every faeron speaks with one another."

Barr shook his head. "It's very different from what I'm used to. I don't know that I could adjust." He nodded in greeting to both guards while passing through the gate. They continued on through the grassy field across from the estate, when Barr added, "Hmm, do I call you Fluora? Or is that some sort of breach in etiquette I don't know about?"

She gave a wry grin. "That is acceptable. What about yours? Is Barr the familiar of something more formal?"

"I think it is, actually, but no one ever calls me by it. Wow," he said and stopped. "This is beautiful."

They stood before the largest spider web Barr had ever seen. It stretched between two broad trees the width of half a dozen arrows and reached again twice as high. Light from both suns played across its silver strands, and danced in time to the shadows cast from leafy boughs overhead. A breeze rose up from behind them and tousled their hair, then passed on through the web with the melodic trappings of a note. Like a whisper of music, it played on with the wind, varying its pitch with the intensity of the breeze.

"I can stand here and listen for hours," Fluora said, smiling with eyes closed. "This spot is one of my favorite places to visit."

I hope its maker isn't home, Barr mused.

We're about done here, Idelle said. *We'll be on our way back in no time.*

"This was not created by a spider." She knelt beside a wooden bowl at the base of one tree, then plucked a hair and placed it inside. "This is pixie art, a sculpture of sorts. Each strand is a piece of hair, dyed by moonlight and enchanted with song. I could show you more of their work sometime."

"I think I'd like that."

Barr knelt next to her, longing to feel her hand in his again, and pulled a strand of his own hair. He put it in the bowl and sat back on his legs. The windsong seemed to thank them with warbling vibrations.

It doesn't sound all that impressive to me, Aren said. *Reed pipes, lute and a drum. That's music.*

Idelle teased, *Maybe it isn't the music he finds so appealing but the company.*

Barr glanced at Fluora for any sign of reaction, but she hadn't seemed to hear. Looking up at the suns, he gauged the time near noon. There was no way of telling how long it would take the seers to find Aislin, but he hoped much sooner than later. Once the sword was back in his mother's care, he would have more time for other pursuits.

Keep an eye out for Dar-Paj when you get back.

"I can show you where he is," Fluora said.

She moved away from the web and waved a hand over the ground. Grass flattened beneath her fingers, then disappeared into dark soil, replaced by a basin of earth. A trickle of water began to form at its center and spread outward in a swirling of vapor. In but a moment, the basin filled with clear water. Its surface rippled with Fluora's reflection.

The hazy tendrils thickened to gray, then pulsed back to snowy white. Her image faded into the backdrop of stars and pitch black, an undulation of nighttime sky. Barr recognized it for the mists, his mother's domain, as he caught a glimpse of umbrals pass through the scry. She wove her fingers over the image, gently guiding the mist, until the ripples of starry sky became a reflection of Dar-Paj beneath her open palm. By all appearances, the gold-skinned apprentice was eating lunch outdoors with two faeron women and a mischievous fey.

"There you go," Fluora said. "He appears to have new friends."

She closed her hand and ended the scry. The image shifted in the span of a ripple and reshaped itself back into a shimmering reflection.

"You used the mists to scry," Barr said, struck by a thought. "I wonder."

Barr leaned forward on his knees and summoned a vision of his own, using both hands to grab at the mist. Where Fluora employed more of a gentle, graceful touch, Barr stabbed outward with his palms and held both eyes tightly closed. He neither coaxed the waters to bend to his will nor did he ask the mists for assistance. He used the strength of resolve to tear through the distance, with only his memory to guide him. Ripples broke apart and violently shook, as the waters gave way beneath his hands.

Within the scry was a reflection of Ealdan.

He was in the shadows of a poorly lit room, talking to a bear of a man from across a large desk, with an armored Guardian standing by his side. Though that one appeared to be human, Barr wondered if illusion hid a skeletal face. Even through the scry, he could feel a terrible power emanate from the Guardian. Ealdan spoke to the larger man like a subordinate.

"How many?" he demanded.

"A dozen," the big man answered. "We couldn't risk more without raising suspicion."

"I want the rest turned –"

The Guardian put a hand to Ealdan's shoulder in alarm and looked about the room. Barr felt a tingling at the nape of his neck, a whisper through the mists that made a ripple all its own.

"That one can see you," Fluora warned and quickly slapped at the water. The image vanished. "That room was protected. I could feel it. How did you force your way in like that?"

We're back at the estate, Idelle said. *Dar-Paj is here with us.*

Aren added, *We're ready to leave when you are.*

"I'm not sure."

Barr rubbed at his neck, troubled by something he couldn't put a finger on. It felt as if that Guardian had sensed who he was.

"He did," Fluora said. "Whoever he is, he followed your scry back to Faeronthalsos. He wields Aislin now, and he saw you as surely as you saw him."

"How can you be sure?"

"I am an oracle. I see many things." She took hold of his hand, looked into his eyes with a deep concern. "They will be ready for you now, if you go after Aislin."

He shook his head. "My mother won't survive long without it. I don't have a choice."

"Then neither do I." Fluora stood and pulled him up. "You need an oracle to traverse the mists, and you need to leave now."

"I know. I just hope my grandmother can find one."

"That will not be necessary," she said and turned, heading back to his mother's estate at a brisk pace. Over a shoulder, she called out, "I will be taking you."

Barr had to hurry to catch up.

– 4 –

hey stood in the courtyard, arguing. Barr had tried to convince Fluora to let another oracle take her place, that the uncertainty they were headed into was far too dangerous. She had refused to entertain the idea. As his intended, it was her right to go wherever he did, and she had every intention of doing just that.

"I will not put anyone else into harm's way for my own sake." She conjured water from the soil and began to scry through the mists, effectively ending the quarrel. "You will simply have to trust that I am not so weak nor inexperienced as you fear."

"Nothing will harm her," Dar-Paj said firmly.

Hidden once more beneath a cowl and heavy robes, the frail apprentice looked ready for confrontation. He had no weapons to speak of, fists notwithstanding, but on more than one occasion had proven his worth.

You said it's just Ealdan and two others. Aren sidled up beside Barr, his head low and body taut. *They don't stand a chance. If she stays in the back, she'll be fine.*

Barr gritted his teeth. *Just because I only saw one of those undead Guardians doesn't mean the other eleven aren't close by.*

An image of Aislin appeared in the water, rippling in the crystal reflection.

You're afraid she'll distract you, Idelle said.

Fluora glanced sidelong at Barr but quickly returned her focus to the scry. The mithrinum sword lay upon a stone dais, with nothing but darkness beyond the glow of its blade. As if sensing eyes upon it, Aislin gleamed in a blue shimmer and thrummed against the stone with a vibration that echoed throughout the chamber.

"Why isn't he wielding it," Barr said more than asked and looked closer at the water's surface. "They left it unguarded. Wherever he is, Ealdan must think we're going to storm in through the front door. Rather than risk using Aislin against me, he locked it away in some vault."

Dar-Paj looked at the image and shrugged. "At least he has no plans to flee. We can secure the blade before anyone knows where we are."

"No revenge," Daesl warned, her voice noticeably weaker. "If you can avoid confrontation, you must. At this moment, nothing is more important than returning Aislin to Faeronthalsos." Dar-Paj turned toward Barr, as if considering, then gave a reluctant nod of agreement. "Please hurry."

"I am ready," Fluora said.

It gnawed at Barr's middle that he was putting her in danger. Though they had just recently met, he felt an overwhelming desire to protect her. He knew what love was, or at least he thought he did. What he felt was more than attraction but not yet those heavy pangs. Besides, the notion of love at first sight seemed irrational. Yet he did feel something. Whether infatuation or the beginning of a deeper emotion, he cared more for her safety than his own.

Unfortunately, there was no other option. Daesi had assured him that only an oracle could carry others through the mists. The level of sheer concentration and attention to detail required to envision every aspect of those coming along, where they were leaving from and going to, bordered on the need for the divine prescience of premonition. The only other person nearby who could take them was his mother.

Under constant attack by the umbrals, her spirit was visibly flagging. Her pale skin had lost its sheen, seemed gray beneath the suns, and no amount of reassurance could mask the pain behind her eyes.

Determined, Barr gave a nod. "Let's go, then."

Mist rose up all about them in snowy tendrils, like arms from deep within the land that pushed through the dark soil and vibrant grass with ghostly appendages. In a glittering spiral, it fanned upward and out, brightening the ground in a circle of starry night. Vapor permeated their bodies and thickened to a fog, drowning out all other senses in a miasma of empty gray. Even Idelle, soaring through the air above them, was engulfed in the dense haze and pulled into the mists.

The emptiness stretched into a void of nighttime sky, a dark expanse of shifting midnight without the radiant silver of a moon. Dark water surrounded them, lapped up against their feet with warmth like a soothing touch. It all lasted for but a moment, as the void renewed its hold, but not before the flash of a shadowy claw could lash out.

Fluora gasped and dropped to her knees before the stone dais, draped in the soft glow of Aislin. Remnants of mist drifted off through the air and dispersed in a fading of light. They stood within the chamber from her scry, a circular room of plain stone, unadorned and without doors. Across her forearm was a series of four gashes.

We've arrived at a stronghold, Idelle said from her vantage above. *There's a city nearby as well.*

Barr knelt to tend Fluora's arm, when Dar-Paj put a hand out for the sword.

"Wait!" She gazed off into the distance, eyes lost to premonition. Barr watched fear rise up inside her like a shadow behind the stare, tensing her grip on his arm until the skin gave way. "Oh no. It is all my fault." She looked up at him, and tears began to well. "Forgive me."

Aren's hackles raised. *What did she do?*

A section of wall straight ahead slid backward and left an opening, where a dozen Guardians rushed in to stand at either side. They wore flowing black cloaks over burnished plate armor. Each had a steel long sword in hand but held off their attack. Two more stepped from the shadows outside the chamber, and the section of stone wall slid back into place.

"I told you it would not take long," Ealdan said to the second man. The other stood quietly, motionless. "I have to be perfectly honest, Barr. I did not expect to see you again."

An image flashed in Barr's mind, of a small girl in torn homespun, struggling to free herself from a black pool of swampy mire. It clung to her body, pulling her down, and her grip upon the surrounding foliage began to waver.

Save me! the girl screamed at him.

He blinked, startled by its abrupt intensity, and then the image was gone. He glanced over at Aislin and knew it was the sword pleading with him to take it. In the past, he could only hear the sword while holding it. That it spoke to him without touch lent a measure of urgency to the plea.

Barr didn't waste time on words but strode right for the dais. Before he could reach out his hand, the entire wall erupted in glowing runes. From floor to ceiling, the whole length of the circular chamber, the fiery sigils tied together to form numerous wards that in unison made up a single glyph. The sudden force it brought to bear shook his body with vibrations, twisted his stomach into knots and overpowered every thought with an incessant buzzing in his mind. He tried to summon the *furie* for a shield, to stave off the onslaught from all sides, but it was too much to overcome. His magic was suppressed, battered down before it could rise.

"What is happening?" Dar-Paj shouted, holding his ears against the thrum.

Aren whined, tried shaking loose the terrible noise in his skull, but refused to leave Barr's side. Fluora winced against the tremors and backed away from the dais. She held trembling hands to both temples and struggled just to move. Barr found it nearly impossible to think, to push past the rhythmic clamor.

"You should not have come," Ealdan said, his voice cutting through the din.

Barr caught sight of enchantment scrawled across each Guardian's armor, small runes that smoldered in ashen black. They seemed unaffected by the glyph and

61

stood waiting to attack. Barr had only a moment to find the linking runes on the wall before Ealdan gave the order. Fighting to maintain a single thought, he drew both kyan and continued to scan the glowing symbols.

Aren growled and leapt forward into the charging throng of men and swords. Dar-Paj snatched up Aislin but made no move to attack. He stood instead with both legs wide, sword held ready to strike, and seemed to wait for any one of the Guardians to try and make it past him to Fluora. The war hound tore into one, crushing armor and bones, shaking the hapless man like a rag doll. Two others swung their blades at his hind and back, but the steel clashed against enchantment with enough force to jar their hands.

With thousands of lifetimes of combat swirling in his mind, like a hurricane of memories funneling down to a single end, Barr was an instrument of precision that melded purpose with calm resolve. He reacted without thought, his body moving of its own volition, and chose targets with a cunning unrivaled in nature.

The first to reach him fell backward, neck punctured by the barest pressure at the tip of his kyan. Blood sprayed outward from an artery, as the man's legs were swept away. Barr completed his spin and turned aside a downward blade, caught hold of the weapon in his kyan's guard and wrenched it away. He drove the other ironwood blade up under the second Guardian's chin, through mail links and soft flesh. Yet a third came at him, but Dar-Paj stopped the man with a kick. The Guardian crumpled and was thrown backward through the air, crashing against the wall with enough force to crack the stone.

I can't get to you! Idelle cried, her voice distraught.

We'll be fine! Aren threw his Guardian at another, sending both men sprawling across the floor. *I just wish that noise would stop! It's grating on my skull!*

Barr disarmed another Guardian, then sliced across the runes on the man's armor. Suddenly clutching at his head, the Guardian staggered back and tripped over a body. A fifth met with Barr's kyan through the exposed area beneath the arm, then crumpled under the weight of a tremendous blow from Aislin's pommel.

"I see it now," Barr said.

He eyed a Guardian with sword raised, poised to strike down at Aren's neck. He flipped a kyan over in his hand and threw it by the blade. It spun across the room in the span of a breath. The Guardian ducked at the last instant, a finger length from being skewered, and looked up at the ironwood blade buried pommel-deep into the wall. It had cleanly parted a single rune and caused a flickering of the surrounding ward. In the time it took for realization to take hold, the glyph had faded to dark and ceased all function. He turned sharply toward Barr, a startled look crossing his features, and silently mouthed an expletive.

The air crackled all around him with the gathering of *furie*, and a helix of living flame rose up from Barr's feet. Tendrils of animated fire, they coiled about his body and climbed toward the ceiling. Stone bubbled beneath their touch, sending out embers through the visible heat. His body alight with spectral fire, Barr turned his attention to the remaining Guardians.

One was thrown against the wall by an unseen force, his armor and flesh succumbing to the intense heat. His screams were drowned out by the whistling of lambent fires, as they charred straight through to the flaking stone beneath his body. Stealing the *furie* from one and using it to crush another, Barr let loose all his pent up frustrations. His mother's life in peril, Fluora terrified behind him and facing Ealdan again was too much for him to bear. He let anger get the better of him, and the Guardians suffered for it.

"Enough," Ealdan said to the Guardian at his side. "Deal with them, Feraesk."

He strode forward without a word, through fire and blinding heat. The illusion woven about him gave way beneath the flurry, burned through by crackling flame, but renewed itself with every step. A white-hot inferno took him full on, eroding the illusion until nothing but a rotted walking corpse was left behind. Passed Barr and into Dar-Paj, the undead creature continued on without relent. His hand outstretched, he tore Aislin away by will alone and battered Dar-Paj aside with a single blow. The apprentice came off of his feet, struck against the wall in time to the crackle of breaking bones, then fell to the ground in a heap of robes and remained still.

The fires fell away.

Barr could see they had no affect on the undead and relied instead on his kyan. Aren growled and leapt at the skeletal creature but was repelled by a shield that pulsed with light as he struck. The hound yelped and fell over, dazed by the resounding shock. Barr met with the same jarring results.

Get Ealdan, he told Aren. *I'll deal with this.*

The hound turned with narrowed eyes and bounded off after the thief, while Barr focused his will on draining *furie* from the creature's enchanted bones. Fluora called up her own magic, as she edged back from the fray. Glittering dust filled the air and formed a shell all about her. The bloodied runes along each bone of the living corpse began to darken. Its shield faltered in a shower of beryl motes.

"Insolence!" Feraesk grated in a hollow voice.

He struck out with a fistful of ebon fire. Barr turned the attack aside, let it scorch wall and runes away, then lashed out with an attack of his own. Though the kyan hit its mark, scraping across the grisly forearm that held Aislin, only sparks and a dissonant shout gave sign of any damage. The creature let out a baleful hiss, empty eye sockets alight, and turned attention to the faeron at his feet.

Aren cried out again, struck in his side by a silver throwing knife. He called upon his collar and vanished from sight, but drops of blood betrayed his movements. He got a hold of Ealdan's thigh and bit down for all he was worth, satisfied by the pained cry and bitter crunch of bone that followed after. Ignoring stabs to his thick hide, he shook the screaming thief until the blade came free and skittered away from them both.

Barr released a flurry of attacks that flashed with sparks at every strike, fighting desperately to keep the creature away from Fluora. Ignoring her ward, dispersing it with little effort, the undead Guardian took hold of her by the neck and lifted her into the air. Suspended by an implacable strength, she dangled with both feet a good distance off the ground. He drove her against the wall, forced the air from her lungs and choked off any hope of another breath. The flicker of dying enchantment rained all about them. Consumed by rage and the mounting fear of looming failure, Barr swung out in an unrelenting fervor. Without pause, the creature thrust Aislin through her shoulder, plunging its blade deep into the wall. She gave a soundless cry of pain, her voice stolen with her breath, and clawed at the remnants of arm that held her fast.

"Hold!" Barr shouted and lowered his weapon.

"Surrender, or she dies," Feraesk commanded. His bony hand edged the blade closer to her heart, eliciting another voiceless cry. "Call off the hound."

Aren let Ealdan drop and turned with a growl. *Can't you do something?*

Don't give up! Idelle pleaded. *If you submit, he'll kill you all! He has no reason to keep you alive!*

She is right. Fluora's voice in their minds was weak with pain. *Aislin is all that matters now. Far more than my own life hangs in the balance.*

The blade moved again, sending spasms through her body. Blood ran down her pale skin, soaked the front of her dress and dripped off her toes to form a puddle beneath her feet.

There wasn't time enough to reason out his decision, to weigh the fate of his mother and all faeron against the life of a girl he barely knew. All he could be sure of was he didn't want her blood on his hands, that if even the slightest chance to save her still existed, he had to take it. He saw no other options, no means to kill the undead and keep Fluora alive.

He had no choice but to surrender.

* * *

Barr woke to the incessant buzzing in his head, felt it thrum down his spine in tremors that shook his body, and overcame the pulsing of blood in his ears. Chained to a wall in the cell, his toes barely touching the frozen ground, it was all he could do to manage his next breath, let alone stave off the pain from focusing too long on any one thought. He felt dried blood on his upper lip, his only reward for the last time he had tried to break free. The manacles at his wrists and ankles glowed in the oppressive dark with runes of silver and fiery blue.

You're awake? Idelle asked. *I'm so sorry. I don't know what to do! I can't get back to Faeronthalsos, and there's only humans around here for miles.* She was quiet a moment, as if worrying how Barr might react. *I went looking for Geilon-Rai.*

No. Barr swallowed. *Too dangerous.* He could no longer recall the last time he had a drink. *Can't risk discovery.*

Aren shifted, pulling at his manacles. *I could break free, if it wasn't for that noise!* He yelped. *Hurts to think.*

A glance up showed Barr little had changed. Fluora and Dar-Paj still hung from their chains, both of them unconscious and dying. The grievous wound left behind by Aislin had stopped bleeding, but it wouldn't be long before infection set in. Worse still, the four cuts made by an umbral had blackened the surrounding skin, and like a wasting disease seemed to be spreading up her arm. She looked terribly fragile, curls plastered to her graying cheeks, like a child pushed beyond all endurance.

Dar-Paj was in a poor state as well, his snowy mane tinged with ash and dirt, as if dragged along the ground by his feet. Though the manacles had not broken the skin at his wrists, patches of dark bruising over his bare chest and sides gave proof of internal damage. Despite what his body had suffered, his mind seemed more affected by the ordeal. He shook in his sleep, wracked by some vision that set his breath to racing and body twitching against his bonds. Whatever demons he faced in dream, he didn't appear to be faring well against them.

Either of them woken yet?

Not yet. Aren shifted again and whimpered. The fur at his neck and back were caked with dried blood. *It's just as well. Idelle?*

Yes?

When we're out of here, will you find me a boar?

Yes. The biggest you've ever seen.

Barr tugged at his chains, struggling to summon enough *furie* to weaken its iron. If he couldn't break through the enchantment, he might be able to sever one of the links. The muscles in his arm and chest burned from the exertion. Sweat beaded on his forehead and ran down into his eyes, touched his lips and mingled with fresh blood. With a feral growl, he pulled with all his might and fought against the violent trembling that coursed over his spine. The vibrations threatened to split his skull, before he collapsed against the wall in defeat. He hung there for long moments, gasping for air, oblivious to the wetness that ran down from his wrists.

"I am almost impressed," Ealdan said from behind the heavy wood of their cell door. He opened it and stepped inside. Feraesk, the undead creature posing as a Guardian, was with him. "To be honest, I half-expected you to be dead by now. Again."

Aren snarled and leapt. Though his chain didn't allow him to go very far, he took satisfaction at seeing Ealdan startle.

"I saved your life once." Barr spat blood at the thief's feet. "I trusted you." He looked at Feraesk. Even illusion could not mask the stench of death all about him. "And these living corpses you command. Who are you really, Ealdan?"

The actor-thief sighed. "Of all my personas, I enjoy that one the least. You may address me as Lord Markus. As for your sense of betrayal, how do you think I felt when I discovered you had Aislin all along? If I had known that in Darleman, I would have just taken it and been on my way." Another dramatic sigh, as if talking with Barr was a complete waste of time. "In any case, these chains were forged by Guardians long ago, when they were still worth a damn. Attempting to break free will only kill you sooner. So, feel free."

Barr leveled a glare at him.

"By the way," Markus continued, unaffected, "those manacles are draining your *furie*. The longer you sit here, the harder it will be to free yourself. I believe the longest anyone has survived is three days." He gave a half smile. "Two more to go. I will have water sent down, if you satisfy my curiosity. How is it you survived? I watched you die, yet here you are! Remarkable. Was it this one?" he asked and raised Fluora's head with a finger beneath her chin. He examined her delicate features, then let her head drop back down against her chest unceremoniously. "It must be the gaping wound that makes her appear so weak now, but I am sure she is usually a power to be reckoned with!"

The cell echoed with his laughter. When no one else joined in, he walked over to Dar-Paj and punched the frail apprentice across the face. Barr pulled at his chains but said nothing.

If I find where you are, Idelle said, *I'll tear him to pieces.*

Aren was mere inches away. *You'll wait your turn.*

"Never did like him. I am going to enjoy asking him the questions you refuse to answer." Markus stepped back to the cell door and nodded to Feraesk. The undead approached Barr and waited. "I know you scried me from Faeron. Is that what happened? This fiery trollop pulled you into the mists and healed you with its waters?"

"You seem to know a lot already," Barr replied. He looked Feraesk in his illusory eyes, recalling the lambent fires that filled those empty sockets. "You're wearing my sword."

Feraesk punched him in the side, cracking two ribs. Barr winced as pieces of bone pinched his lungs with each breath. The undead leaned in close and sniffed at the glistening flesh of Barr's shoulder. Mouth opened, he looked as if he intended to bite.

"Hold," Markus ordered. By the darting of his eyes, he seemed to be listening to something only he could hear. "Leave him. Grab the gold one. We shall allow Barr some time to think."

Feraesk unchained Dar-Paj and dragged him across the floor by the nape of his neck. Markus closed the cell door behind them.

"Try not to think *too* hard, though."

His laughter echoed down the corridor as they left.

* * *

Icy water splashed over his body. Eyes gummed and blurry, Dar-Paj woke suspended from chains, sputtering and aching all over. Each breath brought waves of new pain with the shifting of broken bones, and the white flash at the back of his skull put a limit to how much air he could take in. Aside from his own ragged breathing and the drip of water beneath him, he heard nothing but the thrum in his head. The vibrations down his spine sent tremors through every muscle, gripping him in a semblance of chills.

Despite the assault on his senses, he knew he was not alone. He could feel their proximity prickle his skin, set the hairs on his neck to standing on end. He caught the scent of one, like a slap across the face, and it pulled him from the daze more surely than any water. The one that reeked of death loomed over him, a wraith radiating cold that even Dar-Paj could feel.

More alert, his vision adjusted. A single candle on an upended barrel lit the room, where Ealdan was seated beside it. Anger rose up inside him, a wild beast from his middle, tensed his body and pulled taut the iron chains. He felt the stone overhead give a little and begin to crumble. Showered in dust and debris, he looked up at the crack then back to Ealdan and smiled two rows of pointed teeth.

Powerful blows rained down on him, punches of incredible strength. It stole the air from his lungs, filled his mind with blinding pain, as skin and muscle were battered apart. Tortured minutes passed with no end in sight.

"That will suffice." Through the ringing in his ears, he recognized Ealdan. "I would suggest you not try that again. My associate has no understanding of restraint."

"Traitor," Dar-Paj managed between gasps.

Gritting his teeth, he willed the anger to return. It bubbled up from his belly like the birth of an inferno, a fire devouring wind in an unbridled frenzy. It gave his muscles renewed vigor and fueled resolve into action. He pulled again at the chains with both hands, jerked his body forward and tried to wrench them from the ceiling. He heard the metal whine in protest and faults crack the stone, as a mounting roar tore across the interior of his mind. With muscles strained against heavy iron and the glowing enchantment, waves of fierce tremors shook his body like an earthquake. They raced up toward his neck in an explosion of light and sound. He fought so strongly against the tumult, refusing to give in, that he was sure he would have died if not for the bony hand that reached out and gripped him by the throat.

Two fiery orbs leaned in close and demanded his attention. Dar-Paj flinched at their heat but was unable to look away. Pinned down by the stare, his anger dissolved with the onset of fear and fell away like clothes in the dark. He focused his will on breaking free of the penetrating gaze but felt helpless beneath its weight.

"Unlike you or your friends," Ealdan said, "I know what you are. And while you may not turn, you *will* serve a purpose."

The voice went on in the background, an echo across the surface of blackness all about him. He felt exposed in that dark, his soul opened and laid bare for all the world to come see. Every bit of joy that had lit his heart or touch of sadness that pulled him down, every proud moment and pang of guilt, all his loves and fears, desires and disgraces, each were laid out for the fires to scour.

More frightening than the memories shown were the ones he had concealed, those so painful to endure they had taken everything when tucked away. It mattered little to the fires. They stole into every recess, shed light in every fissure. Nothing remained hidden beneath their gaze. It was only then that he understood, that the eyes did more than merely search. They taunted him with the shadows of abandoned memory, dangled them in the air like spinning silhouettes.

The fires threatened to make him see.

"Good," Ealdan said. "It appears we understand each other now. All you need to do is tell me what you know of Aislin and the other Emblems. Then we can put all of this unpleasantness behind us."

Unable to tear his gaze from the fires, his entire body trembling in fear beneath them and exhausted from his struggles, Dar-Paj could only wince at the tightened grip on his throat. He felt the tip of a bony finger break the skin across his chest. From shoulder to shoulder, neck down to waist, his golden flesh became a parchment for intricate designs. Rivulets of wetness ran freely down his front and both legs, traced sticky lines across his toes and echoed drips into a pool beneath his feet. Though the warmth of life fled from his body and left a growing tundra in its wake, he cared only that the dark remained at bay. He could withstand any torture the eyes devised, so long as he wasn't made to look.

Please, he pleaded in his mind, as tears streamed down his cheeks. *Don't make me look...*

"Tell me," Ealdan whispered in his ear, his voice insistent. "How you did you survive at Lumintor? Tell me, and I will let you go. What harm could come of it now?"

Dar-Paj shook his head imperceptibly, opened his mouth to speak, but no words were forthcoming. He was paralyzed with fear. Inky green vapors began to rise from off his body, clouding his vision, filling his nose with the burning odor of betrayal. When the skeletal hand let go its hold, Dar-Paj hazarded a look down at his front. The golden skin was without mark but for the bruises and jutting ribs he had already endured. He raised his eyes up to Ealdan and swallowed blood to wet his throat.

"Your tricks have failed," he said and gulped another breath. "Kill me. I will tell you nothing."

Ealdan gave a curt nod to the undead. "He is too strong for us, Feraesk. Return him to his cell. We shall see how strong the faeron is instead."

All sense of victory fled at the prospect of Fluora's torture. Dar-Paj tried to protest, to answer their damn questions, but the one called Feraesk no longer listened.

A bony punch sent him back into darkness.

*   *   *

Fluora stirred, fought against the fever in her blood and opened heavy lids. The pain from hanging by her wrists, the quivering up her spine and the chill that rattled every inch of her flesh was nothing compared to the pulsing death that crept through her veins. She felt it originate at her forearm, where an umbral had struck and left its mark.

The cell door opened and let in a bit of light. Dar-Paj was dragged in and chained to the wall on her left by a revenant, a corpse made into a prison for the soul that had once inhabited it. She could see the screaming black of a spirit flitting in and out of its remains. It turned and eyed her with fiery sockets before leaving.

Whatever physical torture the revenant had visited upon Dar-Paj, it paled when weighed against the harm inflicted on his spirit. His aura was littered with gaping holes, outlined in black, with long tendrils of swampy vapor slithering about him. It almost looked as if his spirit was fractured, two pieces of the same whole now housed within his broken body.

She glanced over at Barr without moving her head and caught sight of their captor standing over him.

"You see now," Ealdan said to him with a half smile. "I can take her away and bring her back much the same as your colorful friend here. How would that make you feel?"

Barr looked away.

She saw the images in his mind frantically at work, desperate to find the means to break free. Their eyes met momentarily, and the maelstrom of his thoughts washed over her in a flood of emotion and concern, drowning out all sense of pain for a brief time. She wondered that he could feel so strongly for her so quickly. Despite what she saw of the future, of their love and Barr's passing, she found herself drawn to him all the more. Fear of grief was no way to live, and no future was carved in stone.

Ealdan gave him a playful pat on the cheek. Barr lunged forward, like an animal caged, but the chains went taut and held him back. The enchantment woven about them was very old and burned with *furie*. She could see magic pulsating around the links, spiraling out toward the ends, as if fueling each ward inscribed upon the manacles. She then realized the chains were feeding off them, draining their lives to replenish and empower those wards in a vicious cycle that would only end with their deaths.

"Such foolishness." Ealdan shook his head. "In any case, enjoy what time you have left." He stepped out of the cell and closed the wooden door. From the barred window, he added, "I am willing to wager a hundred gold we will not meet again."

"Make it two," Barr said.

The sound of footsteps down the corridor echoed their departure.

About time he left, she heard Aren say. Though the hound feigned sleep, she could see he was in dire need of rest. *Loves to hear himself talk. Next time I bite him, I'll be sure to finish him quicker.*

"Are you alright?" Barr asked her.

I've carried off half a dozen of their guards, Idelle said. *If you manage to break free, there'll be less for you to deal with.*

Don't draw attention to yourself, Barr told the hawk. *If we don't make it out, I need you to tell Seltruin what happened.*

"I have been better." Fluora was reminded that this whole mess was her doing. If she had stayed behind like Barr wanted, the revenant would not have had her to use as a bargaining chip. "I should have listened. I am sorry I caused all this."

Aren opened an eye. *You two are a perfect match.*

"None of this is your fault." Barr gripped both chains and looked up at the glowing runes. "If anything, this is my fault for leading us into a trap." His face reddened with concentration, as images in his mind swirled about the manacles in an attempt to unravel their wards. "I keep trying... to sever the runes... but no matter how hard I try... I just can't –"

Blood ran from his nose and spattered with each word. It came next from his ears, but he would not relent. She saw guilt weigh upon him like a palpable force, driving him on with no regard for his own life. His breath became labored. His body trembled from the exertion of both muscle and will. Still the runes would not waver. Fluora knew he would not stop, felt it in her heart that he would drive himself to the brink of death before giving in to despair.

"Aren!" she shouted. "Make him stop!"

The hound reacted swiftly despite his wounds and got up to all fours.

What are you doing? the hound demanded. *You're going to kill yourself!* Barr refused to give up. The stone all around him began to crumble, but the runes glowed even stronger. *Idelle, do something! He won't listen!*

The hawk screamed at the skies in frustration.

"Barr, please," Fluora said quietly, reaching out to his spirit with a soothing chant in her mind. "You must relax. Listen to my voice. Let it carry you back." Her chant whispered to his soul but sank beneath the thrum that sought to kill him. "Recall the mists, Barr. Picture it in your mind. Let it soothe your thoughts. Let it fill you with its stars. Let these walls fall away..."

*   *   *

...into the darkness. There were screams echoing all around, but they were distant. Everything was distant. There was only the trickle of water as it dropped from above, striking some unseen puddle, setting time to the eternity of isolation. She remembered family, could smile at the thought of them, as she rocked back and forth on the cold stone floor, but their faces were missing, washed away like so many other memories that had faded with time. She wondered if her own face was still with her, so long had it been since...

...he had any food or drink. He looked frantically about the cell, eyeing the rusted bars and yellowed walls. Not even insects could survive down here. He wanted to shout, but thirst had stolen his voice away. His hands were bloodied and broken from pounding at walls that would not yield. Though he could see others just like him, it offered little comfort. The headman's axe would have been far preferable...

...to the rack. Hearing every tendon pop and bone splinter, as they were slowly stretched out over a wheel. He had lost the ability to move any part of his body, could barely breathe for the shattered ribs stabbing into his lungs, but still he could feel. There was nothing to do for it. No confessions, no questions, no offer of quarter.

He worshipped the wrong gods, and that was an end to it. If only death would come...

...sooner or later, and when it did he would look that skeletal bastard right in the eye! So they were killing him piece by piece, taking a finger here, a toe there, then letting the wounds heal before taking more. Eventually they would be sawing off arms and legs, if the rotting or a fever didn't kill him first. That's alright, he had done far worse. In battle, it's all bloody hands and...

...shining blades, cutting away the flesh, slow and methodical. It was almost a welcome change from the hot pokers. Nothing smelled worse than the burning of flesh, especially your own. Berak could only shrug. They both had jobs to do, after all. He had endured just about every torture known to man, and a few that weren't. He had no fear of breaking...

...every bone in her body, one by one, with a mallet. They began at the toes with what felt like two days past. There were four of them, hooded men with filthy hands that went everywhere. Leather straps held her securely, though she couldn't move if she wanted to. Her bones had been pulverized to the waist. It never ceased to amaze her how cruel a man could be...

...that he would torture a child? Garil told them what they wanted to know, but it didn't matter. They didn't believe him. They threatened to torture his wife and child, if he should die before they had what they wanted. Nail after nail drove into his flesh, parting muscle, striking through bone, but still they did not believe him. Why would he lie? Was it that they truly didn't believe him, or was he just not saying what they wanted to hear? And all the while, his family was forced to watch...

...as the fires climbed up the hem of her dress, like an oily snake creeping ever higher. She was surrounded by people screaming for her blood, throwing rocks,

dancing and laughing as they tossed more torches onto the fire. Even Nora, her friend since childhood, looked on her with disgust, face twisted by a hatred she had never before shown. They teased and taunted, wondering why she wouldn't save herself with magic. If only she had such power. She could free herself of these bonds and escape the flames. But there was no power, just the growing fire and a burning need to break free...

*   *   *

Fluora was confused by all the images in Barr's mind, the numerous people and places that rose up from memories not of this lifetime. He stopped fighting against the enchantment in his chains but seemed lost to the rush of visions, his spirit thrown about in their passing.

All at once, he came back to himself.

She then gasped as Barr's entire body tensed, arcing outward from the wall in a soundless cry. Steam rose up from every inch of him, as if a great heat swelled within and struggled against the bitter cold. When he finally took a breath, it was rapid and hoarse, each exhalation a burst of crystalline frost. Slowly, his body eased, taut muscles relaxing until he hung once more from the chains. He grew calm, letting out streams of icy breath through his nose. When at last he opened his eyes, a burning yellow light fully engulfed them and radiated outward inches from his face. Their glow illuminated the cell, as Barr looked about, studying his surroundings as if for the first time.

He leveled a narrowed gaze at the manacles binding his feet. The enchanted iron began to glow even brighter, each rune flaring across their surface, until a white flash turned them into a shower of sparkling dust. He did the same for his hands and dropped from the wall. He paid no attention to Fluora or the others, his thoughts hidden from her mind, then turned ghostly eyes on the cell door.

"*Disp'aen*," he raised a hand and commanded.

His voice was unearthly, chilling and deep. When he spoke, it shook the ground, and prickled the hairs on Fluora's arms and neck with a wild sensation. It felt as if the very air were alive with power, charged with energy and the crackling scent of a lightning bolt. The stone wall, cell door and all, brightened to a blinding white and burst apart. The spray of ash and intense heat charred the stone wall across the corridor with the shadow of its passing. Without a second look, he stepped forward to leave.

"Barr?" Fluora asked. "Is that you?"

He turned those glowing eyes upon her, setting her porcelain skin alight. Though he looked like Barr, she knew he was not. At least not entirely. His body radiated so much *furie* that she could no longer see his aura. She tried to see past the flesh, to reach him with her mind, but the manacles brought her back to bear, dousing her focus like a flame beneath the tides.

With a wave of his hand, the remaining chains in the cell burst apart in a mist of silvery blue and ash. Dar-Paj fell to the ground in a heap, while Fluora managed only to land hard on her knees. Aren shook off the debris and took a tentative step toward his friend.

Barr again turned to leave.

Fluora got to her feet and called after. She moved to block his path, searching for any sign of his spirit in the blazing *furie* that surrounded him. He towered over her, with an otherworldly gaze that would have wilted any man. Still, she would not move. She reached up a trembling hand and gently touched his cheek.

"What has happened to you?"

Breath caught in Barr's throat, and he collapsed.

– 5 –

arr woke with his head cradled in Fluora's lap. Aren was sprawled out beside him, in a vain effort to keep him warm, but nothing could stave off the biting chill of icy stone all around. He shivered at its touch beneath his back and legs, numbing the bare skin to a dull prickle. He forced himself to sit up, to take in his surroundings, and every muscle cried out against the strain. Though nothing appeared broken or bruised, he was weary to the bone and sore all throughout. The only true pain he could feel, besides the inexorable cold, stemmed from a ravenous hunger that knotted his middle and a thirst that clawed his throat with each swallow. Every bit of him shook in a struggle for warmth, when a trickle of water in the quiet caught hold of his attention.

The buzzing was gone from his mind.

With no chains or manacles in the cell, the only sign they had existed were thin scars at his wrists. To Barr's left, Dar-Paj lay in a pool of dried blood, as if he had fallen from the wall and collapsed. His golden skin had gone pale, to a sickly gray, and matted hair over his face moved in time to shallow breath.

Aren trembled beside Barr, lost to a deep slumber. There was a watery rattling in his lungs and more than a dozen knife wounds spread across the bulk of his thick mane. Whatever blade Markus had used, the collar's enchantment had done little to turn it aside.

He spun and faced Fluora, shocked by what he saw. Slumped over and limp, her back to the wall, she barely moved with the intake of breath. The festering wound at her shoulder was purple and inflamed, oozing telltale signs of infection. Despite the stinging cold, she burned with a fever. Hair dampened by sweat clung to her face in tiny ringlets, and a sheen of perspiration ran the length of her body. The sickness left behind by the claws of an umbral had spread up her arm and continued to reach outward. From fingertips to shoulder, the skin was rigid and black, as if death had taken hold of her by the hand.

They had little clothing to speak of, let alone a heavy blanket, so Barr did what he could to warm the cell. He called up *furie* from within and let it flow from his palm, into the stones of the floor. Each one brightened to a soft yellow glow, tame suns beneath their skin, and chased both darkness and bitter cold from the chamber.

Barr? Idelle asked in a voice still shrugging off sleep. *Are you alright? You blacked out late last night, and it's been hours since I heard from Aren.*

I'm fine, but everyone else is badly hurt. We're not chained up anymore, he said and glanced at the charred wall before attempting to heal Fluora, *and our cell door appears to be missing. Apparently something happened when I blacked out.*

You had a vision, a strong one. Like the time you sparred with Harduen.

How long have we been down here?

It's past noon, so two days now. All but a handful of Guardians have left for the city. Her voice turned grave. *This place is like the temple in Lumintor. Everyone here is a shapeling.*

Fluora's wounds had faded to the barest of scars, all save the blackness that permeated her arm. Barr had never seen anything like it and had trouble discerning what was happening to her body. At first he thought it a disease that ate away at the flesh or a poison that turned her own *furie* against her. This was neither. He sensed no parasites in the blood nor were there any compounds to purge. It seemed as if the magic within her, the very essence of her life, was turning in on itself and dying out.

The ones we faced weren't shapelings, none of them changed. What did you see?

Barr took hold of her hand and opened himself fully, willing the darkness to leave. Rather than fade to pale skin or return to supple flesh, it lashed out and gripped his fingers in growing black. He struggled to fend it off, to stop it spreading through his veins, but it fed upon his *furie* with a creeping insistence. The more he fought against it, the stronger it pushed.

Early this morning, Idelle replied, *dozens of them went down into the courtyard and became wolves. They attacked their own horses, ate or drained every one of them, then left for the city. They haven't been back since.*

The black engulfed his hand up to the wrist and was spreading at an alarming rate. His skin had hardened to ebon leather, and the fingers refused to move. There was no letting go of Fluora, even if he wanted to, and no way of halting the empty pain from spreading throughout his body.

With little of his own *furie* left to expend, Barr turned his concentration downward and sought out the flowing pull of a ley line. Like golden rivers of liquid *furie* that ran deep beneath all lands, the ley lines were both a source of life and a wellspring of magic. Elven sages used them to replenish forests, to breathe new life into the trees. In much the same way, Barr reached down his will through rocky earth and touched his spirit upon a line, let it rise up and flow through him in a wave of cleansing light. The warmth bubbled over in a froth that stole his breath and crashed about him in a spray of honeyed motes of luminescence.

He felt the darkness in his flesh give way beneath a final tide.

Is everything alright? I couldn't hear you just then.

It is now. Barr let go of Fluora's arm and flexed his fingers. *If all the Guardians here have suddenly become shapelings, I doubt Ealdan's presence is a coincidence.*

You mean Markus.

If you're still getting rid of guards, try to save one for questioning.

The blackened skin was gone from them both, and no trace of the umbral's claw marks remained. Fluora opened her eyes, with the weight of dream still upon them, and sighed a deep breath in relief.

You look well, she said in his mind and put a hand to his chest. *I was worried* – she cut herself short with a shake of the head and added, "My apologies. I am weary and forget myself."

His cheeks grew warm at her touch, but he hid the lapse with a smile.

There's no need to apologize, he replied and garnered a smile in return. "I need to heal Aren and Dar. Can you stand? I haven't had a chance to look outside yet."

"I will try."

He tended to Aren first, as Fluora pulled herself up. She stepped out of the cell, beyond the warm glowing stones, hugged both arms to her chest and left to explore. When all of Aren's wounds were mended, his pale blue eyes opened with a yawn and a burst of foul breath. He sat up and was none too amused at Barr fanning the air.

Clearly your sense of humor hasn't suffered. I'm probably dying from starvation, and you joke about my breath.

Barr laughed and hugged him by the neck. *It's good to see you're alright too.* He let go and left off to heal Dar-Paj. *Will you go see if Fluora needs a hand?*

I'll go hunting for you right now, Idelle said.

Something big and juicy. Aren turned and walked off, a trail of drool following after. *Like stag topped with boar.*

Dar-Paj was in a worse condition than Barr first surmised, with numerous open breaks, internal injuries and severe loss of blood. That he still drew breath at all was a miracle in itself. His wounds were so extensive, in fact, that Barr decided not to heal him all at once. Fluora returned and knelt beside him, as he finished the initial pass.

"I tried earlier to bring us to Faeron," she said. "I will need more rest before trying again. I take it the floor is your doing?"

Barr nodded and wiped his brow. "It was getting a little chilly in here. Find anything of interest?"

"More cells and a barred door."

"Other prisoners?"

"None." She pushed aside a lock of Dar's hair. "I see his fever has broken. The rest will take a great deal of time."

He could tell she meant more than the physical. The torture Dar-Paj had endured took more than just a toll on his body.

"Will he be alright?"

She considered. "I see only that the damage done to his spirit is great. If he cannot overcome it, he will never again be whole."

Aren lay down beside the apprentice. *Anything I can do for him?*

It was Fluora who answered, "Be his friend."

Another hour passed before Dar-Paj was fully healed and began to stir. His eyes opened, their soft brown all ringed in a glittering gold, and fell upon Barr. He looked down of a sudden, hand going to his chest, but relaxed when he found nothing untoward.

"What's wrong?" Barr asked.

Dar swallowed hard and shook his head. "It was just an illusion. They cut at my chest, tried to make me tell them how we survived." He struggled with the dryness in his throat. "I told them nothing of your mother."

Barr put a hand to his friend's shoulder, wanted to tell him it didn't matter, that no secret was worth losing his life over. But neither did he want to diminish what Dar-Paj had endured, so instead he gave silent thanks.

"I'm just glad you're alive."

"As are we all." Fluora stood and offered a hand to them both. "I can try to take us home, if you are ready."

Don't leave without me, Idelle said. *I'm on my way back with a late lunch.*

"I can't leave just yet," Barr said. "I need to find my kyan and find out what's going on around here."

Dar-Paj stood before the missing wall, stared at the burn marks across the way and then down at the scars at his wrist.

"I must have missed something." he said. They both shrugged and walked past him, but the massive hound stayed by his side. "Planning on keeping me safe?"

Aren snorted.

"Fair enough."

Barr took a torch down from the wall and called fire to its end, then led them on through the darkness. The corridor ran past three unused cells and ended at a heavy wooden door. Reinforced with steel fittings, bolted with a crossbar from the other side, it was most likely deemed by the Guardians a considerable obstacle. Dar-Paj gave a push with both hands and splintered the wooden beam.

The door swung open with ease.

It led into a small room with a set of stairs going up. The stone hearth on the east wall housed the remnants of a fire, but the wood holder beside it was empty. Aside from a table, two chairs and a rack with no weapons, the room was utterly bare. Barr led them up the stairs into a barracks, where a handful of recruits probably stayed. Their beds were askew, the linens torn and bloodied, as if a terrible scuffle had taken place. Dar-Paj opened one of the cabinets and found clothing his size, while Barr used his tracker's eyes to read markings across the floor and in the smears of dried blood.

"Try this," Dar-Paj said and handed Fluora a tunic three times her size. "Sorry, this is the smallest."

The air shimmered around Fluora with the glitter of rainbow sparkles. The material in her hand shrunk in on itself, softened to a satin sheen and glimmered in the torchlight. When she slipped it on, it looked just as her dress had, albeit in a glossy shade of gray.

Barr held the torch aloft. "This just about confirms what Idelle's seen. The Guardians were all infected by a shapeling."

A sharp look from Dar-Paj. "A shapeling? When they questioned me... Ealdan said something."

"His true name is Markus. What did he say?"

Dar-Paj tried to recall but shook his head in defeat. "I am not sure. I was certain he hinted at shapelings. There was something else, however. He said Aislin and the others. There could be more swords just like it."

"Aislin is sentient," Fluora reminded them, "and very powerful. If others like it exist, they would be valuable beyond measure."

"Worth killing for," Barr agreed, his mind lingering on betrayal. "We still need to get Aislin. Don't forget an umbral was able to attack you. That means my mother is weaker than I thought."

I can follow this, Aren said by a second door, sniffing at a trail of blood. *These are barely a day old.*

Idelle said, *I'm just outside the stronghold. There're only three guards left, but if you give me a minute, I can take care of the two on the walls.*

Where's the third? Barr was already heading for the door. "Let's go."

He's at the gate, Idelle replied.

Dar-Paj stopped him and held out a set of clothes. He took the torch and led the way, leaving Barr little choice but to get dressed. The tunic was coarse and a bit large. The linen breeches he tucked inside a pair of worn boots. Despite the discomfort, they were the best he could manage until his leathers were found.

Through another corridor and the main hall, Barr hurried to catch up. His steps echoed in the silence, despite tapestries and colored rugs, putting a fine point to the weight of emptiness in the air. It hung over him like a shroud, pressing down with unease against the barrier of rationale. It left a sense of gloom in his heart, as if the abandoned stronghold was portent of a greater darkness to come.

He found them in the kitchen, eating bread and fruit from a prepared meal that was never served. Aren lapped up water from a wooden bucket, while the others drank from ceramic cups.

"I found a privy out back," Dar-Paj said between mouthfuls of apple and buttered roll.

There's a nice tree as well, Aren added.

There was a scream from outside, followed by Idelle saying, *I have the last guard alone in the courtyard.*

"Idelle's ready for us outside. I'll be right back."

Barr went out to relieve himself, as Aren left the kitchen for a proper meal of fresh meat. When Barr returned, he put an apple in his pocket, stuffed a roll in his mouth and brought along a cup of well water on his way to Idelle. Even the little bit set his stomach to grumbling, but he knew better than to eat or drink in haste. He stepped out into the courtyard and was struck by an odor of coppery death so strong that it stopped him cold and nearly caused him to wretch.

He saw the pile of horses rotting beside a firepit beyond the stables. To his left, outside the forge, Idelle hovered in the air, dangling a Guardian by one leg. There was a sword on the ground beneath him, as if he had unwisely tried to slash at the hawk. He was bleeding from a head wound, and a matching stain against the workshop showed its cause.

"Put me down!" he shouted.

Where's the boar you promised? Aren sounded put off, and eyed her package with disdain. *I'm not eating that.*

"Let him go," Barr said. He wanted the Guardian to think he controlled Idelle. To Aren he said, "Keep him still."

The man dropped on his head and scurried back. Aren immediately moved in, pinning him against the wall with a drooling growl of hungry promise. Idelle flew off to get the meal she had left outside the walls.

"This is the central Guardian stronghold," he said to Barr, trying his best to speak with authority. He then blanched beneath the hound towering over him. "What are you all doing here?"

"What happened here?" Barr returned, ignoring the question. More to the point, he asked, "Were you always a shapeling?"

The man narrowed his eyes and braced himself with both hands to the ground. His demeanor had changed in an instant, with all sense of fear gone from his face.

"Kill me then."

Dar-Paj strode past Aren, took hold of the Guardian by his front and lifted him up with one hand. With his other, he forced the man's arm to the edge of the forge. The slightest push broke it in two at the elbow. The guard cried out and shook at the pain, gritted his teeth and began to sweat.

"I wager," Dar-Paj warned, "that I have more time than you have unbroken bones."

"It was the emissary from Garand. He... bit me."

"And the others?"

"He bit some of us, and we bit the others." The man eyed Dar-Paj's arm and licked his lips. A jolt against the stones shook that notion from his mind. "I didn't ask to be turned! Please, just set me free!"

It looked as if something he said sparked a memory in Dar-Paj, but the apprentice remained quiet.

Barr asked, "Why did the others go into the city?"

"You know why."

Idelle set down a boar near Aren and left again.

Mind if I eat? he asked and began without waiting for an answer. *I can't think straight, I'm so hungry.*

Fluora put a cautionary hand on Barr's arm. "This man is not what he seems. There is a shadow of another in his mind, guiding his actions."

"Where are my weapons?" Barr asked and followed the faintest glance back toward the firepit. "Fine then. You're free to join your brothers."

"Are you sure?" Dar-Paj let go and stood back. "Is that wise? He might give away our –"

Idelle swooped in and carried the man off.

Ignoring the screams, Barr stalked toward the pit. He found both his kyan in the ashes, blackened but otherwise unharmed. Normal ironwood only burned at extreme temperatures. The enchantment he had placed upon them made that all but impossible. With a sleeve, he wiped away the smudge from their sheathes, then drew each blade to make sure the runes were intact. His armor was in the fire as well, its fur an ashen memory and leather brittle char. Aside from the Maurdon blades, it was the only thing he had left of his time with the sylvannis. The feel of it against his skin, its oily scent in his nose, had reminded him of hunting with Tuvrin. Like so many other memories taken away, that too was gone from him now.

I'm sorry, was all Idelle could say.

Barr hooked the sheathes to his belt and met the others by Aren. The hound continued eating as they spoke.

"Shall we return to Faeron and rest?" Fluora asked.

Dar-Paj replied, "We still need to find Aislin. There must be tracks that Idelle or Aren can follow."

"Or scry him out again," she offered, "though he will most likely have warded himself against it by now."

Barr heard them talking, but their voices were off in the distance, through the echoing din of tunnels beneath a mountain of rock, where daylight strained its way in and the air grew thick. The sound rolled off smoothed walls, down into the city, soaring between the sculpted pillars and bodies of living art. In the black depths of a landslide, a new voice broke the surface, vibrating up through the stones with the ring of mithrinum in his ears.

Free me, the whisper pleaded and carried him up into the air, showing him the ancient city that was its tomb. *Dwendorim. Once yours, now my only.*

Who are you? Barr asked, adrift in the memory of a dozen voices when first he touched Aislin.

I am Khaela.

The world snapped back into place.

Who are you talking to? Idelle asked.

"Barr?" Fluora had interrupted Dar-Paj, and her look was a mixture of both concern and confusion. "What just happened?"

"You were right, there are others," he said, piecing together the faint connections. "I heard them that day in the forest, when my grandmother gave me Aislin."

"What did you hear?"

"The other swords. I know where one is." Struck by an idea, he added, "If we can't bring Aislin to my mother, maybe Khaela will do."

93

Dar-Paj looked toward the gate. "What of the people in that city? Thousands will be infected – or slaughtered. And what of Eald – what of Markus? He could be there with the sword."

He's right. Aren stopped chewing long enough to look up. *We can't just forget about Ealdan – or whatever he calls himself – just because you know where another sword is.*

"Wait," Fluora said. "Your thoughts are all a jumble."

Idelle landed atop the forge. *Worse still. If Markus is behind infecting these Guardians, the city could be just the beginning of an army. What reason then would shapelings in Lumintor have for staying within their borders?*

"And if umbrals overwhelm my mother?" Barr was exhausted and felt the weariness eat away at his calm. "They would have free reign of the mists. All of Faeron would be overrun."

He grabbed at the air and forced water to bubble up from the ground. It broke through the frozen soil in gray tendrils of haze, and a glassy puddle spread out before him. Eyes closed tight, he pulled at the mists with both hands, bending it to his will in a search for Aislin. He pictured the blade in every detail, from a knick at its tip to a wrinkle in the maiden's hand of its pommel. He could feel it in his mind, like reliving a memory, and sought only to catch a glimpse of its surroundings.

A silent shroud of empty black was draped over its presence, like a starless void of night sky rippling with sentience. He flailed against it with his will, raged in fire and lightning, tore at the floating runes that were only visible with each strike. His every attempt was swept aside in a faltering tirade, against a veil of shadow that refused to give way.

He let go that endeavor, calmed his breathing and his heart, then focused his attention on another place. The image of an underground city emerged, rippled over the mirrored surface in a reflection come to life. The dark water of the mists showed him Dwendorim, though his eyes remained closed to the vision. His mind took stock of every feature, as if it had a will of its own, and his desire to go there became a palpable force. It reached out to those around him as vaporous feelers in the air, washed over and through them like a brush over canvas. The painted images became clear, a motionless guide from here to there.

"How are you doing that?"

He sensed confusion in her visage, but the painting never changed. When he opened his eyes, fog danced upon a ring of starry midnight at their feet, rising up toward the heavens in a spiral of argent rain. The gleam of its ascent became a beacon in the dark, where the rush of sudden silence caused a ripple.

Barr took them all into the mists.

*   *   *

Markus sat at the edge of a fountain in the center of Noble Square. Water shot upward behind him, amidst a scene of playful nymphs done in marble and rose quartz. Fading daylight sparkled across the frozen topiary all around him, off walls of leafless bushes that sought to fence those sculpted animals. A framework of living art, suspended in winter's grasp, they reminded him of long ago, when his word had sent armies across the plains, when a nod had ended life or granted mercy for another day. There were times when he weighed all that he had surrendered, lost forever to an impetuous moment, and wondered if Revyn had got the better of their bargain.

"It's done," Grailyn said, a good distance away and waited to be acknowledged. He then moved close but remained standing. "Every suitable guard's been turned. The rest will serve as first meal."

A nod, and his attention went back to the past. He eyed the people of Noria with a detached sensibility, saw them go about their lives in blissful ignorance, like so many had before them.

The boy is gone, Revyn said, sounding pleased with himself.

All this scheming. I should have taken his head. He chuckled inwardly. *Let us see the faeron heal that.*

That would have served neither of us.

Markus winced at the chafing along the inside of his skull and noticed the Guardian had yet to leave.

"What is it?"

"Where's your bony friend gone off to?"

That demanded his full attention. "Lycanthropy has made you brazen."

"Oh, I was plenty brazen before that." Grailyn folded both arms, and his leathers protested the strain. "It just occurred to me you're not one of us."

"Which led to wondering why I command."

"Just so."

Calm, Revyn soothed. *He will make it easier for us to take the other Orders and their cities.*

"I will oblige you this once," Markus said, his hands slipping into either sleeve. "Question me again, however, and you will beg to be killed." The momentary lapse in the Guardian's stare was precisely what he wanted. "I am not one of you because I cannot be turned. I have no *furie* for it to feed on."

"That's not possible. Everyone has some, if even a bit. You'd die without it."

"The things you children believe."

Grailyn frowned. "And the other?"

"The other? Suffice it to say I could have you killed with a thought." Markus stood. "Or I could put a knife through your heart before that dim look fell off your face. You follow my orders because you have no other choice." Passersby began to look, as his voice grew louder. "You and all your kind are mewling whelps compared to my people! When the gods created this world, their next breath gave birth to me! That is why you do as you are told, and I do the telling!"

His shadow had darkened and spread its bulk, each word fuel for the growing black. It stretched behind him like a blanket, an early dusk with crimson eyes. It froze the cobbles underfoot in a widening crackle of snowy glass and touched upon Grailyn with the presence of a god. A frantic glance at those around showed him alone in what he saw.

Somewhat placated by the fright, Markus calmed and gave a smile. His shadow then receded, diminished to its former self, and what looked like ice beneath their feet was merely sunset across the stones.

The Lord High Hunter swallowed hard, regained his composure and wisely chose to leave.

*   *   *

An umbral attacked, swiping long talons at Barr, as if the mists had come alive and lashed out. A patch of darkness dislodged, the creature was a mutable shadow of inky vapor and ebon carapace. It had no eyes on its impish head, just a gaping mouth of serrated teeth and tapered ears that twitched at sounds all about. Another pair joined in, scampering across the waters on all fours, flitting from place to place as black clouds with barbed tails.

Barr instinctively turned aside, his concentration broken, and put off Dwendorim for the moment. He drew both kyan and summoned the *furie* for a shield. A blue half-shell of light rose up behind him, which forced the umbrals to face him head on.

"Barr, no!" Fluora grabbed hold of his shoulder. "We have to leave now!"

All three umbrals stopped, ears shuddering at the use of magic, and turned eyeless heads his way. A trail of water erupted from behind, as they tore through the air, clawing and clamoring to the echoes of delighted snarls.

They fell upon the shield like ravenous animals. Its magic flared beneath their touch and began to dissolve, as if the umbrals absorbed it with their hands. One threw its head back and let out a keen of pleasure, while another fell to its knees and swayed with the intake. The third pushed through the shield and reached a gnarled claw out for Aren. The hound growled a warning, ready to strike, and Idelle was already swooping toward it.

Don't touch them! Barr warned and swung a kyan.

The blade jarred his arm but did nothing, simply bounced off the chitin shell with a hollow ring. The umbral's attention then turned to him in great snuffles of air between them, as if taking in the heady scent of his *furie*.

Aren backed away, pushing Dar-Paj along with him. Idelle swept by overhead but left the umbrals alone. Barr swung again, to no effect, and put himself between the creature and Fluora. He was at a loss as to what to do. His attacks left no mark, nor did the force of his blows move the umbral at all. He sheathed both kyan and called fire to his hands. They might feed on magic, but he was willing to bet that they burned.

"We have tried before," Fluora said and was pulled back by Dar-Paj. "They are not of our realm!"

He bathed them in fire, a torrent of white flame that set the waters to hissing with steam and bubbling to a froth. The umbrals hissed as well and shrank back from the inferno. When it licked across their armored bodies, ebon runes came to life, like a scrawled void beneath the blaze. When he let the conflagration fade away, Barr expected to find charred remains, but the umbrals were still unharmed. The way they regarded him from afar, bodies motionless in the water, gave him pause and prickled his senses to a distant movement all around.

His display had drawn the attention of others.

Dread gripped his middle with an icy fist. He threw fire high into the air, let it cascade down in a rain of burning shimmer that lit a circle all about them. Its light reflected off the chitinous black of a hundred umbrals, all quiet and stillness, twitching ears and eyeless stares. The flames died away with his breath, and Barr wasted no time in frantic thought. He focused his mind on the ruins of Dwendorim and pulled them through the mists in an instant.

The speed with which they arrived sent a wave of queasiness through his stomach and nearly toppled him to the stones. They stood in a vast chamber of polished marble and shaped crystal. White pillars stretched out in all directions, up from an array of square fountains to a grand mosaic of sky. The entire domed ceiling was done in colored tile, from wisps of cloud that seemed to roll beneath the glow of steady sunlight to the blue of a clear sky that faded down into falls of water. Despite the web of subtle cracks here and there, the dulled luster and debris, no signs of aging could diminish the artistry of such a monumental undertaking.

There's small shafts in the ceiling, Idelle noted from above, *with mirrors inside them.*

Barr looked up and tried to see them. *Probably how they get light from outside.* He saw long banners of red and gold along two of the walls, swaying in a breeze above colorful statuary. In the distance, he could hear the melody of silver chimes. *And fresh air. I've never seen anything like this.*

"How did you do that?" Fluora steadied herself with a hand to her middle. "If you were an oracle, I would have seen it."

Aren lay down. *I think I ate that last meal too fast.*

"That was... interesting," Dar-Paj said, with a few blinks and a deep breath. "Not that I am ungrateful for the speedy departure."

"I'm not sure," Barr said to Fluora. "Picturing it all in my mind seems to happen without trying. I could see where I wanted us to go, so I brought us here."

"It takes a great deal of practice before we can carry others through the mists." He wasn't sure if her look was one of disbelief or admiration. "That was utterly reckless and irresponsible!"

Apparently it was anger.

Idelle chuckled and flew higher. *I'd hate to have been there for the failed attempts.*

"Would you rather still be with the umbrals?" Pursed lips were his only answer. He took a seat against a pedestal, overcome with weariness. "What in the world are they anyway?"

She let her irritation go with a sigh. "No one knows for certain, only that they come from the Dark." She took a seat beside him, her body resting against his. "Calling the mists draws on magic from the Dark, and umbrals slip in through the opening that leaves behind."

"And my mother?"

He knew the moment they were attacked that the umbrals had won out. If his mother was still alive, she had given up her fight against them. That, or they had drained her of all life.

"The Matron bonds her spirit to the mists. Her will resists umbrals from entering our realm and keeps the ones that do at bay."

"I meant is she alright."

Fluora was quiet and slipped her hand into his.

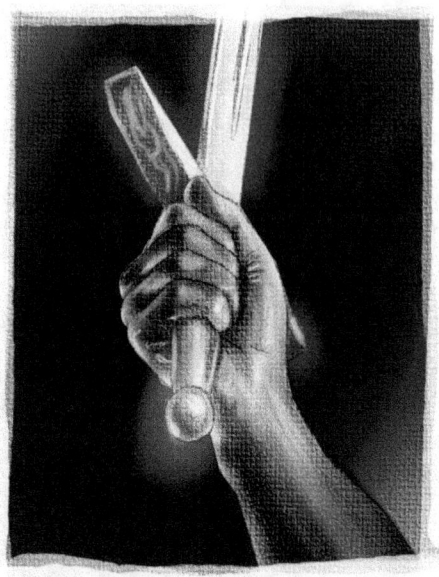

– 6 –

leep threatened to claim him if he sat any longer, despite the urgency that fluttered his stomach. A part of him feared it was already too late, that his mother was gone and the umbrals had won out. He pulled his hand from the comfort of Fluora's grasp, put aside both despair and his desire for rest, then forced himself to stand. Even if his mother could no longer be saved, all of Faeron would soon be at stake.

"This is familiar," Dar-Paj said with a nod to the writing on the pedestal. A collection of spheres and swirls, filled to various degree, each symbol was etched into the stone and strengthened by lustrous silver. "This place is called Skyfall. It is meant to honor those who have passed on."

"You can read that?"

"It would seem so."

Barr watched the way in which Dar-Paj ran his eyes over the text, as if the past could somehow be revealed between the symbols. He was reminded of how little he knew about his uncle's apprentice, though Dar had often proven himself a friend through his actions. Chamal's warning in dream echoed in his mind. *He is not how he appears. Trust only yourself.* It didn't matter that she had meant Markus. The nagging doubts her warning had conjured still lingered in his thoughts.

You worry who he'll be, Idelle noted, *if his memory returns. New memories don't seem to change you.*

Don't they? Aware Fluora was listening, he added, *I'm just wary is all.*

And tired, Aren said. *It's nice here, but I'd rather be back in the trees.*

"This does not feel like my home."

Dar-Paj turned away and walked toward a length of aqueduct, where fresh water streamed down a pathway from one wall to another. Barr moved passed him, to the first of many statues along the arches and alcoves.

"I don't think it is. There's no life here. No plants, no birds, no insects." He saw that same language, etched into the polished flesh of the marble female, again filled with silver, but with the symbols far smaller. They ran lines around her limbs and disappeared beneath the folds of her chiseled clothing. They were everywhere but her face, where only a single rune could be seen. "Maybe something about this place just reminds you of your own home. Ever see a language like that while scribing for my uncle?"

There are plants, Aren said and yawned, with a great stretch of his body, *just not in here. I can smell them, to the east.*

"I have not seen those symbols before."

Fluora got up and looked closely at the pedestal. She ran her fingertips across the lettering, as if she could read them by touch.

"It is a beautiful language, sort of flowing, like water. It reminds me of starlight across the lake by my home."

Aren's right, Idelle said. *There's another chamber to the east, at least three times bigger, filled with all different sorts of trees, flowers and fenced off gardens.*

With a start, Fluora pulled back her hand as if she had been stung. She looked out over the fountains and wrapped her arms about her, shivering against a cold no one else seemed to notice.

"What's wrong?"

"I am not sure." Her eyes became distant and welled with growing tears. "Never have I felt such a terrible sorrow."

Barr wanted to offer her comfort, as she had done for him, to reach out and pull her close until the tears went away. Her demeanor warned against it, as did the hairs on his neck and the growing whisper of magic all about. He caught a glimpse of light in the corner of his eye, a flicker that came from the statue. Sunlight shone off the rune in her forehead, glittering for but a moment, but he was certain he had seen something more. A spark in her eyes, some glimmer of life, there was more than just the sadness he saw mirrored in Fluora.

He reached out and touched the statue, a brush of fingers across her hand. The skin was warm and soft, pliable like his own, but with the texture and firmness of polished marble. Like a masterful replica of life, even the veins in her sculpted flesh seemed to pulse with a steady rhythm, to the beat of a long breath held an impossibly long time. Barr looked up into that sorrowful gaze, his fingers trailing along her arm as if tracing a memory not his own, and in the glossy surface and chilly sadness became lost to the ebb and flow...

...of future life beneath his hands. Fanarin worked the slender wrist, smoothing its dark surface to a glossy sheen by channeling furie *through his grip. The magic was visible as gentle waves of soft light that lit the edge of his thumbs, consuming any excess as layer upon layer was painstakingly removed. With a practiced eye and studied patience, he soon held the forearm of what would become a beautiful woman – albeit one composed entirely of obsidian.*

It would take weeks before he was done, when she would be sent to the rune crafters for instruction wards. As much time might pass again until she was then sent to the silversmiths, where each ward would be carefully filled. Enchanters would then attune her with the ley lines that ran through Dwendorim, enabling her to draw furie *and fuel her existence.*

Yet another Protector, but this one would be theirs.

He laughed and clucked his tongue, then focused once more upon the work at hand. His wife had often told him he was a brilliant shaper but easily distracted. How many times had she found him with a faraway gaze, entranced by one of his own works. Memory of her stung him with a tear, as it usually did, but he put his heart to the task and pushed on.

You will never finish her, if all you do is stare, *he heard his wife say.*

"Yes, dear."

Fanarin ran a hand along the slab where her face would be, imagining he could see eyes looking back. Once finished, she would make a splendid gift for his daughter Shanaran, something to cheer her up and help fight off the sickness.

He paused at the thought of so many falling ill. The eldarath had assured everyone that all would be well and wove a spell over the city to speed recovery along. Though bedridden from weakness, none of the afflicted had yet died. Shanaran had described it as feeling drained, as if she were simply too tired to stand. She slept often and ate little, heard whispers where there were none. Like playful echoes in her mind, they kept her company.

It broke his heart to see her ill, and he hoped his gift would be just the thing to lift her spirits.

You are a good father, *his wife told him.*

"Thank you, dear. I do try."

Though the shaping was far from done, already he could see her walking about in his mind. He knew every detail of every curve, better than he knew his own. It was only a matter of now setting her free. Looking up into her illusory eyes, he decided to call her Hanar...

Barr woke with a gasp of breath and tried to sit up. Fluora was beside him, her hand on his chest, as if her touch might still the rapid thumping. She said nothing but gave him a strange look. Aren and Dar-Paj stood over him, concern in their eyes, but Barr waved them off and took in a deep breath. Though he could see clearly enough, all around him seemed hazy, as if a dream had wrapped itself about his mind.

"Are you alright?" Fluora asked. She looked at him as if he were a puzzle to sort out. "You collapsed without warning. I thought you might have struck your head, but I could find no injury."

"Da'nae, da'nae," Barr said and winced at a sudden headache. *I'm fine, I'm fine.* "Un dey'la na mele ra'n." *I just need a moment.*

Aren blinked. *I know what you just said, but what language was that?*

You don't seem yourself, Idelle added. *That last vision still lingering?*

Fluora opened her mouth to speak but was cut short by a gasp of fear. The statue beside them turned its head their way, as if the sound of Barr's voice had woken it from slumber. It moved far too quickly for its bulk and size, let alone a slab of marble, and knelt before Barr with a frantic look upon its face.

"Tri'lai!" it said in a feminine voice. *Master!* "Su'nae na? En gae'ra su na?" *Are you hurt? How may I assist?*

Fluora backed away from the animated creature and pulled Barr along with her. Dar-Paj moved to stand in its way, while Aren watched on in amusement.

Master?

I'm not sure, Barr replied. *She might think I'm an arachon.*

"What is it?" Fluora asked. "It moves as if alive."

The statue must have sensed their discomfort. She remained still and watched them with interest, listening close to each word with a furrowed brow. A cerulean sheen lit the surface of her eyes and was doused by the blinking of chiseled lids. Though no breath passed her lips, they had parted when she spoke and were now pressed together in concern.

"I think I understood her," Dar-Paj said. "She does not seem to mean any harm."

"No, she doesn't. She's a Protector."

Barr got up and helped Fluora to stand. The statue rose as well, with the grace of an Eneir, but made no move to step any closer. He gave a bow of his head to her in greeting, with both hands to either side of his chest, and waited until she returned the gesture. She stood a head taller, with a slender but muscled build, and seemed for all intents a sculpture of a human female.

You've got more company, Idelle said and landed on the pedestal.

Every statue within the chamber had come to life. In a crowd of living stone, they approached from all around, their eyes locked upon Barr. Fluora let go her grip on his arm and looked out at them with that faraway gaze.

"They have auras but no spirits. How can that be?" She looked at the marble female. "I can see *furie* moving through its body, like blood through veins, but how does a statue come to life?"

In a reverent tone, Dar-Paj replied, "Never would I have imagined such a creature could exist, that such elegance could be found in a weaving."

"They're the pinnacle of arachon achievement," Barr said. The residual thoughts and emotions left behind by his vision were finally subsiding, but he still felt the deep pride and admiration that all arachon reserved for their Protectors. "They're golems, shaped from stones found in nearby quarries and all over Taellus. This one is called Jahd."

Jahd bowed again at the sound of her name. She reached out and leaned forward, put her forehead to his, and filled his mind with warmth. Engulfed once more in the haze of a vision, he felt more than saw the other golems drop to one knee, hands held to chest, in a show of respect. A tingle ran the length of his spine, clouded his eyes with bright flashes and drowned out all other senses in a rising chorus of distant voices. He caught glimpses of Dwendorim, as it was long ago, as the din of merging language fell away.

He didn't realize until it was over he had been holding his breath. He took in a single lungful and let it out in relief.

"You speak a language I have not yet heard," Jahd said and stepped away. "I thank you for teaching it to us."

Golden light spread outward from her feet in a web that lit the chamber and threw shadows against the walls. It touched the other golems and set their bodies aglow, then faded as each of them stood.

"They have returned," one said, a smile broadening his features. "The Masters have come back to us!"

"The Oath is renewed!"

I smell a celebration, Aren said and licked his chops.

Idelle chuckled. *Don't get too excited. They're still statues, after all.*

If there's gardens...

It was some time before the shouts of joy began to fade, when an obsidian female approached Barr. He fought down the lump in his throat.

"Hanar. It's good to see you again."

"You look different," she said and smiled, "but I would know the voice of my shaper no matter his form. I heard you through Jahd."

"Her shaper?" Fluora asked. "I know there is much to explain, but we should not forget what it is that we came for."

"Khaela." Barr clenched his jaw at the thought of his mother dying. "You're right. I'm sorry, Hanar, but I don't have time for a proper reunion. My mother's life is in danger, and I need to find Khaela."

"I know of no such Protector."

I am here, Khaela said, a bare whisper in the stones. *Free me.*

"Wait, I can hear it." Barr turned toward another chamber, through a passage to the south. "It's that way. It's buried so deep, its voice is like a whisper."

He led them to a shattered temple, where every wall had given way and crumbled beneath a vaulted roof. Pillars ten times the length of a man were broken apart and strewn across the rubble. Marble steps cracked beneath the strain in fissures like a cobweb, revealing another level below.

"Down there," Barr said. "There's a caved in vault. I know where it is, but getting to it won't be easy."

"I know the vault you speak of," Jahd said.

She gave a look back to the golems that followed, and a handful came forward without a word. They set about to clearing the fallen stonework and widening one of the fissures. Embarrassed by the lapse, Barr briefly introduced himself and his friends. He caught Fluora studying him then, her eyes seeing past to the person he once was.

"How long ago were you one of them?"

"Hanar?"

She replied, "Well over a hundred generations would have come and gone in our slumber."

"The sickness," Barr recalled. "No one survived?"

"The others have passed on. You are all that remains now of the Masters."

Dar-Paj asked, "What sort of sickness can destroy an entire city?"

To Barr's amazement, a golden tear of *furie* slipped down Jahd's cheek, and her voice trembled with sadness when she spoke.

"It was terrible to behold. It left the body tired and prone to further illness, and all of them were plagued by voices in the end." She looked out at the fallen temple. "Once taken ill, not one recovered."

"Five months and twelve days," Hanar said, "after the first fell sick, the last Master passed away in her sleep. With no one left to guard, we chose slumber over sorrow."

More golems arrived to aid in the excavation.

That's a lot to take in, Idelle said, perched from one of the few pillars that still stood. *Do you remember all that happening?*

It's no different from other visions, Barr said. *I only recall bits and pieces.*

"Tell me," Dar-Paj said to Jahd, "did the arachon ever venture out from this city?"

"Quite often. Once the sickness had spread, though, the travelers forbade it. None were allowed through the portals."

"I see." Hesitant, as if fearing the answer, he pressed on and asked, "Have you ever seen anyone that looks as I do? My memory is gone, and I am searching for others like me."

Jahd regarded him fully. "Your kind is unfamiliar to us, but if it is in our power to assist in your search, we will."

This looks like it might take a while, Aren said. *I'm going off to explore.*

Idelle swooped down and past. *Don't eat anything I wouldn't.*

"What is Khaela?" Hanar asked.

"A very old sword made of mithrinum." Barr looked down at the progress and was surprised to see so much had already been cleared. "So old in fact that it's become sentient. It's difficult to explain, but many lives depend on our finding it."

"Mithrinum is a poor metal for a sword."

"They are close to the vault," Jahd said. "What will you do once you have this Khaela?"

He knew what she was really asking. "If all goes well, I'd be happy to return. I can't promise I'll stay long, but it would be nice to see my old home before I take care of other business."

"Yes," Dar-Paj agreed. "I look forward to settling that particular score."

"I am Protector of your family," Hanar said to Barr. "I should be by your side."

A frown marred Fluora's features.

"That's very generous," Barr said, "but you –"

"They have it." Jahd moved to the fissure's edge and reached down. "I am afraid there was no sword, but this must be what you seek."

She brought out a cuirass of pure mithrinum, from the straps of woven links to the elaborate etching across its surface. The other golems gathered and watched on, as Jahd handed him the armor.

"For you, Master."

*   *   *

Markus stood before a full length mirror of polished silver, in a candlelit corner of the royal bedchamber. A white doublet in one hand, silken black in the other, he debated which of King Torim's clothing would fit him best. There wasn't time for a tailor, and he had grown bored of his own attire. Revyn slipped up from behind, in the form of a young woman, and ran a slender hand with trimmed nails up his arm.

"The black one suits you," the god said, and her ruby lips parted in a smile.

"That is most disconcerting."

It made little difference that Revyn had no gender, at least not in the way mortals perceived it. The god had acted and often appeared as a male. That he now wore the body of an illuminaire, one more beautiful than any Markus had ever seen, felt an insult to the memory of his people. The God of Change, however, wore bodies like clothing and reveled in any discomfort his presence caused.

Striking beauty aside, the soft glow of her skin, it reminded Markus of what he had given up. Without his *furie* or immortality, he was no better than a human. By all outward appearance, the two races were the same. As children of Saernol, however, the illuminaire had been born with an incredible magic that set them apart from all others.

And Markus had traded his without a thought.

"You will only upset yourself," she cooed and nibbled an earlobe. Her eyes were hard emeralds, glittering in the reflection, like Andara's the night he had been forced to kill her. Revyn grinned and turned away in a trail of dark curls. "You should find another woman, one whose goals are more aligned with your own."

She would have been a luminarron, one of the many who had left all behind to follow him in conquest. If only she could have seen what he had envisioned...

Markus thrust aside the useless memories.

"Noria is ours. The other cities will soon follow. I may consider entertainment at that time." He tossed aside the black shirt. "I have been wondering."

"Never a good sign."

"Why do they not stop you? Stop us."

Revyn picked up a jeweled brush and ran it through her hair. Each strand lightened as it passed into a shade of lustrous platinum. When she looked back, her eyes swirled to a startling blue and regarded him with a certain measure of amusement.

"What makes you think they can?"

"Your disease takes the will of their children. Surely that must cause some distress." Markus thought on the last time they had tried to gather the Emblems, when the Father God intervened and hid them away. "What good is their oath if all their children worship another?"

"We take our oaths very seriously. Unfortunately for my brothers and sisters, the wording was poorly done." She sighed and shrank, becoming a faeron in the span of that breath. "I vowed not to interfere in the lives of my children. I said nothing of theirs."

"What if Saernol devises a cure?"

"I know how fond you are of your creator," Revyn said and paid no heed to the dark look, "but if she had the skill to do so, she would have. Lycanthropy is not my first attempt but is the culmination of many trials and errors."

Markus sat and pulled on his boots. An image of their first meeting flashed in his mind, the offer of power, the promise he would rule Taellus. How convenient that Revyn had need of his *furie* and in the process of taking it ensured he could never become a shapeling.

"Is that why you chose me?"

An arched brow, then she was an elf. "It does suit my needs that your will is your own. I suppose it is a happy coincidence that you worship none but yourself. Now, about our other dilemma."

"I should kill him the moment he claims it."

Revyn clucked her tongue. "And ruin such a perfect binding? Think of the missed opportunities. While you focus your efforts elsewhere, he works toward our end." Her clothing changed from a gauzy dress to the leathers of an assassin, from the knife straps at each leg to the steel claws and silken mask. "Not to mention how useful he will be later on. Two birds with one blade."

"As you wish." Markus stood and reached for a coat, then headed for the door. "Shall I have something sent up? Food or a small child?"

In the blink of an eye, Revyn was again Andara. She bit her lower lip as she thought.

"A nice young lady perhaps."

He refused to show emotion. "Plan on changing to a more appropriate form? It will matter somewhat."

"No, I rather like this one."

Markus left without closing the door.

*   *   *

Barr took hold of the cuirass in both hands and felt the presence of Khaela in his mind. It had the distant roll of endless waves sweeping over his thoughts and a calm to the echoes of its depth.

You found me, the blade said, its voice no longer a whisper but decidedly feminine. He could almost see the face of a woman in his mind when she spoke. *I thought I would be lost forever.*

"Is that what you came for?" Jahd asked.

Khaela became fluid in his grasp, came together into one piece and grew to the length of a long sword. Her pommel was a sphere, engulfed in golden waves with an argent shimmer.

When you talk with it, Idelle said, a wary eye to the enchanted sword, *I can't hear its replies. I don't like it.*

"We should hurry," Fluora said.

He wasn't sure if the golems made her uneasy or if she had caught a glimpse of his mother. He should have felt relief that he could now return with a means to help, but he could not shake the grip of a cold dread on his middle.

I cannot assist, Khaela said.

What? Why not?

I am not Aislin. We do not all share the same gifts.

"My mother…"

Barr looked to Fluora, uncertain what to do. He had feared this might happen but spent no time in devising another plan.

"Can we go through the mists again?" Dar-Paj asked. "With so many umbrals last time, who knows how many there are now."

Hanar put a hand to Barr's forearm. Her touch was warm and soothing.

"You can use the portals. They connect to numerous locations across Taellus and will considerably shorten your journey." She gave him a tender squeeze. "I will keep you and yours safe."

Do you know where Aislin is? Barr asked the sword. *Could you show me?*

She is hidden by the one who tries to claim us.

Who, that undead Guardian?

Feraesk is but a revenant, a once king remade into a tool of destruction.

And he belongs to Markus. There were others there, Barr recalled with the bitter taste of remembered blood in his mouth, *when he stole Aislin and left me for dead.*

One for each Emblem, but he too is an instrument.

Barr eased his grip on Khaela and sighed. The others watched on, waiting for him to speak. Failure tightening his chest, he never felt more tired than in that moment.

Who is it then?

The god Revyn, Khaela replied, and the sadness in her voice washed over him like the tides. *Shapelings are his, though not all by their own choice. He would see every race bend a knee to his will.*

The Guardian's last words came back to haunt him. *You know why.* Thousands of lives in danger, and all he could think of was saving his mother. That city would be lost, and Faeron would soon follow. His gamble had been for naught.

What's that have to do with Aislin?

We began as wreaths, Emblems of peace, forged by the children gods to unite their offspring toward a common good. We are tied to the land. We can make it flourish or falter. We are one with the oceans, the skies and all life. Through us the world can prosper and grow, or it can wither and fade back into the Dark.

I have to return to my mother.

Her death is assured if you do not help. Revyn will spare no one. All will turn or be killed. You must gather the other Emblems before he does.

Barr gritted his teeth. *And what of Faeronthalsos? Or the city I just came from?*

Noria is beyond the need of assistance. It was no answer to his question, but Barr knew that there was none. At least none that would satisfy his anger or calm his guilty heart. *The nearest Emblem is in a shrine outside Garand. Many tribes of orc have been led there by the revenant Isdael. He will destroy what Brotherhood are there and lay claim to Vereu.*

How do you know all this? And why didn't Aislin ever warn me?

We are parts of a whole. What one knows, we all know. Her voice began to fade, again a whisper in his mind. *Aislin is a creature of dream, bound by images of the past to draw her words from.*

I can barely hear you. What's wrong?

My strength is lent to another. I grow weary and can no longer speak.

Barr sighed again. "Khaela can't help my mother."

"What do we do?" Dar-Paj asked. "Maybe you can heal her, make her stronger again. It might give us more time to find Aislin."

Fluora shook her head. "That might kill them both. If she cannot keep the umbrals at bay any longer, she has no choice but to pass on her duty as Matron." Barr knew she was trying to console him, to ease the burden that hung over him like a shadow. "She would have done so long before dying."

Back to Faeron then? Idelle asked.

Not yet. "We have another problem and not a lot of time to explain." *Get back here, Aren.* "There's another sword like this one, called Vereu. We have to take it before Markus gets his hands on it."

Dar-Paj clenched both fists. "Markus is there?"

Give me a minute, Aren said. *I found a pond filled with these giant black fish.*

Now, Aren. We're leaving.

"What about that city?" Fluora asked, "The one near the Guardian stronghold. We could warn them about the shapelings and then go after this other sword."

"It's too late for Noria. There's nothing we can do."

Jahd knelt on one knee. "It sounds to me that you head into danger. I am at your disposal, as are any other Protectors you require."

"Please," Barr said and pulled her back up. "I really do appreciate the offer, but we're not going on foot. We sort of travel instantly, through a plane called the mists. I don't think I could bring any of you with us."

"But I must go with you," Hanar pleaded. "My Oath demands it! If you cannot bring me along, then tell me where to go. I will use the portals and find you."

"If you stay here," Jahd offered, "I will send as many as it takes to fetch this Vereu for you."

With a shrug, Dar-Paj said, "That might not be so bad. Fifty golems could prove useful, considering what Markus travels with."

"No, you misunderstand. What you see here are but a few of the Protectors. All the Masters may have fallen, but every one of us has endured."

Memories of life as Fanarin came back to him, of a city that was vast and stretched many levels below. Prior to the sickness, there were hundreds of thousands that lived in Dwendorim. Aside from construction, menial labor and safeguarding the city, the golems were created as wardens for the young. Some were bonded to families and remained with them for generations, while others forever went about their assigned task.

"There were thousands," Barr said, still getting his mind around the numbers and terrible loss the sickness had wrought.

"Fourteen thousand, two hundred and eleven."

That's a lot, Aren said as he arrived. *They could fill a small city.*

Idelle added, *Or form a large army.*

"Hanar can come with us, but the rest of you need to stay. The fewer of us there are, the easier it'll be to slip in and back out." He faced Jahd and bowed his head. "The arachon are no more. Their Protectors are all that remain – their legacy, their children. You are the Masters now. This city is yours."

Jahd looked at him in silence, as if considering his words or speaking with the other golems in thought.

"Then we shall repair Dwendorim, and perhaps one day you will return and call it home."

"I'd like that."

The assembled golems backed away and bowed with a salute. Hands to chest, each one of them watched on.

Barr called up the mists and scried out Vereu.

– 7 –

The image Khaela provided helped Barr find Vereu in the conjured water of the mists. The sword hung upon a wall in a poorly lit chamber, at the head of a long table where men spoke together in earnest. Half were in full plate, burnished and unmarred by battle, while the others wore robes of black with gray trim. Leading the discussion was a thick man of middle years, heavy with muscle and the scars of a grim past. He scratched at his beard, where a dark braid brushed his cloak, and moved one of the wooden pieces across the table. A mockup of the battle outside was arranged before him, with far more green standards in the field than black defenders.

At the only entrance stood a weary soldier, his armor battered and stained from the fray. Once given orders, he turned to leave, and Barr followed him through the scry. Up three flights of stone steps and into the main hall, the soldier stopped and bent a knee to an immense statue of Curoch. Priests ran about, tending to the many wounded, and the echo of mumbled prayer mixed with groans of pain. He stepped out into the turmoil of an icy courtyard plagued by arrows and rocks, where none moved about without the cover of a shield.

As the soldier rushed toward the inner gate with his shield overhead, Barr spied a shadowy corner they could arrive in without being seen.

"Before we go," Dar-Paj said and halted him, "could I use one of your swords?"

"You've never asked for one before."

"That is true." Dar-Paj looked down at the reflection, where hundreds of orcs could be seen downhill, on the other side of the wall. "But neither have we ever faced so many."

"Hopefully, we never will."

Barr had Khaela in hand and regarded his friend. It reminded him of the temple, when Markus fought beside them as Ealdan and had asked to use Aislin.

He's not Markus, Idelle reminded.

"We should go now," Fluora said, "while the way is clear and no one is looking."

With a nod, Barr handed him Khaela.

He called up a protective sphere to shield them from umbrals and focused his will on the scry. With an image of them all and the courtyard in mind, he summoned the mists and brought them through. A screech in the starry black assaulted their ears and was followed by a snap of pointed teeth. Chitin struck against the shield in a spark of grating talons and was gone. They arrived through a swirl of vapor, into the jarring cold of deep winter and the clamor of a siege.

The roar of hundreds crying out in a bloodthirsty rage nearly masked the buzz of arrows on the parapets above. Night was fast approaching, with clouds warning of a storm, and the flares of lighted barbs threw shadows on the walls. Squires carried water from a well to douse any flames that threatened wagons or the stable, while the other arrows were left to burn until their oil gave out.

The clang of fighting on the wall told Barr some orcs had managed to climb up, most likely by way of ladders. The shrine was built upon a hill, which ruled out the use of belfries. He counted less than forty knights moving about and on the wall, with half as many archers firing between the crenellations.

"It worked," Hanar said and looked around in child-like wonder.

"Try to keep your voice down," Barr warned. "And of course it worked. I've done it before."

"I meant I still function."

"Are you saying you just risked your life?"

"In a manner of speaking."

So, *what exactly is the plan here?* Aren asked. *I have a feeling if we're spotted, they'll attack.*

"Be sure of it," Fluora said. "None of us but Barr has a chance of fitting in."

"You might pass as a Guardian," Dar-Paj said and indicated Barr's stolen clothes. A Guardian crest had been sewn into the tunic.

They're going to lose, Idelle said, a sliver of black in the skies above. *There's too many orcs, and those walls won't hold forever.*

As if on cue, a boulder struck against the wall beside them and shook debris from the mortar.

"Age aside, I doubt I'd be convincing," Barr replied. "I actually thought I'd try reasoning."

Fluora grabbed hold of Barr's arm and pointed to one of the squires. The boy was a few years his younger and wore a mail shirt far too large. He moved quickly, despite the added weight, and headed toward the well to refill his bucket. Her fingers tensed as an arrow struck him clean through the neck.

He dropped to his knees and fell over.

Barr was up and across the distance before any of them could protest. A knight was already there, kneeling before the boy. He screamed at a shocked squire to go fetch a priest and did what he could to staunch the flow. Blood pooled beneath the boy in a crimson halo about his head. Arrows continued to rain about them, and one grazed the man's arm.

"Get your shield back up!" Barr told him and looked closer at the boy's neck. Eyes wide and lost to shock, the squire mouthed words but made no sound. "You'll be fine, do you understand? Just listen to my voice. You can only hear my voice."

"Who are you?" the knight demanded, shield raised over a shoulder. The head of an arrow pierced through by his hand. "And don't think for a second I'd believe you're a Guardian."

"I'm the one saving his life."

Barr gripped the arrow near the barb, his knuckles white against the strain, and held it steady as he could. He sent *furie* down his fingers in a wisp of telltale light, burning through the shaft by force of will. The serrated metal flashed and fell away, with smoke rising from the ember left behind.

The man narrowed his gaze. "You're a turner."

In one fluid motion, Barr covered the wound with his fingers and slipped the arrow free, then put his hand to the other side and pressed. Enough to keep blood from spilling out but not so much as to strangle, he closed his eyes against distraction and focused on the boy. Giving in to the ebb and flow of life, he opened himself up to the need that met his grasp. The body knew to heal itself but lacked the energy to do so. In Barr it found the means and took what was required. Waves of aching wrenched his muscles, like hungry fingers all throughout, and drew the strength from deep within him.

"What's the meaning of this!" Another knight, this one seemingly of rank, came up from behind and drew his sword. "Take your hands off my nephew!"

He tried to grab hold of Barr by a shoulder and was thrown wide.

"Sir, wait! I think he's trying to heal Jarvik."

Only peripherally aware, Barr maintained his focus on the conduit between himself and the boy, careful not to give too much and pass out. He held on for the sense of pushing, when the other was fully sated and sought a balance in itself.

The officer got back to his feet. "Archers!"

A moment later, two warning shots landed near Barr, one by his leg and the other by the boy's head.

That's enough of that! Aren leapt out from the corner and took the officer at full stride, sent him crashing to the wall with enough force to bend his platemail. He stood over Barr and growled up at the archers. *If even one of them shoots, I swear I'll climb after them.*

Idelle swooped past the archers and nearly sent one over the side.

Trust me, you won't have to.

Barr let go his hold and fought to stay conscious. The boy's chest rose and fell in a steady rhythm, his eyes closed to restful sleep. The wounds at his neck no longer threatened to take his life but had faded to pinkish scars and the remnant of near demise. Still, it would take some time to regain his strength, but any danger of passing on had come and gone.

"He's lost a lot of blood," Barr said and swallowed, longing for some water, "but he'll be fine, like I promised. You need to get inside."

"I've never heard of a turner that could heal." The knight reached over and lifted the boy in one arm. "For what it's worth, I'll speak on your behalf when they come to burn you."

The matter of fact tone was not meant to be cruel or insulting. Barr saw gratitude in the man's eyes, sincere thanks in his demeanor, but it did nothing to change the way of things. Turners were all evil and hunted at every opportunity. Barr knew he risked his life when he had decided to save the boy.

"I appreciate the sentiment."

As the knight left, Barr slipped over to the other one and checked for a pulse. Two more soldiers approached, shields in hand, and warily knelt beside them.

"We'll take him inside."

"You should come too," the second added, a demand masked as invitation. He turned toward Aren. "Just you. The dog stays out here."

Dog? Aren snorted and went to wait by the door.

They carried the officer inside, and Barr followed after. He was made to wait in a wooden chair, in the entrance of the main hall, where the stench of blood and unwashed bodies filled his every breath. From severed limbs to pierced lungs, head trauma to exposed innards, every manner of open wound stood before him in the knights sprawled out on the carpeted floor. The priests did all they could, with cloth bandages and prayer, but what magic they commanded did little more than soothe a fever.

"Is he alright?" Barr asked one nearby. The knight he tended to had suffered numerous wounds, and sweat covered his pale skin in a sickly sheen. "It looks like infection's set in."

The priest wiped his brow with a sleeve, the front of his gray robe spattered in blood.

"All I can really do is ease his pain."

He said a prayer in hushed tones, and a whisper of magic filled the chamber. It travelled outward on his voice and enveloped the dying knight. It felt to Barr as if he sat before the warmth of a hearth. The tortured look upon the knight began to smooth into a calm, and then he then slipped into the arms of quiet slumber.

From across the hall, two men came walking toward Barr. The heavyset one wore polished steel plate, while the other appeared gaunt and barely filled his dark robes. He recognized them both from his scry of Vereu and took some hope from the fact that neither one held a weapon. He stood when they got close and waited for them to speak.

"Who are you," the knight asked, "and why are you accosting my men?"

The other cleared his throat. "This gentleman is the knight commander Vaumont, and I am brother Dalwyn, High Priest of Curoch. For what reason do you trespass onto Brotherhood soil?"

"I'm Barr, and I've come to warn you."

Vaumont gripped his belt. "We're already aware of the orcs, but thanks all the same. How about you tell us how you healed squire Jarvik, and we'll consider not fetching the Guardians."

Do not let them control the conversation, Fluora said in his mind. *Speak from a position of authority.*

"And what would make different tribes come down from the mountains and work together?" Barr tried to gauge their reactions, to find out how much they knew. He didn't want to reveal what Vereu was if he didn't have to. "Why attack this shrine and not the city nearby?"

"You know of the sword." Dalwyn's eyes narrowed, as if reading into Barr's thoughts.

Vaumont rested a hand on his pommel.

"I came here with Khaela," Barr said.

"You have an Emblem?" Dalwyn looked him up and down. "Let me see it."

"It's safe, which is more than I can say for Vereu." Barr looked out over the wounded. "You won't win this battle. There's a revenant out there, just waiting for a breach."

"You could heal these men," Vaumont said, stating it as a fact and not a plea.

"I can't heal them all, and what difference would it make? They'd go right back into a fight they can't win."

"What are you proposing, that we surrender?"

"No, not at all. I can get both you and Vereu away from this place. The orcs will follow."

"You could help us fight," Dalwyn returned. "With two Emblems on the field, the battle is in our favor."

"He's barely older than a squire." Vaumont sized up Barr and seemed to find him lacking. "Better that he should give up his Emblem and let someone else take it to the field."

Bring everyone inside, Barr told Fluora.

"This is getting us nowhere." The doors opened from behind, and the others stepped in, to the startled gasps of those around. "We came here to help, but you don't seem to think you need any."

"That statue's alive!" Dalwyn said with eyes wide. Vaumont drew his sword. "And the one with white hair has the Emblem!"

"I wouldn't do that," Barr warned. Three knights rushed in from outside, and four more stopped what they were doing to head over. "Keep your men calm. Like I said, we came here to help. My only concern is that Isdael doesn't take Vereu from you."

"No one's taking it," Vaumont said, "including you. Now leave the way you came, or I'll have you all thrown from the walls."

"That would not be wise," Hanar said, her eyes alight with *furie*.

Aren turned about and watched the three, licking his chops. *Is this the reasoning you had in mind?*

"It can speak," Dalwyn said. He looked both in awe and frightened of the golem. "Is there a spirit trapped inside it?"

"She's a Protector," Barr replied, as if that answered any questions. "I could bring more like her, to help keep Vereu safe."

"Does it fight?" Vaumont sheathed his sword and circled Hanar. "Will it follow orders?"

"She, not it. And yes, they know how to fight."

"It might help. I'd rather you gave us Khaela, or at least healed these men."

Barr held out a hand. "I'll heal as many as I can, but Khaela stays with us."

Vaumont considered, sizing Barr up anew. He then gripped him by the forearm and seemed surprised by the strength that met his crushing grasp.

"When can I have them?"

"Soon."

Longing for a warm bed, or at least something to eat and drink, Barr set about the task of healing those most likely to survive. It was difficult choosing who to save and let go, but he didn't have the strength to mend them all. Dalwyn followed as he went, impressed by what he saw. He had bread and cheese brought up, with a cask of ale. Barr chose to drink water but gave his thanks all the same.

"You're not a turner at all," the High Priest said after a handful had recovered enough to heal on their own. "Not even I can weave like that. Who are you really?"

"Just a traveler from Alixhir."

"Not with that accent. Oh, I'm sure you've been to Alixhir at some point in your life, but that's not what made you who you are." Dalwyn handed him another piece of bread. "You should eat more. I'll have some meat brought out from storage."

"If you know about the Emblems," Barr said and took a seat for a bit of rest, "and the revenants, then you know about Markus."

"I know the name. Most of what I know comes from visions sent by Curoch. For some reason, Vereu chooses not to speak with me."

Barr tilted his head and listened. He could feel the sword's presence, like a shadow in his mind. Quiet but alert, Vereu was content to just observe. It seemed odd that he would be so different from both Khaela and Aislin.

"You're right. He isn't very talkative."

Fluora and the others did what they could to help, while knights watched over them from the sides, never too far away. She caught Barr's gaze and smiled, pushed the hair back from her eyes. With all she had endured, she still surprised him with her beauty. He then blushed at the realization that she knew what he was thinking, and the fluttering in his stomach made him turn away. He bit off a piece of bread and stuffed the rest into a pocket. The next soldier was in need of his attention.

"The Knight Commander is quite taken with your statue. She's most remarkable."

"Yes, she is." Barr peeled away the man's bloodied tunic and winced at the grisly sight. "Why hasn't anyone from the city come to help?"

"They did. Four hundred city guard and militia left the gates the first day and met us on the field." Dalwyn lowered his head. "They suffered heavy casualties and were forced to retreat. We fell back into Faith's Spire and have been here ever since."

"How long?"

"Three days and two nights. More Brotherhood will soon arrive from Hope's End. We sent messengers the moment we were attacked. The Guardians at Sanctuary were attacked as well. We have yet to receive word from Marshal Naero."

"I want to stay and help," Barr said, hoping he could somehow explain why he had to leave, "but there's more at stake than this shrine and Vereu."

"There's no need," Dalwyn said with a wan smile. "If our resources weren't stretched so thin in search of the other Emblems, this siege would never have happened – or at least wouldn't have last this long."

Maybe we should stay, Idelle said. *Our goals are the same.*

Barr saw the way his friends were watched, the open hatred and fear on some, the cautious glances on others. He thought it best if they were all away from this place, seeking Emblems on their own. It felt as if some of the knights might turn on them at any moment.

More than anything, though, he needed to find Aislin and save his mother from the umbrals. It was getting harder to think, burdened by worry and driving himself to exhaustion with healing. He didn't know how much longer he could go without sleep and saw the same ragged fatigue plaguing his friends. All he was certain of was that they had to move on. There would be no restful sleep in this place.

Barr! Fluora cried out in his mind. She was frozen in place, staring wildly, lost to a vision. He left off healing and rushed to her side. *Demons in the temple! So many... My mother!*

"What? Calm down and tell me what's wrong." Her eyes darted about, looked through and beyond him. Barr shook her from the images. "Fluora! What is it?"

"Demons," she said and looked up into his eyes. "I can see them attacking Faeronthalsos."

*   *   *

Music broke through the silence, as a door to the main hall slid open. Laughter carried with it, the titters of young women passing time between clients. One such girl stepped through and led a gentleman by the hand. In a violet evening gown of considerable expense, with all the fine trappings of a lady, she could have easily been mistaken for the daughter of a noble. Youth and a bright smile lent her mild appeal, but Markus found it difficult to find beauty in a human.

He sat in a dark corner beside the staircase, in the embrace of a cushioned chair and an aged brandy. The door closed behind them, and they headed up the stairs, leaving the room to quiet shadows once again.

Murmurs echoed through the walls, but only the crackle of a fire made any sound in this room. He thumbed the strings of a silken purse and took a sip.

"I hope I haven't kept you waiting."

The whisper of a woman's voice, it had come from behind the chair, and her lips were close enough that each word touched his ear with passing breath. He could smell the oil of her leathers and the road upon her skin. He knew without seeing that a blade was at his back. She could have plunged it through the chair at any time.

"You really can step through shadows." Markus took another sip. "I am impressed."

"Keep your eyes forward. I believe these are yours."

She held out three signet rings in an open palm. He noted the tattoo of woven sigils about her wrist but knew better than to hesitate. He put down his drink and took the rings, studied their engravings. Two priests and a knight from Faith's Spire, all of the third tier.

"You are sure there were no others?"

"My life hangs upon the tasks I'm given." She sniffed at his hair, an imperceptible gesture. "I am sure."

"This is yours," he said and handed back the purse, holding it within sight.

There was no sign of a blade when she took it. He grinned then, as if winning at a game, and felt certain he could kill her if the need arose.

"About our other arrangement. There's been a slight complication."

"And how much will this complication cost me?"

She was quiet a brief moment. "A quarter more than was agreed."

Markus slipped the rings into a pocket and picked up his glass. The money meant nothing, but respect was another matter. In his mind, no justification warranted a change once a deal had been struck. However, he had neither the time nor inclination to argue. The Brethren would be turned soon enough.

"I would hardly call that slight."

"If you wish, I'll convey your regrets that our dealing is at an end."

"A quarter more." He finished his brandy. "It shall be delivered upon completion."

An empty silence followed, and her presence against his skin disappeared. He had no need to look back to know only shadow remained, that she had come and gone without mark of her passing. That was, after all, what they were paid for.

News, my lord. Solastin's voice in his mind brought with it the scent of rotted leaves. *The raugrin offspring here at Drakanon cannot be turned.*

Markus rubbed at both temples. *Dwarves. They are called dwarves. And what do you mean they cannot be turned?*

I have bitten many. Not one of them turned.

What of the Guardians?

Your man has arrived. The conversion of Stonegrip is underway. A glimpse of forest flashed in his eyes, of a stone city with lumbering brutes twice the size of any human. *I gather a new army. If these dwarves cannot be turned, they will be crushed.*

It annoyed him that his revenants sometimes acted on their own, but he knew that was the doing of Revyn. He recalled the god descending upon Taellus as a black whirlwind of charred debris, a plague that brought death to the immortal kings. Markus had traded the *furie* that granted him eternal life, and Revyn used it to turn the twelve wielders. The god had killed them with one hand and reshaped them with the other. They were the power he had promised, the dominance of Taellus. They were the means of ruling that Markus had bargained for.

He often wondered if that were still the case.

Kraug! Revyn seethed, his words blinding Markus with the pain. *It seems my brother has found a way to ward his children.*

The force of the god's anger dropped Markus to his knees, body shaking with the tremors and ears bleeding between his fingers. He no longer heard anything but the underlying growl that encompassed Revyn's presence in his mind.

What would you have me do?

Kill them all, the god commanded, chewing each word, *every last one. Let the streets of Drakanon flow with the blood of Kraug's children.*

Markus fought for breath in ragged gasps and liquid wheezes. Wracked by waves of pain, his muscles tensed on their own. His eyes burned and blurred, with a mix of blood and tears. He felt the darkness rise up to claim him, in the arms of merciful oblivion.

Only then did he feel Revyn take his leave.

* * *

Surprised at how quickly Fluora called up the mists, considering her frantic state, Barr felt a jarring in his middle and blinked away the sudden dizziness. His eyes adjusted to the shift, to the glow of violet crystal in every facet of the temple. They stood on the central dais, a disc of living gem and floating runes, with two sets of three rings to either side leading up. Pillars stretched toward the stars, in a circle rising at one end, over an altar of shimmering white stone. Long, dark curls spilled down from the front, where the High Priestess Elaedraoni lay bloodied and unconscious. Claws reached over the edge from atop her, the hands of a demon with mottled scales like burning embers, and feral eyes regarded them with disdain.

"Mother!"

Fluora threw faeron magic at the creature in a wave of rainbow sparkle that flashed across its eyes. It gave a shriek and fell back, to the sound of talons across the floor. Barr tried to grab hold of Fluora, but she flew up the steps with *furie* trailing after. Aren and Dar-Paj went up the other side, as he drew both kyan and hurried to catch her. Hanar leapt across the distance and landed atop the altar on one knee, legs spread over Elaedraoni in a protective stance. She clapped both hands together, and a thunderous shock filled the chamber. A sphere of azure light rose up around them, as Fluora made it to her mother's side.

Barr rushed past and chased after the demon.

This is terrible, Idelle said, and Barr could feel her dread overtake him, heard in her mind the screams of innocents being slaughtered. *There's hundreds of them. They're everywhere.*

Aren caught it first and took a bite of ropy leg. He yelped as dark blood burned his mouth but refused to let go his hold. His momentum sent them sprawling across the floor and into the snowy vapor of a runic wall. The demon snarled, flames accompanying each breath, and it tried to kick away from the massive hound. Its claws scraped against him, scrabbling to break free, but left no mark on his hide. Small wings sprouted from its back, and it tried to fly away, carrying Aren along. Dar-Paj arrived and swung Khaela sideways, cutting through a ruddy membrane. The demon's cry was short-lived, abruptly lost to a kyan through its neck and the wall beneath.

Blood spattered Barr and began to burn away both cloth and flesh. He caught sight of a cleansing basin and quickly ran toward it. He washed away all trace of the foul ichor. His tunic was ruined, but it had saved him from severe burns.

I need you, Fluora said, her voice near to tears.

"I have seen these before," Dar-Paj said. He pulled the kyan free and let the body fall away. "I have faced them in battle."

Barr rushed back and took the blade, then hurried over to Fluora. Her mother was badly wounded, from a blow across the head to several claw marks at her middle. Her once pale skin was a mass of burns and bruises. Only tatters remained of her dress, exposing her to the cold, and blood ran freely down both her inner thighs.

Hanar had let her shield drop and watched closely the only entrance. She was first to see the demons step inside. Three of them, all ropy limbs of settling ember and feral maws with dripping flame, they loped up the steps and gave a cry of frenzied glee. She put a hand to Barr's shoulder, telling him to stay, and jumped down at the coming threat with silver runes flaring to life. Aren and Dar-Paj charged in to help her.

"She'll be fine," Barr said of Hanar. Elaedraoni was another matter. "Help me get her down."

They brought her gently to the floor, with her head pillowed in Fluora's lap. Fluora wiped the tears from her mother's face, hands shaking as she wept.

"Her spirit is leaving."

Breathing shallow and ragged, body pushed beyond all measure, it said much for her resolve that Elae yet lived. Barr put a hand to her shredded stomach and the other to her head. He reached deep within himself for what *furie* he could muster. Too weak to draw the magic in on her own, Elae's body began to falter.

"Don't give up," he told her, arms trembling at the exertion. "Don't…"

He forced his will upon her, consuming his own body to save hers. Damaged organs mended first, becoming whole and strong again. Fragments of bone slipped free and knit together with other wayward pieces, as poisons drained away from each wound. Her body resumed its struggle, demanding more with which to heal, but Barr had nothing left that he could offer. His skin cracked and bleeding, devoid of any moisture, Barr struggled just to breathe and felt himself near to death.

Darkness rose up all about him, in a haze of endless black. His eyes grew even heavier, pulled down by the warmth of a growing quiet, and longed to be soothed by the peaceful slumber of surrender. Arms embraced him from behind, the touch of spring against his winter. It cooled his burning flesh with tender hands across his chest.

"Take what you need," a voice offered, lending vigor to his body.

With a gasp, Barr returned from the brink and cast off its cloying grip. The pain in his lungs subsided, and he breathed steady once more. Fluora's cheek against his, her scent and spirit overwhelming, he looked down to see Elae still healing beneath his hands. Bruises dulled from bluish black to a healthy shade of pale, and areas of charred skin became revived and glowed anew. Her chest rose and fell into a rhythm, as her body found its pace. All her wounds closed, with little indication of having been there.

Barr turned around and helped Fluora stay upright. Her usual vibrant pallor had dulled to a tired gray, and damp curls hung down about her freckles. She looked as worn as he felt, on the verge of sweet collapse. Still, her eyes glimmered with relief, and she managed a warm smile. She put a hand to his cheek in thanks, and he reveled in the feel. He took hold of it in his and nodded in return.

Her mother began to stir.

Fluora reached out for the torn fabric that remained. She rubbed her thumb over an edge, and a sheen of many hues ran its length in a burst of sparkle. The dress mended back together, filling holes and joining shreds. Its cornflower blue became bright and free of stains.

By the time Elaedraoni opened her eyes with a weary gaze, only dried blood upon her skin gave any sign of the attack. Fluora helped her sit up and hugged her tight.

"I felt both of you with me," the Grand Seeress said, embracing her daughter. She looked at Barr and gave a weary smile. "Thank you."

– 8 –

emons outside continued their rampage, but the three who ventured in no longer moved. Broken and bloodied, crushed or cut apart, all that remained of their attack were still bodies on the stained floor. The dark sprays of their ichor bubbled across Hanar's front, eating at the obsidian between her runes. Puffs of white smoke trailed behind her, as she made her way up the steps to Barr's side.

I think she's... hurt, Aren said.

"Everything alright?" Barr asked her. He got up and helped the two faeron to their feet.

"For the moment, this chamber is safe."

Elae stared at Hanar.

"High Priestess Elaedraoni," Barr said, "I'd like you to meet a new friend. This is Hanar."

"New only to some," the golem amended and bowed her head in greeting.

The demon blood eating away at her body had finally dissipated, but the marks it left behind worried Barr. He examined the damage, unsure if he could mend it, and decided it was fine for now.

"Pleasure to meet you," Elae said, "and you have my thanks. All of you do."

Her eyes rimmed with moisture but refused to let fall any tears. Lips pursed and jaw set, she was a picture of stoicism. Barr knew what she had endured but resigned himself to silence so long as she did.

"The demons," Dar-Paj said. "I remember them."

We need to stop them. Idelle landed atop a pillar and looked off into the west. *There's more headed this way every minute.*

Barr studied his friend but said nothing of pointed teeth or great strength. If Dar was a demon, he didn't act like these others. He might have been a half-blood, just as Barr was half-faeron.

"Are they the people you've been looking for?"

"No. I fought against them on Danarriden, and even then I was alone."

Fluora shook her head. "That is unlikely. None could survive against such numbers. Be that as it may," she said and staved off any comment, "we need to act while we still can."

"The glyphs have failed," her mother explained. "We are unsure how, but all of them have shattered. Barely an hour has passed since the portal has been breached."

"Then the way to Danarriden lies open."

"What of the guards?" Barr asked. "Can they hold off an attack this size?"

"Not against an endless enemy. We are not a warlike people, despite our conflicts with the dryads and efreeti." Elae seemed old in that moment, weary from a long life. No wrinkles marred her face, but her eyes betrayed a wisdom hard-won. "Too long have we depended on the glyphs for our protection. I fear Faeronthalsos will be lost before dawn."

"I'll do what I can." Barr drew both kyan and looked out to the fires and mayhem on the street.

"That we did not foresee this attack says much. If you reach the central glyph, you may come against an evil far greater than the demons."

"What now?" Dar-Paj asked. "Fight our way to this portal?"

"I had something a little quicker in mind."

"That cannot be done," Fluora said firmly. "If the rift is crowded with demons, you will not be able to keep track of them all."

"I won't need to. Tell me," he asked Elae, "is my mother alright? The umbrals..."

He caught her glance at Fluora before meeting his gaze and wondered at the hidden meaning behind the gesture.

Time is running short, Idelle reminded. *The longer we stay here, the more demons we have to fight.*

There's never a good time for bad news. I need to know.

"The Matron is doing as well as can be expected. She requested to see you both upon your arrival." Elae looked back at the demon that had attacked her, then down at her feet. "That was before other problems arose. She will understand if you cannot see her right away."

"Is there time?"

She considered but did not answer.

"The rift is a more pressing matter. We can worry about umbrals when the demons have been driven back and the glyphs have been restored."

Barr gritted his teeth at the evasion. Before he could speak, Fluora intervened.

"You need to leave. My mother and I will see to the Matron." The lower lip that trembled between thoughts, the look in her eyes, it felt to Barr as if she were saying goodbye. "No, never that. You come back here alive. And you," she said to Hanar, "keep him safe."

"Hanar is going with you." Both of them protested, but he refused to listen. "I'm not asking. You're to keep them from harm and protect my mother when you find her."

"Is Fluora with child?" Hanar asked, in a not so quiet whisper, sounding all too hopeful of a past union.

"Just do as I ask. Please." He headed down the steps to the bottom dais. "Dar and Aren, you're with me."

Elae's eyes widened in alarm.

"My prince, I know what you are planning. You must not go at them with so few!"

He summoned a shield in a sphere of flickering light. Eyes closed to the strain, he focused his will, and the blue flashes that passed over its surface became solid, a glowing beacon that burned through the floor. Brighter and thicker, it crackled the air, sending tendrils of storm writhing outward. Drowning out all sound, the thrum of magic filled the air. The vibrant pulse of crystal dimmed, the temple darkened, and fractures went up along every pillar and spire. Screaming against the power building up in his body, fighting pain and the desire to release it, Barr took in all he could and called up the mists. A mass of umbrals threw themselves at the shield and screeched at the contact, at the shower of sparks that seared their talons and chitin bodies. They were gone with the fading echoes, as the mists fell away, as boiling water underfoot turned to scorched earth.

The sphere arrived in a shockwave of *furie*.

What demons occupied the space where it suddenly appeared were burned away and blown apart into ash. Dark soil lifted outward in a ring that trailed the burst, upending demons and jagged rocks with no regard. The shield disappeared, leaving behind a blackened crater, where the acrid fumes of burned flesh and demon ichor commingled. Feral eyes and twitching claws turned their way.

Idelle soared past and took hold of a large demon, then proceeded to batter all in her path. She tossed it against a boulder and twisted back into a climb, above the cloud of spraying blood and debris.

Aren eyed a victim and growled, with a grin no one should ever face in an elven war hound. Hackles raised, collar alight, he leapt into the sea of writhing limbs and waiting talons.

Two jumped atop Dar-Paj from either side, grating claws across his armor and cackling with eyes wild. He threw one off, but two more took its place, until Khaela began to glow with an aura of frost. Seared by intense cold, they climbed off and sprang away.

Fire lit up the night sky, and the ground shook with the vibrations of steps. Demons flew through the air, in a parting of ember bodies, as a monstrous creature shifted its molten bulk and came forward. Barr knew what it was without thought, through the dawn of a vision, in the passage of one time to another...

... hatchery in sight and the means for a meal to fuel his next change. He could smell them across the lava, see their essence through the rock and winding tunnels

beneath the flow. Such cleverness implied an able queen and cunning offspring. Their scent, as he burrowed, set his senses to tingling. No paltry few thousand here, waiting to devour weaker kin, this den had the heady whiff of the unborn. Salivating at the prospect, in wisps of molten zeal, he burst into the chamber and gorged on their leathery eggs.

With each life that he extinguished, their furie *now his own, his power grew in bounds and brought him closer to a change. At first, when he was young and only hunger filled his thoughts, the metamorphosis came easy. Each conversion then took longer, called for more or stronger prey. He had matured in mind and body, but the need never diminished.*

Become a better hunter or be food for another.

Stronger muscles, thicker armor, dizzying speed and sharper claws, his infant mind had once been flooded with the choices. His struggle to survive had now evolved into a goal. He aspired to the heavens, to be a god like the other five. Not the gods of all creation but the rulers of Danarriden. The Arch Demons had evolved through untold transformations and were worshipped for the bodies they devised.

Such devotion bolstered furie *and granted godhood to a mortal.*

That was what he sought, as he consumed the eggs and then their queen. He could gorge on all the world, but true power stemmed from worship. Why devour the furie *of a paltry thousand when there were millions willing to part with just a little...*

... closer than before. The world reasserted itself in his mind and snapped into place, but the memory of his desire still held fast. The elder stood before him, a mass of molten scale and beefy limbs. It glowered down from the height of ten men. Fist readied to strike, to crack the earth with eager flames, its attack struck against an unseen barrier and shook the ground.

Barr looked out across the landscape, where crimson skies engulfed his mind. He saw the means to indulge his hunger in the mass of brazen lessers and foolish few elders. Eyes grown wild with delight, his widened grin turned to laughter. The booming echo of its dissonance reached out across the land and caused a wary quiet to fall over the gathered horde.

The elder before him fell first, as the *furie* was torn from its body. Caught in the throes of consumption, it knew only pain and a desire to break free. Long tendrils of vapor were stripped from its spirit, leaving behind the dying embers of a desiccated husk. Scales shriveled and sloughed off, limbs shrank into char. The whole of its body collapsed and drifted off onto the wind.

Glowing with stolen *furie* that burned his flesh from within, Barr turned eager eyes on the others.

What's wrong with you!

A giant bird swept past him. *Can you hear –*

The scent of tremendous power assailed his nostrils. He turned toward the source, scarcely aware of those he set ablaze with excess *furie*, and caught sight of an unusual creature across the field. Encircled by an aura of frenzied runes, its presence lit the air with dark fire. In an ocean of demons, it stood out as a man, though one that had long since passed. It barked orders in a hollow voice that others followed without question, and its fiery eyes were intent upon Barr. It wore armor beneath a cloak, both of which should have burned, and rallied those around with a sword that had a voice. More powerful than the animated corpse, the sword radiated magic with a thrum so strong that the sound of it shook Barr by his middle.

He then noticed the rift, a shred of black hanging in the air like wounded sky. An endless flood of lessers flowed through it.

Ignoring voices in his head and the glut of searing *furie*, he began to drain a path toward the creature. All around him demons fell and writhed upon the ground, as the essence was torn from their bodies. He stepped over withered limbs and fading torsos, gathered up the stolen *furie* and sent it out at the next wave. The air became a furnace, a white-hot blanket of hungry flames. Shadows in the fire broke apart and blew away. He took more and burned others, drawing closer to the creature, to its sword and the dark rift it kept open. Not once did his gaze falter but held fast to the fiery orbs that were its eyes.

No amount of lessers could stop him, though not for a lack of trying. Their numbers made him stronger and lent the means of taking more. The growing ember in his middle meant a transformation was upon him, and the promise of another change drove his hunger on. Faster and frenzied, he stole *furie* with one hand and wove destruction with the other. Pained cries and dying pleas became whispers in a storm, drowned out beneath the tumult of intensifying magic.

An inkling of caution rang in his mind, and the grip of past memories began to lessen. The burning in his middle exploded throughout his body, as if the pain had been suppressed and the floodgates broken loose. He looked down at his hands and saw the skin flake away, as the world brightened all around him with a heat that scorched the demons. Nothing could be heard above the rush and crackle of dying earth, through vibrations of magic shaking everything in its path. The ash of drained soil rose up around him in a swirl, mixing in the air with his own debris.

You have to release it! Idelle screamed. *Let it go!*

He could no longer see. The world was but a canvas of empty white and fleeting shadow. Without knowing where his friends were, he couldn't risk letting loose the pent up *furie*. He caught sight of a momentary glimmer, the dim shape of a demon eaten away by the white. One after another, they appeared and disintegrated, with no sound or trace of their passing.

Barr pushed aside the gnawing pain and stumbled toward the rift. He could see it through the brightness, a gash in the air. The passage between planes shimmered with a violet aura, its center blacker than any shadow that came through. Drawing what he thought were his final breaths, he stood before the opening and directed all the *furie* down his arms and toward Danarriden. The rift rippled and wailed, a keening whistle that pierced his ears. His only thought as the *furie* left him, as darkness rose to blot his eyes, was that his friends and family, all of Faeronthalsos, would survive. He collapsed before the rift, weary eyes trained on its center, and felt himself begin to slip into the comfort of dark.

The shadows through the rift had finally stopped.

*   *   *

An archway of light, encased in spinning runes, the portal was a constant temptation. It took little prodding on his part to rally demons around it, especially since he held the Emblem of their forebears. A simple illusion had them believing the glyph was no more, that the passage to Faeronthalsos was wide open. The sword stirred their emotions, drove them to a frenzy and straight into the magical barrier. They burned apart in a flash, without so much as a darkened flake, but to any who looked on, it appeared they had stepped through.

Ombreusk tightened his grip upon Drakha, eliciting a crackle of enchanted bone. He watched with fiery eyes as demons rushed toward their doom, climbing over one another and dying by the handful. The prospect of invading Faeron, a new land to infest with helpless lives to feed upon, slipped into the mind of every demon like a plague. The sword whispered to their spirits, of great power and endless *furie*, of the means to fuel many transformations. More alluring, however, was free reign of the mists and the banquet of other worlds that would follow.

I am impressed, Revyn said, his voice crawling along the inside of Ombreusk's skull. *You know your kind well.*

These may descend from my people, but they are not of my kind.

It surprised him the god did not take offense. These mindless creatures were a far cry from Revyn's first, and no one liked to be reminded of their mistakes. Still, they had the potential for something greater. Not even Revyn could deny the power of an Arch Demon.

They too will be dealt with in time.

Ombreusk nodded, a minor detail in a grand scheme with little care but for existing. All he had lost, what had been taken away, no longer mattered. His people were gone, had been used to fashion the first mortals, and nothing could restore the life he had known before the Emblems. That Revyn's punishment touched them all did not change the way of things.

Hundreds perished within minutes, with twice as many scrabbling to reach the portal. They clawed one another in their eagerness to feed but gave no thought to feasting on those around them. Drakha kept their minds focused, eyes intent upon the rift, and teased with the imagined taste of faeron *furie*.

Runes brightened as they spun, and the glyph began to buckle, caving in on itself and the black at its center. Overwhelmed by sheer numbers, its magic spent upon their deaths, its complex wards unraveled and the glyph was no more. All that remained was the rift, a black gash between planes, and the hollow sound of bodies passing through. Hundreds more fought past, as elders began to appear in various forms and many sizes, each of them deadlier than the last.

Behind them all came Ombreusk, setting fire to the obsidian beneath his feet with every step. The red skies and molten rivers of Danarriden fell away, replaced by the bright greenery of Faeronthalsos. He conjured wards in the air, runes of dark fire, and took a quick stock of the landscape. Nothing but trees opposed them. For as far as he could see, the grasslands bore no soldiers nor any others of concern.

The horde went in search of life to drain.

More poured in behind him, his unwitting army to claim the mists. Demons could not be turned, but they still served a purpose. With the Queen and Matron taken captive, all of Faeron would soon crumble. Travel would become insignificant and the Emblems gathered with the speed of thought. Minutes passed into an hour, with still no end to the flow of demons streaming through.

Be wary, the god warned.

An area off to the left erupted in an explosion of *furie* and burned demons, as if a ball of light had crashed to the ground without moving. Fiery remnants rained down in a shower of ash and blackened bits, with the soil itself being torn apart in a single ripple.

The sphere of light diminished, leaving behind two humans, a large dog and a larger bird.

Ombreusk would have sighed in frustration had he the ability to draw breath but settled for seething hatred and a glare.

The mass of demons around him continued to grow in number, ropy limbs and feral talons keen on rending the new arrivals. The din of magic that ensued sent pain across his spirit, so strong did it shake the air and his long-dead body. Never had Ombreusk felt or heard such power, and it did something he once thought impossible: it sent fear through the horde. Whatever had changed the boy since Markus killed him, it gave reason to pause and consider escape. The loss of Drakha posed too great a risk.

The very air became alight with fire so intense that it blotted out all color, left nothing but shades of waning black and brilliant white. The heat scorched through his shield, evaporating its runes into a fine mist of wispy ebon, and threatened to unravel the divine enchantment across his bones. Ombreusk moved with all speed and pushed through the bodies fighting in from Danarriden, throwing demons behind him to be consumed by the inferno. He stepped through the rift, bones on fire and thoughts inflamed.

His plans had been thwarted by a child.

*   *   *

Her touch drew him from the maelstrom of color and cloying dark with a grasp both soft and insistent. Barr could hear her in his mind, speaking words of comfort, calling him back from the abyss. He followed her voice through memory of other lives and events imagined, heard it fade when he went astray and strengthen when he grew close. His eyes were gummed and refused his first attempt. When they finally gave way, the ache in each orb set his head to throbbing. He felt a hand in his and turned to see Fluora.

The movement wracked his entire body with pain.

Burned from within, his skin blackened and charred, each breath he took was an agony all its own. Open wounds spread across his chest and limbs, where pent up *furie* had broken free. Nothing remained of his hair or fingernails. The few areas that had escaped fire were swollen and red, signs of the damage inside. Each blink brought new pain, his lids sticky with blood, but the look in Fluora's eyes hurt him most.

"Barr!" She sounded surprised, as if she had never expected him to wake. "I will go get the healers."

"No," he said, voice rasped and lips cracking, "don't go. Please."

Are you alright? Idelle asked. *We're protecting the rift, but I'll come if you need me.*

Aren said, *Nothing's come through since you... since the battle. You should keep resting.*

He was inside a pavilion and could see stars through the central hole. Crystal braziers kept the room warm, as blankets would have clung to his wounds. The entrance flap was tied off with leather thongs, but he could hear soldiers moving about outside. The scent of blood and burnt flesh hung oppressive in the air, and he wondered how much of it was his own.

Stay there, he told them. *Don't worry about me, just keep your eyes on the rift.*

"They cannot heal as you do, but they can help."

"I just need... more time."

A tear fell from her cheek and stung his hand. He winced and drew it back.

"Sorry," she said and wiped her eyes. "Will you tell me what happened? There has been nothing but talk and no explanation. Naedrilla, the High Healer, has been in council with the Queen, but I overheard another say your spirit was burned."

Burned? He thought back to the attack and felt a hint of the elder demon from his vision. The screams all around him, the surge of power running through him, it seemed a blur of distant memory, another vision among many. What astonished him more than being alive was that his spirit could be injured.

Fluora's lips pressed together, and the worried blue of her gaze hardened into little sapphires.

"How can one who fights so hard to protect others care so little for himself?"

Barr closed his eyes and summoned what *furie* he could, careful not to take any from Fluora or the land. He didn't know if his body could withstand an influx, so he relied on his own to heal. The lacerations across his chest shrank in on themselves, while others merely drew close together. It helped, but his every thought rode the edge of constant pain. At the very least, he could speak without biting off words.

"I do care."

"Do you? I can see the truth, whether you admit it or not. Whatever guilt rules your life, true worth is found in living for yourself as much as others." Her look softened once more. "Death redeems no one."

"You're wrong," he replied. "I help because I'm able. That's just who I am. If saving all of Faeron meant giving up my life, then I made the right choice."

"It is not the choice that I question but the speed in which you made it."

She let her tears fall unabated and met his gaze with an openness that revealed her true feelings.

"Fluora, I –"

"Is there nothing in this life to stop you rushing toward the next?"

Unsure what to say, he considered the question. Did guilt rule his life? Did he rush into danger in the hope of meeting death? It was true he had once felt blame for his father's murder, but he had put that to rest when he faced off against Ceiran. Killing the elven shapeling did more than avenge his father, it brought safety to Geilon-Rai and prevented countless other deaths.

Barr honored his father's memory by living life as he had been raised, helping others because he could. He did the same for Tuvrin and Seltruin, by acting as the sage he was trained to be. No matter that he no longer lived among the elves, the greater good still mattered above all else. He loved Aren and Idelle, loved life and all it gave him. It was a love worth having and one worth fighting to keep safe.

Eyes closed, she shook her head and gave a sigh, as if all his thoughts served only to confirm her fears. When she looked at him again, a heaviness weighed upon his heart. Just as he thought she wanted to lean forward and kiss him, she let go his hand and sat back in the chair.

"I met with your mother. She was not well but will be soon."

He understood the gesture and gave a slight nod. The pain of his injuries began to pale beneath the loss, but he put those emotions aside.

"Why, what's changed?"

"She asked me to take her place." Fluora got to her feet and headed for the entrance. Undoing the leather binds, she added, "Once I am Matron, your mother will be free of the umbrals."

Fluora stepped out of the tent before Barr could call after. Hanar must have been waiting, came in and closed the flaps.

"You will sleep now," the golem said, in no uncertain terms, and moved to his side. "No arguing."

Barr lay back against the pillow and flinched at the prickling ache that ran across every inch of him. Hanar knelt beside the bed and put a gentle hand to his chest. Despite being able to crush a man with her weight alone, her touch rested upon him with the care of a worried mother. It warmed him from the inside and settled calm over the tumult in his heart. Concern slipped away, like the shedding of clothes, and left him comforted but bare to the rising dark. Though sleep drew him down into the murk, he fought it off a moment longer.

"The rift?"

"Is being tended." *Furie* crept over him, a golden glow at the heavy edge. "It will be there when you wake."

"Fluora..."

"Will be here too. Sleep."

He drifted off into the black, fully immersed within its grasp. Wrapped about him like the waters of the mists, it filled him with dark quiet and the repose of a still surface. No vision or dream cast a ripple through its calm. The only sound he could fathom was the steady rhythm in his ears. Its beat reverberated all around him, was echoed back in a dull thumping. It slowed and lulled him deeper, to where the glow began to fade. He lost all sense of time there, in the absence of light, with neither breath nor beats to gauge the passing. His world became the silence, the dark his only care.

When it finally receded, and Barr was able to come awake, he was certain whole days had been wasted. He opened his eyes and looked about, saw Hanar waiting by his side and smiled at the sight of her despite the pain. The room seemed too bright, as if anything but complete darkness caused him discomfort. His wounds were all gone, both burns and lacerations. The skin left behind though remained splotchy and red. Still tender from healing, muscles sore and screaming in protest, any touch brought with it a sharp intake of breath.

He gritted his teeth and sat up, then was surprised to see hair fall down the front of his shoulders. Aches and tenderness aside, he felt mostly restored.

"Did you heal me?"

"I did not." She handed him a drink and touched a damp cloth to his skin. He hissed and shrank back. "You healed yourself, though I assisted. More rest and further mending should make you whole."

The water was cold. He sipped it and flexed a hand, wincing at the touch of his fingers against the palm. His nails had grown back, but it felt as if the burns were still not healed.

Give it time, Idelle said, *and welcome back.*

How long have I been out? Is everyone alright? How's the rift? "This should have healed," he said, thinking aloud more than complaining.

It's an hour past dawn. Their enchanters still haven't been able to remake the glyphs, though they managed temporary wards. He felt her land on a tree outside the tent. *Aren and Dar are asleep. There's an army of faeron surrounding the rift.*

"I will help you try again, if you are ready."

And Fluora?

Gone, left with her mother in some kind of ceremonial garb. A few others dressed the same went with them.

The hawk paused, intimately aware of how he felt. *I'll go find her.*

No, stay by the rift. The best way to keep it safe while they work may be to go through it.

And face thousands at once instead of two at a time?

That revenant had an Emblem.

Hanar took the cup and put it aside, then held both her hands out palm up. Barr placed his hands atop hers, skin protesting the contact, and used her body to help him focus. He called up *furie* within himself and sent it through the webwork of silver runes across her frame. She mingled it with her own, tempered it toward healing and returned it threefold. A tingle sped over him, then grew to stabbing fire. No matter how much or how long he wove the curative magic, it did nothing to stem the pain or lessen the red marks.

He let go and spent a minute recapturing his breath. His heart raced from the exertion, his body alight with replenished *furie*. Despite the soft glow of good health and a sound body, nothing could explain the burns but what Fluora had mentioned.

"My spirit is burned." He looked up into the glow of Hanar's eyes. "How do I mend my spirit?"

You can't heal the burns? You can't walk around in pain all the time!

I tried, but there's nothing wrong with my body. It's completely healed.

"How can you be sure?"

"I can't, but what else explains burns that won't heal or pain that shouldn't be there?" He sighed and reached for a set of clothes beside the bed. "I'll have to find some other way when there's time."

She stopped him with a hand to his shoulder, but pulled back when he recoiled at the pain.

"My apologies, but where are you going?"

"I have to help rebuild the glyphs. I can't do anything else until the rift is closed, until I'm sure Faeron is safe." She had to help him with his boots. He held his breath and blinked away the tears. "Once I've done that, I can sort this mess I've made with Fluora and go after the revenant that opened the portal in the first place."

"You are a difficult Master to care for."

She stood and picked up both his kyan, then offered her other hand. He took it and got up with a grunt. The clothes chafed against his skin, caused pain each time he moved, but he ignored it and fixed Hanar with a pale grin.

"And you are a good friend."

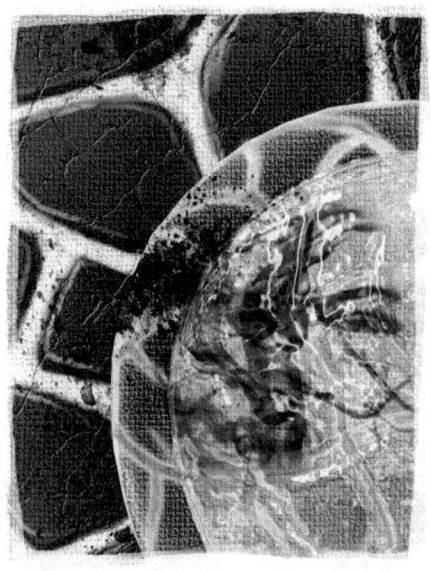

– 9 –

arr could see it in their eyes the moment he left the pavilion, the quiet fear and concern, though for himself or their own safety he wasn't sure. Dozens of faeron soldiers turned his way with open stares. None met his gaze, no warm smiles nor happy greetings. Each one looked away as if afraid to draw attention. A deafening silence filled the area. He looked into the sea of faces and felt a childhood dread rise up to grip his heart.

This isn't Alixhir, Idelle said, *and they're not afraid of magic.*

Queen Ariana approached with another woman at her side, both dressed in elegant contrast to the armored guards that trailed behind. Hanar took a step back to allow for private conversation.

What then? I saved them. He could see the rift in a field of blackened earth, where robed faeron gathered in a circle and wove runes of glowing blue in the air. *The land hasn't healed itself. The entire field...*

"We need to talk," the Queen said. Her eyes betrayed no emotion but looked grave nonetheless. "You are heir to the throne of Faeronthalsos, and I will love you until the day I pass."

"But?"

"I need to know that my people are safe, both from dangers without and within."

Barr swallowed hard. "I risked my life to save Faeron from those demons, and I would never hurt any of your people."

Ariana's gaze softened. He knew his words had hurt her. He hadn't meant to do so, but the sting of her accusation reopened old wounds. For years he had lived among the elves, as both a healer and protector. Not once did he delude himself into thinking he was one of them. Why should here be any different? The faeron blood in his veins did nothing for his appearance. His life was still defined by rounded ears and thick limbs.

"That is unfair," the Queen returned. She reached a hand out to touch his arm, but Barr backed away. "You wield incredible power, like nothing we have ever seen, but you lost hold of it last night. You let the magic consume and control you instead. Dryads were banished for the very same reason. What am I to do if my prince follows their path?"

Idelle ruffled her feathers and took wing. *It's not your fault that some visions are stronger than others.*

"It's not that simple," Barr said. The other woman's narrowed gaze sent a tingle across his skin, as if she saw past the splotchy redness to his damaged spirit. "I don't have an answer, and I can't guarantee anything. All I can do is my best."

"You should not be out of bed," the other stated with authority.

"Prince Barr, this is Naedrilla, the High Healer."

"In this condition," the faeron continued, "you are a danger to yourself and those around you."

"I'm hardly –"

Naedrilla stepped forward and tried to poke him. He swatted away her attempt, but even that brief contact set his hand to trembling in sharp pain. His arm went numb up to the elbow, and he nearly fell to his knees. Hanar rushed to his side and stood over him with eyes flashing. The guards tensed, gripping spears with both hands and readied to strike.

"Are you crazed?" Barr asked the healer, willing the pain to subside.

"Merely illustrating a point."

"No one," Hanar warned in a level tone, "puts a hand on the Master."

Only the Queen remained calm. "Be at ease, friend Hanar. I am sure the High Healer meant no harm."

"It's alright." Barr straightened and took in a deep breath. "I'm fine now. I'd appreciate if no one else tried to touch me."

Hanar backed down from towering over the faeron but refused to go far. Despite the enthusiasm, Barr felt grateful for her protection. Naedrilla, however, had made her point all too well, and he realized something would need to be done sooner than later. He stood no chance against a demon, if the lightest touch brought him down, and any who fought beside him would be at risk.

"We have capable men and women," Naedrilla said, "those far older than yourself and with a great deal more experience. You can trust them to their tasks, while you rest and fully mend."

I agree you need to rest, Idelle said, *but they don't seem to be making any headway with that glyph.*

"How do you plan to assist?" Ariana looked toward the forming portal, as if gauging its progress. "No one knows more of the glyph system than our enchanters."

"I've studied runic structures before, in a number of different languages. I might see some small detail they've overlooked or haven't considered. Besides, what could it hurt to take a look?"

"Having a prince underfoot might be more hindrance than help. They have neither the time to explain nor give instruction."

"I know what's at stake," Barr said. "I wouldn't have offered if I didn't think I could be of use."

His grandmother nodded. "Very well. I will have food and water sent to you. The tray best return empty."

Barr gave a half-smile and headed for the rift.

You really think you can fix it?

I can't make it any worse. Barr winced with each step over the decimated field, where drained vegetation left a layer of grime over charred soil. Awed and ashamed of the destruction he had wrought, no matter the outcome, guilt turned his stomach more than the horrid stench of demon remains. *It doesn't make sense that the land is still scarred. When I enchanted your collars...*

As he drew closer to the rift, he caught sight of the answer. He heard it before he saw but had attributed it to the enchanters rebuilding the glyph. He had felt it from a distance, as a twinge of nausea in his middle and raised hairs on the back of his neck. If the faeron were unaware, it could explain why they had failed thus far.

"*Furie* is being drained through the portal."

"I see it too," Hanar said. "It may not be safe to stand too close."

He had no choice but to do just that. The enchanters wove directly around the rift, runes of gold and blue that hung suspended in air. Each one spun in place and trailed a faint sparkle of its color, which twirled in a lazy spiral before disappearing into the black. A dozen faeron studied the incomplete wards and conferred with who must have been the High Enchanter. A slender man by any standard, he seemed frail beneath the silk of his robe. Others moved about the growing structure, making small adjustments, but nothing new was woven without his consent.

Barr looked closer at the wards for any patterns he could surmise. Though some of the runes were common, used by weavers in numerous cultures, a great many were particular to faeron magic. More than a handful of his incarnations were illuminairen, the first of Saernol, from whom faeron were descended. Dozens more were as faeron, with two being enchanters. From the amalgam of those memories, he knew well each rune, in the shaping of specific wards the glyph they would become. Their intended design, the central and outer glyphs, became apparent.

Unfortunately it carried with it certain flaws.

Dar-Paj approached, still weary and armor bloodied. Since their time in the Guardian cell, he no longer tried to hide his features but walked openly with golden skin and snowy hair. Barr guessed his new friend had either grown comfortable among the faeron or their ordeal had changed him in subtle ways. Or perhaps Khaela at his waist lent a measure of self-assurance.

With a wooden tray of meats, bread and cheeses, a pitcher of cold water and two mugs, Dar joined them near the rift. He placed the food atop a shield, which served as a makeshift table, and glanced at the stack of paper drawings beside it. He poured himself a drink and took a piece of sharp rombuld.

"Good to see you up and about," he said and took a bite. "How are things going here?"

"Not well."

One of the enchanters gave a crusty look.

Be nice, Idelle said. *They've been working hard.*

I didn't mean to hurt his feelings, but little of what they've done can be salvaged. Barr grabbed a drink and a strip of meat. *Have you slept yet?*

I will. I was just waiting...

Go on. You need rest as much as I do. "Are you still having nightmares?"

"Still."

Hanar looked over the apprentice. "I could brew you a tonic. Your sleep would be restful and without dream."

Dar's eyes went alight at the notion.

"Please do. I honestly cannot recall the last time I woke rested." He gripped Khaela by the pommel and sat on a wide blackened rock. "I have been meaning to ask."

"You'd like to know what happened."

"There is that, but something else. How did you take us to the portal without scrying?"

"I... I'm not sure. I didn't realize." Barr thought back to the temple, before he had brought them through the mists. "Fluora's mother. When she spoke of the demons, I saw the portal in my mind. I didn't think to scry its location, because I knew where it was."

"And the battle?"

"A vision got away from me."

Dar-Paj finished his drink. "That must have been some vision. I was told you... burned your aura?"

"Close enough. I think I'll be fine, given enough rest. It only hurts if anything touches me."

"I see." Dar shook his head with a smile. "And here you are, in obvious pain, waiting to lend assistance."

"It's not so bad."

"You are an unusual man, Barr. Your uncle would be proud." He sat quietly for a moment, as if troubled by the thought of his mentor. "I was right to leave."

"You've been remembering."

"Yes. Bits and pieces, sparked by things or people I see. More than anything, I just want to know who I am."

"We are what we do. It's our actions that define us, and your actions have been that of a good person."

"Actions only define us when we can remember what we have done. Still, I wanted to thank you for giving me the opportunity to find my past and my people. I am in your debt." He raised a brow and added, "Although, you nearly burned me alive last night."

He thought Dar might have joked at his expense but saw truth in the jest, whether intended or not. He could have killed them with the demons and until then just assumed such a thing would never happen. What if his grandmother was right? His visions had been steadily growing stronger, lingering in his mind and directing his actions. His thoughts raced back to the Denshyar, at the accusation of being haunted and the fear it had inspired in the elves. He saw the same trepidation in the eyes of every faeron and began to wonder if they were right to be afraid.

"Sorry, I didn't –"

"No, there is no need to apologize. Khaela kept us safe, and I am certain we would have fallen had you not acted as you did." He stood and stopped himself before clapping Barr on the shoulder. "Khaela tried to protect you as well, but your pull was too strong. She feared you might drain all her magic."

A single sigh did nothing to unburden the weight Barr felt upon his shoulders. He may have saved all of Faeron, but the wedge he had driven between himself and his mother's people would not be easily removed. It would only be made worse with what he next had to do. He put his drink down and moved closer to the rift.

"You and Hanar don't need to stay. This might take a while."

"I will stay," Hanar said.

Dar-Paj sat back down to watch.

Barr approached the High Enchanter, an elder man named Rornaelin. Every gathered faeron but one stopped and bowed to their prince. The other, a fellow with gray hair and an ever-present sour visage, merely tilted his head before returning to his work.

"This pattern will unravel," Barr said and stepped up to the spinning runes, indicating a channeling quartet. "The runes around them can't sustain the amount of *furie* that'll pass through this ward. And when it fails, the glyph will fail."

Rornaelin eyed the runes. He may have only done so out of respect for his prince, but Barr could see doubt on the man's face and a hope the claim was false.

"I will be first to admit," he said, "that our lore has deteriorated over generations, from lack of use and the loss of invaluable tomes to efreeti raids, but I do not see the problem you speak of. How can you be certain the ward will dissolve?"

"I've worked extensively with runic structures in the past," Barr explained, ignoring the all too familiar stare of elders who saw only a fifteen year old boy. "If I wasn't injured, I could channel enough power directly into the ward to show you. How about I work a bit on the pattern instead?"

The grumpy faeron gave a snort, which drew a look from the High Enchanter.

"My prince, this is Oloreian."

"With all due respect," the nasal man protested, "we have worked on the glyph all night. To tamper with it now would undo all we have accomplished."

Barr's eyes were transfixed upon the glyph, already reassembling it in his mind.

"Humor me."

A stern look from Rornaelin, and the other bowed his apologies. They all backed away from the glowing pattern to give Barr room to work. He called over Hanar, whose presence unnerved more than a few, and indicated the *furie* being drained through the rift.

"Could you help with whatever's doing that?"

The golem nodded and stood before the rift, legs and arms spread wide. She clapped her palms together with a deafening force. Barr held his ears against the ringing, but a sphere of cloudy blue now encompassed the rift.

"I will hold it for as long as I can."

Barr nodded and began by rearranging the existing runes in broad sweeping gestures of his arm, much to the breathless dismay of Oloreian. With a space cleared before him, he set to inscribing new runes. A fiery trail of golden light followed his finger, as he poked it into the air and used it like a quill. His wards had a simple yet elegant flare, forsaking all but the most basic of runic functions. To the untrained eye, it may have seemed like child's play, as each cluster formed a ward and shrank away to the background. Only when the clumps began to move, twisting around one another, did they appear as parts of a whole.

"What is this gibberish?" Oloreian whispered none too quietly to another, his face pinched together. "Have you ever seen such nonsense? No, *you* shush! Just look at it! Those are not even runes!"

Ignoring his audience, Barr continued to weave a highly intricate pattern of wards within wards, a cunning system of interlocking parts. Each bolstered the strength of its neighboring piece, without relying on them to serve out their function. The channeling runes, which made up the conduit wards, were now comprised of no less than twenty-four separate parts. Evenly spaced and ordered to provide a safe discharge of magic across the entire length of the glyph, nothing short of complete failure in every ward would break the pattern. There were no weak points, as every bit of energy entering into it was evenly dispersed among the lesser runic systems.

A full hour passed before Barr stood back to admire his work. He nodded, pleased with the changes, but felt as if something were not right or missing. What pain he had felt at simply moving with each inscription had not so much subsided as it was nudged aside by a deep focus. His unease, however, gnawed at the back of his mind and threatened to lay waste to his concentration. He studied the glyph in its entirety, from spinning top to swirling bottom, and realized the flaw he sought was in the overall design.

"Why rely on other glyphs?" he asked aloud, to no one in particular.

Oloreian happily answered, though no one paid him any mind. Barr stepped back into the pattern and began weaving new runes. He no longer crafted structural wards but worked to spiral the glyph down it into a chain of channeling runes that linked it to the land. Inscribing runes into the ground in a wide circle of fiery green, he pushed past rock and soil to the flowing ley lines far below. With the briefest *click* of contact on each of the last runes, he bonded the glyph to Faeronthalsos and an endless supply of *furie*.

Never again would the portal open by force.

Rornaelin shook his head in bewilderment, as he walked around the complicated pattern. Barr took a seat to rest, exhausted from the endeavor. He had forgotten how much effort rune crafting took. Oloreian stalked off towards the pavilions in a huff, muttering about alerting the Queen. Hanar maintained her shield over the rift, but its sheen had deteriorated to a dull cobalt.

"Will this work?" the High Enchanter asked, as if unsure of what he saw. "This is either a masterpiece of magic or an utter delusion. I must admit, I am not at all familiar with most of these runes. This looks nothing like the central glyph – or any other glyph for that matter."

"It isn't," Barr told him. "I improvised a little."

"What language is this? For the first time in three-hundred years, I feel like a student."

"That's ankaran."

"And this?"

"Raugrin. Beside it is edarrin, with sylvannis leys and daefarim loops, and up top is an arachon crown."

"Really, my prince, I have never even heard of the last. How could you possibly know all these?"

Barr gave a wry smile. "I'm older than I look. So how about you activate it and see if I'm delusional?"

"I witnessed your battle with the demons," the High Enchanter said, revealing a hidden fear Barr had refused to see in him before. "Certainly you do not require any assistance?"

"It's because of the battle that I do."

Rornaelin nodded in understanding and called the others to join him. They circled the pattern and held their hands palm outward, as Barr directed the High Enchanter toward the front. Eyes closed, they began to focus, directing will and *furie* into the activation rune. It rose up within them all as a glowing fog of deep azure and trailed through the air in bright wisps. It gathered at the bottom and struck against the single rune, setting it ablaze in a flash of light. In the span of a breath, the fire spread to every rune within the pattern. The glyph flared a golden blue, as Hanar let fall her failing shield, and a blinding glow went up around them like another sun.

Its light dimmed to transparency, each ward in the new portal spinning in a rhythmic thrum. The magic ran so strong, it shook Barr by his middle and rumbled its way up his spine. Joy overcame the gathered few, as tensions melted in the wake of a victory cheer. No more demons would pass through, and the fighting was truly over.

The rift had finally been closed.

* * *

Strewn across the hallowed grounds in an array of smoking ruin, charred and broken bodies stained the snow. Shaped stones two men high made up a circle all around them, with the telltale glow of a ley stone in the middle. Floating above the runic anchor and veined with precious metals, a sculpted basin held bubbling clear water that renewed itself with no visible source. Against its polished edge, Caeryk forced the stout neck of the last sankraggan priest near to breaking.

Three times the muscled girth, though half as tall as the revenant, the dwarf dangled in the air like a helpless child. Sputtering for breath through the long braids of a singed beard, the offspring of Kraug fought in vain to break free. Caeryk shook him and asked once again.

"What protects you from being turned?"

"I don't know, ya daft –"

Caeryk squeezed, tired at the lack of progress. In the illusory guise of a Guardian, he had arrived at Silver Downs two days prior. Like the vardikor, their kinsmen at the mountain city of Drakanon, the sankragga had also become immune. Those he bit did not turn, nor did they hear the voice of Revyn in their minds. None of the other revenants had found a clue, but Caeryk was sure the prayer stones played a part.

The grasslands all around bore the touch of divine *furie*, a faint scent that conjured memories of his second making. He could feel it in his bones, where the blood of Revyn filled each rune. It touched his spirit and set to trembling his bony prison. Whatever magic rode the air, it was not the work of mortals.

He let fall the broken dwarf and turned his attention toward Silver Downs.

The sankragga are immune, he told Markus, *but I may have found something worth looking into.*

Caeryk could feel his unease. Few things frightened Markus, but failing Revyn ranked among them.

Then look into it.

Yes, my lord.

171

He left behind the prayer stones and headed toward the fields outside Silver Downs. A collection of hollowed out stones jutting up from the earth, the sankraggan city was surrounded by a river of liquid metal. Though it had the look of quicksilver, it did not poison the air nor the soil it touched. Its heat and vapor, however, wreaked havoc on the living. It posed no risk to Caeryk, but it did present him with another problem. Fifty arrow-lengths wide and twice as deep, the molten silver proved more than an adequate deterrent. It also made it easier for their guards to see beyond where any other city might have had a wall.

Caeryk altered his illusion and from one step to the next became a sankraggan hunter in long leathers and a heavy bow. Snow crunched underfoot, as he made his way through the tall grass. Though browned by winter slumber, it still provided for all the livestock and in turn the many dwarves. He saw others in the distance, more hunters in search of wolf and the occasional crimson burrower. The tingle up his spine grew strong and drew him on, to yet another runic anchor half-buried in the field.

Tied to a ley line far below the frosted surface, the glowing stone siphoned *furie* and fuelled the changes in the grass. He again sensed divine enchantment and even caught a glimpse of the elusive runes that gave life to all creation.

I know what is happening.

Revyn was beside him in an instant, stepping from a swarm of buzzing black that faded on the wind.

Tell me, the god commanded then caught sight of the enchantment. With narrowed eyes, *Celene!*

Just so.

She has tampered with the land. Revyn drove an armored boot into the ley stone, cracking it into pieces and extinguishing its glow. *She thinks by aiding other's children she found a way around her oath.*

Markus said, *Slay all the livestock. Without them to feed on, the sankragga may revert.*

Yes, I doubt she found a permanent solution. I want all these ley stones destroyed. Revyn considered, his brow furrowed as he stared at Caeryk. *This is not the first time she has meddled. Her last attempt, at a cure no less, nearly cost all her children. I drove her elves to the brink of annihilation. Perhaps it is time for another lesson.*

We have agents in all four nations, Markus reminded him. *So long as the elves are not immune, we could turn them in short order.*

No. Without them, Celene has nothing else to occupy her time. I think instead we find a way to keep her busy.

Another war?

That will do nicely.

I will arrange it, Markus said. *What of Barr? He has thwarted the attack on Faeronthalsos. Without access to the mists, our plan will fail.*

My plan does not hinge on any one effort. At worst, success has been delayed.

Caeryk listened and said nothing. Though he agreed the boy should die, his opinion rarely mattered. Once a child of Laeryk, the Watcher God, he and his brethren scried the world in isolation and kept a record of its passing. Those histories afforded him vast knowledge but of a time now long since gone.

Markus persisted. *He has proven too dangerous.*

His reaction to the demons was expected. You do not fully understand what he is. Revyn's tone seemed to say, that too was expected. *Nothing has changed. Faeron and the mists will be ours before long. Barr still serves our purpose by gathering the Emblems.*

Assuming we can wrest them from him once he has the others.

Revyn grinned. *Just leave that to me.*

The sight unsettled Caeryk, inasmuch as his corpse allowed, and for the very briefest of a moment felt a chill deep in his bones.

* * *

Barr reeked of eucalyptus and any number of heady scents. Hanar helped him with the ointment Naedrilla had concocted, spreading the oily substance across his shoulders and back. It left his skin numbed to the touch but tingling all the same, as if a constant cool breeze ran over and through him. The burns, however, continued to pain from within, like a river of lava in his veins. As if his body stood at odds with the spirit that housed it, he felt frozen and on fire all at once. In a short while, that too died away, and the inferno abated to mere embers.

Clothes no longer clawed every inch of his body, and he walked without the stabbing in his feet. He clenched both hands, testing their new limits, and approved of the result. He could hold both kyan and fight if need be, when he tracked down the revenant who had opened the portal. He put that thought aside for the moment. With the glyph restored and Faeron safe from Danarriden, there still remained the threat of umbrals breaking free of the mists.

Hanar took hold of his hand, as if judging for herself if the ointment made a difference. He felt the growing pressure of her palms on either side but sensed nothing of their texture or the warmth he expected.

"That is much better," she admitted. Her tone spoke of a dislike for the High Healer. "Though it only masks the affliction."

"True enough." Barr slipped his hand free and gave her a smile. "I'm just glad I can move without wanting to scream."

He reached for his shirt and a new set of leathers, then finished dressing by strapping on both kyan. The boots seemed to fit him well, but walking with numbed feet took some getting used to. They left the pavilion and headed for the road.

"Where to?" Dar-Paj asked and joined them. He too wore new clothing, light robes with leather vambraces.

"My mother's estate."

With Aren and Idelle still asleep, the quiet in Barr's mind left him alone with troubled thoughts. They walked on in silence, past soldiers standing guard or servants carrying supplies. Each one looked away, pretending not to notice or refusing to meet his gaze. His mind drifted back to restoring the glyph, to the faces of those around him when it had come alive and the danger passed. They had seemed happy at first, relieved and even grateful, but the distance he felt between them had not lessened. He saw it in his grandmother, the hint of fear behind her eyes, the smile tainted by trepidation. Whatever good he had accomplished would forever be overshadowed by the haunting image of him facing off against an army of demons.

"He is still near the portal," Dar-Paj said, sounding eager to go after. "The revenant is called Ombreusk. I can see where he is through the Emblem he carries."

"I thought he'd be long gone by now."

"If we hurry –"

175

Barr held up a hand. "I have to see my mother... and make amends with Fluora."

When they arrived at the stronghold, all that could be seen of the guards and staff were two soldiers at the entry. Though the estate had been spared from attack and spreading fires, clear signs of panic left the grounds in disarray. Chairs were overturned with upended meals and tufts of grass trampled underfoot. Birds picked at the spoiled food, as Barr hurried past. One guard gave a polite nod but looked straight ahead, while the other kept his eyes on Hanar. She and Dar-Paj waited outside, as Barr rushed up the runic stairs to Daesi's chamber.

Despite preparing to face the terrible wounds from an umbral, the creeping blackness Fluora had endured, Barr stood in shock at the doorway and stared. Once full of life and all the vibrancy it afforded, his mother now appeared older than any faeron he had seen. Her pale skin had lost its shimmer and turned from porcelain to ash, wrinkled with dark spots. The ocean blue of her eyes was now clouded by a filmy haze, and her hair had become dulled by snowy streaks. Little muscle remained, as if devoured with her essence. Lying still upon the bed, her withered frame seemed near to death.

"And here I feared for your life," she said, her voice weak but still playful. "By the expression on your face, I am worse off than I thought."

"I'm just surprised." He went to her and sat beside her on the bed. "You've changed so much. You look..."

"Old? I will grow stronger in time, but a great deal has been taken from me. It is the sacrifice we must make to keep the mists."

She took his hand and squeezed.

"And now Fluora will make that sacrifice," Barr said. "How can she survive without Aislin? Is she throwing away her life to buy us more time?"

"Of course not. She is young and far stronger than ever I was. With Fluora as Matron, the umbrals will be driven back and the mists again safe."

"I want to see her."

Daesi looked closely at her son. "Is it wise for you to be up and about?"

"I'm fine," he replied and turned away.

"Even with these eyes, I can see you are not. Fluora has a difficult task ahead. Any distraction could mean failure and disaster for us all." Daesi pulled at his tunic, forced him to meet her gaze. "If she falters, even for an instant, the umbrals will consume her and break free."

"All the more reason for me to see her. I can't leave things between us the way they are. If she dies –"

"Then none of this will matter."

"I can find her on my own if I have to," he threatened and regretted having said it. "Please tell me where she is."

"Do you love her?"

Barr sighed. "We hardly know each other. I just need to tell her –"

"Barr. Do you love her?"

He swallowed and nodded.

"Yes."

"I know you have suffered and fear being hurt." She brought his hand up to her lips. "If you love her, you must put aside those fears and let her know. It may grant the strength she needs to see her through."

"Show me."

Daesi closed her eyes and filled Barr's mind with an image of ten women in robes, their faces hidden within cowls and scrabbling shadows in the dark. They made a circle in the mists, with Fluora at its center, and the blackness all around them swarmed and writhed with tooth and claw. Trails of inky vapor puffed and squirmed between the mass, ebon carapace and twitching ears taking shape. Chitin shells clicked against one another, as umbrals scuttled across the half-shell of protective magic. Their eyeless faces sniffed the air and filled his ears with screeching keens.

From one breath to the next, Barr stood beside her in the mists. He ignored the gasps of protest from the other women and the surprise on Fluora's face. Without a word he stepped in close and kissed her full upon the lips. Though numb still from the ointment, the taste and scent of her consumed him. His need for her rose up from within, and he feared to let her go.

Fluora gripped him by the front and pushed away.

"You should not be here," she said and frowned. "And until we are joined, you will never kiss me unless I kiss you first!"

"I'm sorry. I just couldn't let –"

She pulled and kissed him hard, wrapping her arms around his neck. Her strength caught him off guard, but he returned the kiss with equal fervor. She again pushed him away, though more gently this time.

"Now go," she said and smiled.

The umbrals thrashed about in a heightened frenzy, keening louder overhead.

"Save us all," Barr said and conjured up the mists, "then come back safe."

She gave a nod, and he was gone.

– 10 –

arr hurried downstairs and out past the guards, a dull twinge nipping at each step. The others fell in beside him, as he headed for the road, and kept pace with his sense of urgency. Fluora's scent carried with him, coloring each breath, the memory of her kiss still pressing on his lips.

"Why are you smiling like that?" Dar-Paj asked.

"She kissed me," Barr replied, his smile widening. *Wake up you two. We need to get going.*

I'm awake, Idelle said and took wing. *I'll meet you at the portal.*

Aren grumbled, the only sign he stirred.

A patrol of four went past, spears in hand and eyes ahead. With scales burned and chain links broken, the crimson stains upon their armor were not the blood of

179

demons. More soldiers were marching toward them, most likely returning home.

Dar raised a brow. "Your mother?"

"What? No, Fluora. After I spoke with my mother, I went to see Fluora in the mists. The ceremony was about to start."

"I see."

What was that about a kiss? Idelle teased.

"There is yet hope for a union," Hanar observed. "Is your mother faring well?"

Barr's smile began to fade.

"She'll be better soon." *It was just a kiss, that's all.* He asked Dar, "Can you still see the revenant?"

Like with Lorelei? Aren was now fully awake and gorging himself. The sensation made Barr's stomach start to grumble. *She smelled nice.*

What are you eating?

"Yes." Dar looked off into the distance, as if seeing past the faeron and pavilions up ahead. "But he is no longer near the portal. He is in a place of fire and black stone."

There was a big pot of stew here by the fire, Aren said between gulps. *I didn't think anyone would mind.*

Was? Idelle laughed. *You just ate everyone's lunch.*

They can make more. Can't they?

They arrived to the bustle of servants dismantling most pavilions and carrying the pieces off to supply wagons on the eastern road. Patrols roamed the area and far off into the distance, with light of the noon suns glinting off their silvery armor. Two robed faeron stood by the portal, conversing with the High Enchanter.

The land around the portal had finally begun to mend. Tufts of grass broke through soil and stretched outward all around. Budding trees dotted the landscape and would soon offer shade, while the occasional patch of flowers brought some color to the whole.

Barr shrugged. *Probably not until the land here is fully healed.*

Aren came up to join them, a startled gasp not far behind. Someone no doubt had found the empty pot.

I didn't eat all of it, he said in his defense and hazarded a glance back. *Good thing we're leaving. She looks upset.*

Rornaelin caught sight of their approach and waved in greeting. He dismissed the two enchanters and gave Barr a curious look.

"Your gait seems troubled, my prince."

"My feet are a bit sore." Barr eyed the faded glyph hanging suspended in air, where the rift would open if the portal was activated. "Have you spoken to the Queen recently?"

"She was headed back to Starshrine last I saw." The High Enchanter considered for a moment, scratching at his chin. "You plan to go through."

Dar said, "The revenant who led the assault must be stopped."

"You must know how dangerous that would be. With the portal in place, travel through the rift is one-way, and no one dare use the mists until the new Matron is bound." Rornaelin gave a pleading look to Barr. "Do not throw your life away to avenge this attack."

Barr looked west toward the mounds of fresh graves, where what remained of the demon invasion was now buried. He wondered how many faeron had been lost, how many lives had been forever altered by the loss of a loved one.

"There's more at stake here than Faeronthalsos."

He reached out and turned a ward, activating the portal. A black tear in space appeared before him, as if the air had been torn asunder, and all that remained was a soundless void that drew in light like a voracious creature. The ward began ticking back like a clock to its original position, when the portal would close the rift once again. Without another word, Barr stepped through and onto Danarriden.

The stench was immediately overwhelming, carried upon a blistering wind that assaulted his senses. Hot ash caught in his throat and whipped against his eyes, as the scent of rotted egg and smoking corpses sought to gag him. He fell to his knees and vomited what little food was in stomach. Coughing to clear the ash and spittle, he managed a deep breath that seared his lungs from within.

The others came through, and Hanar helped him to his feet. Her runes began to glow. All about her the air grew less acrid, cooled to the blazing heat of a desert sun at midday. Finally able to catch his breath, Barr thanked her and stood straight. The volatile air had no effect on Hanar, nor did it seem to trouble Dar-Paj. Aren and Idelle made note of the intense heat but were otherwise protected by their collars.

Will you be alright? Idelle asked. *You're in obvious pain.*

It's the ointment. Barr was sweating profusely and wiped his brow with a sleeve. *It was already wearing thin, but now I think it's all gone.*

We can go back, Aren offered. *Through the mists.*

No, that's too risky. For them or Fluora he didn't say. *I'll be fine.*

Barr had expected to find a fiery landscape, a harsh and desolate panorama of molten rivers and blackened rock. What met his eyes, on the other hand, was an alien world vastly different from the one he had imagined.

All he could see for miles were the jagged rocks and glassy sheen of obsidian. Heat rolled across its surface in blistering waves, distorting his vision and reflecting crimson skies overhead. With neither suns nor clouds, it looked as if the heavens had suffered a grievous wound, a bloodied gash that faded down into the bleak of an unforgiving surface. In contrast to the stark, far off in the distance, lush patches of green and yellow grassland swayed in time to a gentle wind. Leafless, thorny trees grew from between jagged crevices, stretching blackened limbs in a prickly embrace. From behind, Barr heard the telltale rush of steaming water moving further off, as if a river cut a path through molten rock.

In front of the portal, however, was a ruin of charred remains and decimation. Countless demons had been burned alive where they stood, seared into the rocks as ashen shadows in the dark. No life could be seen or heard in the smoking arc for a hundred paces, just an endless swirl of ash over broken earth and ghostly remnants.

Dar cleared his throat of ash. "No wonder they stopped attacking."

"Master," Hanar cautioned and pointed to a winged creature in the skies off in the distance.

I've never seen anything that large before, Idelle said from high above. *It's coming right at you.*

Aren growled, and Barr drew both kyan. Though his hands and arms throbbed from the pressure, the rush of impending battle drove back all thought of pain. Dar pulled Khaela from his belt and stood ready beside them.

Though the giant creature was far off, the distance between them was steadily closing at an alarming rate. Barr knew right away what it was. He had read and heard stories of them, even fashioned illusions of their lethal grandeur, but never did he think or even wish to ever face one.

It landed on all fours twenty paces away, shattering obsidian and spraying shards in all directions. The impact nearly toppled them, as its dagger-like claws dug deep into the rock. Covered in glinting black scales, with crimson and silver armor from head to tail that seemed to pulse with an inner glow, its bulk alone would have crushed a team of horses. Its head was the size of a wagon, with two massive spiraled horns jutting back on either side. Spines larger than a man ran down its back and tail, while the barbs along its wings were stunted in groups of threes.

The dragon regarded them with luminous yellow eyes that narrowed and settled upon Dar-Paj.

"You would challenge me?" it said in a rumbling tone that shook the air. Fire dripped from between its teeth and sizzled upon the obsidian far below. "Speak."

"I do not." Dar put away his sword.

Barr sheathed his kyan as well. "We mean no –"

"You have *not* been acknowledged!" the dragon warned, it eyes never leaving Dar-Paj. "As for you, why do you interrupt my hunt? Did you sense my feeding through the rift?"

"In truth," Dar replied, rubbing absently at his chest, "we are not here for you at all. We seek a revenant called Ombreusk. He carries with him an artifact that may endanger all life."

"I know of the wreaths and care little for Revyn's war. We cannot be turned. Let him have all the others if he wants them."

"Ask where Ombreusk went," Barr whispered.

"Speak out of turn again mortal, and I will speed you to your next life." The dragon looked east and snorted fire. "The wielder is that way, no doubt holed up in a fortress. Now leave me to my atonement."

The dragon turned and bolted for an outcropping with blinding speed, tearing away the obsidian top and breathing fire into its depths. A series of horrible squeals followed after, the dying knell of a hundred scrabbling lesser demons. Punching a claw through, the dragon snatched and crushed spiny bodies by the handful then tossed the smoking corpses aside.

"Let's go," Barr said, unsettled by the display. He led the others east, where the dragon had indicated.

I don't think I'd ever want to fight that, Aren said with a shiver despite the heat. *I couldn't move while it was talking. I couldn't even think!*

My feathers are still shaking.

Hanar said, "It is good we did not engage the dragon. I am afraid we might have lost."

"You've seen them before?" Barr asked.

"Many times. We have memories of one who often visited to explore the city and speak with friends."

"I've never seen or heard of one in Dwendorim. I'd think they were much too big for the portals, let alone roaming about the city."

"They can mold their bodies to the form of any race," Hanar explained. "His visits were known to few, as a precaution of safety. They are vulnerable when not in their true form."

Barr thought it odd that anyone would fear for their safety in Dwendorim, considering the sheer number of Protectors. Unless the Protectors were unaware...

"His visits were kept secret from the protectorate?"

"Yes. Only six in total were aware." She was quiet for a moment, and Barr thought he saw a hint of shame in her demeanor. "We no longer keep secrets from one another."

"I see the fortress," Dar said and pointed to a distant mountain. "There is a well-used trail leading up to the top."

The dragon called me mortal, Barr said, reminded of the stories Seltruin had once told him. *They were among the first races. Could it really be immortal?*

Maybe. Idelle went off to scout ahead. *They could just be long-lived, like the elves. Have any of your visions ever been of a dragon?*

No, none. At least none that I can remember. I don't recall ever having seen one either, not in Dwendorim or anywhere else.

I can smell demons all around us. Aren blew ash from his nostrils and shook out his thick coat. *Their stench burns my nose.*

"We are not alone," Hanar said, and the runes along her arms began to glow even brighter.

Barr saw them hiding behind rocky hills and peeking out from holes carved into the obsidian. Their keening filled the air, though none moved to attack. From what he knew of demons, and his lifetimes among them, the ones stalking them were either hatchlings or barely matured. By their size, not one of them had undergone more than a handful of transformations. Without the presence of an elder, something else must have been keeping them from feeding on one another.

"There," Dar pointed out one getting close, his hand fast upon Khaela. "More to the right, and I hear others behind us and to the left."

Barr gritted his teeth, unable to ignore the pain any longer. His leathers rubbed against him, torturing his skin with the same fervor of each scalding breeze across his face. While the pain intensified his senses, he found it increasingly difficult to remain focused upon the demons. He gauged the base of the mountain an hour or two away but expected an ambush long before they could reach it.

"Can you see Ombreusk in the fortress?"

"He is hidden from me now, but I sense Drakha straight ahead."

"I sense him too." Barr coughed, and the pain wracked his chest. "Though he doesn't want to talk to me."

Dar reached out and steadied Barr, despite the sharp intake of breath his touch evoked. His golden eyes were concerned, clearly saw the suffering in his friend, but the apprentice chose not to speak of it.

"How is it you can speak with them, while I can only do so with Khaela in hand?"

He's trying to distract you, Idelle said. *Take your mind from the pain. Promise me we won't go anywhere else after this is over. Not 'til you're fully healed.*

Breathing heavier now, Barr forced his mind from the agony within his body. He knew pain was just a sensation, a warning that damage had been done to the flesh. It could be ignored, controlled, pushed away with the right focus.

Aren looked him over in worry. *Promise.*

I promise. Barr breathed easier now, intent upon the fortress, studying its every feature through scry in his mind. It was much more difficult without a reflective surface, but it was just the diversion he needed. *Keep an eye on that central tower. I can see* furie *emanating from the bottom floor.*

"I'm not sure," he told Dar. "Ever since I first spoke with Khaela, I've just been able to at least get a sense of the others." His mind still fixed upon the fortress, Barr added, "The dragon seemed to recognize your race, even respected you. Why didn't you ask?"

"I – I wanted to." Dar shook his head. "I found it difficult to think, as if a weight were pressing down upon my chest."

"That is fear, friend Dar-Paj." Hanar continually scanned the horizon. "We Protectors feel the same when the Oath is threatened."

"Maybe so."

It was an hour before Barr could see the widened path by eyes alone. Obsidian rubble littered either side, while the path itself was relatively smooth, as if carved from the mountain by a great fire. Reflecting the skies in a glimmering sheen, it held the semblance of a bloody river running down from the fortress. He could make out the southern wall jutting up from the mountaintop, and two of the eight towers peeking over.

Surrounding the mountain was a broken land of cracked rock and ebon trees. Numerous chasms radiated the haze of molten flows, a backdrop for scrabbling bodies and ropy limbs. More and more demons had been crawling out from the rocks, encircling them in an ever-tightening snare. Whether it was distance from the dragon or proximity to the fortress, Barr was only certain of the inevitable attack. He could hear more than see their numbers growing, the claws over rock or the keen of mounting bloodlust.

"We have to run for it!" Barr told them, over the rising frenzied cries. "They're going to attack any –"

Rock exploded all around them, throwing light and leaping bodies from the fissures. Those stalking from a distance threw their heads back in a wail then ran with all speed to join the ambush. Winged demons poured upward from the cracks, great columns of twisted bodies that filled the sky with swarms of black.

Barr reacted without thought, drawing weapons and striking out in one swift motion. Crushing one with a paw and biting down on another, Aren fought beside him, pushing forward through the mass.

There's too many! Idelle shouted, weaving through the blotted skies.

With a thunderous clap, Hanar brought her hands together and called up a glowing shield. Scaly bodies flew in all directions, clamoring through the air.

"Frost!" Dar commanded.

Khaela came to life in his hand, emanating a white radiance with the fury of a sun. His other hand directed outward, the writhing mass of demons slowed and froze in their tracks. Ice spread across their bodies to the crackle of instant winter. Ten across and twenty back became as statues and were shattered by the demons climbing over them.

"Watch the blood!" Barr shouted.

He sliced through countless limbs, dodging claws and noxious sprays. Obsidian bubbled at his feet and grew slick from corrosion. His leather boots began to smolder from beneath.

You have to carry us! he told Idelle. *We can't fight all the way up to the fortress!*

I'll try, she replied, clawing through another wing. She dropped into a dive and headed straight for them.

"Freeze," Dar said and extended his hand before them. The blood upon the ground iced over. "We can do this. Stay strong!"

Demons were breaking through by the handful, but the rest were kept at bay. Hanar's body was a glow with thrumming runes and channeled *furie*. Her shield flared with each strike against it but showed no sign that it would falter. She pulled a demon off her back and crushed its bones with a wrenching twist.

Idelle swooped in and took hold of Aren, carrying him off above the crowd of grasping claws and frenzied cries.

Why me first? he complained and spit out bony limb.

Shut up! She dropped him off inside the fortress without landing and went back for another.

Uhhh, there's demons in here too. He leapt at the armored patrol, sending two of the four sprawling. *Oh well. At least these don't screech like the others.*

Barr wasn't sure how long he could hold out, relying solely on his blades. He feared the use of magic might kill him, burn away his body from within. Or worse. He could lose control of it again and harm those he cared for. Ignoring pain and the temptation to unleash the *furie* at his disposal, he threw himself into the rhythm of combat. His Maurdon blades were an extension of his body, a weapon in itself. Striking out with lifetimes of training, from heel to pommel, elbow to edge, he brought demons down in pairs and threes while avoiding their bloodshed.

"You're next!" he told Dar-Paj.

The apprentice turned and drove Khaela into the ground. Ice crackled in a circle around them and spread outward like wildfire, turning obsidian to frosty blue as it flash-froze everything in its path. He pulled the Emblem loose, as Idelle took hold of his shoulders and carried him away.

Rushing through the frozen corpses, Barr and Hanar covered a fair distance before fresh bodies blocked their way. They continued the fight, and he saw Idelle coming toward them.

Take Hanar next.

What's Dar so mad about? Aren asked.

I will not. Idelle carried off Barr. *That shield will protect her. She can hold them off longer than you can.* Without Hanar's protection, Barr was again overwhelmed by intense heat. He struggled for breath and looked back to see demons swarm over the golem. Hanar punched and threw them off, but more rushed in to take their place. The flicker of dying blue showed her shield about to waver.

I won't leave her! Idelle promised and left Barr atop the portcullis where he would be safe.

The massive steel gate was raised, and the release lever on his right stood beside a wheel with chain links as thick as his arm. Try as he might, he could not free the lever and lower the gate.

He looked down into the courtyard and saw Aren fighting off three large demon guards amongst the frozen and bloodied rubble of at least a dozen more. The central tower door was iced over and shattered, with no sight of Dar-Paj.

He watched Idelle swoop down and rescue Hanar. The demons clinging to her body lost their grip or were kicked away. Despite the golem's weight, Idelle flew them over a thrashing ocean of grasping claws and wild cries. As before, black clouds of winged demons sped in and tried to knock her from the skies. Dodging wicked talons and suicidal grapples, Idelle wove her way through them toward the fortress. So desperate were her attackers that they crashed into one another in their attempts to rend her flesh, dropping from the air like spiny stones.

She was forced to fly lower, to avoid a waiting throng. One among them possessed more cunning and struck from below, tearing at her wing with a triumphant cry. Idelle and Hanar toppled to the ground, churning dust and ropy bodies before the ocean of demons rose up and overtook them.

"No!" Barr shouted, fear and rage boiling within.

An armored demon pulled itself up over the ledge, spittle dropping from a ravenous grin and sizzling the polished black stone. Barr turned and growled, seized the air between them in a fist and lifted the demon by will alone. Paralyzed and bones crackling, its agonizing wail was amplified for miles by *furie*, a promise of doom for its brethren on the field. Countless demons paused their attack and gazed with feral eyes at the source of the death knell.

Don't you dare! Idelle burst free, throwing off her attackers in a wide circle, as a shockwave sent them sprawling. With a firm grip upon Hanar, she sped toward the portcullis. *Don't do it, Barr. Let it go.*

Breathing heavy and eyes burning from ashen tears, he turned and saw them in air. With every demon giving chase, their only hope was for him to lower the gate. He breathed easier then, his hold lessening upon the guard. Fighting to think clearly over the pain and crushing heat, he forced the guard's body up and across the thick chain. He picked up a kyan and struck arteries in its leg and neck. The demon bled out in seconds and lay still.

The chain links began to hiss, eaten through by dark blood. A metallic groan from the stress, and the chain broke apart, sending the gate crashing down into stone. A cloud of dust and obsidian shards exploded out, as the gate twisted in its tracks and remained closed.

Idelle carried him to the courtyard, where Hanar helped him stand. No more guards could be seen, as Dar stepped out from the central tower. His look was one of anger and determination.

Your wing.

I'll be fine, Idelle assured him. She rested beside them and eyed the apprentice. *Something's wrong.*

I'm alright too, Aren said with a huff. *I know how deeply concerned you were for me.*

Barr chuckled inwardly despite the pain. *Oh please. There were only a few dozen.* He scratched the hound behind an ear. *I already knew you were fine.*

"The revenant is gone." Dar looked out at the gate, where demons began to climb, and gripped Khaela all the tighter. "And with it went the Emblem. He knew we would come and deliberately wasted our time."

"What other choice did we have?" Barr looked up at his friend, familiar with the look of guilty frustration, and knew there was little that would console him. "We did the best we could."

"It was not enough! We let ourselves fall into a trap, while Markus is off gathering Emblems unimpeded." The apprentice rubbed at his chest, as if stress or the heat were getting to him as well. "We should focus our efforts on the Emblems Markus has yet to claim."

"That makes sense," Barr agreed. "It might take some time to determine where those are though."

"We must also separate." Dar waved off any objection and added, "Once we are able to use the mists again without any danger, one of the other oracles can carry me through. The revenants only have three Emblems. If we separate and use the mists, we can gather the others much faster than they can."

If we're racing against time, Idelle noted, *it does seem a good idea.*

Aren said, *With that sword, he's more than capable of taking care of himself. Then again, if he lost it...*

Barr frowned at the notion. "How do you know he only has three?"

"From Khaela, of course."

"If I may make a suggestion," Hanar said, "I know any number of Protectors would be glad to assist in this endeavor. Friend Dar-Paj would benefit greatly from the added help. As would you, Master," she added with a solemn bow of her head.

Dar considered. "Any more than one would only slow me down. I do agree, however."

"Alright," Barr said and nodded. "I'll talk with Fluora. For now, we should get back to Faeron, before those demons start killing each other and bleed all over that gate."

He brought them to the mists and was attacked.

Umbrals were upon them the moment they entered, pushing them down into the waters and shrieking in eyeless glee. So many crawled over him, he could see nothing but ebon carapace. Pinned down and helpless, he fought in vain to break free. Their taloned hands were everywhere, clasped tight and draining *furie* from his body. As if the blood were ripped from his veins, Barr grew lightheaded and succumbed to the torturous dark.

Light flashed in the distance and sped across the waters, illuminating swirls of mist into a thickened wall of blinding glow. Warmth swept over his face, in a caress that roused his flagging spirit. The Light fully engulfed him, held him close and granted strength. His body and spirit renewed, Barr opened his eyes to see the umbrals burn away within its touch.

Their cries went unheard, each one frozen in place. Bodies dissolving from within, fractured and collapsing, the umbrals fell apart and were carried off upon the wave of passing brilliance.

*   *   *

Revyn found her kneeling by the stream. Intent upon the reflections across its surface, she had yet to sense his arrival. Falls could be heard in the distance, where the silvery water crashed down from an unknown source of impossible height. He refused to believe it was father. In the other direction, the stream faded from sight, where it fed into the Mirror Pool and acted as a conduit for divine will.

If only they knew what he had done through those waters...

He chuckled and stepped forward, in the shape of a wyndorrin. With leafy braids and painted face, both well-muscled and toned, he looked quite the strapping young elf.

"That is tiresome," Celene noted, glancing up from the water. Her own golden braids fell neatly back over a gauzy dress in hues of spring. "I am not unsurprised by your visit."

"I suspect not," he said, with the teeth of a wolf and eyes a luminous green. Her narrowed gaze showed his point had been made. "All the same, I thought it best to pay a visit. You have so few children left. Why put them in harm's way?"

Celene stood and faced him, eyes hardened by the resolve of having suffered too much loss. He felt the torment within her, could almost taste it on his tongue, and it stirred within him thoughts of physical longing. Fighting down the hungry urge to take her, he reached up to where both his ears had been cut away and held out bloodied hands for her to see.

Her upper lip stiffened. "I would gladly sacrifice all that I am or have, if it meant other children could live free of your curse."

He felt her anger seethe through him. It filled his heart with a gleeful yearning. Within a breath, his form shifted and shrank to a shamarrin child. He blinked up at her with tearful dark eyes and pale skin. Though his tapered ears were intact, large bite wounds began to appear across his flesh.

"Easier said than done," Revyn said in a weepy voice, "but what of those who would succumb or be fed upon? You would be forced to watch each one slip through your grasp, until you faded away from existence."

"Or perhaps I should follow example," Celene shot back, "and let loose a plague upon your demons." She clucked her tongue in mock apology. "Oh dear, I had forgotten. They would rather worship their own than grant devotion to you."

Revyn frowned, marring the child's features. That demons did not worship him was a sore point.

"No matter," she went on and turned away, "they are merely fodder for Curoch's dragons. Now *there* is an idea!" She spun toward him and gave a smile. "What if dragons sought their penitence upon your shapelings instead? That would be dreadful! You would have no true recourse. Attack even one in retaliation, and all of dragonkind would come down from their mountain in a rally against you."

Annoyed, he shifted to a human hunter and admired the necklace of tapered ears around his neck.

"It would be tragic," Revyn said and met her gaze, "if humans were made aware that your elves yet lived." In truth, he had nothing to do with the war between man and elf, but it pleased him to make her think so. "And so close to their homes. I fear to think what they might do to the forests. Hmm," he tapped a finger against his chin, "I suppose that might have an adverse effect upon your centaurs as well."

Celene fumed. "This bantering is pointless! I cannot take back the children you have stolen, but I can stop you from infecting others!"

Tempas appeared in a swirl of cloud and peal of thunder. Fully armored in worn steel, spear and shield in hand, he advanced upon Revyn.

"That is quite enough, brother."

In a blur, Revyn stood as an immense minotaur warrior, with steel-tipped horns and battle dress. He looked down upon the God of War and gave a snort.

"You are not my brother," he said in a deep voice, eliciting a flash of rage behind those gray eyes.

Not born of the father, created by mere devotion, Tempas would not exist but for the strife between races; and few things pleased Revyn more than reminding the fledgling god of that fact time and again. As for the taur, the War God's favored, they were among the mortal races father had shaped from the flesh of Revyn's first children – his punishment for having stolen the Emblems. His feralkin were no more, and Taellus thrived with pathetic mortals. As far as Revyn was concerned, Tempas owed him his existence.

"Tempas!" Celene snapped. "I neither need nor asked for your assistance."

Gripping his spear all the tighter, "He goes too far! I will tell you this, *brother* mine. Oath or no, your end will come by war."

Revyn shifted to a female Brethren in black leathers and smiled behind the silk of her assassin's mask. Only her golden eyes could be seen. She slipped two throwing knives from each hip and expertly twirled them.

"Fear not," Revyn assured, "I do have plans for your Warmasters. Though it seems their Order is in danger of being disbanded – more of that business about oaths, I am sure."

Tempas fairly growled. "That was not my doing! He forsook his vows! Thoryn is no longer a Warmaster."

"How convenient."

Celene crossed her arms and asked, "And the vision that spurred him to action?" She glared at the two gods. "I am done with the both of you."

The goddess vanished in a swirl of leaves.

"Your army," Revyn said with a snarl, shifting to a wolf shapeling, "is doomed. March on Lumintor, and I will decimate every temple that has dared utter your name, let alone offer you praise."

Leaning in close, his gray eyes unwavering, Tempas replied, "You cannot hope to defeat me. There will always be war."

"That remains to be seen," the wolf said and gave a toothy smile, "but there will not always be those who worship it."

*   *   *

Their chanting grew louder but was lost to the din of a thousand umbrals clashing bodies and screeching out in starved frustration. No light penetrated the writhing mass that engulfed the shield in a half-shell of eyeless chitters and grasping claws.

Fluora knelt with eyes closed, focused on her task. She felt the others all around her but through a distance of growing dark. Their thoughts were but whispers in a maelstrom of quiet, suffocating beneath the cold of an unquenchable desire.

Why me? The treacherous thought slipped in, both unbidden and unwanted. She fought it down with firm resolve. Doubt was the killer, the cracks that weakened every armor and the foothold to despair.

Again she reached out and was rebuffed.

Too strong for her spirit, the shadows crowded in. She recoiled from their touch, from the threat of being lost to inescapable murky depths.

You are not ready! the shadows taunted, driving a wedge into her heart.

Too much was at stake to be thwarted by fear. She had no choice but to persevere, to sacrifice all if need be. The dread that gripped her chest fell way to calm in a single breath.

She reached out and pushed beyond the oppressive shadows in the dark, down to the furthest reaches of the mists. Her reflection in the waters looked up with sorrow in its eyes.

You are not worthy.

"You are wrong," Fluora whispered. "It is you who are undeserving – of my strength, of my conviction, of my love for those I share this life with." She smiled and held a hand out to the image. "But I offer my devotion all the same."

The image brightened to a blinding glow that spread up and out across the water, embracing with its warmth and coalescing with her spirit. It washed over and through her body, lit her eyes with its touch, and sang out into the mists as a wave of brilliant Light.

Premonition exploded in her mind, flooding her every thought with images and events of yet to come. Fluora blinked to clear her eyes, confused by the intermingling of future and present, of the images crowding in upon her sight. She saw and heard the others come to her aid a mere second before they acted, and the double-vision sent a wave of nausea through her stomach.

More than images, she lived each premonition as if it were her own. Every sensation, every emotion, all rushed by and were replaced by eager visions without relent.

Through a portal of violet fire, it stepped out of the Dark. Feral eyes and runic skin, spawned of a once god, it sniffed the air to catch scent of its prey. The shiardin sped off through the trees, on the trail of a...

"Fluora?" her mother called, as if her voice echoed down the length of a dark tunnel full of sadness.

... demon child, her own flesh and blood. How could she love such a creature, when its birth had taken away the only...

"Something is terribly wrong," another said, deeply concerned for the small child so like the one she had lost a year from now to an efreeti raid.

... chance he had at redemption. Now forced to relive that crushing grief, no loss of memory would save him...

"Should we move her?" a third whispered, an echo of joy in her voice at the new union. "Her mind feels wrong. Is it damaged?"

... from revelation. Barr turned toward her with eyes wide in wonder, a growing smile upon his lips and sheer joy in his heart.

"Take her to the temple."

"I understand now," he told her, hand slipping from her grasp...

Fluora squeezed tight her eyes and screamed against the madness.

– 11 –

The pain was gone. Still on his back, water lapping against him, Barr felt none of the burning from within or the dull throbbing that had shaken every inch of his body. He opened his eyes to the starry canopy of the mists, a calm black that set his mind at ease. He sensed the others nearby. Whatever light had washed over them, drove off the umbrals and mended his spirit, it had healed their bodies as well.

I feel... wonderful, Idelle said, contentment in her voice. *What was that?*

I think it was Fluora. Barr sat up and saw Hanar helping Dar to his feet. *No umbrals,* he said and looked around with a growing smile. *Everything must have gone well.*

Aren stretched. *Feels like I slept for weeks. Not that I'm complaining.* His stomach began to growl, breaking the tranquil silence.

Don't say it, Barr warned, his own stomach tight and rumbling with hunger.

"Fluora was successful." Dar-Paj reached down and helped him up. "I know she risked much."

Barr could only nod.

He knew failure had meant the lives of all on Faeron, but for Fluora that doom would have been immediate. If the wave of light was any indication of the power she had bonded with, there was no telling how it might have affected her. He just hoped they could find Aislin before Fluora...

She'll be fine, Idelle promised.

"Shall we go see her?" Dar asked.

Though Dar made no mention of the Emblems, Barr could see the eagerness in his friend's golden eyes. For the first time, Barr began to wonder if the apprentice cared more for seeking vengeance than saving lives.

Hanar put a hand on Barr's shoulder. "You are fully healed," she noted. "The others are as pleased as I and prepare for our return. Members of the Aegis stand ready to assist."

Memory flashed in his mind of the Protectors whose sole purpose had been defending Dwendorim, despite the fact the hidden city had never met with a hostile force. Intended for battle, they were ideally suited to help the Brotherhood keep Vereu safe.

"Good," Barr said and began scrying Fluora in the waters. "I don't think we'll need more than ten. They won't be attacking the orcs, just protecting Vereu." An image of her resting in bed appeared across the surface. Eyes tightly closed, she looked troubled by dream. "Any more than that, and I'd probably have to make multiple trips."

"Ten will suffice."

Barr pulled back, and the image receded to the main temple chamber. Crafters were repairing the damaged crystal, as robed oracles conversed with Fluora's mother. Though he couldn't hear their whispered thoughts, he saw fear and concern in each of their demeanors.

He called up the mists and brought them through.

"My prince," Elaedraoni said in greeting, bowing her head and silencing the others with a gesture. "Fluora is well," she reassured, "if but a bit overwhelmed by the experience. She will adjust in time. There is a far graver matter, however, that you must not be aware of, else you would not be here."

"What's happened?" Barr tried to read the images in her mind, but they were chaotic, jumbled by worry over fears she wasn't sharing. "Just tell me."

"The portal is breeched. The Arch Demon Fezuul has taken captive our Queen."

"That's not possible."

"She does not seem in any danger for the moment, but none have been able to break through the barrier he has placed over the entrance to Starshrine."

Barr knew better than to ask why the Grand Seeress was here in the temple and not assisting. He felt torn as well, desperately wanting to see Fluora, to hold her hand until she woke.

She'll still be here, Aren prodded.

"You will be more help there than here," Elae said, not to be cruel but speaking plainly the truth. "Even if the enchanters disable the barrier, none of us can defeat an Arch Demon."

None of us. And there it was, the distinction he had lived with in all his years among the elves. Though faeron blood ran through his veins, he was never truly one of them.

"Barr," she said softly. "That is not what I –"

He waved off her apology. "I'll go see what I can do. If Fluora wakes before I get back, tell her... tell her I'll come see her as soon as I can."

They left the temple and headed toward Starshrine, through the crowded streets of Aranadir. It seemed every sylph, nymph and faeron had heard of their Queen's dilemma.

"She is with child," Hanar said.

Distracted by the thought of any demon having the power to force its way through the portal, through his glyph, he almost paid no attention to what she had said.

"Excuse me?"

"The Grand Seeress. I can sense another life growing inside her."

What if that Fezuul was already here? Aren asked, nudging aside the smaller folk in front of them.

Aren, Idelle balked. *I'm impressed! And here I thought all you were good for is clearing away leftover meals.*

When have we ever had a leftover meal?

That actually makes sense, Barr agreed. To Hanar, he said, "Let's keep that to ourselves for now."

He left the others below and pushed his way up the steps, past frantic advisors and courtesans who both shouted aloud and in thought. Royal guards used their shields and crystal spears as barricades. They held back the crowd, while enchanters and oracles studied a wall of crimson light across the entrance. A captain caught sight of Barr and motioned him through.

"Let the prince by!" the soldier demanded over the clamor.

"What's going on here, captain?"

Looking past the barrier, Barr could see clearly the Arch Demon in faeron form. He stood a bit taller than the average male, with dark skin like the cooling of an ember, and had scales at the neck and both forearms. He wore simple clothing, a short robe and sandals, exposing thick and corded muscles unusual for a faeron. More than the heavy frame, he exuded a power that Barr could hear and feel more than see. There was an aura about him, a shadowy gloom like heat rising from a dark fire. When Fezuul felt eyes upon him, he turned away from the Queen and looked at Barr with a gaze as black as pitch.

There were seers holding hands and chanting before the barrier, while enchanters studied the runes for any weakness.

"He marched in and created this barrier about an hour ago." The captain gave Barr a grave look. "We think he came through the portal."

"No. He was already here when I closed the rift."

Barr began studying the complex glyph from where he stood but found it difficult to concentrate with all the shouting and rhythmic chanting. Accompanied by noisy thoughts all vying for attention, it became clear why no progress was being made.

"Can you get control of this area and clear the steps? I can't even hear myself think."

The captain barked an order. Coming to attention, each guard gently but firmly began instructing onlookers to depart. Barr moved closer, where the enchanters were discussing how best to dismantle the magical shield. An advisor marched up and demanded

J.A. Giunta

to know why the seers have not yet called upon Saernol to shatter the enchantment.

"We are trying," an oracle assured him.

I could take that one elsewhere, Idelle offered.

I don't think he'd appreciate the journey. Barr turned to the elder faeron. "It would help a great deal if you and the other advisors could calm the crowd. Everyone here is already doing what they can."

The advisor frowned but nodded assent. He turned and motioned to the others, as general Qaranillen strode past, his silvery armor reflecting a bloody hue from the barrier. He drew his sword and with both hands struck against the shield. The blade resonated with a *clang* and a flash of spark before shattering. Half went bounding through the air, end over end, and sank deep into a pillar beside a young advisor. It continued to shake violently from the force, a mere inch from the faeron's head. Suddenly quiet and face ashen, the young advisor swallowed hard and backed away.

"My apologies," the general said and threw away the broken blade. He turned to the captain. "Have all these advisors and councilors removed, please. Things could get dangerous here."

Barr shook his head and would have laughed, if the general hadn't nearly killed someone.

Focusing his attention on the barrier, he let his vision pass through the glow to the enchantment just beneath its surface. He could see the glyph spinning slowly in midair, darker crimson outlines of wards within wards. He ran a hand over the shield, felt it crackle with power as it prickled his skin and set the hair of his arm on end. He drew a kyan and placed its tip against the barrier. The blade shot back as if knocked aside by a great force.

206

"Pakrah!" Barr commanded, setting alight the kyan with an azure fire.

He again pushed the tip to the shield and held on with both hands. A shower of sparks flew into the air, blinding in intensity, but the kyan held firm. As if the two magics were evenly matched, neither blade nor barrier would give. With a grunt of effort, Barr stepped back and admitted defeat. There would be no forcing his way through the shield. He sheathed the kyan and looked more closely at the runes.

He could see where they interlocked, spinning individually, as the wards twisted about in a greater whole. Pieces of each ward, however, were dislodging and joining others as they spun and met, then spun again in a different direction. Like intricate clockwork, the wards were changing before his eyes.

The pattern overall remained constant, but it was the smaller runic structures within that altered with each passing moment. Reaching up, Barr took hold of a rune, hoping to unravel one of the wards. It dissipated in a glittery powder of crimson light, but the ward did not unravel. Collapsing in on itself, it transformed into a new structure, shifting from an alternate energy conduit to a protection node. When Barr reached for the rune again, he was struck by a spark of magic that numbed his hand and singed the tips of his fingers.

"Well that won't work," Barr said, shaking his hand and frowning.

"We have tried to unravel it," the High Enchanter said, studying the changing runes, "but to no avail. It must be drawing a great deal of power from somewhere."

Smash it? Aren suggested.

Or drain it until the wards collapse. "Could everyone back up please?" Barr located the central power ward.

"I'm not sure what's going to happen. It'll be safer back by the steps."

As everyone left the area, he took a deep breath and held out his left palm toward the barrier. He then dug fingers into the air, reaching deep into the glyph without touching it. A tendril of bright crimson was coaxed from its center, striking his palm as the *furie* drained away.

Gasps of pain and a collective cry of shock rang out from behind. He turned to see a majority of the crowd doubled over in obvious pain. A guard dropped to his knees and vomited, while others merely clung to their spears with a sickly look.

Barr closed his hand and ended the connection.

How's that even possible? he wondered. *The glyph is linked to those people!*

"You have to get everyone away from here," Barr told the general. "The barrier is drawing its *furie* from them. The more people who stay, the stronger it gets."

A brief look of disbelief crossed the general's rugged features, before he turned on his heel and ordered the area cleared. Rornaelin and the other enchanters looked the most confused and debated how such a thing could exist, let alone be constructed, while being ushered away down the road. Within moments, the guards had led everyone far enough away from the barrier that its sheen had diminished to a filmy red.

The runes spun more slowly on a meandering path across each ward. Their pulse of *furie*, like lifeblood in a vein, no longer filled each one to brimming. He then caught sight of it, how another set of runes had been hidden in the ethereal. They formed wards that governed the interaction of wards in the first set, which is why it appeared some were transforming on their own. With a deft movement of hand, Barr severed the connection between both sets. He began unraveling each power conduit, until finally the glyph fell apart in a ruddy shower of light.

Barr stepped inside and approached, watching their manner as they spoke to one another. Fezuul was intent but calm, with no sign of posing a threat. He had feelings for Ariana. His gestures betrayed him, revealed a longing for affection and approval. Barr could see his grandmother had feelings for the Arch Demon as well, though she tried to hide them behind hard eyes and a firm upper lip. Whatever quarrel or misunderstanding had caused a strain on their relationship, Barr felt sure Fezuul had not come here to harm her.

The Arch Demon turned and regarded him with black eyes and a warm smile that showed two thick fangs.

"How very clever of you." He took Ariana's hand and patted it with the other. "I see our time is already at an end. Please consider all that I have shared with you."

Is everything alright? Idelle asked. *Everyone saw you go inside, and the guards are growing restless.*

Everything's fine.

Never mind, they're on their way in.

"How did you create that glyph so quickly?" Barr asked. "Or link it to the people outside?" Truth be told, the Arch Demon frightened him a bit. The power Fezuul exuded was intimidating. Barr couldn't help but admire his rune crafting, though. "It must have taken at least an hour just to write it out."

"It did," Fezuul replied in a friendly tone. "I scribe them into these gemstones –" he pulled a handful of cut rubies from a satchel at his waist, each one bigger than a thumbnail – "and cast them as needed."

"That's brilliant. I'll have to try that sometime."

Barr tried to see past the illusion encompassing Fezuul but realized there wasn't one. The Arch Demon was a shape-shifter. After countless transformations, his true size would be enormous.

"That's not your true form."

"Neither is that yours."

General Qaranillen rushed in with twenty guards in his wake. They spread out and quickly moved to flank the Arch Demon.

"Good day," the Queen said to Fezuul and walked away.

Fezuul sighed. "Will you require bindings?"

"Yes!" the general answered in the same moment Barr disagreed.

"There's no reason to insult the Queen's guest," he said, giving the general a meaningful look. "Give us a few moments alone before you escort him to the portal."

"Yes, my prince." The general nodded to his men, and guards cleared the room. "We will be just outside."

"You are a bright one," Fezuul noted with an arched brow. "All Ariana has told me of you must be true."

Barr bowed his head. "I don't think the general or any of the others here truly know what it is you are."

"And you do?"

"I know what you're capable of. Tell me, why the need for all this? Why not just ask to see the Queen?"

"She refused," he replied and frowned. "I was merely trying to explain that I was not responsible for the attack on the portal. One of those revenants enlisted a baron of mine to orchestrate the assault. I have already dealt with the baron, but as for the revenant –"

"He got away," Barr finished for him. "We chased it to a fortress on Danarriden. There must have been a

210

portal in the main tower. The Emblem it carried is gone too."

"Yes, I know all about Markus and his desire for ancient trinkets."

What's taking so long? Aren asked with a groan. *I'm going to see about finding some dinner.*

Me as well, Idelle said. *Whatever happened to us in the mists has left me starving.*

"The mists," Barr said. "That's what this attack was really about. Markus wants to use the mists to gather Emblems faster."

"That could very well be." Fezuul agreed. "His next attempt, however, will not come from my realm. I intend to build a temple around the portal." His smile faded and grew hard. "Nothing will get past my children once it is built."

With that, the Arch Demon tilted his head ever so slightly, in what Barr assumed was a bow of respect. He then left the Court, where a command of faeron cavalry patiently awaited.

Three oracles stepped in, after his departure, one in a heavy white robe and the other two in blue initiate attire. Barr knew before she spoke that it was Fluora. Her hood, trimmed in silver runes, hung low and left her face shrouded in shadow. Neither hands nor feet could be seen beneath the folds, and the two young women gripped her by the elbows as if guiding her steps.

Is she alright? Aren asked.

"I am fine," Fluora said and stopped before Barr. He reached out to touch her hands, but the initiates warned him not to. "My sight is clouded, confusing. I seem to be caught between visions of future and present."

He had so much to tell her, concern for her well-being left him unsure where to begin. Foremost, he was glad she was not harmed by the ritual. He felt a pang of guilt at the flush of relief, that his mother was no longer in danger from the umbrals. But at what cost? Without Aislin, Fluora would –

"I know." She took a seat beside the throne. "I have also spoken with Dar and have agreed to teach him to use the mists." Fluora held up a hand before Barr could speak a word, as if her seer sight had already heard the argument. "He has been trained to scry and will learn far more quickly than usual." She looked up at Barr, and he caught sight of her lips. "Dar has innate talent he has not even begun to explore. Most likely, he has forgotten how to use it."

"What of you?" Barr asked and knelt, fighting the urge to hold her. "Is there anything I can do?"

"No. I am not wounded or broken, as some seem to think. I must adapt on my own, learn to distinguish the future from the now." She rubbed at her temples. "It is like living in echoes, with the ripples too close together. And at other times, it is as if I am not myself, in this place or this moment. It feels like –"

"Losing yourself." Barr was all too familiar with the feeling. "It's one of my greatest fears."

Fluora nodded. "Just so. Some things are blocked to me, and I cannot see if my sight changes for the better." She stood and lowered her hood, her eyes closed as she spoke. "You need to move quickly. Isdael has gathered more tribes for his siege. Word never reached Hope's End for reinforcements, and I fear Faith's Spire will fall before morn."

We'll be ready in a bit, Idelle said. *I think I've found a dinner worth catching.*

Aren's heart beat faster, as he raced to keep up. *You should eat something, too,* he said to Barr. *Maybe one of those feasts they like so much. I'll even help you with it when I get back.*

A smile creased Fluora's lips. "Return to the temple. I will have food and drink provided."

Before Barr could leave, she leaned in and kissed him, a brief touch that lingered in his thoughts. She pulled low her hood again and was led outside by the initiates.

Try to eat quickly, he told them. *Every minute we spend here could mean a life lost at Faith's Spire.*

He found Hanar and Dar-Paj waiting outside.

* * *

Markus rode through the forest toward Geilon-Rai. Despite never having seen the elven tree city before, he had met with sylvannis agents in the past. Five in all, the elven shapelings had long ago attained high ranking in all parties but the Valar. Over the years, even before Barr had been taken in, they have dealt with those Revyn deemed a threat to his plans. Now it was time for a more overt action on their part.

I have found Caorynor, my Lord.

Though many centuries had passed since they were at odds with each other, he still felt that old anger each time he heard Wyllnuor's voice.

Why have you not claimed it? Markus snapped. He caught sight of the tree marker and turned left off the path. *Does King of the Illuminaire require assistance?*

It was a petty jibe, but his mood had turned foul.

The Emblem is buried, the revenant replied, ignoring the taunt, *in the ruins of an ankaran city.*

213

Ankarans. Markus glared as he led the horse toward another marker. *Is it anchored?*

No, it floats freely over the lava pits in Harandor.

Once an illuminaire, a child of Saernol like Markus, Wyllnuor would have reveled at the sight. The ankaran cities were forged of enchanted elements, alive with the runic systems that flowed through each wall. Cobbled water that shimmered between buildings like a river, fiery walls that clashed with air in a cloudy entangle or stone pillars that turned crystalline as they spread out in domes to cover all.

As an illuminaire, one born and bred to weave, the accomplishment would have stolen the breath away. As a revenant, a walking prison for the soul, the monument to magic was nothing more than an obstacle, an artistic endeavor he could never take joy in.

Markus smiled at the thought.

"You seem in good spirit," Landrin said and stepped out from behind a tree.

I am sure you will find a way.

The elf led a horse with two others tied over the saddle, a young female and male gagged and squirming their discontent.

"Somewhat." Markus dismounted and approached. "And how is the Speaker's son this fine day? Ready to assume his mantle?"

"As always," the Eneir grinned, his eyes flashing a beryl sheen. "All has been made ready. We will strike at night and be prepared for the humans come morning."

"The orcs?"

Markus took a handful of sable hair from the elven female and yanked her head up. Her pained glower made him smile all the more. She was attractive for an elf, with gray eyes and a straight nose, but she caused no stirring within him.

"All turned and awaiting instruction at deila falls." Landrin regarded the female. "She is Kiere, daughter of a minor Narohk. Feel free to use her, if you have need."

Letting her head drop, Markus punched her across the temple. She instantly went limp. The male elf beside her stopped struggling against his bonds and became quiet.

"I do not need you," Markus warned in a dangerous tone, "to tell me what I can and cannot do."

The elf swallowed and gave a nod. "Of course not. I meant no disrespect. This other is Beiron. He has served us in the past but of late has outlived his usefulness."

Taking hold of the reins, Markus tied the horse to his saddle and climbed up. Heading back toward the path, he called back over a shoulder.

"What will you do with the Valar when the council is replaced?"

Landrin shrugged. "He is our only sage. The Illumin Valar will die with him."

"See that it does."

An hour passed before the sun reached its zenith. Markus judged six more before he would see the city gates. He thumbed the silver hilt of a throwing knife, mentally preparing his speech for the people of Alixhir. He brought with him proof that their enemy yet lived, that their fire tales had come to life to endanger their children. He imagined them rising up in unison, torches in hand, to lay waste to the forest –

An angry cry tore through his mind, like a flash of blinding darkness. He fell backward in the saddle but managed not to fall.

My temple! Revyn roared.

The god appeared in a swirling of black motes like a plague, burning the frozen earth with his rage. The air around him wavered with intense heat, and his eyes were burning fires in the dark.

Markus blinked furiously and grabbed hold of the reins. The horses skittered away, neighing in fear, as the swarm rushed forward and lifted him into the air. His body arched in terrible pain that gripped his spine with fingers of thorny ice. It shook him like a ragdoll, before the fiery eyes drew in close and blistered his skin.

Summon the Brethren and turn them all! Each word blew back his hair, sent the blood from his nose and ears down in rivulets across his neck. *Then set them loose on the House of War!*

Revyn threw him to the ground. The black mass took on a shape, a knight in ebon plate.

Kill the initiates, the god demanded, clenching a gauntleted fist, *and turn his precious Warmasters!*

It will be done, Markus promised weakly, his mind and body trembling in torment. *I swear it!*

The knight broke apart into a swarm and buzzed a final time, cracking rock and earth beneath it before slipping off into the distance in a swirl of fevered wind. Revyn's voice echoed back, each utterance a torturous scrape along the inside of Markus's skull.

Tempas will have the war he so desires.

* * *

Alarmed by what he saw in the scry, Barr brought them through the mists and immediately gave orders to bolster the failing walls. Ten golems of bloodstone, the Aegis set to work with no heed to the cries of surprise and confusion among the defenders. Fiery arrows lit up the night sky and rained down into the courtyard, where knights had fallen and forever remained still. The outer wall was lost, shattered by catapult and scorched at its jagged edges. Orcs filled the outer courtyard, screaming for blood in a battle frenzy, while battering the iron gates and climbing up the walls where there was room.

Less than two dozen Brotherhood yet fought against the rising tide, knights and warrior priests tired beyond endurance. Bloodied from their own wounds, comrades and fallen orcs, they pressed on in a hopeless endeavor. Commander Vaumont was among them, long sword in one hand and knocking orcs from the wall with a shield in the other.

Uinahd, the lead golem, took two Aegis and headed for the gates. A stomp of one foot set the earth on the other side roiling in upheaval, exploding orcs outward onto the spears of those behind. The two golems placed hands upon the gate, reddening the iron in a wave of growing heat and silver runes. Crossbow bolts came through and struck harmlessly against them, as sword and axe met with the same failure against their hands. When they let loose their hold, the gate cooled to a jet black, restored and hardened by enchantment.

"It's about time you got here!" Vaumont shouted. An axe struck against his shield. The old knight turned on his attacker, angered at the interruption, and cut off the orc's arm. His eyes still on the orcs, he said to Barr, "I hope you planned on bringing more of those walking rocks!"

There's hundreds of them, Idelle said from above. *The shrine is completely surrounded.*

Aren leapt atop the wall and attacked. *I wish Dar was with us. He was pretty handy against those demons.*

Aren took an orc by its legs and flung it from the walls. *Not that this won't be fun all the same.*

Hanar swatted an arrow from the air before it came near Barr, showering the ground with flecks of fire.

"Perhaps ten will not suffice after all," she noted.

"I was just thinking that myself. Do what you can while the others enchant the wall." Barr looked around. "In fact, go find Dalwyn and make sure Vereu is safe."

Barr disappeared in a swirling of mist, only to return moments later with ten more Aegis. Three more trips to Dwendorim had the courtyard and walls secured, but he knew the tribes would not relent so long as the revenant spurred them on.

Dressed in the black robes of a Justiciar, Isdael sat atop a norian warhorse overlooking his army. Beneath the hood and ebon mask, his eyes glowed with crimson fire that set his frame awash in a bloody light. He was surrounded by a tribe Barr had never before seen, and the air around them crackled with dark lightning from a dozen totems. Lighter skin, like mossy water, these orcs were larger by three hands and bore shamanistic tattoos across every inch of their scarred bodies. More worrying than their appearance, they stood quietly waiting. While the horde gathered around them shouted and fought to get closer to the walls, caught in the throes of bloodlust, this entire tribe stood intently staring but still.

And their eyes were all trained upon Barr.

"We can't hold out here much longer," Vaumont told him, as arrows struck and bounced with a flash of light off a barrier. "We have food and drink for a few more days, but our arrows are spent. If we want this lot gone, we'll have to take to the field."

"You're right."

"Well I'm glad you think so!" the old knight snapped. "I have done this before, you know. Just so there's no confusion, I'm still in charge here. I appreciate the help, but this is a Brotherhood shrine."

He's a cheery one, Aren said and looked down at the orcs trying to dig under the wall.

"Of course." Barr noticed the commander had fresh blood dripping from his cuirass and wondered how many wounds the armor hid. He could heal all the knights, but that would leave him with nothing left to face the revenant. "We need to kill that one. Kill Isdael, and these tribes will leave or simply turn on each other."

"Easier said than done," said a knight at Barr's side. He recognized the man as squire Jarvik's uncle. "We'd have to wade through his entire army just to face him." The knight offered a hand to Barr. "About the last time we met..."

"I understand," Barr said and shook his hand in a firm grip. "My apologies for any harm my hound might have done to you." Aren snorted and looked away, as if to say *he* was not apologizing. "How is Jarvik doing?"

"Well enough," Vaumont answered, pointing to the east wall. An armored figure, albeit much smaller than the other knights, stood alert with sword and shield. "As for that undead creature, he came here with a purpose. We can use that to our advantage."

"Bait him with Vereu?"

I'd snatch him off his horse, Idelle said, *but I don't think I'd get very far with him. The air around him feels charged, even from up here.*

Brother Dalwyn and Hanar walked the steps up to the wall. He had the Emblem in hand and carried it like a veteran soldier.

"I was thinking much the same," the warrior priest said.

His eyes flashed with a deadly confidence Barr didn't recall seeing when last they met. Dalwyn looked out across the sea of enemies, at the ladders that flashed to cinders upon touching the barrier, and had the look of a man that welcomed an insurmountable challenge – not because he sought his own death, but for the delusional certainty he could not be overcome.

"You seem... different," Barr noted.

"I am now attuned with the sword. Its powers are mine to command." Dalwyn nodded toward the revenant and grinned. "I will destroy him, if he dare face me."

He's on our side, right? Aren shook out his thick coat. *He gives me the chills.*

It must be Vereu, Idelle reasoned. *Dar seems affected by Khaela as well.*

Not like this.

Brother Dalwyn turned and headed down the steps. There was no doubt what he had planned. Vaumont called out orders to rally at the gate, and more than a dozen able knights moved in answer. The others would most likely stay behind to guard the portcullis, in case the orcs tried to rout them and take the shrine.

"We stand a better chance," the commander said, "if we hold them off in the portcullis, limit their numbers."

"No," Barr said, weapons drawn. "We'll need room to fight, and the point of going out is to reach the revenant. If we choke the gate with bodies, we won't be able to close it."

"Seems you've done this before, too."

"Raise the gate!" Dalwyn shouted, his mithrinum sword held high. To the heavens he cried, "Hear me Curoch! Enemies tread your holy ground! Grant us the strength to strike down such insolence!" In lower tones, biting off each word as he eyed the raging orcs beyond the rising gate, he added, "Or I'll damned well fight them without you."

Aegis gathered atop the wall and over the portcullis, as Uinahd led the others beside Barr. Hanar and Aren stood ready as well, the war hound's muscles tensed and set to pounce. Idelle flew over the outer courtyard with a barrel of oil in each claw. The iron gate continued its torturous climb, creaking with the strain of metal links. Impatient orcs grabbed hold and tried to raise it more quickly, while others scrabbled across the bloodied earth to squeeze beneath.

"Burn," Dalwyn commanded, his left hand held out toward them. "Burn!"

Vereu sprang to life with a ghostly white fire, and it seemed the image of a gleaming knight three times the size of any man had imposed itself over Dalwyn like a towering spirit. It mimicked his actions, blurred the air all around him, and looked down upon his enemies with a gaze that cracked the earth.

The armor and weapons of every orc for twenty feet began to redden, hissing with wisps of smoke as they burned through rugged flesh. Axes and swords fell from charred hands, whitening upon the ground into puddles of molten slag. Orcs screamed in pain and fear, fought vainly to pull away the melting armor.

The waiting throng was all too eager to step over the fallen, crushing bone and fading breath beneath their heels. Wooden barrels crashed against them from above, raining oil on their heads and across the ground. Each stopped for but an instant, eyes wide in recognition, before igniting into a tumult of rising flame.

Nice! Aren said and leapt over the burning corpses. *My turn for some fun.*

"Now!" Barr yelled. Golems stepped forward and off the wall. Earth and bodies broke beneath them, as the onslaught began. *Aren, stay close!* "Keep them away from Dalwyn!"

Crossing both kyan and thrusting them forward, Barr sent an unseen force ahead that threw wide the fiery remains and cooling slag. Knights followed behind him, as he led the assault with keen precision, cutting a swath through heavy limbs and crushing blows that never landed.

The Aegis pummeled ahead, their runes alight with glowing *furie.* Weapons bounced harmlessly against their bloodstone frames or shattered from the force. Orcs leapt upon the walking statues, bringing down a few by sheer numbers alone, but could not break apart the living stone.

Brother Dalwyn calmly walked behind the storm of whirling blades that was Barr. Knights fell in beside the priest, struggling against the overwhelming strength and unbridled rage of every orc that sought to end them. The sight of Vereu had spurred them on to heights of frenzy beyond the norm, where orcs slashed and crushed one another in their growing fervor to claim the sword.

"Forge!" Dalwyn shouted. The image standing over him reared back its head and bellowed at the skies.

Iron spikes as thick as a man jutted up from all around them, impaling orcs from below, and dropped back into the earth. Again, farther out, the wicked barbs tore through another wave. The icy ground beneath their feet grew slick with the pooling mire of orcish blood.

The way to Isdael soon stood clear, but for the odd tribe of light-skinned orcs. Why the revenant watched on from behind them, without intervening, became all too clear as the Aegis reached their ranks.

Half-naked women stood the edges of the tribe, their hair tied back with bones and blood, their skin carved and marked with shaman runes. Some held totems as they danced in place, shaking the ground with their calls to the spirit world, while others coaxed totems from the earth and fallen orcs. Twisted rock or woven bone, *furie* rose up and engulfed them in a fire black as night. The runic tattoos upon the warriors began to mirror those dark flames, like liquid come alive across their skin. In unison, they calmly watched the golems approach, axes in hand but held waiting by their sides. The Aegis were nearly upon them, when a single word from Isdael sent the orcs rushing to attack.

No longer calm but directed by disciplined rage, the orcs struck fast and with the exacting of veteran soldiers and ordered troops. They worked together, choosing with care who and when to strike without stepping over each other or endangering one another with reckless assault. More surprising to Barr was the damage they caused. Axes bit deep into bloodstone, chipping away at the golems in a way he never thought possible by mundane weapons. Runes split and broke apart beneath the axes, severing wards of protection and unraveling stony life.

One by one, the Aegis were being hacked to pieces.

Black lightning flashed from overhead and struck out, cracking frozen earth and steadfast golems into heaps of smoking ruin. The ground beneath Isdael came alive with ebon fire, undulating with flashes that dulled the glow of Aegis runes. Through the clash of magic and steely axe, Barr could see the outline of a fiery glyph. He knew at once why the revenant had refused to move and that the Aegis had walked into a trap.

Dalwyn let loose his own magic upon the orcs and stood dumbfounded when it refused to heed his call. The shamans danced with greater fury, clawing the air above them and directing their combined will toward the priest. The knightly image that engulfed him flickered and grew dim, as if the spirit were being sapped or driven back. A final flash of lightning sent it reeling, shattered to a mist upon the wind. Dalwyn fell to his knees as if struck, doubled over in pain and clinging to Vereu.

"Stay with him!" Barr ordered the knights. More orcs were pouring through the broken wall and battered gates of the outer courtyard. "Vaumont! Don't let them take the Emblem!"

The commander stood protectively over Dalwyn, his visage bloodied and grim.

"Nothing will get through my men!"

Idelle took hold of a shaman at full speed and let her loose over the wall. The orc careened in a tumbling arc, as her scream faded out of reach. Aren smashed through the elite orcs, crushing one across the middle with a bite that went through armor and bludgeoned those around him with the bloodied carcass. With a paw pressing down on one's faltering helm and crackling skull, he spat and took hold of another. Axes struck against him, through enchantment and rigid muscle. Driven by a rage of his own, he growled with bloody froth and savaged all that dared to face him.

I need you! Barr told Idelle, dodging attacks from two elites at once. *Hurry!*

Isdael cast bolts of shadow at the Aegis, and the sound of his magic was like the keening of a thousand voices in despair. Uinahd held the others back, mindful of the glyph, and relied on Hanar's protective wards to help turn aside the shamans' *furie*.

Snatching up Barr, as he cut the leg out of from under an orc, Idelle carried him past and into the air.

Sweep back and throw me at Isdael.

You'll be killed!

Barr eyed the revenant and the glyph all around him. *Don't argue, just do it. Please.*

Barr sheathed both kyan and readied for the impact. Wings straining against the speed, Idelle cut through the air with all her might and let him go. Like a bolt from a ballista, arms out and weaving *furie*, Barr smashed into Isdael and took hold around the waist. In the moment before they tumbled into and through the ground, he put a hand out with a barrier to break their fall. In a half-shell of frozen earth, like a meteor from the sky, his magic tore the glyph apart in a torrent of spent *furie*. It exploded upward in a column of debris and blackened fire, throwing runes that burned like embers from a flash to fading wisps.

Fire scorched Barr's shoulder, and he turned to face the full attention of each shaman. He moved forward to tear the *furie* from their bodies, but a skeletal grip took hold of his ankle and bit deep into flesh. The crimson runes along each bone flared to life in a bloody glow. Before he could draw a kyan to deal with the revenant, Dalwyn was there and thrust Vereu through the undead king's chest. The remnants of heart parted in two like a cleaved stone.

"You're free now, King Isdael," Dalwyn told the soul trapped within. "As High Priest of the Brotherhood, loyal servant of Curoch, I break the binds that hold your spirit to this prison."

The spirit of King Isdael lifted gently from the corpse, a transparent figure of a raugrin – the thick-limbed creatures from which dwarves were descended. Stroking his beard, he looked up at the moon and stars with a childlike wonder. As if seeing them for the first time, he smiled and gave a nod. He bowed his head to brother Dalwyn then faded from sight.

Without his magical influence, the orcs came to their senses and lost interest in the losing battle. Vaumont allowed them to retreat and go their separate ways back into the trees and distant swamps. With so many lost and so few remaining, there seemed no room or strength left for vengeance.

"You were right," the commander said to Barr and clapped him on the shoulder, though it seemed more like the old knight was leaning on him for support. He nodded toward the handful of Aegis that remained. "They can fight. And I'm damn glad you brought them."

Uinahd bowed her head. "It was an honor to assist the Master. If you will excuse us, we must gather our brethren for burial."

Are they dead? Aren asked. *Or can you fix them?*

Barr could only shake his head at the loss.

"I will assist them," Hanar said and left to help.

"Ho there!" a man called out and approached. He wore the battered armor of a Guardian. "I'm Jakob, from Sanctuary. I thought I'd come to lend a hand but looks as if I missed the battle."

With dark hair and bright green eyes, the young man looked nothing like Barr would have expected of a true Guardian. He was obviously a soldier, had recently seen battle, but his demeanor was almost affable.

"From the looks of you," Barr said, "I don't think you missed the battle at all."

"No," Jakob agreed, his brow furrowed, "truly not. I'm afraid there's nothing left where I came from. They tore down the walls and killed everyone inside. I caught the tail end of things coming back from patrol."

Dalwyn blinked. "Are you saying you're the last Guardian at Garand?"

"I'm afraid so. We'll rebuild, of course..." He let the thought trail off. "I sent word to the other Marshals. Until I hear something back, I'm at your disposal."

"We could certainly use the help." Dalwyn sheathed the Emblem and led his guest toward the shrine. "Tell me everything that happened."

Commander Vaumont gave a nod to his men, and they followed after Dalwyn. The old knight walked over to what was left of Isdael and toed the broken bones with a boot.

"What will you do now?" he asked Barr. "Technically, I should arrest you, but I'm just not up to it at the moment. Besides, I suspect your furry friend there would eat me whole."

Aren looked the commander up and down. *Not even with a side of potatoes.*

Barr laughed, and suddenly every cut and bruise he had sustained in battle cried out for attention.

"I'll go home," Barr said plainly, "for now. I intend to find the other Emblems and put a stop to whatever Markus has planned. That, or kill him. Whichever I can manage first."

Vaumont held out a hand, and the two shook.

"You've made a friend of me, turner Barr. If you ever need my help, you know where to find me." He smiled and gave a wink. "And if your statue friends there need a home, I have just the place in mind."

"They have a home already," Barr said and chuckled despite the aches, "but I'm sure they'd appreciate the sentiment."

"Well, you can't fault an old soldier for trying."

– 12 –

fter tending to wounds, both the knights' and his friends', Barr barely had the strength to call up the mists. So few Aegis had survived that he was able to bring them all home in one trip. He thanked Uinahd and the other Protectors, without whom the battle would have been lost. Barr offered heartfelt condolences for those brought back in pieces, their stony remains carried upon the shoulders of their brethren in sacks of burlap. He retired with Hanar, Aren and Idelle to the stone cottage and workshop that had once been his residence in the city so many lifetimes ago.

The next morning, a breakfast of steamed vegetables and sliced fruit waited for him at the table. Idelle and Aren were already awake and apparently feasting on a catch of rockfish. The creatures were bred for size, and at one point were a staple of the arachon diet. Gray like stone at the head, with blue and white striations, the large fish had the look of subterranean rocks found nearby. After only three, Aren was so full he had to rest beside the water for a short nap.

As if he doesn't sleep enough. Idelle perched atop a thick wooden beam over the water, from which a net and heavy rope was tied off. She cleaned each of her feathers and eyed her lazy brother. *And not so much as a 'thank you' for catching his breakfast.*

Aren yawned and dozed off.

"There will be a memorial," Hanar said and sat down at the table, "this morning, at Skyfall. All would be honored if you would attend."

"Of course." Barr put down his tea. "I'm responsible for their loss. I didn't think they could –"

"Do not," Hanar interrupted and placed a hand over his, her touch warm and caring. "Many lives would have been lost if not for their intervention. To feel blame for their deaths is to dishonor the sacrifice each of them willingly made."

Barr nodded in understanding. "When do we go?"

"As soon as you are finished."

It was warm outside, Barr assumed for his benefit, and the soft golden glow of enchantment ran the length of the cavern ceiling far above. Though no sun moved across the smoothed dome semblance of sky, countless runes etched into its surface gave the appearance of early morning.

"They've been busy," Barr noted.

Not a single home was in disrepair, with stones free of mossy growth or overgrown ivy and wooden trimming freshly coated with colorful paints to match the flowers. It seemed every topiary, every garden, every flowerbed or box hung upon a sill had been coaxed into full bloom and filled the air with scents of spring. The cobbled road bore no cracks, each street lamp gleamed a steel blue up to the crystal globes upon their tops, and a path of bushes shaped like children led to the park where his daughter – Fanarin's daughter – used to play.

"We have slept for far too long and thought it time to bring our home back to life."

"It's beautiful." *Are you two coming?*

I am, Idelle replied. *Good luck waking Aren, though. He's already snoring.*

They passed through the central square, where over a dozen different districts met together like spokes of a wheel. Unlike the white stones that made up the roads leading from every arachon home, a wide path of gray and blue cobbles marked the way toward market shops and industry. That road branched off into various colors, earthen brown for the farms and fisheries, emerald green for the groves and gardens, golden yellow for the library, schools and university. Many others they passed, and it felt to Barr as if his life within the city had never ended. All that were missing were the people and Protectors, the sounds of laughter and toil, the thrumming buzz of living enchantment that encompassed everyday life.

It's so quiet, Barr said, with sadness in his tone, *so empty. It feels wrong to walk these streets without a single Protector in sight. Other than Hanar, that is.*

I know why the streets are so empty, Idelle said from up ahead. *You have to see this.*

Moments later they entered Skyfall, and Barr was struck with a profound sense of wonder and remorse. For as far as he could see across the chamber, of every class and colored stone, the entire protectorate stood in silence. Through the sea of living statues, to the center of the assemblage, he saw each and every one of them facing an obelisk of polished bloodstone. It stood ten times the height of any golem and three sizes wide. Barr knew without being told that is was shaped from the pieces of those destroyed in battle.

The mass of Protectors before him stepped aside to make a path. He and Hanar walked past thousands of golems, each head lowered or glowing eyes turned his way. Around the base of the memorial, upon the wide circle of grass lined with white stone, golems male and female knelt together in sorrow. Others stood next to the monument, a hand upon its surface, and as Barr drew close enough to see their faces, he saw tears of *furie* run down their cheeks.

That's... not possible.

Barr stopped and looked at those around him, as if truly seeing them for the first time. He noticed it then, how some stood in pairs, hands clasped together in offered comfort. This was more than honoring the loss of Protectors upholding the Oath. This was love that he was seeing, golems stricken by grief as if family had been taken from them.

"They're mates," Barr said in quiet revelation.

He looked at the monument and swallowed hard, fighting down his own grief, as the enormity of their sacrifice sank in. He had always thought of the golems as alive but not in the sense of those who had created them, with a capacity for love beyond the Oath. They had somehow evolved over the centuries, transcended their instruction runes, and became every bit living creatures as those who had bled or died upon the field.

In a swirl of cool air and ivory mist, Fluora was beside him and slipped a hand into his.

"I would have been here sooner," she said in way of apology, but her words trailed off into silence.

Barr struggled to find words that might ease the suffering of those before him. He realized at last, much like the loss he had suffered throughout his life, that only time would heal their wounds and fill the hole left behind.

"They were brave," he told them, almost choking on the words. "They fought without fear, put themselves in harm's way and saved the lives of countless people."

He saw names etched upon the bloodstone, though they were difficult to make out. Letting go his hold of Fluora, he stepped forward and drew a simple glyph upon the obelisk and tied it to a ley line far below. The names sprung to life with a golden glow, as if sunlight shone from within the polished stone.

"If there's anything I can do," Barr said, looking to each golem that had lost a loved one, "please let me know."

"There is one thing," Hanar said, her eyes downcast, as if ashamed to ask or in fear his answer might be no.

"Anything."

"Please, follow me."

She led Barr and Fluora back toward the workshops, and to their surprise every Protector followed with them.

"How are you doing?" he asked Fluora. He noticed her eyes would often dart back and forth, as if seeing past what lay ahead. "Has it gotten any easier to sort the future from the now?"

Fluora smiled and squeezed his hand. "A bit. I have at least gotten somewhat used to letting others ask a question before I answer it."

"What about Dar?"

"He is still in the mists," she replied, and her voice betrayed concern. "He has not slept or taken rest but practices without relent. It is as if he is driven to master the mists. I understand the need for urgency, but his desire borders on obsession."

"I just hope it's not Khaela affecting him that way." Barr allowed Fluora to step through the open door before he entered the shapery ahead of Hanar. "I noticed Vereu had a similar affect upon brother Dalwyn. Will he be able to do it?"

"Yes and very soon. He was already quite skilled at scrying, whether the skill was merely forgotten or mostly unused. As far as traversing the mists, he has an innate talent for it I cannot explain." They both walked up and circled a rounded block of obsidian. "He was able to carry himself through the mists with little trouble. It is bringing others along with him that he struggles with. Oh," she said and put a hand upon the rugged stone, "she is... beautiful."

Barr looked confused. "What is this, Hanar?"

"This is what we hoped you might help us with."

The block was far too small. He eyed its dimensions, falling easily back into his craft as a shaper. It was a solid enough piece to work with, just not of much use as a Protector.

"No," Fluora said, "not a Protector. They do not want you to shape for them. They want you to teach them how."

Hanar touched the block, where finger marks had shaped away the upper edges.

"Will you?" she asked him.

"You're not trying to make more Protectors," he said, again struck by how much they had grown. "You want to make children."

"More than anything."

Can they do that? Idelle asked. *Or would they just end up being tiny Protectors?*

I don't know. "I can show some of you what I know of shaping, but that could take a long time."

Hanar looked to those gathered in the doorway and the road beyond.

"That is all we ask. We have been studying what texts remain at the university, of shaping, enchanting, smithing and our creation." She put a hand to either cheek and drew his head in close to hers. "You could teach us so much more, if you would but open your mind."

"Alright," he promised. "I'll try."

Their foreheads touched, and the world around him disappeared into a void of soundless white...

A multitude of voices rose up from the distance, a sea of whispers and echoed longing that crashed over him in a flood of memories. He was Fanarin again, just a baby in his mother's arms. Time sped by in a panorama of shifting images all around him. She set him down upon his feet, and he walked forward through his life, growing with every step as the memories evolved all on their own. His parents aged before his eyes, from school to craft, always proud of their only son. He kissed Elora, and they were wed, reveling in laughter. In his arms he found Shanarin, his baby girl looking up with green eyes that caught his breath. So many then fell ill, stricken with a fever, and Elora's hand slipped from his grasp as his grief drove him to madness. The memories blurred past him, a reprieve from fading sorrow, only to end in rising darkness to the beating of his heart.

His eyes opened once again, further back through dark and light, and the memories played out in scenes that wove his life with growing fervor. From birth to sleep forever after, his time as Yaerin seemed a glimpse. A practiced gardener and loving husband, father to three

*strapping sons and a beautiful daughter, his recollections
came and went all too soon.*

*Each time the darkness overcame him and the light
was born anew, his eyes opened to another set of
rushing memories from the past. Horadrin the mason was
a short collection of scenes abruptly ended by collapsed
rock, while Illinara sped by more slowly in her lengthy
collage as an enchanter. A carpenter in one breath, a
silversmith in the next, the visions bled together in their
eagerness to live again. A fisherman, a seamstress, a
scholar then a painter went by with dizzying speed. A
traveler forging silver portals, a rune crafter building
glyphs, an enchanter teaching the Art or an eldarath
allaying sickness, each one played out and was gone,
but the last one brought with it his consciousness to the
surface...*

Tens of lives had gone past, each with a craft and
family all its own. It was when Barr noticed that some
of those lives had been lived out at the same time that
he became self-aware, focused once more upon the
present. He knew many of his lives had occurred
simultaneously, that all were pieces of the same whole,
the higher self we call the soul. Only when he was faced
with that certain knowledge, that glimpse of inner
understanding, did the light loosen its hold and fade
away into the distance.

It was the memories of Calara that stuck with him,
her years as an eldarath. Though alive at the same time
as Fanarin, Barr was able to separate the two sets of
recollections and emotions. It was what she knew of the
fever that caused such alarm, her discovery and failed
attempts to cure the enchanted disease. Meant to break
an entire people, subjugate them with delirium and the
persistent whispers of a god, the plague succeeded only
in their demise.

Barr knew with dreaded certainty that it was Revyn behind the scheme. The God of Change had tried to bend the arachon to his worship, steal their devotion by altering their very nature. He had killed every last one of them, as surely as if his shapelings had descended upon Dwendorim and tore them limb from limb.

Worse still, every Protector now knew it as well.

* * *

Markus pushed the young girl aside and sat up at the edge of bed. Morning light seeped through the closed shutters, casting rows of dusty gold across her hair and bare skin. From how roughly he had used her, she would sleep until afternoon. Her beauty had caught his attention between bouts of sharp aches that drink would not quell. More than willing to ease his pain with her body, he took out his frustrations on her youth time and again. There was no pleasure in the act, no solace from the emptiness that haunted his every thought. Just the sight of her only served to remind him of what he had lost. And like most humans, in the end, she disgusted him.

He reached for his pants and glanced at the mirror on the floor in the corner. Memory of what he had seen reflected back only angered him. The shock of white that marred his hair, the wrinkles around both eyes, the mere notion was enough to drive him mad! His people grew from baby to child, adolescent to adult, but they were forever vital with the strength of eternal youth. The time since Barr had been born, when Markus had woken from forced slumber, was nothing compared to the years taken from him the day before. The illuminaire were for all intents and purposes immortal; only violence could bring their lives to an end. If he was no longer one of them, then what was he?

"I have *aged*!" he roared, startling the girl awake.

She slipped free of the blanket and came up behind him, her hands soft against his shoulders and lips upon his ear.

"You're beautiful," she told him, hands moving down across his chest and pulling back toward the bed.

Markus turned and took hold of her by the cheek, drew her close and stroked the other with the back of a finger. Her skin was soft beneath his touch, firm and aglow with youth. No more than fifteen, full lips, bright eyes, brimming with happiness and life, she became the object of his hatred, the embodiment of his loss. His hands slipped down to her neck and squeezed, cutting off breath with a frightened gasp.

"Don't, plea–"

He choked harder.

It took much longer than he remembered, before the struggling finally ceased. Long moments passed, but he persisted, crushing the airway for good measure. Vacant eyes stared upward, the faded blue of a worn dress, and the lips were parted in farewell. Markus bent forward and kissed them, then got up from bed and dressed.

He felt weaker, physically and in spirit, as if a piece of him had been forever torn away. The loss of Isdael left him both numb and in pain, in a state of living more dead than alive. He feared his hold upon this world was slipping from his grasp. He could feel it in the others as well. His unwilling servants were diminished by the link that bound them to his essence. Their power had waned when his spirit faltered.

Markus could not afford to lose another. The reality of his situation had finally sunken in, and it made his need for the Emblems even more urgent.

Soon enough, Revyn cooed in his mind.

How could this happen? His tone was accusatory, on the verge of an outburst he might not recover from. *You promised me nothing could stand against them!*

I said they would be nothing like your world had ever seen. There was a warning in the god's voice, and Markus took heed with a few calming breaths. *The loss is unfortunate, but another of my plans is coming to fruition.*

Our friend?

Is already on the move.

Revyn sounded pleased. It caused a sensation in his middle that greatly unnerved Markus.

How did you manage that in one night? He finished dressing and headed for the door, stopping to drop a handful of silver coins on the bed. *Surely they must be suspicious.*

Suspicion does not interfere with my plans.

Markus left the inn and headed west, away from the stables and his horse. The presence of Revyn was gone from his mind, leaving quiet and dull pain in its wake. The crowded streets were alive with talk of elves and coming war. He could smell the charred remains before entering the central plaza, where two bodies hung from the outstretched arms of a statue. Swinging beneath the chiseled visage of Tempas, what remained of the elves was burned far beyond recognition.

What progress? he asked Dhalak.

Hope's End is ours, the revenant replied in a voice that echoed in his thoughts, like talking into the wind and having the words thrown back, *as is the Ivory Sanctum. The total conversion of Alixhir is underway.*

And the Brethren?

I met with Jyotika hours ago. She should have already infected the conclave. Markus had the sense of quickly moving across rocky terrain, and knew Dhalak ran on all fours with due speed. *I am headed to the House of War as we speak. I will meet the Brethren tonight and assist with their endeavor.*

Good, Markus thought. *We could use a few dozen Warmasters to lead the armies we've been gathering.*

*   *   *

Sera leapt over a fallen log, keeping pace with the two ahead but not so close as to draw attention. She felt the morning sun, as it touched the horizon and cast the forest in a haze of winter light. It took only a moment for her eyes to adjust.

More than obvious signs of passage, the upturned snow or tree markings, she relied on the geas to track her prey. She could feel its proximity, gauge the distance between them by the intensity of pain, hear its heart beat in her ears, feel the blood flow in its veins. Its tracks were of secondary importance, details that told her of the battle to come. Its gait revealed a height two times an average man, while the depth of its prints were from a weight some forty stone.

She'd been following for three days, across mountain and as of last night into dense trees. More than capable of closing the distance, Sera chose instead to keep back and observe. The fire in her middle had been growing at a steady pace, but the years since her Awakening had trained her to endure.

Never had she heard of or encountered a creature like the one chasing her prey. Its touch melted snow and blackened the earth beneath, rotting any growth in its wake. It left a scent of decay on the air that overpowered any trace of sulfur or burning flesh. She had come across a deer that had had the misfortune of stepping upon that path. Its hind legs twitched in the short moments before death, as its head and forelegs grayed to black in a state of rapid decomposition.

With morbid curiosity, Sera had stepped upon the fetid path. Shocking pain that had stolen her breath for but a moment and the runes upon her bare feet glowing more brightly had been the only result. So she followed, and she watched, waiting for the two to clash. With any luck, the monstrosity would kill her prey.

It didn't matter why or what else was giving chase. She only knew the geas wouldn't let her rest until either she or the demon was dead.

Not that she needed sleep or ever tired. Rest was an indulgence at best and, much like eating, one she would often go for days or weeks without. Wiry thin and corded with muscle, her body was a weapon, an instrument not her own. She'd lost it long ago, to a gift that had taken everything.

So thin as to appear sickly, starvation was only one of the many ways she had tested its limits. At this distance, the pain was just an ember in her belly. If she slowed or fell too far behind, her blood would start to boil, her muscles ache and then burn with the inner fire. She had tried it once before, let it ravage her body just to see how much she could take or if the geas would actually kill her. Though it had felt like burning alive from within, every fiber of her being inflamed with divine consumption, still she could grin at the defiant memory.

It was all she had left to call her own, the pain when a demon drew near and her defiance of the two gods who had seen fit to inflict their blessings upon her.

Steam rose off her body, intermingling with each steady exhalation of frosty breath. Exposed to the biting cold, wearing the barest of shredded cloth across her chest and on her hips, the discomfort reminded her she was alive, that it was her choice to feel its numbing sting. She also believed the lack of any armor kept her more focused and alert, gave greater freedom of mobility and added challenge where usually there was none.

From the soles of bare feet to the roots of cropped hair, divine runes no bigger than a thumbnail ran the length of her body in even circles, glowing with a silvery blue like moonlight off of water. Atop those were larger runes, just above the skin, shimmering and rotating with a black fire. From ankles to thighs, across her waist, up her back and chest, over shoulders and down each arm to the wrist, with a final set like a mask around preternaturally sapphire eyes, the runes marked her for all too see as both their savior and a warning.

Imbued by Herne, God the Hunt, and fueled by Curoch, God of Honor and Truth, the geas granted her inhuman speed and strength. It protected her from most harm and made her very hard to kill. Her decision not to carry weapons, relying on her body and its ability to enchant by touch alone, lent another added challenge to the task she never asked for.

As she raced past a ravine, a leafless branch on the other side struck her cheek and scraped along her head. The ensuing sting was momentary, each cut instantly closed. She could have avoided it, of course, but had chosen not to. It reminded her of the hair she used to have, long enough to touch her waist and in braids so elaborate it took her sister two hours to finally finish. So blonde as to seem white in the summer sun, soft to the touch and smelling of daffodils, she was sure it had been one of the reasons Denifar had ever taken notice.

Now it was cut so short the runes across her scalp could be seen between the muddied strands. Aside from the braids having gotten tangled in brush while she chased, a demon had nearly yanked her head off by the roots. A reminder of what she had lost, they became more of a burden than a joy. She had cut them off not long after the cancelled wedding.

Digging into a tree, she tore away dried bark and splintered wood while propelling herself forward. She gritted her teeth and glanced down at her fingernails. Once neatly trimmed and polished, they were now raw and bitten, ringed with dark soil and stained by blood – her own or a demon's she wasn't sure.

Sera had been thirteen summers when her dad had told her of the news. Denifar's father had asked for her hand, on behalf of his son, and their marriage agreement had soon been arranged. The memory had once been the only happiness she could remember, but even that had become clouded by long bitter years, until the painful aftermath was all that remained.

Her Awakening had followed the week after. She would have been married to a man she truly loved, and even more rare she believed he had cared for her as well. All of it had been burned away in the wretched fires of a blessed curse. She recalled the searing pain, as each rune had etched itself into her flesh from within, how all had come running, only to look upon her in fright and then sad realization.

Demon hunters were left barren by the geas, and with no prospect of a child, their arrangement had been ended. To Denifar's credit, he had insisted they still marry. Be it for love or her dowry, she liked to the think it was the former. It had mattered little in the end, when demons tore through town to find her, through friends and family, through all she had ever known. She had no choice but to leave or risk endangering those she loved.

Even now, when she succumbed to the need for food and brief company, she could stand no more than a few hours of the fearful stares, the terrible wondering when – not if – a demon would appear, inexorably drawn to her presence, and lay waste to all around.

A flash of warmth rose up from her middle, prickling her skin and alerting her to another. She reached out with her senses, still chasing her prey faster than a horse at full gallop. It took only a moment, an instant of absolute quiet and concentration between heartbeats. Sera felt the essence of every life within an hour's run in all directions, from the burrow of snowtails a hundred paces on her left to the shalewing nest high in the branches of a white fir far behind.

She stopped and looked ahead, confused by what she felt. Or rather, what she didn't feel.

Whatever chased her prey was not alive.

Cursing herself for not noticing sooner, she resumed the chase. There were times when she had grown lax, when she hadn't bothered to use every advantage at her disposal. It was said in taverns she had visited that a demon hunter was considered lucky to survive more than a year, where most were torn apart by their first prey. Sera had stopped counting the years. Either the stories were false, or she was doubly cursed, for nothing pained her more than the necessary solitude. A lesson hard learned, she would rather die herself than watch another person killed for being near her.

There were two a hundred paces on her right, young but blooded and headed straight for her. Mature demons would have been able to resist, though in the past some had sought her for the challenge. Neither of these two felt more than a dozen stages old, which made her wonder how they had managed to find a portal.

Fire sliced through a tree in front of her, erupting a wall of steam from snow and ice suddenly gone. She rolled and faced them in a crouch, glaring with intense hatred. She couldn't rid herself of the geas or strike out at the gods who had cursed her with it, but she could unleash all her anger and frustration at every demon foolish enough to stand against her.

They both had yellow eyes with a sliver of violet, most likely spawned from the same queen, but their similarities ended there. One stood on two legs, with four arms and a wide chest. Covered in thick plates of fiery orange, with spikes along each arm, its claws ended in grasping talons the length of daggers. The other looked more an insect, skittering across the earth upon a dozen legs beneath a segmented carapace. Its sharp mandibles dripped molten saliva an emerald hue, much like the spots across its abdomen when it reared up on six hind legs.

"Jhu re fa nema!" the bipedal demon said, more delighted than surprised. *It has no weapons!*

Sera felt dirty at the fact she could understand it, as if the language soiled her skin or infected her spirit. Her disgust, however, paled in comparison to the indignation that boiled up within her, that her chase had been interrupted by such unworthy prey. She stood, arms at her side, and walked directly up to the first demon.

"Barok!" she demanded. *Attack!*

She made no move to defend, as its talons cut deep across her chest. Her blood and flesh spattered over the snow. The four wounds went through muscle and bone, searing the edges of each gash in wispy smoke. Though pained by the attack, her gaze never wavered. She stood firm, defiant, and endured the mending of her body with mounting rage. Her bones knitted back together, muscle fiber painfully rejoined, and her skin closed over without a trace of the assault.

"You'll have to do better than that."

The runes upon her body came alive with blinding light, immersing the entire area in holy fire. Snow, earth and demon flesh bubbled beneath the conflagration, as if a star had descended from the heavens and burned a crater in the soil. Rearing back and shielding their eyes, both cried out in gurgling anguish. The air itself was alight with shimmering flames, a white-hot inferno that spun around them in a sphere.

Sera stood at the center of the holy blaze, untouched and eyes aglow. She kicked the demon's leg, shattering its protective thigh plate and exposing fractured bones. The demon dropped to its knees, screaming and lashing out, but its talons could no longer penetrate her skin. She grabbed it by the throat and pulled close its toothy face.

"Kha nema a fala," she said, *I need no weapons for you,* and punched a fist through the rigid flesh of its abdomen.

A pale fire erupted from within and ravaged its body. She let the demon fall over, twitching in a pool of molten rock and its own burning blood.

The other demon turned to flee, its clacking body still on fire and screeching from the pain. Cracks ran the length of its carapace, revealing orange flesh beneath that blackened as it burned. Sera reached down and tore a claw from the first demon, spraying blood across her face and enchanting the severed hand with her touch. Runes flared around and up each digit, set each talon aglow with *furie*.

She calmly walked toward the second, watched it stumble over charred legs that refused to move. With a hand between two segments, at its neck and bulbous head, Sera brought the demon up short as if it weighed no more than a human child. She drove the claw, talons and all, through the back of its head and let the body fall away into holy fire.

Even the weakest demon could be deadly, as Sera had learned early on, but her patience had worn thin at the intrusion. Leaving the two smoking corpses behind, she resumed the hunt and easily caught up to a safe distance.

The forest ahead exploded with black streamers, a maelstrom of wailing tendrils that shredded trees and shook the ground. Frozen earth and rocks began to rain down, as Sera leapt and clung to a thick tree limb some fifteen feet overhead. From her vantage she could see the demon flailing back from blasts of shadowy fire that tore and froze its flesh with icy flickers of nether magic.

Its pursuer seemed to be a lich, the spirit of a weaver who used dark arts to bind its soul to what was once its mortal body. Long dead flesh clung to its yellowed frame, where little more than bone showed through the black armor and tattered cloak. She could sense more than see the blood-red runes across its bones.

Sera dropped to a crouch and ran closer to the fray, her ears assaulted by the clash of deadly magic. It was rare for her to see a demon of such age. She studied its every move, as she ran from tree to tree and took cover behind the remains of a smoldering stump.

The demon towered over the undead caster, a mass of thick muscle beneath chitin scales and rigid plates. Its mouth opened at four points, where rows of teeth ended in curled fangs at each corner. Two massive horns jutted up from its forehead, ebon tipped with white and sharp as dagger points. Chitin barbs sprouted the entire length of its spine, while bony spikes protruded from the end of every joint. Aside from the black fire, its body emanated flames of its own, a whirlwind of flickering crimson like a sunset bleeding out. In one hand it clutched an unusual sword, a heavy mithrinum blade with two edges and a hollow middle.

Unrelenting in its attack, the lich pressed forward, eye sockets alight with an orange glow. It spoke in an alien tongue, an echoing litany of words that scraped the inside of her skull. More shadowy tendrils rose up and lashed out, each streamer led by the ebon face of a soul wailing in anguish.

Sera could feel the demon's exhaustion from having run for days on end, its ravenous hunger, its thirst for blood and an obsession bordering on madness that focused solely on the sword. Despite the pain of grievous wounds, where armored flesh continued to crackle and fall away from icy fire, revealing jagged bones and ravaged muscle beneath, the demon stood its ground, refusing to buckle. In one hand it conjured fire, the soul-charring flames that only a demon could master, and in its sword hand the mithrinum blade sparked to life.

A beryl mist ran the sword's length, with shocks of lightning a deeper hue of brilliant emerald reaching out. Vines as thick as a man's leg sprouted up from the decayed and broken earth, up and around the lich's body, entangling every inch. Fist-sized thorns erupted from the vines, piercing armor and yellowed bone and eliciting a skeletal cry.

The earth around them seemed to mend, its soil darkening in a shimmer of falling moisture from the sword. Lush grass pushed through, thick tufts of vibrant life that blanketed the ground, fighting against the aura of death and decay emanating from the lich's touch. The demon unleashed its fire in a jet of screaming ruby, as if the voices of Danarriden carried with it. The vines went up in flame, igniting the lich as well, melting armor and dead flesh in a living furnace. When the fire bled away, all that remained was an aged skeleton, a collection of dead bones that refused to fall over.

The crimson runes came alight, and the lich's eyes glowed again. It took a step forward, instantly wilting the vines that sprang up to entangle its feet and legs. All growth withered beneath its touch. Fire bathed its every bone but couldn't pierce the glowing runes. The demon swung with a mighty roar, but the blade never struck. Caught in the lich's bony grasp, the demon's wrist began to blacken. As if infected by a voracious plague, the rot began to spread, eating away at living tissue with the speed of certain doom.

In moments, the demon fell away a lifeless husk.

Free of pain and the geas, at least for the time being, Sera could have walked away. The demon was gone. No longer did its presence compel her to action. Still, part of her yearned to face a challenge worth succumbing to. In the company of demons, her power grew. It was widely thought that only a demon hunter could face an Arch Demon in combat and survive. Conversely, without a demon nearby, her power waned. To face the lich now would be madness.

Sera stepped out from behind the stump and calmly approached the undead weaver. It picked up the sword and faced her, shrouded once again in the illusory visage of black armor and a long cape.

"You should have stayed hidden," the hollow voice intoned, though its jaw never moved beneath the helm.

"Fancy a go?"

She grinned and attacked, easily dodging the now shortened blade. Reaching through illusion, she grabbed hold of a rib and pulled. It came free in an explosion of blinding light that threw them both wide. The crimson runes on the bone died out, replaced by her own glowing blue enchantment. With a laugh, Sera kicked her legs out and stood in one fluid motion, then launched herself at the lich with godlike speed. Before the creature could even rise, she was upon it, striking down time and again with the jagged bone. Sapphire sparks flashed out with each strike, as she rained down destruction upon its corpse without relent.

A wave of dizziness overcame her, a sudden pulling at her middle. Her attack wavered, slowed, long enough for her to notice that the runes across her body began to dim. Her flesh went paler still, as if all the blood had drained away. Where her legs touched the lich, the skin wrinkled and grayed, grew numb with a rising cold. She swallowed and blinked, a touch of fear at the back of her mind, the terrifying doubt of a prayer that might be answered. She halted her attack, the bone falling from her grasp.

"You can hurt me," she said in disbelief, before the weakness overcame her.

Thrown aside, body limp, Sera watched the lich rise. It clenched a fist, crackling aged bones, fiery eyes alight with murder, and stepped toward her with a promise of release. A cloud of mist erupted behind the lich and dissipated, followed by two dark blades protruding outward from its chest. Embers came alive from the severed heart, spread across its body and ate away at each crimson rune like papyrus in a fire. Stripped of enchantment, all illusion torn away, the lich collapsed in a heap of bones before the form of a young man.

"Time to rest, King Kaidyn," the man said.

Rising up from the remains, a transparent body of pure light turned its head to regard her. Though she could once again move, Sera was transfixed. To her, the image was of a being both beautiful and sad. The sorrow wrenched her heart, caught her breath in a long moment before the spirit walked away. Light faded, and it was gone, but the sorrow remained.

"Why?" Sera demanded quietly, refusing to shed a tear. The sword lay beside her. She picked it up and stood, facing the stranger who had appeared from out of nowhere. "Why did you save me?"

"You would have died," he answered.

He still held both swords and eyed her warily, as if expecting her to attack. She had no more fight left. All her strength, all her will, seemed lost in an emptiness she could never hope to fill.

"I died a long time ago."

The sword shimmered like silver liquid, shrunk in on itself and crawled up her hand. Settling upon her wrist, it became a bracer with ornate etchings.

"I know what you are," he said, "and I can help."

"It's not safe." Sera studied the mithrinum, running a thumb over the strange markings. "It won't be long before a demon finds me. It never is."

"I can take you to a city where no demons can enter. You can rest," he said, emphasizing the last, "truly rest, without worrying about the geas."

Skeptical, Sera met his gaze. She had never heard of such a place, if it were even possible, where no demon could find a portal through the ether. It didn't matter. Her desire to be free was no longer buried deep inside. It was out in plain sight, a sorrow that bound her as surely as any curse.

"Alright." She crossed her arms. "Lead the way."

Mist rose up all around them, and the forest fell away into a realm of starry black.

– 13 –

They walked back toward Barr's home in uneasy silence. Fluora walked slower than usual, sorting through the flashes of vision that overtook her present. It felt as if she were somewhere else for a brief moment, someone else, living events that may or may not come to pass. Though she focused her attention on the here and now, her mind was tired from the constant struggle. It sapped her body of strength, made her weary all too soon, and even sleep did not refresh her as it once had. She feared losing herself in those lingering visions, where the present returned unfamiliar.

How long, she wondered, before she could no longer tell the difference between her own life and those she glimpsed through her seer sight?

"I wonder what they'll do now," Barr said, *and she was dodging his attack, moving to the martial rhythm of the dance he was teaching.*

His voice was sad, filled with the loss of an entire people. Fluora felt it in his words, in his thoughts and in his hand. She squeezed it in comfort, just glad for any contact. It helped her stay anchored, reminded her who she was and what she felt in her heart.

"I cannot see," she told him and enjoyed the empty black of uncertainty. "They must not yet have decided."

Did I miss anything? Aren yawned in Barr's thoughts, *the smell of fish in her nose, gentle water lapping nearby along the shore...*

Shapelings assaulted the docks, taking down sailors and workmen with tooth and claw. Some they left bitten, screaming in agony against the disease now coursing through their veins, while others were feasted upon in a bloodied wholesale slaughter. Mostly wolves, though some among them were hulking bears or thick boars with bristled hair and tusks streaked with gore, they were all monsters of terrible proportion. Their victims were helpless to stop it, killed by the turned guards who had sworn to protect them. It was too late for Noria. The feasting had begun, as parents succumbed to the disease and fed upon their own children. The elderly and those deemed weak by judging scent were no more, drained of all furie *and life. From the Guardians at Haven to the Brotherhood at Mercy's Light, the entire city was gone, blotted out by the shadow of a god.*

You just missed lunch, Idelle teased.

Be nice, Barr said. *You'll get him all upset. You only missed the memorial, Aren, and an unexpected request.*

You feel tired, the hound noted.

Barr sighed, more sorrow than weariness. *I am tired. The golems asked me to teach them shaping, and through visions of past lives, I'm afraid I taught them more than even I thought I knew. It was Revyn who had infected the arachon and killed everyone in the city with his disease.*

Fluora closed her eyes to the carnage, but memory of it haunted the once comforting black. Pain-filled screams of the dying rang in her ears, echoed with the moans of souls being turned.

Garand was next. The city guard and officials had already fallen. Revyn tugged at their strings, and they carried out their macabre tasks. The noble Guardians at Sanctuary had been turned first, and one among them, Jakob, set his jaws upon the Brotherhood. Despite their victory against the orcs, the remaining knights and warrior priests would be defeated by a single wolf. Vereu would belong to Markus after all.

"Are you alright?" Barr asked, *blinding her with golden light. He was the sun in human form, brilliant and breathtaking, divine in presence, wrenching at her heart.*

"No, I –" she faltered, and he steadied her. "I just need a moment." Fluora blinked back the tears, shaking her head. Her chest tightened against breath that came in labored gasps. "Visions. Terrible, terrible visions."

Fluora wept.

The conversion of Alixhir was underway. As with the other cities, the Guardians were turned first. Hope's End fell in a single night, its magic hunters now bears with the rare chaodyn in their ranks. They headed into the city, to the guardhouse and guildhall, the King's estate and the academy. Most of the Brotherhood at the Ivory Sanctum were gone from the tower, off searching for Emblems. The few left behind were no match for the diseased hunger. Its voracity was unparalleled, ravaging the body and spirit of its prey until the lump of humanity had been shaped into Revyn's dark desire.

What's wrong with her? Aren asked, *haunted by the fear that her baby was not well.*

"Fluora?" His voice called from the distance, begging her to come back. "Do you know where you are?"

He stood in the center of the shapeling temple, at the heart of Lumintor. His army was dead or dying, replacing the infected they had burned or cut asunder. It did not matter. He was a Warmaster, chosen by Tempas. Divine magic filled his spirit, burned his body from within. More than willing to sacrifice his own life, Thoryn had agreed and was granted the full might of a god. Though the magic consumed him, the temple would fall.

"I am in the House of War," Fluora replied, her voice sounding strange in her ears. "The students are bound. Once the Warmasters turn, they will feed on the young and old."

They would have made invincible leaders for Revyn's armies, she mused, had the Brethren stayed to ensure Tempas's favored children had indeed turned. Enduring the Battle of Self, each one to a man would take his own life rather than serve another god. Of the Brethren, only their leader Jyotika would be spared. The others would be torn apart by an avatar of their goddess. Zilania could not free them from the disease, but she could grant them final rest. She too would fall prey to Revyn's plague...

"No, you're in Dwendorim. You are Fluoralandylae, Matron of the Guiding Mists, daughter of Elaedraoni, the Grand Seeress."

"She is with child?" Fluora asked, confused by the thought that came unbidden to Barr's mind. *The demon*, she remembered. "That cannot be. It will kill her from within. I am going to lose my mother."

Fluora felt his uncertainty, his mounting frustration. She knew he wanted to help, but there was nothing to be done for it. The sorrow and despair were hers alone to endure. It was her sacrifice to the balance that must be maintained. The mists were a gift for her people, and she had chosen to pay its price.

Or it had chosen her.

Humans marched on the sylvannis, while the elven council subverted its own people from within. No longer truly elves, they would soon all belong to Revyn.

Put her to sleep? Idelle offered. *It breaks my heart to see her like this.*

Barr put his hands to her cheeks, warm and none too soft, hardened by battle, by years of training she herself would pursue with an unrelenting and firm resolve. As if her body were broken, he tried to heal her.

"You cannot heal madness," she said and laughed, crying against the despair.

The nomadic ogre clans were united once more, under the revenant Solastin and its Emblem Faelsha. Though the ogres would not turn, they worshipped nature and were drawn to the Emblem. As a lumbering army, they marched on the dwarven city of Drakanon. Standing twice as tall as any man, and three times the girth, the ogres were but a shadow of their forebears – the titans. Beside them strode eyeless pets, feline creatures called stalkers. They were taller than a horse and twice as long. Sniffing the air for prey, as ogre magi wove enchantments and war blessings upon the whole, the first stalker crested a grassy rise and caught scent of the mountain city. Two more days of hard marching, and blood would fill the river.

"You're not insane," Barr said, sending *furie* through his fingers, but the thought hung upon the air, two little words that spelled her doom. *Not yet, not yet,* the words filtered on the breeze, whispers of a promise. "Let me help you. Stop fighting me."

The world fell away, replaced by a Taellus barren of life. The desolate landscape stretched out behind Markus, beyond the fading smile, the broken promises and empty sacrifices. A shadow rose up from his heels, a darkness that stretched outward across the entire land. She saw his eyes in the shapeless mass, saw Revyn for what he was. Destruction, the death of all things, the god was both an end to their worlds and a horrible beginning.

"I cannot stop him," Fluora said and looked into Barr's eyes, a tear dropping on his hand. "No one can."

"I refuse to believe that."

Reflected in his eyes, she saw the revenant Kaidyn standing over a fallen woman. The Emblem Amintro was in his grasp, and the undead king reared back to end her life.

"Barr!" Fluora sent the image to his mind, showed him where to go. "You must save her! We *need* her!" Barr's eyes darted back and forth, seeing every detail. "Go!"

Without a word, he disappeared into the mists.

* * *

Barr returned as quickly as he could, walking at a brisk pace from the plaza to his old home. He could have used the mists but wasn't sure if doing so put undue pressure on Fluora. Without Aislin, it was just a matter of time before umbrals slipped through and began to drain her. He pushed the thought from his mind, as the house came into view. Fluora sat on a wooden bench, head in hand. Hanar was beside her, holding the other.

You left without us, Aren said evenly.

Sorry. There wasn't time.

Idelle ruffled her feathers, looking down from the top of the house. *He's just upset that he didn't get to fight,* she said in a playful tone.

Barr could feel her hurt and a little angry as well. *And you?*

A bit. But I understand.

"Sera?" Fluora asked without looking up.

"How did you know – never mind. She's fine. She's been given a place to rest, and a Protector's nearby if she needs anything." Barr raised a brow. "But you knew that already."

She looked at him then, shook her head and smiled. "I can see many things, but I am not omniscient."

Hanar said, "Friend Dar-Paj arrived at Skyfall and is already gone. He is accompanied by Jahd. An excellent choice, in my opinion."

"Did he say where they went?"

"A mountain," Fluora said with a faraway look. "A cold and snowy place."

"The Baeryd mountains," Hanar confirmed. "He is searching for the Emblem Ghaireuk."

We should be going soon, too. Aren walked over and lay down beside the bench. *We can't sit around waiting, and we can't take her with us.*

Fluora rubbed behind his ear. "He is right. Until my seer sight is firmly under control, I would be a burden and endanger you all." Barr opened his mouth to speak, and she added, "The visions come and go, some stronger than others." She crinkled her brow. "My apologies."

Barr laughed. "That's alright. Before I start scrying where to go next, I thought we could take a walk. I may have an idea that can help you with the visions."

He went into the house, down the hall and to a dresser in the master bedroom. He took a handkerchief from the top drawer, white linen and still soft, stuffed it into his pocket and headed back outside.

He offered a hand to Fluora. "Shall we?"

Her smile made his heart skip a beat. Fiery braided hair, a deep crimson touched with gold, bright blue eyes ringed in midnight, pale skin that glimmered beneath the pseudo-sunlight and a dusting of freckles, she was more than simply beautiful. Fluora was elegant and graceful, both fragile and strong, with the diminutive stature of a full-blooded faeron. The mere thought of her flushed his cheeks. She took his hand, and her touch was much warmer than he had expected.

To the others he said, "We'll be back soon."

He led her to the park, where afternoon light shone across the misted grass. It felt oddly quiet without the laughter of children.

"I've been a seer and an oracle," Barr told her as they walked, "many times in the past. I don't think I've ever had quite the ability you do, but..."

She squeezed his hand and leaned in closer. "I like this. It puts my mind at ease."

Whether she meant the scenery or holding hands, he wasn't sure.

Fluora giggled.

Blushing, Barr had his answer. He enjoyed being with her too, the feel of her against his arm, the scent of wild flowers in her hair. He stole a sidelong glance, could look at her for hours, and sighed inwardly at the time slipping from his grasp.

He dreaded having to leave so soon.

"What are you going to teach me?" she asked, as they stepped onto the grass.

"You tell me," he replied with a half-grin.

She poked him in the side, eliciting an *ow!* and smiled despite the teasing.

"I do not need to see the future to know you brought me here for a reason." She stopped and faced him. "Or did you just want some privacy to try and kiss me?"

He was suddenly unable to think of anything else.

Fluora gave him a playful shove. "Boys! You are all the same!" She crossed her arms and tilted her head. "I am almost offended."

"Almost?"

She held up a thumb and forefinger, slightly apart. "This much."

"My sincerest apologies," Barr said with exaggerated flourish and gave a bow. "I shall endeavor to be more gentlemanly in the future."

"I can *see* the future, and there is no such evidence of this endeavor you speak of."

She stepped forward and kissed him, her tongue brushing his lower lip. Caught off guard but pleasantly surprised, Barr returned the kiss with gentle fervor. She tasted like strawberries. His cheeks burned and chest pounded, as she slowly pulled away.

"There," she said and touched her lips with a smile. "You have your kiss. Now you can focus on why we are here."

I knew it! Aren said.

Idelle laughed and flew above.

Oh, shush! Both of you.

"Alright," Barr said and moved to stand beside Fluora. "One of the ways I learned to focus my sight and strengthen concentration is an exercise very similar to a martial dance." Before she could ask, he added, "A series of precise movements, it's a combat rhythm used to attack and defend. Once adept at the dance, you can reorder the sequences to fit any situation. As an exercise, it works every muscle in the body and distracts the mind by focusing elsewhere."

He began showing her the dance, a long series of both simple and complicated moves, where each fluid action led one into another. Slowly, allowing her time to mimic his every move, Barr stretched and worked his muscles through the dance, felt stress fall from him in waves and drew strength from his center. Minutes went by before the dance was complete. The final move, both arms pushing forward as the body turned and swept a leg, led back into the first, where hands touched palms flat and went out to either side.

Two more times Barr led her through the dance. It would take hours of practice before she could remember each move, but before long her body would know them without prompting. Unfortunately, time was short. What Barr wanted to see was if the exercise helped her focus, freed her mind from the seer sight, if only for a moment.

"Let's try something else." He pulled the cloth from his pocket and tied it around her eyes. "Use your other senses." He took hold of her hand and pushed against the bottom of her palm. "Your body is a weapon."

She nodded, looking toward his voice.

"But like all weapons, it has strengths and it has weaknesses. Never strike with a fist. The fingers are too delicate. You use this," he pushed again on her palm then tapped her above and below the elbow, "or these. Above the knee, the heels of your feet, you use the parts of your body best able to absorb impact." He lifted her arms, bent at the elbow. "Always protect your head. One hit, and you're finished. All around you, to the length of your arms, is your kill zone. Never extend beyond it. What comes into this area, you turn aside or strike. You move forward, putting enemies in your kill zone, but never overextend, never compromise balance."

Barr began teaching her to spar, regardless of the blindfold, forcing her to rely on any sense but sight. The sound of his breathing, hands parting the air. The feel of his proximity, the vibrations of his steps upon the grass. The scent of his presence, the sweat and oiled leather. He went through a series of three basic strikes, one to each side and one overhead. He went slow, giving her time to gauge where the attack would come from, and gently brought to bear the flat of his right forearm.

She missed many times in the first few minutes, blocking some only by coincidence, but steadily grew more confident and relied less on guessing, more on her senses.

"Does Sera have Amintro?" Fluora asked, arms bent and held firmly ahead. She pushed aside a strike with the outer edge of her right arm.

"She wears it as a bracer," Barr replied. "Just like Aislin. I already asked the Emblem if it could help you. She said no." Barr turned aside a counterattack and almost laughed, so surprised was he by the attempt. "Kaidyn is dead."

Fluora nodded. "What of the runes on her body? I know she is special and plays an important role in the future, but I have never before seen her like."

"Sera's a demon hunter."

"You feel sorry for her." Another counterattack.

"I do. Only once before was I one of them, and I don't envy her at all." Barr slowly moved his palm toward her middle and was surprised again when she blocked. "How did you know to do that?"

"I could feel it." She shrugged. "You cheated."

Barr laughed. "I was testing you. Let's add that in then." He had been gradually attacking faster, but still she kept pace. Rarely did she miss a block, which truly impressed him. "You're very good, you know."

"What exactly is a demon hunter?"

Recalling what he knew of them, both from lore and having lived shortly as one, he pieced together what he thought to be fact and what seemed at least believable.

"I can only say for certain that there are five at any given time. If one dies, another somewhere is awakened."

Barr blocked a counter, but Fluora touched him on the shoulder with her other palm.

She grinned.

Though she seemed to enjoy any strike she could land, Barr noticed the visions were not troubling her while she fought. He was forced to block more often and increased his pace.

"They have a geas upon them," he continued, his breath steady despite the exertion, "a curse that compels them to hunt nearby demons. It physically pains them to ignore the hunt. The geas also attracts demons, which means a constant struggle to survive. From the moment of my Awakening, I never slept again."

"How is that possible?"

Her body was now covered in a thin layer of sweat, which caused her dress to cling. Barr forced himself not to look or even think about her body beneath the light cloth and gauzy wrap.

"The geas draws power from the gods, Curoch to be precise. Though the curse is Herne's doing, it's Curoch that fuels the magic."

Fluora paused to catch her breath. "I have never heard of such cruelty in any god but Revyn. Why would they do such a thing?"

"I can't say for sure," Barr replied, wiping sweat from his brow. "I only know the old stories. Revyn was set on stealing Curoch's first children, the dragons. When that failed, he sent an army of demons against their home at North Haven. Curoch asked Herne for assistance, and the Hunter God gave him five anaire, one for each Arch Demon. The anaire were Herne's first children, a race devoted to the art of tracking and the hunt. The arachon and humans are descended from them."

Fluora motioned she was ready once again. "And the curse?"

"They devised it together. They consider it a blessing. It's anything but. The runes burned into her skin protect and compel. Nothing can undo them but death." Barr was attacking and defending with greater speed. "I was twenty when it happened. I died less than a year later."

Barr purposely moved too close and attacked with both arms to either side. Fluora blocked them and poked him hard in the stomach.

"Now who's the cheater?" he accused and rubbed his soon-to-be bruise. "You're using your seer sight!"

She clucked her tongue. "Sorry, was I supposed to let you beat upon a blind, defenseless girl?" She laughed at what he felt was a betrayal. "It just happened. When we fight, I can see what you plan to do before you do it. I did not set out to deceive you." She patted him on the cheek. "You did help me though. I have not had a single vision since putting the blindfold on."

"Well, that's something then."

More astounded than truly hurt, Barr marveled at what a fighter she could be. It almost made him jealous, which of course caused her to laugh again. That was fine. It felt good to hear it, to see her happy. She stepped forward, kissed him then stepped back and put her arms up.

She's trying to throw you off guard, Idelle said from her perch atop the central fountain.

How long have you been watching?

Long enough to know she'll win if you let her keep distracting you like that.

"What happened next?" Fluora asked without trace of a smile, as if she hadn't heard what Idelle said.

Barr resumed his attacks. "The five killed every last demon there, thousands, which left none on Danarriden that worshipped Revyn. Rather than attempt to create new children –" Barr blocked a low attack, one that was *too* low for his liking – "he tried subverting other races. He created a disease like the geas, one that compels the infected to worship him. That's how shapelings came about."

Given enough time and training, Barr knew he could turn Fluora into a deadly fighter. It was not his intent, but the thought occurred to him more than once. He was glad they had found a way to keep her seer sight in check. In a past life, as an oracle named Kavra, he had worn ceremonial wrappings that blinded her to all but the seer sight. Kavra had not been able to see everyday life, as Fluora could, but was restricted only to glimpses of possible futures.

With more ferocity, Barr struck faster, pushing to see what she could do without formal training. Fluora was young and in good health, with a supple body tone born of faeron strength. He could see her growing tired, dripping with perspiration, but she refused to give in.

She pushed on with an unrelenting determination that made little sense to Barr. He didn't see a need for her to fight quite so hard.

Afraid she would go too far and get hurt, Barr moved in and slipped under her right arm, hooking it as he put himself directly behind her. He pushed the back of her knees, taking her down to the grass, then held up both hands in a call to stop.

They both lay side by side, catching their breaths. Back soaked from sweat and wet grass, warmth upon his face from the runic light of afternoon, the thick smell of flowers and trees in bloom, Barr took in a deep breath and smiled. Her fingers found his, slipped between and interlocked.

"You have spoken of past lives," she said, looking up through her blindfold at the sky of golden runes and the gauzy illusion of floating clouds. "How many have you had?"

Barr considered. "Thousands."

She was quiet for a time, her thumb rubbing against the back of his hand.

"How is that possible? Given the length of an average life and history of the known worlds, there would not be enough time for that many."

"Most were simultaneous. I was literally two or more people at once." Memory came flooding back, a cursory glance of his entire past. It seemed much clearer than at other times, when he had tried to sort them out. Before this life, he knew with absolute certainty that he had been twenty-four separate people, across five different worlds. "A lot more. Except for my first." He thought back to the silver-haired woman with runes upon her brow, the illuminaire named Serce. "There was just the one life with my first."

"That is significant." She said it as fact, though he wasn't sure if it was opinion or something she had seen. "Since then you have always lived more than one?"

"Yes," Barr replied, tracing the path of his lives in a mental map, "gradually more and more. Until this one, that is."

"Maybe you are not aware of the others."

Barr shook his head. "No, I can feel it in the pit of my stomach. There are no others."

"That, too then, is significant. Like the first, perhaps this life is your last."

Barr made a face. "Enlightenment? I don't feel very enlightened."

Memory of a vision came flashing back to his mind, of countless people stretched out behind him, all bound by a silver cord that ran through their middles from back to front. All but the first. And he was the last. *Join us!* they had cried at him. He was not much for religion or worship of the gods, but many of his past lives had more than a passing knowledge of theology. If each life was a lesson, leading up to ascension, then what if the final life is meant to glean a culminating knowledge of all that had been learned? What if he was meant to do just what they had asked, join them together into a single thought of enlightened knowledge?

Is that true? Idelle asked.

"Impossible," he said, almost angry at the notion.

There were too many to sort out, too many to even *think* of at once. That level of scrutiny would drive him mad!

"Calm," Fluora told him. "You will know what to do when the time comes."

Something in her tone caught Barr off guard, and he wondered if she was hiding something she'd seen.

Fate was malleable, he had long ago learned, like quicksilver across the surface of a flowing stream. The future was a series of choices, and each choice changed the course of one's life. Barr knew better than any how misleading the sight could be, but still he wanted to know what she'd seen.

Fluora sat up and removed the blindfold. The sorrow returned, weighed upon her shoulders. She looked down at the grass and would not meet his gaze.

"Barr, before you left to save Sera," she began, her voice trembling. "I saw...

"There are some things you should know."

*   *   *

Revyn arrived in a massive chamber of obsidian. Its walls stretched up a thousand feet, to a dome of rippling black. Runes were carved all the way through the dome, letting in the crimson glow of Danarriden sky. The waves of ebon haze falling down like sheets of rain should have been his. Though none of the mewling demons could see it, the raw *furie* gained from devotion, Revyn saw it all too well, and anger raged deep inside him. Columns of black marble, flecked with glittering gold and platinum, ran the length from polished floor to runic ceiling. Four times as wide as it was tall, the single chamber itself was as large as any citadel. Towering gilded arches showed it was not the only one.

In the center of the chamber, filling more than half the open space, was a pool of hissing ooze. It bubbled from the heat, sent up putrid clouds of vapor from its inky depths, and basking in its contents was a mountain of tawny flesh. Nothing below the waist could be seen of the Arch Demon, which meant the chamber was most likely as deep as it was tall. Black ridges and spines covered the outside of its four appendages, while thick veins ran a web-work beneath sagging leathery skin. Each arm ended in something different, a fist with talons the size of wagons, a pronged sucker with tendrils that groped the air, pincers edged with serrated chitin and a skeletal blade that protruded outward from the wrist. Its chest stretched across the chamber, a field of muscle beneath scales of rune-etched chitin and prickly flesh.

Hundreds of demons were tending the colossal body, while others were dragged in by chain and bled into the pool. Demons hung from strands attached to the ceiling, spun from bulbous torsos, and crawled about the living mountain on various forms of leg. Some spiderlike, some like centipedes, others with sticky claws, they cleaned away the brackish muck of shedding skin and other remnants of transformation.

Revyn looked up at the Arch Demon, purposefully in the form of a slender faeron woman, and caught sight of multifaceted eyes lost in the flood of exultation. Spikes jutted from the shoulders, towers of ebon bone, and the thick neck was ringed with bristles that seemed to dance beneath the shower of devotion. Hairless, without ears, its head was a stunted rock of heavy chitin plates and a gaping mouth. Behind the rows of jagged teeth, a mass of tentacles writhed, feasting on a lesser demon.

Four demons noticed Revyn and charged, flailing ropy limbs and howling in maddened glee. She looked past their mortal forms, to the divine runes that bound them to existence. She undid the glyphs of all four with a thought. Their bodies turned to ash and were carried forward by momentum across the floor.

The eyes looked downward. "Revyn."

"Asmodan." The god inclined her head. "You look... lovely, as usual."

Distracted by the thoughts of those who worshipped and served – there was a distinction – Revyn frowned for the slightest of moments. Khulfa, her High Priest, was still scheming revenge for the fallen temple. Strega and her cadre were anxiously waiting, urgent whispers of impatience that grated on the nerves. Markus, once again, was fuming over another loss. Revyn could hear the individual thoughts of them all clearly, thousands upon thousands, but some whispered more loudly than others.

She put them all from her mind.

"What do you want?" the Arch Demon demanded.

"I have a problem. And an offer." Revyn tilted her head, letting ebon hair spill down her shoulder. Faeron were a particularly tasty desire for her second children. "Would you care to listen, or shall I leave?"

"Go on."

"I assume you know of my chaodyn?"

A deep chuckling filled the chamber. "What a sweet irony that you infect other races with demon blood to garner worship."

Revyn ignored the barb, had expected as much. Her guise, the diminutive stature, had been chosen with care and played to the bloated demon's arrogance.

"My other children have their advantages. My wolves are quick and agile. My bears are strong and relentless. My boars are ravenous and cruel." She looked about the chamber, at the children that were once hers. "But only my chaodyn combine the traits of all three." She sighed and looked away. "Unfortunately, mixing demon blood with other races is unstable. Barely a twentieth of those bitten survive the turning."

"Get on with what it is that you want."

"I seek the means to steady the turning, to make the blood more reliable... or replace it altogether." Revyn looked up and smiled sweetly at the pseudo-god. "You could help me with that."

Asmodan laughed. "A single drop of my blood would subvert the blood of any mortal."

"I am well aware."

"Why would I shed a drop for you?" The Arch Demon leaned forward, hovering. "Not that I do not enjoy your asking. You would use my precious blood to create more demons, force them to worship you against their will. What could you possibly offer in return to warrant the birth of demons into bondage?"

"The one thing you truly want." Revyn's hands came alight with blue flames, in a semblance of holy fire. "To be rid of the demon hunters."

"We have tried many times and failed. Kill one, and another awakens. Just what is it you propose?"

The flames died away. "I will turn them, make them into chaodyn." With a dramatic sigh, "If only the turning were more stable."

The chamber walls shook with the reverberation of Asmodan's continued laughter. The pool of blood began to tremble at the commotion, splashing out onto the floor in hisses of smoky protest.

"That is the most beautiful irony ever conceived! The veins of all five would flow with demon blood." Asmodan chuckled again, mouth wide in unholy mirth. "They would be forever in anguish, *compelled* to take their own lives but unable to do so! Wonderful!"

Revyn inclined her head again. "I am glad you think so. They will be unable to hunt, wracked with pain, and unable to die by their own hand." She shrugged. "If one of them should somehow die, I will simply turn the next to awaken."

Asmodan made a small incision with one talon and lowered the wounded arm down to Revyn.

"Take what you need."

Revyn pulled a crystal vial from a pouch at her belt. She released the stopper, careful not to let the beveled lip touch her skin, and placed it into the wound. Her flesh melted away, down to the bone, where it touched the acrid blood but healed so quickly as to barely draw notice. When the vial was full, she removed it from the wound and watched ichor on the outside of the crystal fade inward as if absorbed. Revyn put the stopper back on, fighting back the urge to grin, and secured the container in its pouch.

The Arch Demon's wound closed.

"How soon?" Asmodan asked.

"The first of them shall be turned shortly. I will send word when the others follow suit." Revyn smiled up in triumph. "Goodbye, Asmodan."

She could still hear the demon's laughter, as she stepped into the astral.

*   *   *

Dar woke in a lightless tunnel, though he could see clearly the jagged walls and muddied puddles underfoot. Chiseled marks showed the passage was not natural. He shook the sleep from his head, worried and unsure what was happening to him. Another blackout, the third since leaving Dwendorim. Dar was certain it had something to do with the mists, some adverse effect to his having trained so quickly. He felt torn between telling Barr and thwarting Markus, because if told, Barr would demand he return at once. Dar was driven by the need to disrupt whatever plans Markus had for the

Emblems, but more so, he wished to find the actor-thief and kill him.

He gripped Khaela and frowned; he didn't recall drawing the blade.

Sounds echoed from ahead, chopping wood, a steady drum, the clang of metal on metal and the guttural voices of a thousand gathered trolls. Dar followed the sounds and knelt beside Jahd, hiding behind an outcrop of rock along the path. Below them, a tribe of trolls went about their daily business.

"Did you find anything?" Jahd asked quietly.

"I did not."

He knew better than to tell the golem what had happened. She would no doubt relay the information to the protectorate, which would find its way to Barr through Hanar.

The trolls were large creatures, much taller than a man, though the females were noticeably smaller. All wore animal skins around the waist and over a shoulder, from large cats to bristly goats, snow bears and even owlkin – though Jahd had to tell him of the last. He had never heard of the manlike owls before. Each troll was painted with wide swirls, lines and dots. Dar assumed the different colored paints denoted status within the tribe. Only one among them, by far the largest, was marked in red. The males wore either blue, gray or green, while the females were in white or yellow. Dar noticed that every one of them had a weapon of some sort. From the double-edged stone axe across the back of one blue to a granite dagger at the belt of a yellow, they all looked formidable and not to be trifled with. Few among them carried iron, though a smithy could be seen at the far end of a central fire pit.

"It is excessively cold here," Jahd said. "Are you sure you do not need to be warmed?"

The cavern was quite large, a bowl-shaped bottom of broken stones and icy walls that reached to a ceiling so high that even Dar's unusual vision could not penetrate the black above. A number of tunnels exited the cavern, and three paths led to more areas with stone dwellings. Dar felt wind against his cheek, admittedly cold, but was more intrigued by where it might be coming from.

"I am fine," he replied, each word a frosted cloud. "Thank you, though." Dar eyed the largest troll and saw the sword, Ghaireuk, across his back. "It would be folly to try and take it by force."

Jahd gripped his arm. "There," she said and pointed to a man in black armor, hidden in the dark. "That one emanates great power but no life. He is a revenant."

Nomosch, Khaela told him, *once king of the titans – the first children of Veralnon. He was Ghaireuk's wielder and has come to reclaim my brother.*

What can he do with it? Dar asked the sword.

He can bring down this mountain all around us and survive.

"What shall we do?" Jahd's runes began to glow a soft white across the sheen of bright silver. "An open confrontation is not in our favor."

I can conceal us, Khaela said. *You would be able to sneak up on the wielder, freeze all in the area and wrest it from his grasp.*

What about Nomosch?

You must hurry.

The revenant moved through the cavern, obscured by enchanted shadow. For a creature long dead, he moved with great speed.

Dar willed himself to move, wanted to rush down the path and take the Emblem before Nomosch could reach it first. Something inside him screamed against it, sent a fear down his spine that froze him in place. Images of them being torn apart by angry trolls played out in his mind. Watching the revenant below them and trembling with the desire to act, Dar's body refused to move until it was already too late.

"It is too risky," he said, breathing heavy as if from some exertion. "They would easily overtake us if we drew attention to ourselves."

"That is wise," Jahd agreed. "However, we could risk drawing attention to the revenant."

With a wave of her hand, the shadows around the undead king slipped away. His armor began to glow in a radiant hue of gold, a beacon in the darkness for all to see. His fiery eyes turned upward, looked directly at them. Dar winced as if he could feel the creature's anger stab at his chest.

The cavern exploded in dark magic, sending cracks along the floor and shaking debris loose from the walls. Nomosch drew black fire to his hands and walked with grim purpose toward the wielder. The nearest trolls burst into flame, an ebon fire lined with emerald that shriveled their leathery flesh in great swaths. Screaming, they fell to their knees and died. The very air around the revenant seemed alive with hungry fire, lighting wood and hanging skins as he passed them, cracking stone huts and throwing wide the unwary.

As stone axes and swords were drawn, the blue trolls rushed in first. Ghostly spirits rose up from their tall frames, flexed transparent muscles and dove back into bodies now infused with shaman magic. The females in white continued to dance, jangling bone totems and augmenting the warriors. Spears flew through the air, striking the ground around Nomosch or bursting into flame before reaching him.

Weapons rang down on the revenant, clashing with fire and illusory armor. He sent black tendrils out to grab the necks of two, draining them of life in an instant. His fire ate at those around him, scorching their flesh to the bone. Each one fought without relent, until death overcame them, and was replaced by another fervent wave.

The wielder held Ghaireuk and charged among his brethren, unaffected by the ebon fire. He brought to bear the mithrinum blade, striking down with both hands in a mighty roar of challenge. Nomosch raised an arm to block the blow, and the limb fell away in a blast of pallid radiance. Bodies went flying in all directions, some dead, some gravely wounded. A pale fire ate at several gashes across the wielder's chest, and even Nomosch had been knocked back from the discharge of magic.

His illusion gone, the revenant scrambled to his feet as a skeletal nightmare. Rotted flesh clung to him, and the runes across each bone flared in a bloody light. He rushed forward and grabbed hold of Ghaireuk. The two of them struggled to wrest it free from one another, as stone weapons rained down on Nomosch from behind. The fires around him were fading, and the spirits that reached out from each warrior and attacked left scorch marks across his ancient bones.

As if winning a battle of wills, the troll pulled free the Emblem. Stone rose up and encased Nomosch's feet. A stalagmite shot up and sheathed his remaining hand. Unable to move, the revenant reared back his head and let out a cry of undead rage. The fire around him flared, but it struck against a barrier of blue light.

"Did you do that?" Dar asked.

Jahd smiled and watched on in silence.

The wielder motioned for everyone to move away. He swung and severed the other arm, ignoring the explosion that tore flesh from his forearms. He swung again and lopped off the revenant's head. Still the bones refused to fall. He looked more closely at the creature, heard a shout of advice from a shaman behind him, and nodded in understanding. He drove Ghaireuk straight through Nomosch's chest, piercing what had once been his heart. A breath of release filled the cavern.

A spirit stepped forward from the toppled bones, a cerulean phantom that stretched upward so high only its thick legs could be seen. With a hush of wind, the spirit vanished, and all trace of fire in the cavern went out in a final gust.

"He is dead," Dar said in disbelief. "I – I did not think they could be..." He looked at Jahd and put a hand to her shoulder. "That was good thinking. I am glad you came with me."

Jahd bowed her head. "I am honored you asked."

"I think it best we leave Ghaireuk here. If Markus is foolish enough to try again, he will only lose more of his precious revenants."

Ghaireuk is safe here, Khaela agreed.

Dar saw a nearby puddle and moved to kneel over it. He began trailing his fingers just above its surface, his mind reaching out for another Emblem. It occurred to him to contact Barr, to let him know what had just happened, and he sought him out through the scry. An image of him appeared, rippling across the water. He was still in Dwendorim, scrying in a fountain.

Barr?

Dar-Paj! It's good to hear from you. Despite the happy tone, Dar could see sadness hanging over his friend. *It's amazing how quickly you mastered the mists.*

You did so without a teacher, Dar pointed out. *I think Fluora, however, had much to do with my success.*

Not to mention how hard you practiced. I see you have Jahd with you. Barr smiled and looked away. *She'll keep you safe if she can.*

We found Ghaireuk, Dar explained, *but there must be close to a thousand trolls in this cavern.*

That's odd. A tribe's usually no more than fifty.

The revenant Nomosch appeared and tried to take it. He did not survive the attempt.

Barr nodded. *Good. Isdael and Kaidyn are dead as well.* Their eyes met, and Dar saw hope come over his friend – as if their success hinged upon fate or some other such nonsense. *We just might stop Markus after all.*

Dar did not smile. *I never had a doubt.*

Where will you go next?

Khaela said, *Muornay is hidden beneath a temple at the peak of Naerat Sanae. North Haven. His voice is distant, weak, but that location is closest to where we are.*

North Haven, Dar answered. *To find Muornay.*

Alright, good luck. Let me know if you need any help at all.

A frown darkened Dar's features. Though he knew Barr had meant well, the suggestion he might need help only angered him – and much more than it should have.

That will not be necessary, Dar said coolly.

He ended the scry without another word.

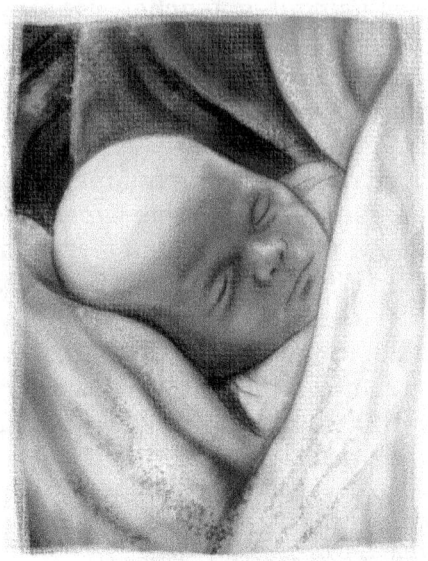

– 14 –

he scry ended abruptly. Though Barr could see subtle changes in his friend's demeanor, the short temper and growing obsession for vengeance, too much already weighed on his mind. Fluora had told him of her visions, of Revyn's building army and the fall of major cities one after another – one of which was still home to his uncle Therol. The sylvannis were in danger of subversion as well. If shapelings turned the council, each party would fall in short order. He thought of Tuvrin, his elven father, who had taken him in when a shapeling wolf had killed Daroth – his first adoptive father; and Seltruin, the old sage who had been both a friend and a mentor, who had taught him to weave as an Illumin Valar.

They were both members of the council.

Humans had somehow learned that elves yet lived and knew the location of Geilon-Rai, the sylvannis tree city in the heart of Darleman forest. If shapelings didn't kill off the sylvannis from within, the army marching toward them surely would. That soldiers from Alixhir were gathered at all meant the walled city had not yet fallen, and his uncle was safe. A small consolation but the only one Barr could see.

Dar seemed angry, Aren said.

Both he and Idelle had heard Fluora. The war hound walked over to the fountain and settled down upon his paws. Idelle flew far above, stretching her wings and deep in thought.

I just hope we're doing the right thing. Barr waved a hand over the water and called up an image of his uncle. White-haired and aged before his time, Therol sat at a wooden desk with a quill and blank parchment. A drop of ink marred the surface, though his hand remained steady. His eyes never strayed from the window, as if he too were looking out and sought Barr. *Part of me feels we should be fighting shapelings. What if searching for the Emblems is a waste of time?*

If it were, Idelle replied, *Markus wouldn't want them so badly.*

I know, still. Barr shook his head. *People are dying. Gathering the Emblems feels like the right thing to do. More than keep them from Revyn, I think we can use them to defeat him. There just has to be something else we can do!*

Do you mean kill him? Aren asked and looked up. *Can a god be killed?*

If he can't, I don't see much hope for those turned.

Idelle asked, *You think killing Revyn will cure his disease?*

I'm not so sure lycanthropy is a disease any more than the geas upon a demon hunter is. And if I'm right, killing Revyn will undo the curse. Barr ended the scry and clenched a fist. *Shapelings would be free, but those they'd fed upon and slaughtered would still be dead.*

There's just a handful of us. Idelle landed upon the statue at the center of the fountain. *As much as I want to, we can't save everyone.*

Aren got up and put his head on Barr's lap. Barr loosened his fist, let out a sigh and rubbed Aren behind an ear.

Ruffling her feathers, Idelle asked, *Why is Revyn the only god who seems to do anything? The elves worship Celene and others, but what have they ever done?*

Barr had nothing to say. There was a time when all the gods had walked among their children, cared for the worlds and life they had created. Those days were long gone now. If the other gods still existed, he saw no sign of their presence upon Taellus or any other world. They either slept or were gone – indifference seemed too cruel – which gave Barr hope that if Revyn could not be killed, the god could at least be imprisoned elsewhere.

Something deep inside him, however, no matter the logic or reasoning, told him all would be well once he gathered the twelve Emblems.

We have to warn my father, Barr said and stirred the water with his mind. His fingers trailed over the surface, trying to coax an image, but he couldn't see past the veil of wards over Geilon-Rai. In frustration, Barr broke off the attempt and slapped at the water. *I can't get through the wards. We have to go back. I can't scry into the city.*

You'll be killed! Idelle said, like a mother scolding her child. *Or did you forget you were exiled?*

I never forget. What else would you have me do?

I'll go, she replied. *You get back to finding Emblems, and I'll warn Seltruin. Just take me to the forest, and come back for me when you can.*

Alright. First things first.

Barr scried out Vereu and saw the Guardian Jakob in the courtyard of Faith's Spire. Jakob held the sword and barked orders at the knights and war priests that remained. Barr saw commander Vaumont and brother Dalwyn, and beyond them sprawled the bloodied and broken body of squire Jarvik.

Aren growled at the sight, mirroring Barr's anger.

They were through the mists and in front of Jakob in the span of a thought. Barr took hold of Vereu in one hand and crushed the man's throat with the side of his other fist. Jakob let go the sword and fell over, gasping for air that wouldn't come. The men Barr had fought beside all looked upon him with feral eyes. He heard their animal growls, felt the hatred and lust for blood building up inside them. Aren returned a growl of his own, daring one of them to move.

Barr said to commander Vaumont, "Sorry I let this happen."

In a swirl of mist, Barr brought Aren and Idelle into the shrine. They could see the cursed men through the open doors and stood waiting for them to follow after. Drawing sword or mace, each one cautiously stepped in, eyes trained upon Barr and the Emblem he had stolen. He waited until they were close before disappearing right before their eyes in a swirl of mist and returning to the courtyard with Aren and Idelle. Barr closed the doors and held them fast with a quick ward.

"Anything you can do to keep them in there?" he asked Vereu.

The sword said nothing in return, but shards of iron as thick as a man erupted from the stones and jutted at angles through the shrine. They had caught Aren off guard, and the hound jumped back with a yelp.

Barr heard chuckling in his thoughts.

"That should take them a while." Barr expanded his ward to encompass the entire shrine. "You alright?" he asked Aren.

Very funny. The hound glared at Vereu.

Idelle fought down the urge to laugh. *Don't be so sensitive, little brother. I'm sure it was unintentional.*

Who are you calling little?

The mists rose up once again, and Barr carried them to the northern outskirts of Darleman.

We'll be back in a few hours, he told Idelle, who had already taken wing toward the tree city. *Keep an eye out for Narohk.*

I'll be fine. You two stay out of trouble.

Barr slipped Vereu into his belt and called up the mists. He and Aren arrived at his uncle Therol's scribery in Alixhir. They stood just outside the door to the third floor, Therol's living quarters. Barr didn't want to startle him by just appearing right before him. Unnaturally aged by overuse of magic, Barr's uncle was a man some forty autumns that looked to be well into his seventies.

Barr knocked and opened the door. "Uncle?"

"Barr? Is that you?" Therol turned in his chair and put down his wire glasses. Barr wondered if they were still missing lenses. "It is you!" Therol hobbled across the rug, where a water stain marred its center, and hugged his nephew for all he was worth. He stepped back and gave a shrewd look at Aren. "I don't see my apprentice. Did you feed him to your horse?"

Aren narrowed his eyes and gave a single bark.

"Don't take that tone with me!" Therol scolded and wagged a finger. Aren whimpered and turned away. "Now that's more like it. And you," he said to Barr, poking him in the chest. "Tell me everything, but start with how you got Dar-Paj killed."

Barr rolled his eyes and brought them all through the mists, to a bedroom in his home in Dwendorim. Therol swooned as they arrived. Barr helped to steady him and sat his uncle down on the feather bed. Aren left the room, his feelings hurt, and went outside to sulk.

"I don't have time for a talk," Barr said, "but soon. I promise. You'll be safe here."

Hanar entered the doorway. "Shall I arrange for a Protector to come see to your new friend?"

"Saernol's wards!" Therol's eyes grew wide, and his hand was reaching out across the bed, as if searching for his cane. "That statue's alive!" He took off his sandal and jumped up before Barr. "Get behind me! I'll hold her off while you climb out that window!"

"Uncle Therol," Barr said, and gently put down the arm holding him back, "this is Hanar, a very good friend of mine. She's a Protector, a golem, sworn to keep safe the people who once lived in this city."

With a bow of her head, Hanar said, "It is a pleasure to meet a relative of the Master. Is my honor to welcome you to Dwendorim."

"I know that name..." Therol said, shaking his dirty sandal, lost in recollection.

"Please put that back on." Barr sat his uncle down on the bed again. "Your apprentice is fine. Hanar will try to answer any questions you have, but right now I have something very important to take care of. Will you be alright?"

"Of course," his uncle said with a wave of his sandal. "Why wouldn't I? This is the best dream I've had in two years! I could tell you about my last one..."

"Maybe later." Barr smiled and gave his uncle a pat on the shoulder. "We'll talk soon." He gave a sympathetic look to Hanar and said, "Good luck."

I thought I liked him, Aren said, *but I changed my mind.*

Barr left the house and started walking toward the fountain. He felt the urgent need to be out looking for more Emblems. The longer it took to find them, even if just to keep them from Markus, the more people died or were turned by Revyn's plague.

I think my uncle's a bit senile. You just startled him is all. Barr looked back and saw Aren on his side beneath a tree. *Quit brooding and go get yourself some lunch. We'll be leaving soon enough.*

He better not be coming with us.

Barr snorted a laugh and sat down at the fountain's edge. He focused on the water, conjuring in his mind an image of Markus, still hoping to catch the thief off guard. Nothing but cloud and murky dark appeared across the ripples. Neither were there wards or painful stabs to fend him off. Confused, Barr sharpened the image, picturing every painstaking detail he could recall from their last encounter. Still nothing. Either Markus was dead, or his protective wards far exceeded Barr's ability.

Or his appearance had changed...

Relaxing the image to a blurred memory, focused more on feeling than visual accuracy, Barr reached out through the scry and found him. Markus came into view, a shocking contrast to the young man he once was. His dark hair was receding, shot through with wiry streaks of dull silver. His skin sagged beneath the chin, with deep wrinkles that lined his mouth and brow. Sunken cheeks gave him a gaunt look, one both aged and in poor health. Dressed in black, hunkered down, his thief's clothing did little to hide his new frailty.

He's aged, Barr said, *like my uncle.*

When Markus posed as Ealdan, the actor-thief, he claimed to have no *furie* or knowledge of weaving. Yet one more lie among many, as evidenced by the changes. He had either abused magic, eating away his own *furie*, or something else...

The thought trailed off, as Barr considered recent events. By his count, three revenants were now dead – or rather set free from undeath. What if their destruction had effected the change in Markus? Barr was familiar with the notion. A master of the Art could live on after death, as a lich, by binding the spirit to an inanimate object. The jade monks of Tanakara bound their spirits to animals, creating a symbiotic relationship for life. Could Markus have found a way to bind his spirit with the revenants? More likely, it would have been Revyn's doing.

Only one way to find out, Aren suggested. *Kill more revenants.*

What about the other way around? Barr asked, eyeing the image of Markus. *Kill him, and we might destroy all the revenants.*

Five others were with him, dressed in similar garb, faces hidden and painted black. A red sash tied at the waist marked them as Crimson Order. They were in a forest outside a large settlement.

A heavy wall of steel-reinforced timber circled the collection of longhouses. The standing guard, outside and on the wall, as well as others beyond the gates were minotaurs, creatures both human and bovine. They stood half again as tall as a man, walked on two legs, had cloven hoofs and a tail. Born and bred to war, their upper bodies were corded with thick muscle. Barr knew from memory they possessed enormous strength. Their bull-like heads sported horns three feet long, some sharpened to points and capped with steel, while others were blunted for ramming. Nose rings varied in shape, size and material, denoting rank within the clan as much as the herald brands burned into their furry flesh by shamans.

Daumon, Barr said, recalling the people so much like human southmen of the tundra. *That's Elenthor. How did he get so far northwest? That's at least twenty days from Noria by horse.*

Maybe Revyn transports him around, like the mists? Aren bit into a fresh catch, and the taste soured Barr's mouth. *Sorry, I thought you like fish.*

When it's cooked, yes. Barr watched the six of them sneak toward the back of the settlement.

My brother, Vereu said. *Uinbro.*

As if sunlight warmed his cheek, Barr could feel the Emblem inside the Great House. Centrally located, it was by far largest of the eight longhouses. It could have sheltered two hundred warriors. Home to the clan's Warlord, the mightiest among them, every warrior would feast at his table. Unlike the kheos, their fanatical brethren that lived in stone cities and temples further north, the daumon were born to the axe and battle hymns. If Uinbro was inside the Great House, there was only one way for Markus to acquire it.

He's going to steal it. Barr ended the scry and rushed back toward home. *Let's go, Aren, we may not have much time.*

*   *   *

Hanar met Barr outside. "Fluora said you have need of me?"

"Yes, we need to leave. Now."

Aren ran up as the mists enveloped them all. They passed through starry night and into the trees outside Elenthor. Barr could no longer see Markus or the other thieves from the Crimson Order.

"They must already be inside," he said, looking to the gates far off in the distance. "Will you stay here with Aren? I'm going to use illusion to sneak into the Great House. If I can catch Markus in the act, I'll just let the minotaurs deal with him."

"As you wish," Hanar said. To Aren she added, "You could do with a bath. You have been spending far too much time catching fish at the pond."

She can smell? Aren asked in surprise.

"Of course she can smell," Barr replied aloud for her benefit and chuckled. "The only sense they don't have is taste, for obvious reasons."

"We often cared for children," she explained to Aren. "A sense of smell is essential for that task alone, yet –"

"I'll tell Aren if I need help," he interrupted and left them to each other's company.

I liked her better when she was quiet.

You're just worried about Idelle, Barr said. *I am too.*

The air around Barr shimmered as he walked, and the image of a daumon warrior imposed itself over him. Its eyes were so far above his, he found himself looking through the transparent haze of chiseled middle covered with soft fur and a broad leather girdle. His armor was a mix of steel chain and boiled leather, with two double-bladed axes at his back. Relying on memory, his brands were that of a veteran Conqueror, a clanless warrior that hired out for honor and lodging.

Both guards at the gate gave a salute, banging the haft of their great axes against the ground and touching them to chest in a swift motion. Barr stopped and bowed his horns in a show of respect. As was the custom, he waited patiently for one of them to speak.

"We've not seen a Conqueror for many weeks," one said, appraising Barr and finding approval. "You will find Warlord Jhorgan Skullcrusher, of the Gold Horn clan, seated in the Great House. He'll be anxious to hear your tales."

The guard had told him all he needed to know, with a subtle hint that he should not wander without seeing their Warlord first.

Barr nodded smartly. "You have my thanks. Honor to your clan."

"Glory to your battles."

He walked past the gate and headed to the center of the settlement. Young taurs went about the menial tasks of daily life, gathering water, cleaning fresh kills, beating dust from hide rugs, all while keeping a watchful eye on the children at play. Barr knew once chores were done, those budding warriors would spend the remainder of day's light training until they'd earned a meal and sleep. One led a black strider past him, toward crafters carving baskets and fletching arrows. Horses even larger than Noria's famous warhorses, striders were bred for the sole purpose of carrying armored taurs into battle.

Barr approached the Great House, a wide longhouse of thick spruce reinforced with steel bands and stone pilings at steady intervals. The entry was massive, with heavy doors three times the height of a daumon. Smoke filtered out from a sloped hood on the thatched roof. He could hear pipes and drum beneath boisterous laughter, the banging of cups and cheers from midday meal.

Out of the corner of his eye, he caught sight of a dark shape slipping behind the building. He quickened his pace and pushed open the double doors.

Brother! Vereu said, flushing Barr with exultation.

The pull of Uinbro was strong, as he stood waiting to be acknowledged by the Warlord. Barr scanned the hall, past the five long tables where flagons of honey mead, breads, meats and cheeses fed dozens of lively warriors. They drank deep, ate hearty and tested each other's prowess in contests of strength and agility. Two wrestled to his left, hoofs firmly planted, using both hands to pull or push the other off balance. Another pair stood atop two rows of wooden barrels, and at a signal raced from one end to the other. One of them fell halfway, eliciting consolation from the crowd, and was soon handed a flagon which he raised to the woman who had bested him.

At the far end, where a veteran clansman spun a tale illustrated by scars on his arms and chest, Barr saw Uinbro hanging on the wall. Hidden in shadow, beyond the light of the double hearth, the Emblem was shaped as a great helm. Poorly suited to a minotaur, it would have never been worn in battle but hung as a treasure that bolstered clan fortune and glory.

At the head of the central table sat the Warlord. No larger than any other, he was a grizzled minotaur with shrewd eyes that surveyed all around him, even now while in drink. He had seen many battles, judging by the array of scars and herald brands. Though his fur was graying, his body looked strong as a young taur. His horns were mottled black, capped in polished steel and tips of gold. That neither was broken said much of his prowess, as most veterans had lost one or both by the time their fur grayed.

Jhorgan caught and held Barr's gaze, studying him from afar. Drums beat out the rhythm of a warrior's tale, accentuated by pipes and booming laughter. Rising up from within him as a gathering dark, memory of times long past washed over. Stirred by the regaling, Barr felt his senses dull and fade away, replaced by...

... an arrow in his shoulder. Fantar Fireheart roared with delight, the song of battle in his throat and the fate of enemies in the haft of his axe. The second son of Warlord Kharn, he was a proud daumon that took to the field with the same vigor he brought to his bed. It mattered little that they fought over a stretch of marsh neither clan used, or that shamans augured a terrible loss for that morn. What mattered was the thrill of cleaving horn and bone, driving a mailed fist through helm and teeth. He fought for honor and glory, because his Warlord had called, and Fantar answered that call with every...

...muscle in his body ached from wounds and days of battle without rest. There was too much to be done, and far too few for the doing. Rhok the Cleaver, they called him, but this day his axe lay quiet. Placing brother and friend upon the pyre, he said a silent prayer for the fallen that would be sent to the Great Lands with honor. Their armor and axe went with them, among treasures gained throughout their lives, floating down the river as flames licked ever higher...

...up her staff, crackling with blue furie against the darkness of early morn. Growling, she slammed a bone totem into the ground, sending a wave of cerulean flames out before her. Lenae Firecaller, High Shaman of the Blue Rivers clan, gave the enemy more than steel and horns to fear that day. Stomping her hoof and shaking her spirit-

caller, *Lenae fed the totem furie and sent wave after wave of pulsing fire across the trench. The few who managed to make it to her were cut down...*

...by the rolling trees and jutting spikes pegged into them. Some managed to jump the oncoming massacre, but most fell prey to the well-timed tactic. A cheer went up across the line, and a song filled Enthar's ears with the sweet sound of victory and the promise of mead...

... before battle. Naera fastened the horn at her belt and nudged Baleful on with her thighs. Clansmen beside her as she rode, the bloodlust rose up and came loose in a feral cry. She fired six arrows before the enemy closed, slipped the bow over her saddle and drew both axes from her waist. The first was too eager, leaned in as he rode and caught the edge of her axe against a shoulder for his error. A scar to mark the battle, should he survive. Naera turned in her saddle and blocked...

... the attack with a forearm. The assassin's dagger nicked an ear, as it drove deep into the bedding. Bhorok grabbed the human by the throat and crushed the life from him. He tossed aside the refuse, nostrils flared in growing rage, when the dizziness came upon him. He dropped to his knees and lost the contents of his stomach. The attempt on his life was not a failure after all...

Barr snapped awake from the visions, but they clung to his mind like tangled blankets pulling him back down to sleep. His eyes focused and widened, saw two humans in the shadows of a cellar stairwell. Outraged that any but a blooded warrior would set foot in the Great House, he drew both illusory axes from his back and raised them in a cry of challenge.

"Intruders!" he shouted at them in the daumon tongue and charged.

Other taurs dropped their mugs in haste and moved with battle-hardened speed toward the humans. Barr was there first, leaping tables and shouldering past all in his path. Dressed in black from head to toe, the two had drawn knives and crouched to attack. Barr avoided their blades, wary of poison, and drove his axes into either shoulder of the closest man. He pulled them free, spun low and took the other down with his full weight behind an elbow to the middle. Barr had disabled them both as a handful of daumon rushed to his side. They subdued and carried the humans off to be questioned.

Neither of them was Markus.

"You have my thanks," the Warlord said in a thick accent, standing at Barr's shoulder.

Barr bowed his horns in respect. "It was only by luck that I saw them first."

"Saw them first and charged passed a dozen others." The shrewd eyes softened to friendly mirth, and Warlord Jhorgan Skullcrusher gave a hearty laugh. He clapped Barr on the shoulder and almost toppled him over. The illusion, however, never moved. "What are you called?"

"Bhorok Stonefist," he replied without thought, the memories still upon him.

"Some drink for our new guest!"

"You should search for others," Barr said. "Such an attempt in midday would be foolish without diversion."

Jhorgan nodded, and a handful left to go search.

A flagon was handed to Barr. Jhorgan led him to the center table and took a seat at its head. He motioned for Barr to sit on his left. The other daumon resumed eating and sharing tales over drink, as if nothing untoward had happened.

"Honor demands I grant a boon," the Warlord said so all could hear. "Any woman or treasure, that is mine to give, shall be yours for the asking."

Barr looked about the room at the female warriors. Those with no bond had stood. One raised her mug to him, licking at the foam of her ale with a devilish glint in her eye. Men chuckled at the gesture, as if they knew well her fire. An image of Fluora came to mind, her red hair across the grass, lips soft against his and tasting of strawberries. Any residue of daumon mannerisms the visions had left behind fell away beneath the warmth of her remembered touch.

"Perhaps that?" Barr asked and indicated the plate helm hidden in shadow. "I will one day bond but have no treasure of my own. If tomorrow I traveled to the Great Lands, I would have no riches to carry upon my pyre."

"So be it," Jhorgan agreed. He motioned for the helm to be brought over. "Let this then be the first of your treasures. May it keep you in the afterlife!"

Barr took the helm and bowed again, in thanks and respect. "Honor to your clan."

"Glory to your battles."

A cheer went up across the hall, as every daumon raised a mug and drank to his honor.

Well played, said a young man now seated beside Barr.

He looked like a faeron, though taller and with ears that sloped further back. Sable hair fell over his slender shoulders, ringed with silver bands on either side, with the center strands bound into an intricate knot. His eyes were fully blue, a glowing bright blue that spoke of *furie*. His body fluctuated in the light, became transparent as if illusion.

Uinbro? Barr asked.

Who are you talking to? Aren was growing impatient. *And how much longer do I have to wait out here?*

The man bowed his head. *You might want to look away. No one else can see me, and you are beginning to draw attention.*

I have the Emblem, Barr told Aren. *Two of the thieves were caught, but Markus wasn't with them. Did you see anyone come out of the settlement?*

Barr looked back to the Warlord. "Could I trouble you for a place to rest?"

Not through the front gate.

"Of course," Jhorgan replied. "The house nearest the gate is open to you for as long as you should need it."

A warrior returned from outside. "Three more were found and taken to the others. One of them was about to burn all our oil."

With Uinbro under one arm, Barr stood and bowed. He waited for Jhorgan's nod before taking his leave. He headed outside and saw the men tied to a rack where pigs were normally gutted.

All five of them wore red sashes.

Barr went into the longhouse Jhorgan had indicated. When he was alone, he summoned the mists and was back outside with Hanar and Aren. He cancelled the illusion, willed Uinbro to become a sword, and secured it to his belt.

"Markus got away," Barr said and knelt, conjuring a pool of water to scry. "Their attempt might have worked, but it makes no sense. Why not wait until dark? He didn't even have any of his revenants with him."

"This Markus grows desperate," Hanar said.

Balaen is not far from this place, Uinbro said, again in his illusory form. Barr focused on the scry. *To the east, in the Forsaken Forest. The elves of Karon-Rai have her, though they know not what she is.*

The wyndorrin? That could be a problem.

Aren snorted and gave a look that clearly stated his feelings on being left out of the conversation.

Try as he might, Barr was unable to find Markus. It irritated him to no end. He had little enough trouble an hour ago, and now it was as if Markus was gone from the face of Taellus or warded so strongly that Barr could not even see the protection runes. He slapped at the water, and it faded back into the soil.

"I can't find him."

Hanar looked up at the fading sun. "We have a few more hours before nightfall. Shall we return home and rest?"

"No." Barr sighed at Uinbro's image. "Idelle's waiting for us at Darleman, and there's another Emblem in that forest." He nodded to the tall trees a two day ride from where they stood. Even from this distance, he could see a massive, single tree jutting up from the forest's center. "It's in Karon-Rai," he said to Aren. "Let's hope their Narohk don't try to kill us before we can speak."

Mist rose up all around them.

*   *   *

Markus cursed his luck and the five imbeciles he had hired. Desperation had made him careless, but at least he had had the foresight to wait out in the forest. He blamed Revyn for his anxiety, for the frustration and urgency that plagued him. He squelched the thought in an instant. That he had allowed it at all was a sign of his deteriorating mental grip. A slip noticed by Revyn would mean his life. He unclenched both fists and reined his anger in to a dull seething.

With three of his Brood unmade, his life was literally passing before his eyes. Now he would either have to go back for Uinbro himself or send one of the others for it. Of the remaining revenants, only three carried Emblems, and only *two* were even searching for more! The others were off amassing armies and turning the world into a shapeling graveyard. When none were left to turn, what then? Lycanthropy left its host infertile. They would be forced to feed on animals, and when those were all extinct, each other. Markus would rule at the right hand of Revyn, over a world dying from greed and starvation.

Wondering why he was not dead, struck down where he stood by a god's wrath, Markus stepped from the ancient ring of tall stones and into the snow. Magic filled the air, buzzed in his ears and set the hair on his arms to standing. The earth around the stones was free of snow and ice. Dark soil gripped tight the gray slabs, and the circle it formed was lined with yellow sprigs and white mushrooms. In the center was a collage of colored rocks, chipped to fit like puzzle pieces into a symbol that had long since lost all meaning.

Snow crunching underfoot, Markus headed toward the shard of glacial ice just ahead. It jutted up from the canopy of white, oblivious to wind that stole warmth in its grasp. Humans knew this place as Astoria, but in the time of the illuminaire it had been called Suncrest. The flowers that had once gone on for days had long given way to crushing ice and frozen winds. Magic had once flourished here, saturated the soil with its touch, birthed hundreds of plants and animals never before seen on the face of Taellus. Now a wasteland of withering cold, only the harshest of life still managed to exist here.

As he plodded through snow up to his knees, toward the tomb of dense ice where Luorn was buried, Markus sent his thoughts out to his Brood. Dressed in a black cotton tunic and trousers, determination was all that kept the cold at bay.

How close to Muornay? he asked Lochlaen, the once king of the ankara.

Very close. The revenant's voice was colder than the damn snow in his shoes. *I may need to destroy the golem to claim it.*

Good. I grow tired of these schemes. He drew *furie* from Faelsha, through his link with Solastin, and it warmed him until the snow began to steam. *We could have had all twelve by now, if our efforts were focused. In fact, take Khaela as well. I think it time to pull tight that one's leash.*

It will be done.

How soon will your army reach Drakanon? he asked Solastin.

The dwarven city will be under siege in three days. It was fitting that a child of Celene would lead the army that crushed those she had foolishly tried to protect. *It will fall in less than another.*

Markus reached the glacier, where the jagged tip had torn through rock and earth. It had a blue cast to the frost he had not expected. Inside the clear ice were tiny bubbles, thousands of them, and deep within its grasp he could sense Luorn calling.

My army will reach the rallan nation in two days. It was Feraesk, his voice hollow and grating. With Aislin in hand, he had been able to muster and unite thirty-seven different tribes into a sizeable horde of unturned. Most were mountain orcs from the northern steppes, but a good portion of the army were goblins come up from the Ember and Ashwyn mines. *If the nagas cannot be turned, they will be driven from existence.*

With a throwing knife, Markus began chipping at the glacial ice. The warmth he stole from Drakha caused ice nearest to his hand to melt, but he had a long way to go to reach the sword.

What of the Warmasters?

All have been bitten, Dhalak answered, *and will soon fully turn. The Brethren are on their way into the desert. They should reach the first dervish province by nightfall.*

And you? Markus could feel the revenant crossing a rocky and arid landscape.

I am headed west to Sun Hold. Once a dragon, his disdain for running was a palpable force. Dhalak longed to be in the air, but his prison would not allow it. *If the gnomes are not protected, I will begin subverting the city.*

If not, leave immediately. I need more of you to help reclaim Emblems. Markus cut his hand against the ice and swore. It was a small cut, but sight of his own blood made him angry, a reminder he should not be the one digging. Gritting his teeth, he pressed on. He asked Wyllnuor, *Have you retrieved Caorynor from the ankaran ruins yet?*

I have not. A few moments passed, and it seemed as if the revenant would say no more. *Glimmerkin occupy the ruins. It will take some time to claim the sword, lest I meet the same fate as Nomosch.*

Something in his tone told Markus the once king of the illuminaire would welcome such a release. The bond between them would not allow it, but the thought ate at his resolve, nagged at the back of his mind. Markus had no power of his own, nothing to command but unwilling servants.

Caeryk interrupted his thoughts. *I have destroyed all the ley stones at Silver Downs, but the sankragga still will not turn.*

The same is true of the krevallan, Khalydaos intoned, in a voice that stung like reddened burns from the sun. *Every ley stone at Ironfall has been crushed, but the raugrin descendents remain unchanged.*

Markus sighed, waiting for the headache sure to come. When Revyn did not bellow in his mind, he began to wonder what occupied the god.

Both of you focus on reclaiming Emblems, he told them. *What cannot be turned, we will enlist or conquer.* He was getting closer to the sword. It was so deep inside the ice he was forced to reach his arm passed the elbow to keep digging. *Have you found your old home yet?* he asked Trafaelos.

I have, the revenant replied, his voice echoing sorrow from the crushing black of ocean floor. *The last of the daefarim still sleep in their crystal cocoons. Kierna has either forgotten them or is still unable to cure Revyn's failed attempt to turn them.*

Just think, Markus said, *had you not been king, you would be in one of those cocoons right now, instead of setting them free.* The inkling of hatred almost caused him to chuckle. He knew there was no freedom in what came next. *Get on with it.*

He chipped away the ice around the mithrinum grip, finally able to touch a finger to the Emblem. He focused his will upon Luorn, called up its powers and the ice began to melt.

Ombreusk? Markus asked, eyes closed and smiling in triumph. *Have you finished forging a new army?*

We are headed to the portal, he replied, *though from the far side of Danarriden. They will be ready when the Arch Demon turns.*

Splendid! Markus cried and pulled Luorn from the ice. *I believe I have a gift for you, Trafaelos.*

He turned and faced three elves, though unlike any he had ever seen before. Two were barely covered by cloth embroidered in crystals and seashells, and both of them carried long staves carved of a single bone. The other wore emerald scale armor over her chest and loins and carried a trident forged of the same metal as her armor. All three were female, with opalescent skin that shimmered beneath the wintry sun. Blood-red runic tattoos ran the length of their bodies, from crystal circlet to webbed feet. He could see silvery blue scales on either side of their necks and up each arm, ending in webbed fingers as well. Their hair, long and bright, was tied back and a stark contrast to their skin. One's was ocean blue, another coral red and the last a sea green.

Though somewhat attractive, for elves, they had a stern demeanor that put Markus on his guard. His grip on Luorn tightened, and he felt its magic at his disposal. He gave a disarming smile, a charming remark upon his lips, but before he could speak, the one with a trident rushed forward and punched him with such speed and strength that he scarcely had time to realize he had been struck.

The sky fell forward, icy blue gone to black.

*   *   *

Eanid was one of the oldest among them, one of the first to be shaped. Her runes were not as sophisticated, not as elegant, as the thousands given life after her. The needs and expectations had been simpler then, but over time more and more had been required of them. Still, her runes had served their purpose. The Oath had remained unchanged, and never once had she failed it.

She loved and cared for all her brothers and sisters but had no mate to speak of. Far from unintelligent, her thoughts were just not as interesting as the others'. Or so it seemed to her. She could listen to them for days on end. They had slept for so long, she had no use for rest now.

When the protectorate had begun speaking of a plan and a volunteer had been called for, it was Eanid who answered first. She considered herself a logical choice for such a dangerous undertaking. She had far less to risk. With so many questions unanswered, there was no telling what might happen when the runes were shaped away.

Would she die? *Could* she die? If she was Eanid no more, what difference would that be from destruction? She supposed she would still serve the protectorate, an empty slate to create new life upon. The memories she had garnered over the centuries would still be housed in their collective minds. She just would not be able to feel them anymore.

There was no certainty her new runes would even activate. The decision to shape a rune crafter first had already been made. If successful, Eanid would store not only all the knowledge of rune crafting Master Barr had shared with them, but every bit of knowledge stored in the Academy archives as well.

She would be the first among them to specialize in a craft, forsaking her instruction runes and all her power as a Protector. Worse still, she was forced to make a terrible choice, to preserve the knowledge of the Masters or continue to serve the Oath. There was simply no room for both. With the placement of every new rune plotted out by the combined efforts and understanding of the protectorate, not a hair's length of space would be wasted. Even the soles of her feet would bear runes. Each one half the size of a thumbnail, the runes were already as small as they could be.

Eanid had chosen knowledge in the hopes that her sacrifice would better the protectorate. With any luck, once completed, she might find a way to improve upon the runic design, so that her brothers and sisters would not be faced with the same choice. She would rune craft the remaining volunteers: enchanters, shapers, silversmiths, travelers, every craft learned from Master Barr and the archives. At least one golem per craft had been chosen, and more had decided to join them.

Many, however, had not.

Forsaking the Oath meant more than giving up her life as a Protector. It meant losing her place within the protectorate. Her mind would no longer be linked to those she loved. An individual, she would forever be alone with her thoughts. In truth, the notion frightened her. That which gave her the most joy would be gone, replaced by the isolation of her own mind. Despite the trepidation, it was a sacrifice she was willing to make for her people.

Are you ready, Eanid? Anara asked.

The others were quiet, an unsettling feeling. She could only manage a nod and closed her eyes.

Eanid felt warmth, and then her silver began to melt, slipping from her body like a baby sheds its blanket before a bath. She focused on the smile, the delighted cry of Rosella. Memories of her first ward came flooding back. What a joy the child had been, a baby girl of such beauty and happiness and unconditional love it filled Eanid with the pangs of affectionate loss.

She felt fingers upon her, smoothing her skin, and the world behind her eyes slipped away into light. Their voices had returned, and she reveled in their thoughts.

Floating among them, buoyed by their spirits, she was loved and in return loved them all the more. Memories floated with her, clung to her like a corona of golden light. Each one played out at her whim, as if she lived her life in happy moments, scenes captured in vivid detail that could be played and replayed again.

The disparity became apparent, how her life at first was not how she remembered it. When she looked back on it now, it warmed her with joy, but the living of it had been devoid of feeling. How could that be? The past was an absolute, what had occurred was not malleable. What she felt was not from the memory itself but from what it evoked inside her. What then had changed, that she should be so different from the first time her eyes had opened?

At some point in her life, Eanid had become more than her instruction runes. Her name had become a person. Her body had become a vessel. If her body was not Eanid, then what was? If her thoughts cannot exist without a mind to give them voice, could her mind then exist without a body to give it life?

There was no measuring time in this place. She had lived out her life many times, revisiting each memory as if it happened for the first time. It felt like an eternity had passed before a voice broke through her reverie.

"Can you hear me?" it said aloud, feminine, lovely, grating.

Eyes opened and blinked. Bright light stung with its intensity. A face loomed in front, eyes glowing and wide, worry written on the brow. Not a sound could be heard, a deafening silence that filled the world with empty air. Surrounded by faces yet alone. The sorrow descended, a crushing weight of fear and inescapable despair.

Eanid began to sob uncontrollably.

– 15 –

hey arrived in Darleman, as the bloodied orange haze of setting day touched across the treetops. Columns of black rose up through the trees in the east and west, marring the sky with signs of fire. Barr could hear the shouts of battle as Idelle flew over the carnage, clanging steel against armor, the bestial roars from the throats of war hounds and bears. What the sylvannis lacked in numbers, they made up in ferocity and combat prowess. Hampered by dense trees, alixhiran soldiers had given up their mounts and pressed forward on foot, claiming tapered ears from the fallen, setting fires by oiled arrows, killing an enemy they had thought were extinct.

Why are there fires in the east? Barr asked Idelle.

307

She was flying toward them, far above the trees. *Set by the orc tribe we saw at deila falls. They're aligned with the shapelings. I saw huge wolves and boars standing with them at the eastern road.*

Boars? Aren asked, his interest piqued and stomach rumbling.

That means they're all turned, Barr said. *But why block the eastern road? That makes no sense, unless...*

You wouldn't want to eat these boars, Idelle warned her brother. *I doubt even you could stand the taste, by the smell of them.* She asked Barr, *Unless what?*

The shamarrin.

Idelle landed and ruffled her feathers. *You think they'd come up from Tehkon-Rai to assist?*

I do, Barr replied, *and it's almost nightfall. The orcs and humans wouldn't stand a chance.*

"Will we be joining the battle?" Hanar asked.

Balaen is more important, Uinbro said, standing beside Barr once again. *You could stop this war, but you cannot save the elves from being turned.*

Barr sighed. "No. Both Alixhir and Geilon-Rai were once my homes. I don't think I could bring myself to hurt anyone from either side, and the Narohk would probably shoot us on sight."

"What of the other elves," she asked, "The ones in Karon-Rai? We could alert them and hope they can get here in time."

Were you able to warn Seltruin? Barr hoped the old sage might turn the tide of battle in the elves' favor. At least until the shamarrin could arrive from Undersea.

I couldn't find him, Idelle said, her eyes downcast. *I looked everywhere. I'm sorry.*

"Karon-Rai it is then."

Barr knew better than to try and scry inside the tree city. It was warded the same as Geilon-Rai.

Instead, he conjured a pool of water and scried the forest around it. They would have to approach on foot, which meant an inevitable encounter with their Narohk.

Hanar suddenly dropped to both knees, streams of golden *furie* slipping down both cheeks.

"Are you alright?" Barr asked and knelt beside her. "Why are you crying? What's happened?"

"Something wonderful," she said, smiling as tears of joy fell to the snow and melted through.

She seemed unable or unwilling to say more. After a moment, she stood and wiped her eyes. Hanar nodded to Barr in readiness, still smiling at whatever *wonderful* thing had happened.

What's that all about? Aren eyed the golem. *Why won't she say?*

Respect her privacy, Idelle said. *She'll tell us when she's ready.*

Whatever it is, Barr said, calling up the mists, *at least it isn't bad news.*

They arrived in the Forsaken Forest, what the elves called Tarrandor – *one life* in the old tongue. They stood upon a Maurdon hunting trail, where tree markings told of a nearby stream and a bear den to the east. Most trees were broad at the trunk, wide enough for ten men to circle them touching hands together. There were smaller trees, sprouting up between their tall brethren in what little space could be found. Brush, forest flowers and mushrooms filled the rest, though winter held them all in its grasp. Snow and icy brown leaves littered the forest floor. Barr could see no sign of elven hunters along the path.

He led them toward Karon-Rai, where the boughs of an enormous tree loomed over the forest. Unlike the bare limbs interwoven overhead, thwarting the sun's attempt to breach the treetops, this one stubbornly held onto its leaves. Fading green and golden orange, with tarnished yellow in the mix, it had the look of spring and summer in a quarrel.

Only minutes had passed before Hanar held up a hand in warning. "I sense others in the trees ahead," she said in low tones, "moving quickly toward us."

They stood patiently waiting. Barr scanned the trees overhead, with Idelle far above. He could see no one on the branches, crouched and looking down, but felt their stares upon him.

"I have come to see Teldein," Barr shouted up at the trees in elven, "Speaker of the Stars."

An arrow sunk into the ground near his foot.

"I am sage Barr Shintae," he continued, unshaken by the warning, "of the Illumin Valar. Geilon-Rai has need of your assistance."

A wyndorrin leapt down from a tree ahead and to their left, a fall of at least thirty paces. His ironwood bow slung over a shoulder, he eyed Barr with open disdain. Others dropped down, effectively circling them.

The elves were shorter than the sylvannis but still taller than Barr. With long tapered ears and wild dark hair strewn with broad leaves and braided feathers, the wyndorrin were outwardly different than their brethren in more ways than mere appearance. Their demeanor was almost feral, as if they had more in common with the animals than the elves of Geilon-Rai. They didn't wear much, strips of leather and dark hide, but elves never did much feel the cold. They were painted head to bare feet in a berry dye that blended them with the forest. Earthen browns, clay reds, moss greens and ashen lines hid their features from the pale light.

Shapelings, Aren said and fought down the urge to growl. *I can smell them!*

"You were exiled," the first elf said, his voice severe and cold as the winter wind.

Aren sniffed the air and narrowed his eyes. *He's one of them. There's three more around us.*

"I was." Barr met his gaze without flinching. "I risk much by coming here, but Geilon-Rai is under attack. Soldiers from Alixhir –"

"We already know of the humans," the Narohk said. A female, her bow drawn, approached and whispered in his ear. "And how do you suppose humans learned elves yet live, so shortly after your exile?"

"Not by my doing."

Are they going to attack us? Aren asked. His hackles rose, and he looked for the one most likely to strike first.

"Be that as it may, we sent aid days ago. They will arrive shortly."

That or try to keep us from Karon-Rai, Barr said. "How could you have known –"

"That does not concern you," the Narohk replied in an even tone that suggested Barr was no longer privy to the affairs of elven nations. "If that is all you came to say?"

The female whispered to him again, more urgently. He turned to regard her, angered by her insistence.

"There is another threat," Barr replied, "one that may affect you as well. Shapelings have infiltrated Geilon-Rai, intent on turning the council."

"Ridiculous."

Barr, Idelle warned, *the one behind and to your left.*

He could feel the tension, heard the muscles in the elf's arms tighten upon bow and string.

"It's the truth," Barr told him, sorrow in his voice. He feared the worst for his father and Seltruin. "Revyn is overthrowing the elven nations from within. He converts all with his disease, with his *filthy* plague –"

The arrow fired and stopped in air a scant inch from Barr's head. Barr turned and looked at the elf who had fired it, saw the flash of beryl in his eyes. The arrow's shaft reddened to ember, and the whole fell away as ash upon the wind.

"There is your proof," Barr said.

Two grabbed the elf by either arm, but he easily threw them off. He dropped to all fours, skin rippling and bones crackling beneath. His scream turned to a roar, as the largest bear any of them had ever seen now stood before them. Two more changed as well, both wolves, as the Narohk who had been speaking sighed at the display and transformed into a boar. He swatted at the female by his side and sent her sprawling through the snow. With rage-reddened eyes, he squealed and charged Barr. The other three shapelings attacked their once kin.

Barr drew both kyan in an instant.

Bad form! Uinbro complained and crossed his arms. *My brother and I are better than those!*

Vereu chuckled and impaled the frothing boar with a sudden eruption of iron spikes the length of a man. Held stationary, lifted in the air, its dying body twitched in shock. Bloodied metal then receded back into the frozen earth. The ravaged boar carcass left behind became an elf once again.

Uinbro winced. *Well, there will be no questioning that one, I am afraid.*

Aren leapt at a wolf and bit into its neck. Though his teeth didn't pierce the thick hide, he refused to let go and shook his head with all his strength. Idelle swept in, her claws raking the back of the second wolf. While howling its pain, the Narohk pinned beneath it drove an enchanted knife into its neck. The female was on her feet, loosing arrows with the skill of a veteran. She took one of the bear's eyes, as Hanar faced off against it. Strong as the Protector was, she had a difficult time pushing back the bulky animal. The bear was a taut mass of thick muscle, finger-length claws and jaws that threatened to undo her stony body.

Barr stole *furie* from the dying wolf bleeding out at its neck and let it loose in a stream of fire at the other. Aren's collar protected him from the flames. Yelping at the intense blaze, bristled hair and hide giving way to char, the wolf scrambled backward to get away.

Let go! Idelle yelled and swooped in.

She picked up the wolf, as Aren let go his hold, and carried the creature off into a tree. By the time it fell back to snow and frozen ground far below, its broken body was again that of a Narohk.

Arrows filled the desiccated remains of the other wolf, its shriveled form shrinking further inward to a gray mass. The Narohk beneath slipped out from his diseased brethren, as a final breath escaped its body. An elf once again, it lay still in a pool of its own blood.

The bear reared back, swatting at the air, as every Narohk fired arrows into its belly. Its remaining eye was wide in fear, roaring at some unseen enemy, as wounds opened across its hide from no apparent source.

Poor thing, Uinbro said and clucked his tongue. *He seems to be frightened of something.*

Illusions, Vereu scoffed at his brother.

Hanar drove her fists into the bear, smashing bones with each strike, but the gaping wounds that tore open, revealing muscle and organs, were not of her doing. Its hide and body literally shredded before their eyes, the bear collapsed into a bloodied heap upon the snow. What it reverted back to looked nothing like an elf.

"We must warn the council!" the female said. By the tone of her voice and how the other Narohk fell in step at her command, Barr assumed she was now in charge of the scouting party. "I am Allana," she said as they ran. She cleared her throat and wiped something from her eye. "I am now First of the Narohk."

A bright shade of gray, her eyes looked luminescent beneath the fading light of day. No amount of soil or leaf could dull the brilliant gold of her hair. Thrown behind her in wisps of fluid sunlight, slipping behind tapered ears, she had an almost regal look about her. For a brief moment, she reminded him of Lorelei and the pangs of a childhood love he was never able to pursue.

"A human sage," a male Narohk said on Barr's right. He seemed younger than the others, though age was a difficult thing to gauge among elves. "You may have well brought the downfall of the sylvannis."

"I had nothing to do with that," Barr said, breathing heavy and struggling to keep pace. "The only way you could have known about the attack before it happened was a warning from someone who knew it was coming." The elf said nothing. None of them did, which could have meant they didn't know or simply refused to confirm his suspicions. "Knowing Revyn is somehow behind all this, I think it's safe to say Celene was the one who warned you."

"We have no Valar," Allana said, which left only their Speaker to commune with the gods. "And the warning did not come from Teldein."

"Jeruid could be one of them!" another Narohk said, his eyes wide at the betrayal. "With almost all of us gone to help the sylvannis..."

Allana closed tight her eyes, as if warding off the grief looming ahead in their future. When she opened them again, she ran even faster.

Barr could not keep pace, and Hanar had already fallen behind. He slowed to stay with her, knowing they were close to the city. Two Narohk turned and saw them, slowed their pace as well and ran by their side as the lifts came into view.

They were told to wait while Allana and four others went up to ask permission for Barr to enter Karon-Rai.

"I thought you a sage," one of the two elves left behind noted, "yet you travel with the companions of a Ballar." His hair was grayed at the sides, and his grizzled voice spoke of one with many years upon his bow. "I have heard tales of the sylvannis war hounds, but never did I imagine them to be so large. Our own panthers and wolves would be jealous."

Did he just smile? Aren asked, incredulous at the thought of a Narohk with any humor.

The other elf chuckled. "True enough. And a hawk as well! The Ghaoylens are too long of a journey from here, though many of our Ballar have considered the trek."

These are not like sylvannis Narohk, Idelle agreed. *They're almost likeable.*

"My father," Barr said, "my elven father, Tuvrin, is a Maurdon. I was given Aren and Idelle as gifts from the Speaker and trained with a Ballar in my spare time. We grew up together," he added with a smile.

"I truly wish you were not in exile," the first said. "The last of our Valar died many years ago, and our Niyaen is fading by the day. The forest will not survive the next winter."

"I can help with that."

"What of your other friend?" the older elf asked. "She is a work of enchantment like nothing any of us has ever seen. And she *fights!*" He smiled in admiration. "Did you craft her?"

"He did," Hanar answered in perfect elven and bowed her head. "It was an honor to fight beside you."

The lift touched down, and Allana motioned for them all to step on. As they were raised upward by a system of pulleys and enchanted vine, Hanar leaned in close to Barr and spoke so that the others would not hear.

"They are an immodest people," she said in common, "more so than the faeron."

Barr quietly replied, also in common, "It's one of the reasons they separated from the Celedharrin. The four elven tribes once lived together as a single nation."

When the lift reached the top, breaking through a woven layer of leaf that hid the platform from sight down on the forest floor, they were greeted by the Speaker and six Gharak armed with dual ironwood kukris. Similar to the Maurdon kyan, the kukri was bent at an angle in its middle and only edged on the inside, which made it ideal for chopping rather than stabbing.

Teldein, the wyndorrin Speaker of the Stars, was by all appearances an elder elf. His gray hair, braided into three lengths that were bound in thick silver hoops, still held the wild mien of his kin but lent itself to an aura of authority. Tanned and muscled, trim at the waist, this was a leader accustomed to rigorous activity – hunting, running, and most definitely weapons training. Unlike the sylvannis Eneir, which was composed of noble born and bred to diplomacy, only the most accomplished of the wyndorrin were invited to their Eneir. They were the elite, noble by actions, and Teldein would not have been crowned Speaker without having been one of them.

His Gharak were unusual. Their face paint was more ornate than the Narohk, with markings done in silver to denote house and rank. Personal guards to the Speaker, they would be the best the Gharak had to offer. Most likely each of them had renounced their invitation to the Eneir for the very purpose of serving the Speaker.

Barr bowed low to the Speaker and stood waiting to be addressed. Both his hands were clasped before him. As an Illumin Valar, a weaver of *furie*, it would have been considered disrespectful to hide his hands.

Teldein eyed Hanar with curiosity then turned his full attention to Barr.

"I appreciate the formality," he said plainly, "and your adherence to custom, but I am told there is a matter of grave importance."

"There is," Barr said. He looked into the eyes of each elf, trying to catch a glimpse of the familiar beryl sheen. Teldein's eyes were pale steel, like Allana's, and Barr began to see the resemblance. *Do you smell anything?* he asked Aren.

No, none of them are shapelings.

Uinbro appeared and sniffed at a Gharak. *I could have told you that.*

Then why didn't you? Barr frowned at the illusory man and realized everyone was waiting for him to say more.

You did not ask. Uinbro walked off to study symbols carved into the tree wall.

"No one here is infected," Barr told the Speaker. He could see the guards visibly relax. "I came here for two reasons, to warn you of a possible attack on the council and to ask for a mithrinum relic."

The Speaker nodded. "You can detect them? Good. We must go to the council at once. They have already been summoned." As Teldein turned and led the way through the corridors of shaped tree, woven branch and packed earth, he motioned for Barr to walk beside him. "We have no Denshyar and no Valar to create one. I can have resources made available, should you possess the ability to craft one."

Globes of smoky glass were fastened to the walls in regular intervals. Giant fireflies within provided a warm yellow light, as the insects fed off a honeyed biscuit inside.

"That lore is lost to the sylvannis as well," Barr said. "That's not the relic I need, in any case. What I'm looking for will either be a sword or a piece of armor."

"Help us root out the infected, and you can have your pick of anything in our armory." They turned left and headed for guarded double doors. "Precautions have been taken should any of the council be turned." Teldein stopped at the doors, grief written upon his face. "Do you know of a cure? Is there no other way but death?"

I'm outside the window, Idelle said.

More than anything, Barr wished he did know of a cure. They could subdue and imprison those infected, assuming their numbers were not beyond containing, until a cure could be found. How long that might take, Barr was afraid to even guess.

"I don't know of any," Barr said quietly. "You could imprison them until a cure is found..."

"If one *can* be found." The Speaker straightened and pushed open the doors. "A swift end is the more merciful choice."

They entered, and Aren froze in place. Three men and a woman were seated at the council table, each with a Gharak standing behind them.

What is it? Barr asked but caught sight of the beryl sheen as he faced them.

Every one of them, Aren said. *Even the guards.*

"It's a trap!" Barr yelled, too late.

More rushed the guards at the doors from down the corridor, weapons drawn and snarling. The eight behind the table pulled free their blades and leapt over to attack the Speaker. Those fighting through the doorway began to change, nearly filling the entrance with their bulk.

The six Gharak surrounded Teldein and attacked the nearest enemies. Allana and her two Narohk fell back, drew bows and fired arrows from the far end of the room. Aren turned with a growl, swatted an elf against the wall and bit deep into the shoulder of another. That one cried out and rippled between Aren's jaws, changing to a wolf in mere moments.

Barr saw Teldein had no weapons. He drew both kyan and handed them to the Speaker, who took them without thought and thanked him with a grin. The eight elves struck against Hanar's shield and fell back. One tossed aside the heavy table as if it was kindling, and his body trembled into the form of a bear. The others began to change as well, a boar's snout and tusks taking shape while a wolf's ears and muzzle extended.

With both hands out before him, Barr took *furie* from all eight, halting their transformations. They writhed on the ground, screaming against the pain of life being torn from their bodies. Withering beneath the assault, each one's skin grayed and wrinkled, pulled taut over bones. The air between them shimmered in a fiery distortion, waves of luminescence that engulfed Barr in a growing light.

The *furie* burned beneath his skin, set his veins alight in a golden glow that matched his eyes. Barr persisted, his spirit stronger, more resilient. The sounds of battle behind him were dulled by the wind of *furie* roaring in his ears. When nothing remained but brittle ash in elven form, he turned and faced a dozen more. Golden fire ran the length of his body, blurred his vision with *furie* and a desire to release it.

A bear hovered over one of the Gharak, its claws an inch from the elf's face and forcing his weapon further down. Barr held a palm toward the shapeling, and its body flash-burned from claws to tail. Its fur and flesh, muscle and sinew, were consumed in an instant by the wave of ember, leaving behind an ashen skeleton that crumpled into dust.

Two more burned away. Others were riddled with arrows, blinding and bleeding out from a dozen wounds that refused to stay open for long. Still the golden fires enveloped him, charring the earthen floor. Three more screamed abruptly, devoured as so many cinders upon the breeze.

– *alright? ... hear me?* a voice called through the gale in his mind.

A transparent man stood before him, studying him with interest. Barr held a palm in his direction. A wolf behind the man wailed and burned.

Four more flared and were gone. Still the fire was not sated. One sprawled across the floor, in a spreading pool of thick blood, as men continually stabbed it. Barr looked to the doorway, and its emptiness saddened him. A hand touched his shoulder. He looked her way, into the brightness of steel gray concern.

"It is done," she said, calm, soothing.

When the golden fire abated, it felt as if the world came back into focus. Barr could hear clearly, see the remains of every shapeling and the wounds sustained during battle. He held up his right hand and sent *furie* out toward them. In moments all were healed, surprise and thanks upon their looks.

Barr? Aren nudged his arm. *Did you have a vision?*

He blinked, twice. *No. I didn't.* He looked down at the two Emblems he never drew. *I – I'm not sure what just happened.*

Uinbro was gone. Neither one of them spoke.

"Our sage," the Speaker said, at a seeming loss for words, as he handed Barr back his kyan. "She could do nothing like what I just witnessed. I understand now why Roedric took you in, though he is a fool for casting you into exile. I never did like Ceiran."

Talk of the sylvannis only reminded Barr that the same fate had probably occurred to their council – to his father and Seltruin. Is that why he let himself be talked out of going? Did he know he would have had to burn them as well?

"There could be more," Barr said finally. He smiled at Allana, at the gentle touch that had brought him back. "Aren will go with you to sniff them out."

I will?

Don't argue, Idelle said, *and I'll go fetch us dinner.*

"What will you do?" Teldein asked.

"I have a Niyaen to restore. It may take some time, and I'd prefer to be alone." Barr walked to the door at the Speaker's approval. "I can find it on my own. I'll let you know when I'm finished."

*   *   *

Barr walked the corridors with fingers trailing the shaped wall, feeling his way through the warmth that radiated outward from within. Karon-Rai was not much different in appearance. It was the feeling of its walls, the woven branch underfoot, that gave a sense of something more in the whole.

Barr found it at the center of the city, its boughs reaching up and blotting out the sky. A walkway circled its entire girth, at least a hundred arm spans wide, and wyndorrin walked or sat around it with the wonder of children. There was a glow about its bark, a vibrancy he could see and feel as he approached. It beckoned to him with its warmth, cutting through a cold wind that shook limb and leaf in calm rhythms. His presence startled a few, but he was used to ignoring stares and idle whisper. He walked for some time, choosing a spot shadowed in the dark of falling night, where no one would threaten his concentration.

He placed both hands upon the tree and closed his eyes. Immediately he felt and saw with his mind's eye what was wrong. The Niyaen, the Great Tree, the Pillar of Life, was central to each elven city. Its roots went far down into earth and rock, immersed in the ley lines to draw *furie* for the forest. Over time those roots touching the ley lines would burn away. Each year, a celebration was held, as the Valar coaxed new roots to reach back into the ley lines. With only one root barely immersed, a great deal of time must have passed since the wyndorrin last celebrated the Restoration.

Barr could feel trees on the outskirts of the forest weakened and succumbing to sickness. Their illness was spreading. It wouldn't be long before it reached Karon-Rai, rotting the city from within. Barr realized then that the roots of this Niyaen touched upon every tree, wove itself through their roots until the forest as a whole was a single living organism. Tarrandor, the elves called it. One life. Focusing his mind, Barr followed the central roots deep underground, seeking the ley lines, the rivers of *furie* that ebbed and flowed in an intricate pattern throughout the world.

Geilon-Rai stood upon six ley lines. Twelve crossed directly under the wyndorrin Niyaen. Most likely it had lasted this long because so many of its roots had been immersed in different lines. The Niyaen felt tired to Barr, frail and saddened. The images it sent to his mind were of longing for an eternal spring. Sharing himself with the ancient tree, Barr lent it his essence and became one with its roots. He stretched his fingers, willing them to grow. He reached down through rock and earth, parting frozen soil, until the first tingle of liquid warmth filled his body.

Touching the first ley line sent a thrill of energy over his body, prickled hair and embraced him with sunlight from within. It gave him strength to push further, to extend roots into two more lines. The rush of power and pleasure threatened to overwhelm his senses, vibrating his limbs with the surge of raw magic. He willed more roots to grow, thickening as they went. Three more lines, and *furie* pulsed upward. It shook him to the core, lit a fire in his middle.

A final push, and he touched upon all twelve.

His consciousness travelled down the tree, through its roots and into the flow of golden *furie*. Awash in the river, carried along by its current, he saw the world all around him in a different light. Minuscule runes filled the air, empty of *furie* and swirling along with him. He saw them in everything, the rocks, the earth, roots and grubs, the tree city and its elves, the Niyaen and himself. Never before, not in any of his past lives, had he seen such a language, and he believed it was the language of creation. Divine runes, they were the words and will of the gods.

The river surface was full of them, crowded together in a layer of spent magic. The pull was growing stronger each moment, tugging at his spirit with an unrelenting promise of fulfillment. Racing toward him was a tunnel of black, an impenetrable darkness his new vision could not pierce. Forced along by the current, in a swirl of empty runes, Barr felt his spirit near the Dark and recoiled from its cold. Fighting against its pull, arms desperately swimming backward, he watched runes slip into the void and become filled in the instant before disappearing from sight.

Barr wondered for a brief moment, fought with less vigor. Would the Dark fill him too? What would become of him, in that breath of an instant when his spirit filled and disappeared?

His body arced of its own accord, muscles tensed with an excess of *furie*. Dragged back up along the roots, his consciousness struggled to remain in the flowing warmth. He felt himself being torn away, pushed back into the cold of his own body.

In what felt like an eternity of agonizing bliss, Barr exploded the limits his spirit and body could endure. Slowly, steadily, the Niyaen began to pulse with great strength and glowing light. Its hold on Barr lessened, released his spirit with a hush of thanks. *Furie* flowed through the forest, from the closest hole to the furthest shrub.

Barr's eyes opened, and he slipped to the ground.

The vision stayed with him, all the world comprised of tiny golden runes. Everything, everyone, he saw as a single glyph, impossibly complex patterns in a language he didn't know. He looked down at his own hand, trying to understand.

You did it, Idelle said. Through the tone of her voice, he could see the forest brighten with life anew.

We've only found two others, Aren said. *We should be done searching in a bit, or so the Narohk says. I heard Teldein promise us a feast!*

"Are you well?" the Speaker asked and helped Barr to his feet. For some reason, Barr didn't expect to see the elf so soon. His patterns were dizzying. As they walked out of the darkness, Barr saw that a crowd of wyndorrin had amassed. Hundreds of them had come to see him restore the Niyaen. "I cannot thank you enough for the happiness you have brought my – brought us. We shall remain forever in your debt, sage Barr."

Barr blinked away the strange sense of vision, and looked once again in the normal spectrum. He found by focusing his will, he could call it up again, but in truth it only gave him a headache.

"I pledged my life to protect the elves," Barr said and looked out at the gathered families, the people who had nothing but joy and gratitude for what he'd done. "I will never forsake that vow, exile or no."

"A celebration in your honor is underway."

I told you! Aren laughed like an excited puppy.

"The honor is mine." Barr felt his strength returning, and he walked with more ease. He also felt the pull of Balaen. They were getting closer to the Emblem. "Do you mind if I ask how you have no Valar? Wasn't anyone called upon to serve?"

Teldein's smile diminished, as they turned down a sloping corridor. "There were none with the ability to pass the test. Now it is too late. Even if we were to find one with the aptitude to weave, we have none left to teach the old ways."

"You don't need to be special," Barr told him quietly, "to weave *furie*. You have my word as a Valar, any one of you can weave. Think of the Narohk, who enchant their arrows to fly true, the Ballar that weave signal wards in the forest to alert against intrusion, the Maurdon and Gharak that enchant their blades. All of us have the capacity to weave. Like anything else, it's just a matter of knowing how and lots of practice."

"I wish it could be so," Teldein said, a wistful smile at the thought. "Why would sages insist on the test for so many generations if it were otherwise?"

"Pride? Control? I don't know. I'll prove it to you one day, though." Barr's eyes widened as an open chamber came into view. Stars loomed overheard, as song played out on bells, mandolins and drums. Tables laden with food and drink stretched out with enough to feed the entire city. "There's something I need to take care of, but I give you my word. I'll come back and teach anyone to be a sage. The wyndorrin will have Illumin Valar again."

Allana approached and bowed her head. "I thank the stars that we came across you today in the forest." She was carrying an item bound in leather. Barr was certain it was Balaen. "This is the sword you asked for. Please take it in good health."

Barr accepted and bowed his head in return.

Greetings, the Emblem said, her voice solemn.

Pleased to meet you, Balaen. Barr ignored Aren's huff of indignation. *Why aren't you here?* he asked the war hound. *You're missing out on all this food.*

What! Barr and Idelle could feel Aren barreling down the corridors. *That Narohk said I should wait here for you!*

Idelle laughed. *Don't knock down any children! There's still plenty of food. Hmm, or at least there was a moment ago,* she added, teasing. *These people must be famished. Look at how fast they're eating everything!*

Aren growled and ran harder.

"You and your friends," Teldein said, "are welcome to stay here for as long as you need. What aid we could spare was sent days ago to Darleman. I only hope they arrive in time." He clapped Barr on the shoulder, and many cups were raised in his honor. "Please join us in celebration!"

"Thank you," Barr said, humbled by the Speaker's sincerity.

He took the cup Allana offered but didn't drink. Wine would only sour his stomach after all the weaving he'd done. What he needed was water. Barr looked around for a pitcher, as Allana took a seat and patted the spot next to her. He joined her and put down Balaen and his cup.

"Where will you go now?" she asked.

"Back home," he replied and caught her studying him. A swirl of mist appeared before them, and Fluora stepped through. She wore a blindfold of green faeron silk. "Fluora!" Barr grinned, stood and took her hands. He remembered what she had said in the mists about kissing her first and fought down the urge. "You look rested. Fluora, I'd like you to meet Allana, First of the wyndorrin Narohk and daughter to the Speaker of the Stars." Allana stood and gave a respectful bow of her head. Barr continued, "Allana, this is Fluoralandylae, my intended, Matron of the Guiding Mists and daughter to the Grand Seeress of Faeronthalsos."

Fluora bowed in turn.

"I see," Allana said and put down her cup. "It is an honor to make your acquaintance. If you would please excuse me, I must tend to another matter."

"Of course." Fluora stepped aside, and Allana left to the other end of the chamber. "What was that about?"

"What was what about?" Finally, Barr spied a pitcher of water and poured himself a cup. He offered some to Fluora. "You're just in time for the celebration."

"I am wearing a blindfold," she said, "and even *I* can see that... girl likes you." Fluora looked out across the gathered elves. "You hurt her feelings."

"I didn't mean to."

Good! Aren said without pausing. He'd been eating from a tray of carved venison, potatoes and onions since arriving. *She's the one who told me to wait for you, when I could have been eating all along.*

"Poor dear," Fluora said with a wry grin. "He might have starved."

Sarcasm is lost on Aren, Idelle said from above.

"How are you doing?" Barr took a seat, and she sat next to him. "You're still wearing a blindfold. Does it help much?"

"I am fine," she answered, "and yes it helps. I can still see with it on, though not with my eyes – which is a bit confusing at times." Fluora had been looking down at her hands, but she raised her covered eyes to his. "I have been with my mother."

"She knows?"

"Yes. She refuses to remove the unborn child. Even though birthing it will kill her." Fluora balled up both her hands into fists. "Of all people, she told me, I should know best the future is not written in stone."

Barr dreaded saying it. "She's right." He endured the stabbing look of betrayal. "I'm sorry, I'm not trying to defend her decision. What I'm saying is not every vision you'll have will come to pass."

"And in the meantime," Fluora said, grief hidden beneath the blindfold, "I can see her die over and over until it happens."

"Let's go back to Dwendorim."

No! Aren began to eat faster. *I'm not finished yet!*

Hanar stood against the wall behind him. She was never far from sight. At Fluora's nod, Barr picked up Balaen and summoned the mists.

In the moment between, when they reached the starry plane, he paused. He could see the rift he'd just opened, hanging suspended over the waters. He exerted his will and held it open. It led to absolute darkness, a void with no light, no sound, nothing but the promise of empty runes and replenished *furie*. He focused upon the Dark, switching his vision to the panorama of divine runes that bathed the world in golden light. A corona of fiery gold encompassed the rift, but no runes could be seen in its depths.

Barr looked closer, leaning forward.

"What are you doing?" Fluora demanded, and her voice carried fear, brought power and will to bear. His rift rippled and faded. "Are you mad? Do you know what you just did?"

He blinked the vision away. "I was curious. I don't really know much about the Dark, but today –"

"*Never* do that again!" She calmed herself, as the others looked on. "You left open a portal to the Dark. Not only could umbrals have sensed it and passed through, the Dark could have claimed you forever." Fluora put a hand to his cheek. "You must never stare into its depths, never dare touch it, not even for an instant. It will make you its own, with no hope, no escape. Do you see what I contend with every moment of every day? These rifts to the Dark are the

counterbalance to the mists. My will is all that keeps it
from consuming Faeronthalsos."

Right, Uinbro said beside him. *Make a note of that.
Stare into the Dark, lost forever.*

Barr ignored him and brought them to Dwendorim.

"I won't do it again," he told Fluora and led her by
the hand into his home. "It's just that I saw the most
amazing thing today."

Fluora leaned in, put her head against his shoulder
and wrapped her other arm about his.

Softly, she said, "Tell me."

*　　*　　*

Her sleep had been restless and haunted by
demons she had slain and yet to meet. Drenched with
sweat, her nerves rattled and stomach knotted, she had
given it up as a lost cause.

Demon hunters weren't meant for restful sleep.

Despite her agitation, the young man Barr had
been right. This underground city of a forgotten,
ancient race was quiet and peaceful. The enchanted
statues, golems he had called them, kept mostly to
themselves, all of them busy with some endeavor.
Fruits, nuts, cooked fish and a pitcher of water had
been waiting for her when she woke.

Sera had slept in someone's home, a family of
three. Toys filled the little girl's room, with a feather
bed, down pillows, colorfully stained shutters that let in
the scent of flowers outside the window. A painting over
the hearth showed a moment of their happiness,
captured forever on canvas. Whether they had lived
that way daily, none but the statues knew. She couldn't
find a single cobweb or mote of dust. Nothing tarnished
their shrine but her presence.

It was an odd feeling, walking through the park with no pain in her middle, directing her steps. Water sprayed from fountains, clear and clean. Lush grass gave way beneath her feet, tickled her toes. Though she knew the city was far beneath the surface, under rock and earth, she looked up and marveled at the vista of stars. How day and night could exist underground she didn't know, but neither did she know how statues could be given life. A cool breeze touched her cheek, caressed her bathed skin through the gossamer dress she had woken up in. Her hair was washed as well and moved with the wind. Like two lovers soon to wed or a child's dream on the maturing cusp of disappointment, it all seemed much too wonderful to be true. And like a crossbow aimed at her head, those feelings nagged at her senses, cast a shadow over the tranquility she was certain couldn't last.

The crossbow fired and wrenched at her middle.

Demons were in the city, five of them. Though their scent was unusual, Sera could hear the blood pumping through their veins with every erratic beat, felt the lust for murder rise up inside them. It was rare for so many to hunt together but not unheard of. Cerulean fire lit her body as she ran, a ghostly glow in the underdark. She knew where they were, as if she could see the outline of their bodies through the homes and trees in her path. They waited in ambush, lambs with sharpened teeth bent on facing a wolf.

Sera covered ground faster than any horse, leapt an inhuman distance to a thick branch and propelled her body through the air. She landed atop a house, clay tiles shattering beneath her feet, and continued running and leaping across rooftops. When she drew near the cobbled circle where each demon awaited, a burst of *furie* shot down her legs and bunched her muscles into a jump. An eruption of tile and stone trailed behind, as her body arced and careened the length of three houses. Stones cracked, giving way to a small crater, as she landed on all fours in their center.

They eyed her as they circled, but not one of them was a demon. Three men and two women, moving about her like hunters rounding prey, none had a weapon to speak of but tensed their bodies in preparation to leap away or attack. The geas tore at her insides, raked her spine up to the nape of her neck. Her fingers twitched of their own volition, anxious to get on with the killing.

"What is this?" she asked.

One laughed, a woman. A scar ran the length of a once pretty face. Her laughter was feral. Light flashed across her eyes, a beryl sheen of *furie*. The woman began to change, and with her went the others. Their hands elongated, ending in black talons, while skin hardened into scales like embers blown to life. Leather armor and clothing vanished into the transformation. Fascinated and eager to rend them limb from limb, Sera watched all five grow both in girth and height. They had the look of young demons, rigid plates at the head, jagged teeth and pointed ears, but her senses warned that what she faced was far more deadly.

Fully changed, one dared an attempt to swipe talons across her back. Sera ducked and spun, took its legs out from underneath it and drove the length of her forearm into its chest before gravity could take hold. The demon crashed into the stones, broken and bleeding. Its blood bubbled the cobbles and sent wisps of acrid smoke into the air. Sera had long ago grown used to the rancor of sulfur.

A nod from what was once the woman, and the four remaining attacked. Sera easily dodged their attempts, twisting her body to avoid talons from all directions. She sent fire along her hands, burning them as she blocked or struck out with glancing blows. The nagging returned, scratching at her mind with the sense of something out of sorts. One lunged in too close and got an elbow to the face for its efforts. She realized in that moment, studying the others' moves, that none of them was trying to kill her. They sought to bleed, subdue...

Her arm caught the edge of a fang.

It had barely cut her skin. The wound closed before she could look down. A rivulet of her own blood dripped down to her wrist.

The four demons backed off at the same time. They circled her again, watching, waiting. It didn't matter to Sera. They could bide their time. The holy fires would claim them soon enough. The one she had already slain had changed back during the fight. A man once more, in leathers and woolen clothing, his appearance caught her off guard. For a single, shocking moment, she wondered if she had rid Taellus of another demon or murdered an innocent man. The pool of blood that haloed his body no longer ate away at the stones.

Dizziness overwhelmed her, rose up from her middle and assaulted her mind. Her blood boiled, as if the geas had gone awry. Falling to her knees, body wracked by unrelenting pain, every muscle taut against the burning from within, Sera felt as if she had been cast into the depths of Danarriden. Vision blurred by a haze of agony, she retched upon the stones.

The woman laughed again. "Welcome to an eternity of torment."

Sera was engulfed in holy fire, but the flames burned away at her own flesh, as the geas then healed her in turn. Her hunter senses cried out at the sound of her own heart, at the rush pulsing in beats through her body. Demon blood ran through her veins. Compelled to destroy her own body by fire, she was also physically prevented from causing herself harm. The geas that burned her alive from without and within would not allow her to die by her own hand.

"Do you know what you've done?" she rasped at the laughing demons. Gritting her teeth, Sera forced herself to stand. She shook against the anguish of dying and renewal. "Do you?!"

The woman grinned and stepped in close, an inch from Sera's face. Her breath reeked of ash and rotted eggs. In the reflection of the woman's eyes, Sera saw the bright blue of *furie* that once marked her as a demon hunter had turned to a luminescent bloody red.

"We've made you one of us," the woman said. "We've made you a demon."

Sera felt power coursing through her in tandem with the pain. Just as the presence of a thousand demons would immerse her in torment beyond the endurance of any mortal, it would also grant her the divine *furie* to kill them all.

"No," Sera said, and her eyes narrowed to a look of burning hatred. "You've made me a god."

The area erupted in holy fire, a pillar of intense flame that consumed all four demons in momentary screams and blinding *furie*. Their bodies blackened amidst the light, thinned and faded away to motes of ash.

Yes, a voice said in her mind, a cooing voice of the triumphant, one she knew without asking was called Revyn, *but a god that answers only to me.*

"I answer to the curse."

The pillar subsided, but holy fire still surrounded her. It burned away the flesh between her runes as fast as the geas could heal, left her naked and hairless, in a struggle between the throes of euphoric power and the suffering of undying damnation.

You serve a new curse now, Revyn said, momentarily soothing the fires when he spoke. *There is an old man not far off. Go to him.*

"No," Sera said firmly and began to walk.

No matter how hard she struggled, she could not move in another direction. Her gait slowed and stopped. She smiled at the victory, though pain far worse than the geas compelled her to keep walking. Her defiance lasted a brief minute before the new curse won out.

She had no idea how long she walked. Cobbled roads and colorful houses passed by in a stream of empty hope for release. Grass went by underfoot, but it no longer tickled. Sera felt nothing but the fires and the impulse to hunt. She found him seated at a bench, watching water spray from a fountain and dribble down a series of shells into the hands of a maiden.

"Well now," he said and stood, facing her with open curiosity. "That's something you don't dream about every day. I don't mean to be rude, but you're on fire." He gave a nod towards the fountain. "Perhaps you should step in?"

Sera laughed and cried, as Revyn's voice slithered through her mind. *Feed on him.*

"I will not!" She moved closer. "I refuse!"

"Oh. Alright then. Maybe you shouldn't stand quite so close, though." The old man tugged at the white hairs of his long, scruffy beard and winked. "These do take a while to grow, you know."

She took him by the shoulders in an unshakeable grip, trembling as her face drew in close.

"Interesting!" he said when the flames didn't burn him. "Rather warm, almost pleasant." She bit into his shoulder. Weakly, he said, "Oh my."

Sera screamed in her mind that she would not kill the poor man, over and over as she drained him of all *furie*. She let go of him and sobbed, wiped blood from her mouth with the back of a hand. She stared down at the stains in self-loathing. Nothing remained of the old man but a desiccated husk, a gray shell with wispy white hair and a long beard.

A swirl of mist appeared before her, much like what Barr had used to transport them to the city. A young man stepped through but none like she had ever before seen. His skin was frosted gold in color, from sandals to snowy hair. He stood transfixed before her, lost to some trance, and stared blindly ahead with eyes a filmy white. Without a word, he moved a hand, and the mists rose up around them. He took her from the city, back to the realm of starry night.

Away from the old man she had just murdered.

*   *   *

Dar woke from another blackout, unable to move. He was seated beside the broken remnants of an altar, in the temple ruins he and Jahd had found the Emblem. His last memory was of them both trying vainly to free Muornay from a crystal prison. Embedded into a wall of the expansive chamber, the sword was at least an arm's length deep in the amber rock.

A smashing sound broke him from his reverie. Dar looked up to see a revenant driving the pommel of a blade into the rock time and again. Chips of amber fell at the creature's feet and sprayed out behind. Though it wore the black robes and mask of a Guardian Justiciar, Dar had seen the illusion before and knew what sort of monster it hid.

He is taking the Emblem, Dar thought. Khaela was silent in his mind. He looked closer at the revenant and realized with sick horror that it was Khaela being used to smash the crystal. *How is this possible!*

He knew the answer but refused to believe it. Until his eyes fell upon the shattered and molten remains of what could only be Jahd. The revenant had killed her. Dar grew angry and tried again to move. His chest felt on fire, reminding him of the torture he had endured in the Guardian dungeon.

No, he thought and knew it to be true. *My blackouts. I helped them.* He looked up at the revenant, eyes wet with the sting of a betrayal he could not fathom: his own. *I brought that thing here, and it killed Jahd.*

"Do not fear," the revenant said in a hollow voice, the fiery orbs of its eyes glowing through the illusion. "You will not be harmed so long as we still have need of your assistance."

It reached a hand inside the hole it had gouged from the crystal, and ice emanated outward along the wall in a sheet of crackling frost. Another smash of Khaela's pommel, and crystal fell away in great chunks. Three more times it repeated the process, freezing the crystal and smashing it to icy pieces. The revenant eyed its handiwork, reached in, took hold and tugged with all the strength of an undead. Dar could do nothing but watch in helpless frustration, as cracks shot out along the wall and thickened into crevices. Crystal exploded outward in a shower of jagged amber, some fragments no bigger than a gemstone, while others were small boulders that fell and rolled across the floor. Muornay was pulled free from its tomb, and the revenant turned to face Dar with both Emblems in hand.

What have I done? was his only thought.

*　*　*

"Barr!" Fluora ran into the room, waking him from a sound sleep. Starlight through the window cast the room in a pale light, and he saw that she had removed her silken blindfold. "Your uncle, he has been killed!"

"Uncle Therol?" Fully awake, Barr thrust aside the blanket. *Idelle, Aren! Find my uncle!* "What happened? Where is he?"

Idelle opened her eyes and shook the sleep from her feathers. Aren roused a bit slower. He was padding along the cobbled street as Barr got out of bed, when the acrid bite of sulfur twitched his nose. Hanar rushed into the room, nearly taking the door from its hinges.

"It gets worse," Fluora whispered, her eyes haunted by sorrow.

"Master!" Hanar moved to his side, tears of golden *furie* welling in her eyes as she spoke. "Jahd has been slain by a revenant!"

"What?" Barr could scarcely hear her, still focused on the thought that his uncle was dead.

I see... something, Idelle said. *It can't be –*

It's him, Aren said. *The shapeling's gone, but I can still smell it.*

Shapeling? "What about Dar?" Barr asked.

He's been... fed upon. Idelle shivered. *I'm sorry.*

"We have no way of knowing." Hanar knelt, her head against his middle. "I felt it, felt that creature tear Jahd to pieces. If only we were ready!" She looked up at him, and Barr was torn between consoling her and dealing with his own grief. "If only we worked faster! Harder!"

"Stop." Barr pulled her to her feet. "Tell the others to search the city. My uncle's been killed by a shapeling."

"It was Sera," Fluora said, her head hung low, as if the blame fell upon her shoulders. "A group of chaodyns attacked and turned her. She found your uncle in the park. He..." Fluora swallowed hard and could say no more.

"How could shapelings get into Dwendorim?" Barr asked angrily. He could see his tone had stung Hanar. He left his other question unanswered, but it burned in his thoughts. Where were all the Protectors while his uncle was being murdered? *"How?"*

"We have failed you," Hanar said quietly. "We were so caught up in our endeavor, that –"

Fluora said, "It was Dar-Paj. If I were not wearing a blindfold, I might have seen it sooner."

"You can't see everything," Barr said, fighting the urge to go fetch the blindfold and force her to wear it. "Even if you could, would you want to?"

She shook her head. "He brought the chaodyn here, through the mists. He has been helping Markus, using the mists against us! It was Dar-Paj who brought the revenant to North Haven, where it destroyed Jahd and now has Khaela." Fluora clenched her eyes shut. "In any moment, Lochlaen will free Muornay and have both."

That makes no sense, Aren said. *Dar wants to kill Markus as badly as I do.*

Idelle agreed. *He would never help Markus.*

Not willingly. "I have to find Dar." Barr went outside to a water basin and tried to scry the apprentice. He could sense the vast mountain, felt Dar-Paj deep inside its bowels, past tunnels of scorched stone and crystal formations, but the image refused to focus in the water. "Wherever he is, it's warded."

"I can take you," Fluora offered. Her eyes were bare, looking for absolution. Her lips stiffened in refusal before Barr could suggest she put the blindfold back on. "There is no time for that."

Uinbro appeared and touched Barr on the forehead. "He is here."

The image filled Barr's mind, vast ruins of a dragon temple long lost to disuse. He saw Lochlaen pull free the sword. With no word of explanation, Barr called up and stepped through the mists in a single breath, shoved the revenant back in a burst of *furie* that sent it sprawling a hundred paces over stone. It landed hard and slid across a thick layer of dust and debris. Its hold on the Emblems remained fast.

As the undead king stood, ice crept out from its feet and spread across the stone floor between them. The ice raced towards Barr, crackling with frost, and struck against a molten barrier of jutting iron. Steam rose up in plumes, distorting the air. Lightning crackled from its depth. A flash of blinding white struck out and hit Barr on his right shoulder. The blackened flesh sizzled, and a shock went through his body with such force it nearly floored him. Illusory warriors stepped from nothingness around Lochlaen and attacked, landing heavy blows that set off sparks in the darkened chamber.

Crystal veins in the walls glowed with dull shades of amber and sapphire, as if the mountain housed the light of a dying sun. Barr grabbed the air between them, tore the *furie* from Lochlaen with a building rage that would not abate. Iron spikes erupted from the ground, impaling the revenant from numerous angles. Ice shards whipped across Barr's cheek, shredding the flesh in a spray of bright blood. Still the warriors swung their mighty axes and swords, filling the chamber with sounds of battle but not penetrating bone.

An aura of black fire enveloped Lochlaen. It melted the iron spikes, burned away the ghostly soldiers and cast aside the revenant's illusory guise. A corpse made prison, with walls of decayed bone and rotted tissue, a soul could be seen flitting between the ribs, desperate to be free. Midnight tendrils grew from the aura, thick as an arm, writhing with malevolence. One lashed out with blinding speed and secured Barr's arm.

It numbed him to the bone, spreading ice through his veins. The connection between them was severed. Try as he might, Barr could not break free of the shadow magic. Another whipped out and grabbed his leg. Its touch deadened his flesh, plagued his body with growing cold. Wounds opened where the tendrils had touched, blackening the skin as blood fled him in dark rivulets, taking with it further warmth. Like strands born of the Dark, more tendrils struck and parted flesh across his chest, thighs and middle. As if eaten by a hungry plague, his body was blackening, losing the strength to resist. They all lashed out at once, dozens of tendrils grasping hold. One about his neck caused his breath to escape in streams of icy cloud.

With little enough blood left, Barr closed his eyes and sank down into the darkness of rock, packed earth, glowing crystal, empty pockets of dense air, molten flows and a river of golden sunlight. Liquid magic splashed his cheek, bathed him in its warmth, and the vision of divine runes filled his senses. It reminded him of the Niyaen, the layer of spent runes atop the ley line, flowing toward the Dark, filling to the brim in that instant before simply vanishing into nothing.

Barr could feel them now, flowing through the ley lines, like lifeblood through the veins of the world. In they went as vessels depleted. Out they came the other side as life reborn. The ley lines were just conduits, Barr realized, not the source of all magic they were thought to be. The true source of *furie*, the heart that fueled all life in the Light...

...was the Dark.

He too could be a conduit. Barr grabbed a portion of the ley line, forced it to flow up and through him. When he opened his eyes, they lit the chamber in golden light. The tendrils fell away, burned by the glow of building *furie* within him. His wounds healed and closed, with no sign of the shadow plague.

Both hands extended, Barr loosed the *furie* toward Lochlaen. The revenant was running at him, closing the distance between them, and threw itself forward with both Emblems readied to strike. The hum of coalescing power was deafening, the swirling mass of liquid magic that met the undead king head on. As if struck by a wall of golden light, the flow of runes stopped Lochlaen mid-stride. The aura of ebon fire dissolved, as *furie* showered every pore of the undead king's runic bones.

The strain of calling and managing so much power could be seen in Barr's tightened jaw and the lines of his neck. His body was taut as a drawn bow, pushed near to breaking. When the burning at the pit of his stomach began to expand, he knew he could take no more.

Lochlaen's scream echoed down the long tunnels, as each runic bone engraved in godsblood gave way to the burning. Its skeletal body darkened and thinned, then burst apart in a spray of ash. So strong was the flow of *furie* that it continued past, melting crystal and rock. It formed a new tunnel that stretched out and breached the mountain. The magical din resonated down the new tunnel with a thunderous clap that could be heard by weavers the world over.

Barr let loose the ley line and collapsed. He fought to catch his breath, blowing away the ashen remains of Lochlaen's prison. All that was left were the Emblems and a body of pale mist. Lightning blue eyes regarded Barr for a moment, then the once king of the ankara disappeared. Despite what it had almost cost him, Barr now had a plan for Revyn. He just needed time to make preparations.

Dar-Paj walked over and picked up the Emblems. He knelt beside Barr, looked over at Jahd's shattered body. "When they tortured me at Noria," he began, voice weary and uncertain, "they did something to me, marked me in some way that allows them to control me."

"We can undo it," Barr told his friend, and sat up. His body still trembled, but he felt strength returning. "You'll be fine in no time."

"And what of Jahd?"

"Some things can't be undone."

Dar laid both Emblems in front of Barr. "I can stand this loss of memory no longer. Your grandmother said I should seek the Mirror Pool." His eyes searched Barr's, as if hoping their friendship had not died along with Jahd. "Will you take me?"

Barr nodded and stood, left Khaela and Muornay for Dar. "I would do anything for a friend. You should know that by now."

Dar took up the Emblems and stood.

"Thank you."

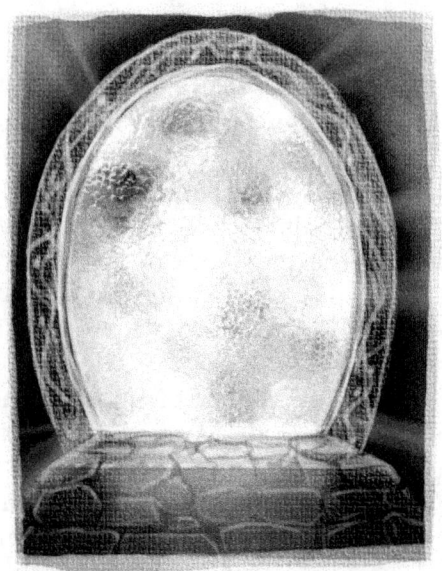

– 16 –

ist parted in eddies all around them, twirls of reflected moonlight. Dark clouds hid stars on the horizon, promise of a coming storm. They stood upon a sandy shore, surrounded by forest but for a road on the opposite side of the Mirror Pool. Pale water stretched out before them a thousand feet to the road and half again as wide, bubbling at its center. It was said a stream from the heavens fed into the pool at that very spot, causing the argent maelstrom, and the pool itself was the conduit from which Taellus and all life upon it had been created.

Dar had his doubts on the whole notion of gods.

"I'll scout around," Barr said and quietly walked off.

Looking into the water's surface would be a personal experience, one meant to be undertaken alone.

344

Besides, there was little threat of him leaving through the mists. Fluora would have seen to that. Dar rubbed at his chest, at the unseen runes he knew were there, and headed to the edge of the pool.

He knelt and leaned forward on both hands, looked down at his reflection in the shining surface. The water had a silvery cast, like a fickle quicksilver on the verge of translucence. Nothing of sand or rock showed through from the water's bottom. Stranger still, Dar saw nothing but his own image reflected back, as if the night sky had been swallowed by the water's pale glow. A solid mass of mutable light, the Mirror Pool seemed alive, a presence felt from its depths but unseen in the calm of its face. As Dar watched for ripples or any sign of life in the pool, his image began to change. The color of its skin softened to the pinkish hue of a human, and the white of its hair fled before a wave of earthen brown. The eyes were like fresh-turned soil, no longer ringed in gold. Its lips parted in a smile, though Dar remained grave, and its teeth were two rows of straight perfection.

Water began to gather and rise up before Dar, in the form of a man. It stopped when its eyes were level with his, its waist and legs hidden beneath the ripples of pale light. Its surface shivered for a moment, and the face settled into handsome features, broad cheeks, a straight nose and strong jaw. Dar saw veins in its watery skin, a muscled chest and arms.

The Mirror Pool bowed its bald head.

"You have returned, old friend." The pool's mouth moved when it spoke, and it blinked, looking at Dar with an equal curiosity.

"Do you know me?" Dar asked. The pool nodded with a wistful smile. "Could you help me? I seem to have lost all my memories."

"I will not," it replied sadly.

Dar was taken aback. *Will* not?

"Have I offended you in some way? Why would you not help?"

Water rippled in a sigh. "You asked me not to."

"I never asked..." Realization dawned, and Dar said, "You took my memories." The pool nodded. "And before you did, I asked you not to give them back."

"That is correct." The pool touched his shoulder, and Dar's body changed to match the reflection. Gone were the gold skin, white hair, and sharp teeth. "You ran off frightened before I could help adjust your new form."

"I need my memories," Dar pleaded, grateful for the appearance of normalcy but still incomplete. "Without them, I am lost. I have no idea who I am, what I have done, but feel I was meant for something more. Please, if ever we were friends, you must give back what you took. I will not go on living without them."

The pool frowned at that last. "Have you considered what brought you to me is worse than not knowing? You had no other choice. Taking your life is not an option."

"I was wrong," Dar said, his brow furrowed. "I cannot understand why I would ask you to take them, but I can handle any memory, anything but this emptiness inside me. I was weak to ever ask. I am stronger now."

"You were not and are not." The Mirror Pool crossed its arms and regarded Dar for a long moment. "If I grant this request, know I will not again take them. Truth be told, I no longer want them. They have pained me for centuries. I only suffered their presence in honor of our friendship, though doing so had cost me that as well." Its body began to recede back into the water. "Look upon your reflection, and you will again be whole. I only hope we are still friends when it is done."

"Centuries?" Dar asked, but the body was gone. He was alone with his reflection, the glimmer of his other self awash in silver glow.

Dar stared down into the eyes. Light flashed at the back of his mind, a whirlwind of tangible memory that began to fill the void. The world brightened and fell away into pale light...

Among the first of Curoch's children, he was also the last Patron – a title bestowed upon the dragon males who had fathered the first eggs. The name given him was Dhar'paogi. It came back to him of a sudden, as if it were there all along, within sight but out of reach. And just as he knew his own name, he knew his mate was Eoraini. Just thinking of her caused his heart to soar, filled his body with a flush of longing that burned his cheeks and forced joyful tears to fall. In all his long life, their millennia together, nothing and no one he had ever witnessed could surpass her noble beauty. She was magnificence refined, a sunfall taken wing. The mere glint of her eyes would steal his breath.

Only one other had come close to Eoraini's elegance and grace, the warmth and love that wrapped about her like a blanket of sunshine.

Their daughter, Eorana.

Thought of her brought him further back. Images of the past, emotions once felt, washed over his senses in a collage of vivid colors and textures...

Though dragons were one of the few elder races that still remained, Dhar could see clearly in his mind the day when they had first sprung to life by the will of their father and friend. The God of Honor and Truth, it had been Curoch that gathered wind and water, earth and fire, and brought dragons forth from the limitless depths of his imagination. As a home for his children, he had forged the enormous mountain of Naerat Sanae, an expanse of rocky peak that endeavored to touch the very foundation of the heavens. While the mountain had given them warmth and shelter from without, the wide open skies had granted freedom of flight both absolute and theirs alone.

In time, dragons had seen much of Taellus, enjoyed its splendor from their unique vantage high above. Having spent countless years in search of new places to discover, Dhar had found that the land was still beautiful to behold but offered little in way of fresh exploration. It was then that he had turned towards the other children races, intrigued by the differences and similarities they shared. Most were pleasing to the eye, in their own right, and not without a measure of intelligence. With the ability to mold his own body to mirror theirs, Dhar had found it a marvel to walk among them without the substantial bulk of his winged form. He had enjoyed the various shapes of the brother races so much, particularly the raugrin and anaire, that he would often walk as one of them in the great halls of Naerat Sanae.

It was in the minds of these new acquaintances that Dhar had found a renewed joy in exploration. Changing his form as easily as his new friends might don a new set of clothing, Dhar would seek out debates on matters of worth or wile away the hours over some minor frivolity. He would sometimes find absolutely fascinating a topic that another would deem mundane at best. One of his fondest memories was a discussion he had had with an anaire woman named Gaela, and of all the things they could have spoken of, their discourse turned towards sneezing.

"Bless you," she said to him offhandedly.

They were ridding her turnip garden of troublesome weeds. Dhar was wondering why she did not simply forget the turnips and eat the weeds, since they seemed to grow stronger and without aid. Dust had shot up into his nose, and he had convulsed against the tickle.

"Why do you do that?" he asked with a puzzled look.

"Do what?" Gaela pulled a silver-edged root from the ground with a beefy arm and tossed it into the bucket. "Bless you? It's the polite thing to do when someone else sneezes."

"Yes, but why? You are not a priestess."

Gaela huffed. "Since when do I have to go around in a robe, burning candles and lighting incense, to give someone my blessing? I'll do what I please, thank you very much."

Dhar raised a brow. "That is not what I meant. Why bless someone when they sneeze as opposed to blessing me each time I pull one of these weeds?"

"That would be a lot of blessing."

"And?"

Adding another to the bucket, she said, "And I think I'd rather get these pulled than bless you all day. You might as well ask me why I say 'thank you' when someone does something nice for me."

"I understand that it is polite," Dhar explained and gave a grin. "I am just curious why. Is it something you are taught as a child?"

"I suppose it was." She sat back on her knees a moment and wiped dirt from her cheek. "I recall hearing a tale that if a person sneezed, it meant they were under attack by an unseen evil. It's the body fighting back, you see. So to help them ward off the evil presence, you bless them. See? It's polite. No one likes an evil presence."

"Aside from other evil people, I suppose."

"Nope," Gaela said firmly and pulled another weed. "They don't much like each other, either."

He had had thousands of conversations in a similar fashion, all ranging from the varied topics of governance or masonry to cleaning one's shoes or the proper way to fold a towel. Dhar would spend entire days idly watching craftsmen at work, building a wheel or forging a tool. Whether it was a painter's brush or a sculptor's chisel, he would sit quietly observing the art taking shape. Of all he had surveyed, his favorite medium of expression by far had been music. A deft hand plying an instrument would set his heart to fluttering, and never would he have imagined that such emotion could be conveyed by the drawing out of one's voice in song.

All that he had learned with each passing day, he had taken home to Eoraini and shared with her his joys. Often he would try to convince her to join him on his outings, but she had playfully told him she found more pleasure in hearing him speak of the day than ever she could by enduring it. Her adventures were in the skies, and she needed nothing more than the wind upon her wings and the sun across her back to feel as he had on his journeys. Eoraini had been glad he could find the same happiness as she. What had mattered to her most was that they could seek out their own separate amusements and share them together at day's end. Eoraini had her dizzying currents and swift streams of warm air. Dhar had his many friends stretched out across Taellus.

Light shifted the images to high atop Naerat Sanae, where Dhar had been teaching Eoraini to mimic the shape of a human. Ungainly, clumsy, fragile and weak, she had immediately disliked the feeling. Dhar had persisted with a smile, found her stunning in any shape. He had taken her by the hand and led her in a dance, a slow twirling of limbs still growing sure of their odd footing. They had continued to dance as he sang, providing rhythm to their spins and hops, a cadence for their bodies intertwined at the elbows or extended hands. Her laughter had bubbled up as they circled one another. The sound of it shot down his spine with remembered joy, overshadowed by the jolt of a horror yet to come.

"Why look you so sad?"

The voice was his daughter's, the echo of a distant dream confused by stolen memories.

Eoraini had slipped.

Dhar raced forward before she began to fall, though in truth he had stood crippled by the sight. Motionless, unable to breathe, he had watched a bare foot slip on the rocks and tumble her backward, over the mountain's edge and out of sight.

He screamed and leapt, transforming in air. His wings beat with all speed, soaring downward toward the image of her breaking upon the rocks. Dhar roared in anguish, filling the air and his heart with a blast of fire and endless sorrow. Too much to bear, he shoved the image away.

He had spent decades in despair, unable to fill the emptiness left behind, unwilling to find happiness in all but the cherished memories he had of her. They had been treasures to hoard, shiny moments he polished by reliving them in his mind.

"Why look you so sad?"

She had known. Grief had turned love into an ashen taste in his mouth, a bitter rancor in his throat that ate him from within. Dhar had been little more than a hollowed shell by the time sorrow finished devouring his spirit.

He had taken wing and flew with all the strength he could muster, soared higher than any dragon had ever dared. Ice had frosted his scales, choked the breath from his lungs and frozen air crushed in against him... until finally the dizziness had won out.

Dhar had plummeted toward the rocks. Bloodstains worn away by time, marks only he could see, had called out with a jagged and patient embrace. The wild howl of banshees had ridden the wind, rending membrane from his wings, tore scales from his chest, set fire to exposed muscles straining against the fall. It had sought to open him up fully, to fill the void in his heart, the emptiness in his spirit that left him as broken and incomplete as the remains of his only –

"Father, no!" Eorana had yelled and took him from the side.

They had toppled end over end through the air. Hard earth had rushed up to meet them, unrelenting in avarice, unwavering in resolve. She had struggled to right their fall with young wings giving way. Fear of yet another loss had woken Dhar with its chilling grip, filling his senses with the dread of urgency. Helpless to act, nothing left of his wings by tattered remnants, he could do little but look into his daughter's eyes as they fell.

He had seen it then, the realization she could not stop or even slow their descent, watched the decision unfold and take shape behind her gaze. Eorana had gripped him with her claws, twisted their bodies at the last, as rock and earth shattered beneath their impact in an explosion of scales and debris. Both broken and severely wounded, it was she who had sustained the brunt of their fall.

"Our lives... are a gift," she had said, eyes wearily opening and closing, as if each time might be the last. "Mother's death... was a tragedy, but you dishonor... her passing by throwing away... your own life."

"Eorana," he had said and nearly choked, on blood and the fear of losing her. "I am sorry! Please... forgive me... and stay." Dhar could not fly, but his legs would still bear his weight. "I will fetch a healer."

"I will be fine." She had managed a smile. "Hold me."

Dhar had slipped an arm beneath her neck, cradled her head and looked down into her eyes. "Stay," he had pleaded, hating himself for his unwillingness to have done so for her. Her eyes had closed – "I love you." – and did not again open.

Lost to despair but refusing to dishonor his daughter's sacrifice for his sake, Dhar had chosen to seek penance upon Danarriden. It was the way of dragons. Those who transgressed went to the home world of their enemy, and for days or even weeks would slaughter demons or fall to the howling masses. Dhar had spent years on the fiery plane, unleashing guilt-driven rage in the buried hope that his end might be found in the talons of another's claws. Last of the Patrons, he was not like other dragons. He had dwarfed his brethren, who grew smaller every hatching. Dhar had faced endless hordes, stood his ground against Arch Demons. Though none of them had the strength or prowess to grant him death, they instead gave him a name: Demonsbane.

When they had chosen to avoid him, rather than rush into his waiting claws, Dhar decided his penance a fool's errand. He had sought out his old friend and asked a boon.

Thankfully, the Mirror Pool had agreed.

Dhar'paogi, the last Patron dragon, had stepped into its waters and emerged an empty vessel. His body had been changing, altering shape to that of a human male, but his confusion at the unfamiliar surroundings turned to worry and finally blind fear. He had fled into the forest, a man-shaped remnant of a gold dragon, with a whisper of faint memories still lingering in his ears.

He had wandered the world with no grasp of time's passage. As an elder race, he was immortal, could not die by any means but a violent end. Hunger and thirst had been his companions, always with him, driving him on, but never threatening his strength. When he had arrived in the walled city, the heart of mankind called Alixhir, he found nothing but taunting hatred and bitter laughter – save for one aging man who picked him up from the gutters and gave him a home and family.

"What do I call you, son?" Master Therol had asked, washing the grime from a golden cheek with ink-stained hands.

"Dar... Dar-Paj."

The images disappeared into fading light. The Mirror Pool was silent, and Dhar's reflection was gone. He was once again whole. At some point, he had changed to his natural form and stood over the waters as a gold dragon. Four times the size of the black brother they had come across on Danarriden, the sheer weight of Dhar's body sunk his claws into the sand.

Dhar threw back his head and roared, breathing a gust of flame that sought to burn the heavens from its starry cradle. He then shook with choking sobs. Rivulets of fiery tears ran down his maw, turned sand to glass beads and hissed a cloud of smoke from the water.

The Mirror Pool rose up in man shape. "Do you wish now that I had honored your first request?"

"No," Dhar rasped, his voice trembling the sands. "I should never have asked you to bear my pain for me."

"We are friends then?"

Dhar dissolved the binding runes on his chest with a wave of his claw, burning them away in a brief flash of golden light. He knelt upon his forelegs, bowed his head to the pool so they could look one another in the eyes. His voice was heavy with sorrow, but Dhar was resolved to carry the burden of loss on his own – with the help of his friends, of course.

"Always."

* * *

Asmodan was no taller than a human. Each life he had fed upon, every demon in his retinue, had shrank his massive body inward. Smaller, more compact and potent, his form had changed with each influx of *furie*. Skin and scale had sloughed off, muscles thickened and grew dense. He had felt the etching of runes across his bones, burned into their surface by the *furie* he ingested. There was only one explanation, but the Arch Demon wasn't sure if he should be angered or feel grateful.

Already the whispers echoed through his mind.

"What have you done to me?" he asked the god in tones like a growl. He looked down at his arm, one of only two now, and recalled the vial pushed deep into his wound. "I should have known better than to trust you."

He walked toward the rift, drawn to an allure born of murmurs beneath his mind's voice. Night was falling in a drawn shadow of bloodless dark, graying the golden field of sweetgrass beneath his feet. Obsidian haunts rose up in the distance, crags of black fingers that gave sign of watchers. Their body heat betrayed them. Ambush holes beneath the soil were misshapen rings of silver to his eyes, as if a new sight had supplanted the old. Scent of a hatchery caught his attention, the charred aroma and grizzled taste of rugged shells. Far below the lava vents to the south, their *furie* beckoned to him. The rift's pull was even stronger.

So much smaller, seemingly frail in appearance, his own worshippers did not recognize him. They too fed the disease coursing through his veins. No matter how many he had drained, the hunger deep inside him would not abate. It groaned with the wailing of eternal emptiness.

Asmodan disappeared in a wisp of black, a buzzing swarm of clicking beetles left in his wake. He appeared a hundred paces ahead. The world trembled for a brief instant, as the swarm settled to a chill quiet in the frosted trail left behind. Again he became the black, a mass of clacking chitin with abdomens afire and tiny wings tracing eddies of frost through the air. Distance lost all meaning. He traversed the landscape in the span of thought, a wraith born of icy fire and rasping hunger.

The bulk of a mature soldier distorted sight of a feast with the heat of its pulsing lifeblood. It sprawled atop a warren, shoving bodies in its mandibles with bloodied arms as thick as trees. Asmodan passed through its upper body and appeared amidst the carnage. Ice spread across the soldier's thorax, cracking the rigid plates. In a blur of ebon motion, to the sound of wails beneath the swarm, Asmodan gorged upon all their *furie.*

Wiping blood from his mouth, unsatisfied, he looked in the direction of the rift. Leagues passed by him in the frozen silver of new sight. Molten rock stood still, fiery wind lost its voice, and currents of ash and dust hung suspended in the calm of muffled time.

Lessers were constructing foundations far around the rift. Their secretions softened obsidian, so they could shape it to their needs and place the glassy rock into a pattern for it to harden. Mature weavers coaxed lava from the ashes and molded glowing slag into pillars of cooling black. Their scent was intoxicating, blinding him with need.

Each one fell prey to his hunger.

Asmodan felt on the verge of transformation. A few thousand more, and he would change, evolve beyond the constraints of his demon body.

And you will. The whispers settled to a single voice. Revyn slithered through his mind like grubs staking a claim. *The choice is yours. Feed and submit, wield the power of a true god, or starve and die a free corpse.*

The revenant Ombreusk led an army his way. He could smell the enchantment woven into the prison of undead bone and rotted flesh, saw the feralkin's tortured spirit flitting in and out between the ribs, the bars of its unliving cage. The heat of ten thousand bodies rose up on the horizon, ropy limbs and howling cries, thumping hearts and glowing *furie*.

"That is no choice at all," Asmodan said and grated his teeth through the roar of mounting hunger.

There is always a choice, the god whispered, but his words were lost to the maelstrom.

With elated abandon, awash in blood and *furie*, the truth of freedom revealed itself. It was not the illusion of choice, the desire to control, but the liberation of body and spirit from consequence. In submission, he found power. In succumbing, he found free rein.

Asmodan slaughtered them all, fed on their essence as an icy wind through their hearts. Though the hunger was sated, he saw no need to relent. A specter in the dark of bloodied night, he touched them with the black, engulfed them in the swarm. He wrenched *furie* from the chaos of writhing bodies, from the throng of maddened turmoil, and left a quiet harmony in the ashen remains. The army fell apart in a swell of debris, a choking wave of charred remnants beneath the hush of silenced cries.

The transformation overtook him.

There now, Revyn soothed. Asmodan was down on all fours, screaming against the pain of change tearing through his essence. *You can already feel it.* His body and spirit strained against the alterations, pushed near to the limits of unmaking. *The mantle of godhood is now upon you.* His skin fell away for the last time. He looked down at his hands, human hands, and saw through the layers of flesh and blood the divine runes etched upon every inch of his bones. *Stand and be recognized, first of my new children.*

Asmodan stood, naked in the warm breeze, and was fully clothed in fine silks and cotton breeches at the notion. He looked down at his human body, and it too shifted to a likeness of his old form, albeit human-sized. Just as he traveled by thought, his body too shaped by whim.

"That is convenient," he noted, studying the world with new eyes. His senses were keen far beyond mortal imagining. He saw life in the form of *furie*, from the revenant heading west to the maggots within a corpse a thousand paces behind him. He felt Danarriden beneath his feet, the pockets of gas, the flow of molten rock and liquid metal, the odd spinning of its axis around a sun no one could see, the heavy clouds of crimson and fiery gold that blanketed its girth. He tasted pollen in the air, sulfur and ash from a hundred leagues off. The world was filled with lingering scents that brought images to mind, each demon that had labored upon the temple around the portal, the young boy of human and faeron descent, the black dragon that sought redemption, the gold dragon in human form, the living statue of obsidian, the Arch Demon Fezuul... "Now what were you doing here?" he wondered.

"It worked," a female shamarrin said at his side. The elf had long sable hair and eyes like violet fire. "Not that I had any doubt."

"Revyn," Asmodan said and inclined his head. "You are crafty beyond measure. It is an honor to serve."

"I am not quite done," she said and smiled. Revyn looked up toward the heavens and called out, "Nanindar! Would you be so kind as to grant an audience?"

The god appeared in a puff of smoke and the tinkling of bells, like a charlatan magician in a travelling show. He was wiry thin, with a long nose and pointed chin. He wore black and yellow leggings, a checkered satin shirt and a floppy hat over earthen hair in desperate need of combing.

"Brother," he said in greeting with the flourish of an exaggerated bow. "How may I be of –"

Revyn vanished in a swarm of black and appeared behind the god. She quickly grabbed hold of his arms.

"I knew I could count on you," she said in his ear and nibbled at the lobe.

Nanindar laughed. "I love you too, dear brother. Now what is the meaning of all this?"

"You are not born of father," Revyn sneered. She tightened her grip, and the god winced. "And I am not your brother."

"Well, clearly. The bosom against my back is quite firm." He chuckled and eyed Revyn over a thin shoulder. "What is this all about? You cannot kill me, and I can do nothing for your eternally soured disposition."

"I have no need to kill you. I just need you to be still for a moment."

Asmodan's body blurred to a swarm and froze the air between them. He stood before the foolish god, or God of Fools as he was known, and bit deep into the flesh above the collarbone.

"Gah!" the god shouted in pain. Asmodan backed off, wiping blood from his lips, and Revyn let the spindly god free with a shove. "What did you do that for?" He healed the wound and clothing as if brushing away dust. "You asked me here so you could have me *bitten* by one of your shapelings? I mean really, what did you think was going to happen? That I would drop to all fours, turn into a wolf and bow to your every whim?"

Nanindar's eyes fluttered with dizziness, and he fell to his knees.

"Well, not a wolf, no." Revyn grinned. "How do you feel now, *brother*?"

"What have you done to me?" The god's body began to tremble and shimmer a wan light. His eyes, once blue, now swirled a bright emerald. "I am changing."

Asmodan shook with laughter. "Oh the irony!"

"As with my werewolves, wereboars and werebears," Revyn explained, "I needed more. I created chaodyn, my weredemons if you like. Now Asmodan," she said with pride, "he is entirely new, the first of my wrathborn – what I suppose you might call a weregod."

Nanindar looked up from all fours.

"You," Revyn said, "shall be my second."

*   *   *

Markus had aged before their eyes. One of the fish-elf guards had been running a coral blade across his chest when Lochlaen was destroyed. She had paused, a mild look of surprise across her pallid face. They had watched his body wither, his skin wrinkle and grow age spots, his hair whiten further and fall away at the brow. One of the priestesses had shrugged and ordered the guard to keep cutting.

Over and over since he had woken, they cut at his naked body with coral blades. It continued to burn his skin, even after the priestess had healed each wound. They asked him of Luorn, where his revenants could be found and how many Emblems he possessed. The same questions, all pointless, he refused to speak a word to any one of them.

They had known where he was.

He studied the chamber, its high ceiling of azure crystal flickering with golden light, like seeing the sun from beneath the ocean's surface; rows of gray and blue marble columns, gilded in swirls of fanciful design from top to bottom; a pearly white floor with no seams or sign of mortar, polished to the brilliance of a mirror. Of all the stonework and enchantment, what struck him most of all as a work of art were the walls. Bright red coral, full of life, ran the length from floor to ceiling. Ocean water lapped against and through it, shimmering in vast liquid barriers. Occasionally, light from above would illuminate a series of runes across the water, rippling silver wards that kept the ocean at bay.

"I know you understand me." Another guard cut at his middle, the female who had punched him with the force of a mule kick. She would be attractive if not for the dark scowl that perpetually marred her features. The maniacal gleam in her eyes or the smile that promised him pain were almost as enticing as her lithe body outlined in scant armor. "How do your ears feel?" she asked with that twist to her full lips.

She had cut them off earlier. A priestess had put them back, healed the flesh enough to stop any bleeding, but they both still pained him a great deal. Markus met her gaze and smiled, wondered what she might taste like beneath that armor. The coral blade dropped lower and touched against his growing excitement.

"Enough," a priestess said from behind the guard and tapped her bone staff against the mirrored floor. Two guards from the grand archway on the right, female of course, approached and saluted, tridents to chest. They were all female, in fact. Markus had not seen a single male since his arrival in Anoran-Rai. The thought made him smile again. He had learned more from the foolish elves than they ever would from him. "Force him to eat and drink but only enough to keep him alive. No sleep. I will return in one hour. Let him bleed a while."

The priestess too was somewhat attractive, despite the ice in her veins. She was too much like a fish for his tastes. His bloodthirsty admirer left without a word. One guard held his head still, while the other forced raw fish and dirty water down his throat. Chained to two pillars, his arms and legs spread wide, Markus had no choice but to stand. His muscles cramped and burned, almost as badly as the coral, but he had suffered far worse in the past and would no doubt do so again. He blinked against the horrid breath of the first guard. It smelled as if a fish had taken root in her mouth and died weeks ago.

How long are you going to let them keep me? He had been asking Revyn to help him for hours. The god either chose not to answer or was otherwise occupied by his endless scheming. *Are you anywhere near the illysidaen city?* he asked Trafaelos.

I am not, the revenant replied, his voice prickling the skin. *The daefarim, however, soon will be.*

Markus hoped Revyn would not keep him waiting that long. Not to mention he would be stranded beneath the ocean. His golden puppet had stopped answering his beckons. Likely Barr could be blamed for that. That was the problem with mortals. They didn't always stay dead when you killed them.

And how many more of my Brood must I lose? His dreams of domination were slipping away. He began to wonder, not for the first time, if he had been foolish to ever trust in Revyn.

"You wound me," the god said, her breath causing him to wince again. Revyn took hold of the other guard's hand and bit down at the wrist. Her eyes immediately flashed a beryl sheen. "Would you be so kind as to go fetch our friend's sword?"

"Straight away!" she replied and left.

"You were here all along?" Markus asked in disbelief. "Why did you wait to set me free?"

"I was busy elsewhere." Revyn shattered the emerald metal shackles with a touch of her finger. "As for your revenants, soon it will not matter. I have found a way to restore your *furie* and immortality, to revitalize you with such power that your undead kings and the Emblems combined will pale in comparison."

Markus had smiled wider with each word, and the old lust for battle and conquest rose up within him.

"How?" he asked, as the new shapeling returned and handed him Luorn. "And when?"

"Be patient," Revyn said and changed form to a high priestess. She tapped her bone staff against the floor and grinned. "Have faith in my scheming."

"Revyn!" a female voice shouted, cracking the floor and marble columns with its strength.

"Greetings, Kierna." Revyn bowed, and he became a fearsome knight in black armor. Dozens of female elves came rushing in from both archways. "How does this day find you?"

"How *dare* you attack my children?"

Coral red lips, silken hair black as night and in a flowing gown of fine white linen, the Goddess of the Deep was not amused. She clenched a fist, and blue lightning crackled between her fingers.

"I think you are confused," Revyn replied, his voice echoing within the depths of his helm. Illysidaen Gharak and Eneir began to surround them. "These creatures are descended from Celene's first. *Your* children are still on their way."

Tridents, spears and staves were leveled at the god. Markus stepped aside, his grip on Luorn firm. If the fish-elves wanted a fight, he was more than willing to repay their hospitality.

Revyn vanished in a blur of trailing black. The buzz of insects followed his path through the room, as he bit three elves in an instant. All three turned in the blink of an eye, dropping to all fours as massive beasts born of nightmare. A wolf, a bear and a boar, they attacked their once brethren in blind rage. Kierna tossed lightning and jagged ice, upending stone in deadly blasts of debris, but Revyn was too fast.

Another three were bitten.

More elves charged into the chamber, their crimson tattoos alive with *furie*. Narohk, Maurdon, Ballar and a single Valar rushed to the aid of their goddess.

Show me power! Markus demanded of Luorn.

As you wish, the Emblem replied and thrummed in his hand with the combined might of twelve deities.

A nimbus of ebon cloud formed around him, shot through with flashes of gray. Markus strode forward into a waiting throng and felt *furie* coursing through his body like a current. A guard stabbed a trident at him, as three others moved to intercept his advance. The metal froze and shattered upon contact with the growing cloud. The blackness spread and engulfed those foolish enough to get too close. They dropped their weapons and grasped at their throats, no longer able to draw breath. Their skin darkened in black splotches, marring the scaly flesh with a sickness that consumed them. The Valar stepped forward in robes of flowing emerald and a deep sapphire. She sent healing magic forth to intervene with the cloud, to push it back upon Markus. The attempt was futile at best. Four more fell to the wasting black, as Markus leapt at the sage and stabbed her through a lung.

"No more chanting for you," he said, leaving her to drown in her own blood.

The chamber was in chaos. Revyn turned elves as quickly as they arrived. Kierna had struck him a few times with magic, but none of her attacks did any lasting damage. In the end, she was forced to destroy her own children, lest the disease in their veins contaminate the whole city. In the carnage that ensued, Revyn took hold of Markus and led him out through an archway.

"Damn you, Revyn!" the goddess screamed, and her voice shook the corridor.

Shrieks of the dying followed behind them.

They walked briskly, killing or turning those they met along the way. Revyn led him through a series of twisting corridors to a vast hall. Two rows of portals ran from one end to the other, panes of silver light encased in oval crystal. The portals stood three times the height of an elf, were wide enough to ride a carriage through and still had ample room on either side.

"This one," Revyn said, indicating a portal halfway down the right-hand side. "Go through."

Markus walked up the stone platform and into the silver light. It felt cool against his skin, as he stepped from Anoran-Rai into a chamber carved inside a tree. An elf was waiting there for him.

"Markus," Lorelei said curtly.

The Ballar tossed him a set of sylvannis leathers and headed for the doorway without a word.

You know what to do, Revyn told him.

– 17 –

arr returned that night alone, still shaken by the notion that his friend Dar-Paj had been a dragon all along. Barr had watched him change shape and grow to an unfathomable size. Dar had stood taller than the trees when he reared up, with a broad wingspan that made Idelle seem like a sparrow. Even the dragon from Danarriden was but a child in comparison. Barr assumed that meant Dar was far older than he seemed as a human. Dar had bowed his great head and spoke in a voice like tumbling rocks, thanked Barr for helping to restore his memories and said they would meet again soon. He had taken wing and disappeared into the night sky before Barr could say goodbye.

Fluora was suddenly crushing Barr in an embrace, trembling with fear and anger. She gripped him tight around the middle. Her face pressed hard against his chest, and he could see she had been crying.

"You almost died," she accused, squeezing harder. Her eyes closed tight beneath a soft brow marred with frowning. Barr couldn't help but hug her back, nose buried in her fiery curls. He had no words to explain. She had seen it all. "You cannot leave me," she said in a quiet voice and loosened her grip. Fluora looked up into his eyes. "Not like that. Not ever."

He kissed her, wondering not for the first time what she had seen of his future that frightened her so much.

"I won't," he promised. "Not if I can help it."

It was a close fight? Idelle asked. He had expected her and Aren to be angry with him, but neither showed anything but concern. *We know there wasn't enough time. Lochlaen and Dar would have been gone with the Emblem if you didn't leave right away.*

What about Dar? He could tell Aren was hurt by the idea of Dar's betrayal.

He was marked with a binding glyph while we were held captive in Noria. Markus was using it to control him and through Dar use the mists. Barr hung his head, as the image of Jahd's remains came to mind unbidden. *We went to the Mirror Pool to restore his memories. He flew off afterward, saying we'd meet again soon.*

"Will you tell me what you've seen?" Barr asked her and pushed a wayward curl behind her ear. "Not my fight with Lochlaen. Whatever vision has been bothering you since we first met."

"No," Fluora replied firmly, as if she feared speaking it aloud would make it come to pass.

He flew? Aren asked. *What does that mean?*

Dar's a dragon, Barr said. Of course Fluora already knew. *I didn't get to speak to him before he left, so I'm not sure what happened. I just know he was big. Very big.*

That actually makes sense, Idelle said. *I always felt something more inside him, like his body was just a mask.*

Aren padded up from behind and nuzzled Barr with a wet nose. Barr let Fluora go, knew there was nothing he could say to change her mind, and turned to face his furry companion. He hugged Aren around the neck, but the hound rose up on his back legs and toppled Barr to the ground. Buried beneath the bulky show of affection, barely able to breathe, Barr gasped and tried to push him off his chest.

Aren, get off me!

Not until I'm done with my turn hugging you, the war hound said. While Barr was helpless, Aren licked him across the face. *I'm not mad, but I still wish I could've gone with you.*

Idelle laughed at the two of them, nearly falling from her perch in a nearby tree. Another groan from Barr, and Fluora joined in the laughter. She patted Aren on the head and got a lick for her troubles. Fluora backed away, shocked and blinking from the unexpected bath.

"Aren!" She wiped her face with both hands. "How could you?"

He gave a questioning look, as if he'd done nothing wrong. Barr continued to struggle beneath him.

Fluora laughed all the harder.

* * *

Barr woke early the next morning. Though still tired, too much weighed on his mind. He stopped at Fluora's door, watched her toss and turn, her brow furrowed in dream. Not even sleep granted reprieve from her visions. Careful to move quietly, he slipped down the hall to the kitchen and found breakfast waiting on the table. A bowl of cut apples and honeydew, with three types of berry, had been prepared while they slept. He poured himself a glass of water and began to eat. All that weaving had left him famished, but he only just now felt the empty pangs of hunger. There were no wheat fields in Dwendorim, so in the past bread had to be traded for. Yet there was a loaf of darkbread and a tin of butter on the cutting block. Barr wondered how it had gotten there and had eaten half the loaf before realizing he should save some for Fluora.

He felt more refreshed with his belly full. The haze of tiredness burning at the edge of his consciousness faded beneath the burst of renewed energy. He went outside, where light from the runes above brought early dawn to the city. Hanar sat upon the edge of the central fountain, twirling a finger in the water.

"Good morning," he said. Aren and Idelle were still asleep. "Thank you for breakfast. I was curious about the bread –" He could see something was wrong. "What's troubling you?"

Uinbro appeared, sitting beside her. *She looks sad. For a statue, I mean.*

"It is nothing, Master." She looked up at him with a weak smile. "I just have a difficult choice to make."

I thought you might like to know – Uinbro began to say and was quieted at a look from Barr.

"Is it anything I can help you with?" He held out a hand, and she took it. Though she was so very different from the Hanar he had known as Fanarin, his feelings for her had only grown since they'd met again. "You've always been there for me, Hanar. I'm here for you too."

She stood and led him toward the street's end, past a rock fence where Barr recalled was a graveyard. His wife and daughter were buried there, as well as... himself. They walked to his family plot. A fresh grave had been dug with a blank granite headstone.

Barr suddenly felt terrible. He'd almost forgotten.

"Uncle Therol," was all he could say.

"We buried him while you were away. We thought it best to wait for your return before inscribing his stone."

Uinbro sat down with a heavy sigh and rested an arm across the bare headstone.

What do you want? Barr snapped at the Emblem.

My brother Drakha has been wrested from the fetid corpse called Ombreusk. Uinbro leaned back his head, as if basking in the warmth of the false sunlight. *The Arch Demon Fezuul took him captive last night.*

"I appreciate that," Barr said and squeezed her hand. *That's good news, I suppose. I doubt Markus could take it back from him, though I don't know how much Fezuul can be trusted either.* "That reminds me. I'll go back to the cavern and gather Jahd's remains. I'm very sorry for her loss."

"There is no need," Hanar said in a tone grateful for the offer. "We have already retrieved her remains and buried her near the memorial. She was brave to the end, despite the evil creature she faced alone."

Uinbro cleared his throat. *Speaking of evil creatures, Wyllnuor has also claimed my brother Caorynor. He is on his way back to Markus as we speak.*

You know where Markus is? Barr wanted to throttle the apparition.

Of course, the Emblem replied and wiped dust from his transparent silken shirt. *He wields Luorn at this very moment, though sister is loathed to bear his touch.*

Why didn't you tell me sooner?

I was a little busy, if you recall. Uinbro turned a lazy head Barr's way. *Saving your life and all that. And we do sleep, you know.*

He asked Hanar, "How did you know where –"

"Good morning," Fluora said from behind them. She was wearing her blindfold again, and belted at her waist was Balaen. "Oh, I am sorry. I did not know you were mourning your uncle."

"It's alright." Barr turned her way, wanted to reach out and pull her close but was still wary of that line he feared to cross. With all his past experiences, as both men and women, he thought handling their relationship should have been easier for him. "How are you feeling?"

Fluora kissed him on the cheek and smiled when he blushed. "You mean the blindfold. I needed rest from the visions –" she placed a hand on Balaen's pommel – "and thought we could spar a bit more before leaving for Drakanon."

"The vardikor city?" Barr asked in surprise. "Why would we need to go there?"

"Solastin plans to sack it this afternoon with an army of ogres he has been gathering for some time now." Even blindfolded she seemed to look past him. "He used the Emblem Faelsha to unite their tribes. Without our help, the dwarves will not live to see morning."

More fighting? Aren asked sleepily. *Guess I woke just in time.*

Some of us are still trying to sleep. Idelle sounded grumpier than usual. *And don't you dare ask me to fetch you some fish.*

No worries, he told his sister. *I'm sure we won't leave before everyone eats.* His voice went up a notch in mild concern. *Right?*

Barr shared a grin with Fluora. "Thank everyone for doing this," he said to Hanar. "If you need anything at all, we'll be at the park."

"I apologize for how I acted last night," Fluora said as they walked. "I get very emotional when the visions come upon me, as if I am both myself and the people I see."

"No need to explain. I understand." Her arm went around his waist, and she leaned in closer. Barr put an arm across her shoulders, felt her hair against his chest. The boundary he feared to cross blurred even further. "I see you've got Balaen. Does it bother you the way she talks directly in your – oh, never mind. Sometimes I forget that's how faeron normally speak."

They entered the park and walked across the grass to the spot they had last sparred.

"It can be unsettling to hear a voice without seeing or knowing who spoke. I can only imagine how confusing it must be for you, what with Aren and Idelle sharing your thoughts and having two Emblems as well." They squared off to warm up with the martial dance, moving in time with one another. "Although a room full of faeron might be worse."

Barr laughed. "It was. That first night we met..." He let the thought trail off. Memory of that encounter only served to remind him of the terrible vision she refused to share. "It was difficult."

"About our joining," Fluora said, twisting her body in a fluid motion. "Have you given it any thought?"

In truth, he hadn't. "I'm not against it." She stopped and arched a brow. "I mean, I'd welcome it." His stomach fluttered as he spoke. "I do love you."

"I know that," she said with a smile and resumed the dance. "I just wanted to make clear that I too love you and welcome the marriage." Something in her tone... "However, I do have one condition."

She can't have me, Aren said flatly. *Not unless she plans to feed me more often than you do.*

Shouldn't you be trying to catch breakfast? Barr was beginning to sound irritated. *You don't need to listen in on every word we say.*

Aren pouted. *I don't like to miss anything.*

"As much as I love Aren," Fluora put in smoothly, "I had something else in mind. We will not be wed until the day I can best you in combat. And I mean *truly* best you. If you hold back in the slightest, I will know."

"We'd kill each other," Barr protested. "I don't just fight with weapons, Fluora. I use whatever it takes to come away alive."

She spun her arms through a block that led into an elbow strike, still matching Barr's practiced moves. "I am aware, which is why you must train me to win. We will both have to work very hard if we want this."

"I do want it," Barr said, "but learning to weave can take a lifetime." He knew why she was so adamant on this demand. Whatever grim vision of his future she had seen, his death mostly likely, she hoped to avoid it by being skilled enough in combat to save him. "Is it really that important?"

The dance ended. Fluora faced him with hands out, raised and ready to block or strike. Silence was his only answer, that and the fervor with which she trained. Barr knew he could teach her to be a better fighter than he, to master any weapon she chose, but weaving was another matter. The seer sight would give her no advantage in learning magic.

He feared their joining would be a long time coming.

*   *   *

After hours of unrelenting exercise and training, the two of them needed a break. Fluora left to stretch tired muscles and find something to eat, while Barr headed for a fountain to scry. He tried finding Aislin, as he did at every chance, but the Emblem was guarded by wards. A thought occurred to him.

Uinbro?

Uinbro appeared within the fountain, studying its sculpture as water passed through his body.

You want to know where the others are, he said with a nod. *Some are very distant, hard to see, but I can try.*

Can you tell me where Aislin is?

She is with Feraesk, Uinbro replied, *marching at the head of an army through Salianne. Their goal is the jade city, at the heart of the rallan nation.*

Nagas, Barr said. *What about Markus?*

He is in Geilon-Rai.

Barr's heart sank. His fear of the sylvannis council being turned had come to pass – his father, Seltruin. He had no way of saving them but by fire. How many friends would he be forced to slay? Speaker Roedric, Lorelei and countless others...

He pushed the thought aside. *Can you see Amintro?*

She remains with the demon hunter on Danarriden.

Barr's eyes went wide. He couldn't imagine the pain of a hunter with demon blood in her veins, let alone being surrounded by millions. The burning compulsion of the geas would be crippling. He didn't begrudge Sera the death of his uncle. She had been infected. Her will belonged to Revyn now. Blame fell squarely on the god's shoulders.

Barr? A voice interrupted his thoughts.

It was his grandmother. He waved a hand over the water's surface, and an image of the Queen appeared.

She sat upon her throne in Starshrine. Fezuul was by her side, with Drakha laid between them on the throne's arm.

What's wrong? he asked. Despite what he considered to be a happy occasion, wresting another Emblem from a revenant, she looked grave. *I see you have Drakha.*

Fezuul bowed his head to Barr, not only sensing the scry but the direction from which he was being viewed.

Yes, Ariana replied, *and Ombreusk as well. Fezuul captured the revenant last night. He contacted me, and I brought them both here. I think you should come right away.*

We'll be there shortly. He ended the scry and headed toward home. To Aren and Idelle, he said, *It's time to visit Faeronthalsos.*

Fluora and Hanar were outside waiting for him. As Aren and Idelle approached, Barr asked Fluora, "Isn't it a little boring when nothing surprises you?"

He poked a finger at her middle in an attempt to tickle. She swatted his hand away before it touched, and Barr swore he saw her eyes roll behind the blindfold.

"No," she replied at his antics, "and if you even try to tickle me there, you will regret it."

Where? Aren asked immediately and chuckled.

I have no idea. I wasn't even going to try again, Barr said. *Although, it would be funny to wait 'til she turns and – oh.*

Fluora gave him a sweet smile.

Barr brought them to the Queen's Court. The hall was unusually quiet, empty but for his grandmother, the Arch Demon and a handful of guards.

"Welcome home, my prince," Ariana said and stood. They embraced, and she kissed his cheek before letting go. She hugged Fluora as well, kissed her forehead and said, "You, my dear, are always welcome. As are you all," she told the others. She touched Hanar on the shoulder in a gesture of friendship and even tousled the furry hair on Aren's head.

What, no hug? The big hound huffed. *I like hugs too.*

I remember, Barr said dryly.

Idelle said, *You'll get her pretty dress all covered in hair. You may want to consider a bath sometime soon.*

Alright, that's the second time someone's said that to me!

The Queen sat back down and pretended not to hear them. She gave Fezuul permission to speak with a nod.

"Prince Barr," the demon said and inclined his head. A bow would have been too much respect, a concession that Barr was the greater between them. "A pleasure to see you again."

"Asaen Fezuul," Barr said and bowed, using the title reserved for Arch Demons in their own tongue. "I'd like to thank you for aiding our efforts."

Fezuul indicated a room to his left with disdain. Barr assumed it was where Ombreusk was held captive. "The revenant is bound in the strongest glyphs I know." He clenched a fist and bared his teeth. "Revyn has gone too far. He has somehow infected Asmodan, one of the other Asaeni. The disease has driven him mad. He slew and fed on his entire retinue, proceeded to the rift and then destroyed the temple my children were building. None survived."

"That is not all," Fluora said quietly, studying the demon without her eyes.

"No," Fezuul agreed and his jaw tightened, "it is not. All five hunters are on Danarriden." He shook his head in true concern. "I fear my home and my people will be lost."

Fluora stepped closer, as if to console him, but did not touch. "They are chaodyn now, with the blood of Asmodan in their veins. Rather than incapacitate them with pain, the Arch Demon's blood has strengthened them." She cast her eyes downward, as if what she had seen of the future was too grim to face head on. "As for Asmodan, he has become something far worse."

"Damn that fool Revyn!" Fezuul spat, scorching the pristine floor. "Him and his petty jealousy! He cannot bear the thought of demons worshipping another, so he will destroy every one of us out of spite."

"Not destroy," Fluora said, "turn."

Barr said, "That's not possible. Demons are immune to the disease."

"They were. Now they are not."

Fezuul sat down hard upon the steps.

Every demon will worship Revyn, Idelle said, giving voice to the dreaded thought on everyone's mind. *If he finds a way to bring them to Taellus...*

As if werewolves weren't bad enough, Aren snorted.

"I cannot see what will happen to the others," Fluora said to Fezuul, "the other Arch Demons. Yours and their fate hang upon a choice you have all yet to make."

Looking to Umbreusk's cell, Barr said, "We need to know what else Revyn has planned. Clearly Markus is just a pawn, and the Emblems don't play as large a role as I'd thought."

Do not be so sure of that, Uinbro said, lounging on the other arm of the Queen's throne. *We are more now than we were when the twelve children gods forged us.*

"Here," Ariana said and took up Drakha. She handed it to Fluora. "May this keep you safe until Aislin is again ours."

Fluora took the Emblem from her Queen and bowed in thanks.

"Before I leave," Barr said to Fezuul and headed to interrogate the revenant, "I'd like a little time to talk with you about something."

"As you wish."

He found Ombreusk chained by magical bonds, links of cerulean light that rose up from the ebon tile and held fast to bony ankles and wrists. More so, Barr could see the crimson and golden outlines of glyphs encompassing the revenant, a series of twisting and interlocking wards so complex that it was difficult to focus on the runes as a whole.

He stood face to face with the undead king, looking into its eyeless sockets with contempt. It was a mockery of life, an animated corpse that survived off the blood and *furie* of others. He could see the tortured soul fading in and out of its rotted shell. No matter how hard it tried to shake free of the prison its body had become, it could do nothing but rage in eternal frustration.

Looking deep into the fires that were its eyes, Barr mustered his will and let his mind lose focus. He drifted into the glow, forcing his consciousness through. Images flashed from both sides, flitting out of the darkness and taking shelter behind the flames. The less Barr focused his thoughts the more images arose, until a vision of both past and present settled in his mind.

A vast shapeling army rose up like a beast of night and fell upon Noria with all its hunger. It left a mountain of bones in its wake and was not sated. Other armies were gathering as well, like a tide of darkness perched upon the precipice of mankind. Spurring them all on was the shadow of Revyn, his relentless whispers fueling their thirst for blood and *furie*. The cries of war echoed in his ears, a deafening clamor...

... that shook the ground beneath his feet with the strength of an earthquake. Skies rolled from gray to black, as the storm of booted feet marched across the land, trembling cracked earth with their numbers. Kheran saw them all from the vantage of a seer's eye, the future armies that would call down the end of time. Nothing could stand against them, as they consumed enemy armies and spat out renewed darkness.

And in that ocean of shadow would one man stand, clad in the plates of a silvery-gold armor. A shining beacon would he be, casting off the dark, as the sun brings new day, brightening the fields of battle. The whispers of twelve that shielded his frame would then melt beneath the skin, infusing his body with the light of the gods, until only one voice remained.

He was the master of mortals, a slayer of gods. With the power and furie *to rule all worlds and all life, he would aspire to the heavens and see past the starless cloak at the root of all creation...*

The connection broke. Barr stumbled back, gasping for air. He blinked away the vision but couldn't shake the image of the man in his mind, the glowing eyes, the aura of pure *furie* that emanated from his body like blistering waves of heat from an inferno.

His power was both absolute and terrifying.

"Markus will *not* get the Emblems!" Barr said in a near snarl.

The vision had unsettled him, flooded his senses with fear and anger. He had no way of knowing if the revenant had somehow tampered with the images. Barr couldn't see the man's face but felt a terrible dread at the premonition of Markus wearing all twelve Emblems.

Barr refused to believe he could fail, that everyone he loved might be turned or killed. His anger fell away to a deadly calm.

"And neither will you," he added quietly.

Barr placed both hands upon ribs etched in bloodied runes. Ombreusk was helpless to resist, unable to move, held fast by the glyphs. The fire of his eyes faded to dim embers.

"Do it," the undead king said in hollow tones. His jaw moved with each word, but it was magic that gave him voice. "Set me free."

Drawing *furie* from Ombreusk and himself, Barr put up a hasty shield and pulled with all his might. Bones splintered beneath his hands and broke free. A blinding yellow light burst forth and threw Barr across the room, smashing him into the runic wall behind with the force of a battering ram.

Hands torn and bloody, slumped to the ground, Barr felt a wetness seeping down his back. He crawled toward the revenant, reached inside its chest and pulled free the remnants of its heart. It turned to ash in his hands and drifted down to the charred tiles. The bright form of a transparent spirit rose up and stood over him, looking down with a faceless mask. It then faded from sight, leaving behind the golden image of a memory. Before darkness rose up to claim him, all Barr could see was a remnant of the premonition...

The man sheathed in silvery-gold light.

*   *   *

Left at the next rise.

She had never met the other four, but Sera knew they were on Danarriden. She could feel their presence somehow, as if their link through Revyn was far stronger than the bond they shared through Herne's geas. She hated them all, the gods. No matter how much power they thrust upon her or divine will they used to bend her, Sera would never break nor would she ever stop hating. It kept her sane, focused on survival. Unlike the other mindless shapelings, which she could sense as well, she had not succumbed fully to the disease.

Sera did not worship Revyn.

All in good time.

She did his bidding, mostly to avoid the torment of refusal, but Sera was long used to obeying compulsions. In complying she had found the geas less painful, almost tolerable. Its ache was dwarfed by her need to feed. Sera felt the lust for blood and *furie* in the others. She shrank from it like poison, saw it for the trap that it truly was. Succumb to the hunger, and her devotion would be his.

Chuckling in her thoughts chilled her spine.

The other hunters scoured the demon plane in their shapeling form. Sera would not surrender. To take the form of a demon was anathema to her existence, went against every fiber of her being. Besides, it was what Revyn wanted. She had instead settled for allowing bright crimson and ebon scales to cover the immodesty of her transformation. The holy fire that encompassed her body burned away all but the gleaming scales and divine runes. Changing to a demon would spare her the pain of burning flesh and its rejuvenation, but as in all things in Sera's life, pain was both her bane and her savior. Some she shrank away from, as if their touch would rend her spirit. Others she embraced to persevere.

Pain is good for the soul, it is true. Cross that lava flow and continue west.

Hatchlings and lessers could not survive her aura. They perished within seconds, consumed alive in feral screams of fading anguish. It was the way of this new world they were forging. There was no room for the weak. The young, old and infirm were fed upon or discarded. Only the strong were turned, and only the heartiest demons became chaodyn.

See, you are doubly blessed.

Sera had fed sparingly, just enough *furie* to keep at bay the breaking of her will. It was a precarious line to walk. Those she had bitten and let go changed with all speed. They had fallen writhing and screaming against the disease, only to rise moments later with a beryl sheen in their eyes. They had run off in all directions, seeking out their once brethren. The disease had been spreading like wildfire across the land, exponentially growing with every pack she encountered. Soon all of Danarriden would be his, with an infertile army at his command.

Our army.

None of the others seemed to care they had become barren with their changing. Sera knew it was more than foolish to cling to hopes of a family as a demon hunter. The geas brought nothing but suffering and death to all around her. Still a part of her longed for it, for a child to bear her love. That piece of her heart had died when she turned.

I will bear your love now.

The others were too blinded by hunger and *furie*, but she could see the true design behind the plague. There was no mistaking that Revyn desired to rule all worlds, every living creature, but his disease was not the means toward that end. It was meant to wipe out all life within a very short time, killing everything off within a single generation. When there was nothing left to turn or feed upon, his shapelings would die out. The gods would be his, unable to help or hinder. Only then, when all life had passed, when the worlds were an empty canvas, would his plan draw near to fruition.

Sera reached her destination, a stronghold of basalt and obsidian. Its walls loomed above her, so high they blotted out the orange skies. She punched a hole wide enough to pass through, sending rock and debris flying outward. In the expansive courtyard leading to the keep and jutting towers, the Arch Demon Balizar awaited her arrival. Her blood surged with his presence, inflamed by the geas. The legion of demons standing with him would be turned, while he was meant for another.

"He is mine," Asmodan said for his own benefit. She had no need for his instructions. The wrathborn stood by her shoulder. Sera gave a curt nod and fought down the bile in her throat. "I am to have your little trinket as well."

She removed and handed him the bracelet without hesitation. The legion of demons roared and charged as one. Amintro lengthened to a sword in his hand, and the once Arch Demon stalked forward. She cared little for the loss. The bracer had been silent since her turning. Enchanted weapon or pretty jewelry, it didn't matter.

Sera never had need of either one.

* * *

Naerat Sanae, Seat of the Gods in his native tongue, the name of his home had been bastardized over time by other races. North Haven they called it, as if dragons had need of a sanctuary. They were all that remained of the first children, despite time and evolution dwindling them away. All the others had died off, having met with violent ends, or had changed through the millennia into entirely new species.

Dhar could see the mountain far off in the distance, hours before he would reach its peaks. It pained him to think of home, what he had lost, the sacrifices, the dull aches of what could have been. All of Taellus was headed toward destruction. Dhar was not sure if he cared, if he could bring himself to care.

He had new friends. They did matter to him, and he was certain they cared for him. He once thought it would be better to forget, to expunge himself of the pain. Only a small part of him had fully realized what he was truly giving up to be free from despair. The happy memories, the love relived in thought, moments that could raise his spirit higher than the sun, fill him with such joy that no obstacle could bar his path, all that was best in his life had gone away with the pain. It had left him hollow, a shell, with a new set of fears and pains.

Dhar was no better off than he had been before his memories were taken. He was back in the dogged grip of despair. It tightened his chest, strangled his heart, froze him from within until his only salvation was a numbing distance from it all. Thrust it aside, no hiding it within anger. He could not revel in their smiles, feel the warmth of their embraces, enjoy the melody of their voices, fill his heart with their love, without reliving the sickened horror of their deaths. For the sake of his mind, for those he called friend, he would tuck away what he treasured most until the time both joy and sorrow could reconcile in his heart.

He arrived at the mausoleum, an immense chamber at the tip of Naerat Sanae. Carved from the blue granite by fire and *furie*, the ordered collection of vaults spread through the mountaintop with rows of ornate columns to support it by stone and enchantment. Each one, be it white or black marble, bloodstone or jade, sandstone or granite, was crafted and imbued by the loving claws of both Patron and Matron dragons. The vaults of each house were done in precious metals and gems, depicting lineage, calling and tier, as well as any notable deeds and contributions. A dragon's final resting place for the body was a tribute to how they had lived and to those they had shared their lives with.

The vault of House Uindanarri loomed before him. It was intended to hold numerous generations, stretched off into the dark where no runes upon its walls lit the way in pale light. Only two had been laid to rest, their bodies encased in gilded stone. Longing to be with them, Dhar rested his bulk between their tombs and fell to sleep.

When morning set the outside chamber alight with flecks of swirling gold, Dhar opened his eyes and found a silver staring back. She stood looking at him from the entrance, her dark eyes sad and still pining. So much smaller than he remembered, Kaolanni was much like the rest, diminished in size from one hatching to the next. There was no denying her beauty, the bright eyes and smooth maw, high ridgelines and violet scales along the edge of her ears. Her chest scales were polished with meticulous care, and the scent of her roused feelings he would not pursue. Dhar knew she moved with subtle grace, as if the wind were always with her, and had an agile mind to match her lithe body. It had once been her desire to bear his seed, be it for love or the welfare of their species.

He could see in her eyes that had not changed.

She struggled to draw breath, shivering with little quavers along her scales. The sight reminded Dhar of his duty as the only living Patron, to reinvigorate his people with stronger stock. Their home within the mountaintop, a colossal city of lairs, shaped stone and enchantment called Naerakeilan – Godsbreath – had been abandoned by offspring no longer able to survive its frigid heights. A new city was shaped from the mountain, half way to the ground far below. Its lairs were much smaller, too small for one his size, and not quite as grand. Its stones served function, not aesthetics, and the enchantments that ran its length were diminished in scope and elegance, much like the scions that inhabited its halls.

Dhar had never felt at home in the new city, what its shapers had dubbed Wyaerakeilan – Dragonsbreath. The remaining children of Curoch were so proud of the home they had breathed into the cold stones, oblivious to what Dhar felt was their arrogance. He had chosen instead to live alone in his old lair, rather than slight the god who had breathed life into his body.

"You should not be here," he said in a fatherly tone. In many ways, he saw them all as his children. Though taking her as mate would strengthen his people, he had no room in his heart for another.

"I saw you arrive," Kaolanni said, the delicacy of her voice marred by wheezing. "I waited until morn to come find you."

"You always were respectful." Dhar brushed his maw against hers with affection as he passed, mindful of the stirrings it caused within her. "Let us fly to a more comfortable height."

She followed him down to World's Edge, a wide ledge jutting out from the southern quarters of the city. Many gathered there to warm their scales in the sun or meet before flying off upon the winds. They landed together and were immediately noticed. Dhar endured the happy whispers of his return, refuting with a shake of his claw any rumors of his demise upon the plains of Danarriden. Though he did not want to dash their enthusiasm, he politely asked for some time alone. Knowing nods and toothy smiles ensued as they left, the hopes of an entire race in the loins of a lone silver.

"There was no need to send them away," Kao said and blushed, darkening the scales beneath her eyes. "Your presence lifts their spirits. Gods know we could use some joy in these times."

"I wanted to speak plainly with you." The slightest furrow touched her brow, and he could see her bracing to be crushed. "I have been gone for so long because I had my memories taken from me. I was in the shape of a human, with no idea of what or who I was. Last night my memories were returned to me, so I too have returned."

"And I am glad to see you well. I would also like to speak plainly, if I may?"

"You may."

"I am aware our feelings are disparate, but neither are they wholly opposite." Kao looked up into his eyes for the strength to continue. "Time is of no matter to us. I have waited in the past and willingly do so in the future. Unless you tell me to stop waiting."

Dhar felt the void in his heart skip, as if a gust of warm air had passed through it.

"Do not stop waiting," he told her, lowering his head so that their eye ridges touched at the ends. "Please."

"Welcome home!" a gruff voice called out, as a red approached them with the deadly gait of a warrior. Fire ran in the veins of every dragon, but it was said the blood of reds burned hotter than others.

Dhar raised a brow. This place was never his home. "Good day, Emissary." To Kaolanni he said, "If I do not see you again before I leave, know that I will not be long gone."

She nodded and backed away before turning to fly off. Khronaerrin stopped at a fair distance, so he would not have to look up while the spoke. He wore the runes of his office, silver markings across his chest.

"Have you returned to head the conclave?" Khrona asked, his desires poorly hidden. Ambition ruled his existence. "I would of course not oppose it."

"Neither would you welcome it," Dhar replied evenly. "Your position is safe, Emissary. I have no aspiration for politics or city life."

"Many will be sad to hear it." Khrona's tone indicated he would not be one of them.

"There is a war coming to Taellus. I will be gathering my battle armor and taking part." Dhar's tone was also clear, and it brooked no argument.

"That is a decision for the conclave."

"Feel free to discuss it," Dhar said. "This world is in its final death throes, and it will not be long before the war arrives at our doorstep."

"With so few of us left, you would risk our existence with war?" The red scoffed. "Why endanger ourselves in the matters of lesser children? No mortal war can reach Wyaerakeilan."

"I will await your decision on the field," Dhar said, his eyes bearing down on the young leader.

His intention was clear. Dhar would fight with or without them. The only decision left to the conclave was whether they would honor the old ways and join him.

Dhar flew off to gather his battle armor.

crying in the water of the fountain outside his home once again, Barr sought out the other Emblems. All but two of the six were warded: Ghaireuk, which he knew was in the Baeryd mountains, guarded by hundreds of trolls, and Luorn. The second was with Markus at Geilon-Rai. Barr watched him in the water's surface and saw he had aged even more. He was seated at the council table in the rounded chamber where Barr had fought against Cciran – in the same cushioned chair Speaker Roedric sat upon when he exiled Barr from Geilon-Rai. Chained to the eastern wall of the tree was his father, Tuvrin, on his left Lorelei and to his right Seltruin. That Barr was able to scry into the city at all, that the wards had somehow vanished overnight, was no coincidence.

How are you feeling? Idelle asked him. She already knew. He sensed her deep concern, the struggle with her own grief, and knew she just wanted to talk.

I'm fine. Just a bit overwhelmed.

Barr clenched a fist and continued to stare at the scry. His wounds had been easy enough to heal once he woke. It was everything inside him, in his mind and heart, that caused pain. Doubts were eating away at his resolve, taunting him with the vision of the silvery-gold man, proof of Barr's inevitable failure. Seeing his father and friends bound in chains, entire cities infected, only strengthened his fear that time would be better spent in halting the disease's spread, rather than chase any more Emblems. They already had six, between himself, Fluora and Dar. Wasn't that enough to ensure Markus couldn't gather them all? The prophetic vision that haunted him seemed to show otherwise.

You need something to eat, Aren suggested. *When was the last time you had a meal?*

Barr wasn't interested in eating or resting or wasting any more time while people across Taellus were dying or being turned.

Idelle landed beside him and slapped the water with the tip of a wing, ending the scry. *There's only so much we can do. If you set your expectations too high, you'll never be satisfied with anything you accomplish.*

"Revyn is the true enemy," Fluora said from behind them. "The Emblems are the only way to destroy him." Hanar approached carrying four burlap sacks, each the size of a baked ham. They bulged with small jars of fired clay in blacks and reds. "We need to leave. Hanar and I have made preparations."

The Protector handed two to Fluora, one with red jars and the other black, along with a heavy belt of thick leather tooled with locking rings.

"Others are organizing," Hanar said and fastened her belt, "to join us on the field." She secured the bags on each hip for easy access to the clay jars. "They too have prepared flash bombs and scented oil."

Aren joined them with a questioning look. *What's a flash bomb?*

"Just where are we going?" Barr asked and stood.

"Drakanon." Fluora finished securing her arsenal, and she looked as if the added weight might topple her. "Solastin's army is almost to the bridge. We can save the vardikor from annihilation and take Faelsha at the same time."

"Alright." It was exactly what Barr wanted. "I wasn't able to scry Faelsha though. How will we –"

Mist rose up all around them and carried them into starry black for a brief moment. They arrived to queasy stomachs and a stone bridge four carriages wide.

Aren gagged, on the verge of losing his breakfast.

"A little warning next time," Barr said and made a face at the taste of bile at the back of his throat. "You could do with a little more practice."

"Excuse me?" Fluora arched a brow. "Do you mean to imply you traverse the mists better than its Matron?"

"Archers!" a dwarf shouted from the gate behind.

Two steel gates at either end of a portcullis kept the northern end of the bridge secure. A stone wall, some hundred feet high, stretched across the river for as far as Barr could see. Its eastern end followed the mountain Drakanon was built into and disappeared over a fall. The city was a collection of winding walls constructed along the face of the mountain, comprised of homes and shops that twisted ever upward. Large gates had been built at every turn. Fighting up toward the top would be nothing short of impossible. Defenders could fire down into the streets with little fear of retribution and retreat back to the next wall if a gate was breached.

Scores of archers fired, filling the air with the sounds of plucked bows and whirring arrows. Each shaft struck harmlessly against Hanar's barrier, eliciting flashes of blue light. Arrows fell to the bridge with an odd clanging.

"Stop that!" Barr turned and yelled at them. "You're wasting arrows!"

"Hold!" the same dwarf ordered. The archers ceased, as their general looked down at Barr with eyes like gray stones. He stood between two crenellations, so that only steel pauldrons and an ebon beard were visible beneath his helm. "Who are you little man, and what evil magic have you brought?"

Little? Aren sounded incredulous. *He's one to talk. I could eat him whole.*

"We're friends," Barr returned, "and magic is not evil. People are evil." He looked toward the skies and reached down through the earth for a ley line. Will brought to bear, he conjured dark clouds from the distance with the rumbling flashes of a terrible storm. "This is not a wall fight. Lose this bridge, and your city falls."

With that Barr turned on his heel and headed out to meet the army of ogres and stalkers clearing the horizon. There were more than he could have imagined existed in the hills, thousands of the lumbering brutes. They wore animal skins, boiled leather, iron chain and fur boots. The weapons they carried were the size of small trees – stone or wooden clubs, mauls and great axes. Stalkers ran between them, hunting companions too small to ride for the giants. Some would stop to sniff the air with twitching whiskers and sightless stares.

They snarled and bared teeth that could be seen even at this distance.

"He's daft!" Barr heard a soldier say. Another one called out, "Have fun dying!" and others laughed along with him.

"Uinbro," Barr said to the Emblem. The apparition appeared and began walking with them. "We could use some reinforcements."

The sort everyone can see, I assume? The Emblem gave a chuckle.

Ghostly soldiers clawed their way up out of the soil on the river's edge. Water thrashed behind them in time to their moans and clanking armor. Hundreds of spirit knights in bloodied full plate soon stood ready to fight, wielding swords as tall as a man or tower shields with war maces and bastard swords. Covered in armor, their faces were hidden by helms and dark visors. Despite their transparent bodies, they left heavy boot prints in the soil as they began to march.

The sky darkened overhead beneath a shroud of growing storm. The first drops of rain touched down in visible splashes, heralding a downpour to come. Barr and the others continued toward the end of the bridge.

"Some bulwarks please, Vereu," he told the Emblem, leaving its construction up to the sword. Molten spikes of iron jutted up from the earth along the river, stabbing into the rain with hisses of gray smoke. Like a second wall of reddened metal, it stretched out from the falls to thousands of feet toward the west. "Very nice."

"Wait!" the general called after. "What would you have us do?"

Barr drew both kyan and looked back. "Bring every juggernaut, disciple and evoker you've got, and join me on the field. Then put whatever shielders you can at the end of this bridge. They can hold off the entire army if they have to, and it will keep the ogres busy while your archers pick them off." Barr looked at each dwarf along the wall. "Ogres can't swim. If I see the gate under siege, I *will* destroy the bridge. I refuse to let Drakanon fall."

The vardikor cheered, raising their axes and voices in defiance of a larger enemy army.

"Raise the gate!" the general commanded with a grin. "By Kraug's beard, we'll be drinking from ogre skulls this night or warming the earth with our blood!"

"Stay close to Hanar," Barr said to Fluora. "I'm going to fight through them to the back and kill Solastin." *You stay with her too*, he told Aren. *Idelle is with me. If all else fails, she can fly me over them and throw me at the damn revenant.*

Not that again! she said with a shiver of feathers.

The heavy sounds of steel boots on stone rang out behind them, as dwarven soldiers and weavers marched out in ordered columns. Juggernauts led the way, all bristling steel and angry stares. Armored head to toe, with only braided full beards in war regalia showing through, they shook the bridge with the weight of their marching. Some hefted wicked looking double-bladed axes and swords, though most chose to wield two of the dual-edged war axes vardikor were renowned for. Their disciples wore heavy robes of brown and black, thick padded cloth reinforced with steel bands. They carried war mauls and blackened heaters, but their true weapon was more devastating – the divine *furie* at their disposal. The evokers were an unusual sort for dwarves, weavers so devoted to stone and fire that their Art bordered on worship. Unlike turners, who wove for personal gain, evokers had pledged their lives to King and Craft.

The general and a command of juggernauts caught up to them at a jog. The ground had gone muddy from rain. Barr hoped it would give them an advantage by causing the ungainly ogres to lose footing as they fought. Dwarves were even shorter than faeron, but their limbs were thick and muscles dense. It would take more than mud and slick grass to throw off their balance.

Banners from the three major clans were carried out to the steady rhythm of steel against shields. Stonefist, Ironbeard and Ireheart clansmen marched together as units, proud dwarves with the look of a forge in their eyes. Dozens of other banners were interspersed through the army, all colorful heavy cloth, many bloodied and torn from past battles.

Barr gave a sidelong look to the general. He had introduced himself as Tark Stonefist. "You might want to consider a drawbridge."

Tark scoffed. "Vardikor work stone, not wood. Even our bloody arrows are made of stone!"

"What? What about the bows?"

"We *buy* them!" the general answered and laughter ran the ranks of his men and women soldiers.

The ogres began running at full speed, screaming in bloodthirsty rage and shaking the ground as if a quake threatened to tear it asunder. Stalkers ran out in front, set loose to kill as they pleased. Rain dulled their senses, but it was not enough to blind them to scents and body heat.

Fluora grabbed a red clay jar and smashed it against the ground. It easily shattered, spilling heavily scented oil over grass and rock. It took seconds to permeate the air with its heady musk, a sweet odor so strong dwarves a hundred paces off immediately complained.

"Oi, girl!"a juggernaut called Burtok shouted to her. "Quit stinking the field with your bloody perfume, ya daft wench!"

A stout female beside him glared at the lack of courtesy and gave him a hefty shove with her left arm.

"That is the whole point!" Fluora shot back. "Stalkers see by scent, you fat runt of goat!"

"Who she callin' fat?" he said to no one in particular. Burtok looked down at the wide girth of his armored waist, then gave Fluora a shrewd look. "Oi! Gimme one of those!" He walked over to her and added quietly, "If you please."

Hanar and Fluora began passing out clay jars to the others, hoping to spread the scent as wide as possible. "These are incendiaries," Fluora said of the black jars, "flash powder. Ogres are sensitive to light. The flash may stun them long enough to get a strike in."

"Hmph!" Burtok thumbed the jar, unmindful of the ogres nearly upon them. The stalkers had all stopped in their tracks and looked around confused. "Guess yer not so daft after all – for a blind girl."

She pulled him aside. A stone club came crashing down, missing his shoulder by a hair.

"I am no more blind than *you* are!"

"Oi!" Burtok yelled at the ogre then stomped his foot down on the club, tearing it from the creature's grasp. "Watch yer manners!" The burly dwarf drove his mace into the ogre's unprotected middle, doubling the twelve foot tall monster. He grabbed the ogre by its collar and pulled down hard, forcing their eyes to meet. "Never interrupt a lady!" he shouted and smashed the clay jar into its face. A flash of white sparks exploded between them. "Kraug's balls, I'm blind!"

Aren pushed him aside and bit into the ogre's neck for a quick kill. *These dwarves are kind of fun!*

Barr ran ahead through the enemy, dodging stalkers and striking out with practiced ease. He feinted, slipped between the legs of an ogre, and sliced both arteries in its inner thighs. The creature fell to its knees and bled out in seconds. Barr was already gone, running as fast as his legs could carry him. He leapt and spun through the air, jumping over a stalker and killing two ogres by cutting the corded veins in both their necks. Landing in a roll and sliding across the rain-soaked field, he took another swift kill. Blade flat, it went through the ribs of an ogre and into its heart. He quickly pulled the kyan free and continued forward. Weapons hit the ground beside him in great splashes of muddied rainwater, always but an instant too late. Hands the size of shields tried to grab or knock him over. With the fluid grace of an acrobat, he stepped through evasive patterns from the martial dance as he ran.

Battle raged behind him. The dwarves were like iron given life, fighting without relent, shrugging off blows that would have crushed any human. Illusory knights fought beside them, cutting away ogre limbs with giant swords. If struck, the knights vanished into wisps of air, only to reform and attack again. Light flashed across the field, bright bursts from clay jars or *furie* unleashed by the wrath of disciples. Fluora wielded both her Emblems, Dalaen and Drakha. The raging storm answered her call with lightning strike after strike. They forked down into the enemy with crackling destruction that arced from one smoked body to another. Barr faltered, slipping in the mud as he looked back.

She's fine! Idelle cried from above him. She'd been swooping in to rake claws across the backs of stalkers or carry them off to be dashed against the rocks of a cliff. *Just focus on getting through to Solastin!*

An ogre punched him as he hurried to get back up. It was a glancing blow across the chin but enough to send him sprawling. Blood and muddied water splashed around him as he landed on his back. The battle went quiet, with a light buzzing in his ears. Ogres snarled and moved toward him as if slowed, their motions blurred by the haze in his eyes. Barr blinked and rolled away from a stone axe. Its chipped edge went into the earth up to its haft where he had been just a moment before. Wiping mud from his face with the back of a sleeve, he slipped between the grasp of thick fingers. His muscles burned, and his lungs began to sting from the cold air. Ignoring it all, he pushed on, slicing legs and wayward hands with his ironwood blades. A stalker came too close and felt the momentary sensation of a blade across its neck. The blind creature fell, tripping an ogre in the process, and spurted lifeblood over them both.

A pane of silver light appeared before Barr. It was oval in shape, slightly taller than he, and was barely a hair's breadth thick. He paused only for a second before turning aside, dove and came up facing the light. A Protector stepped through, one unlike any he had ever seen. He then realized the silver light had been crafted by a traveler, an artisan portal maker the arachon used to journey out from Dwendorim.

The golem bowed and joined the fray without a word. Other portals began to open across the field. Even the ogres stopped to wonder at this new change but renewed the fight when living statues came walking through.

What's this all about? Aren asked.

Idelle dove at a stalker. *Just keep your eyes on the ogres and keep fighting! This is a battle, remember?*

"Friend Barr," one said to him, and he could have sworn it was Uinahd – but different. Her runes were all changed, much smaller, and they covered every inch of her body. That she hadn't called him Master also seemed odd. "Behind you!"

He ducked the swipe of a club, and Uinahd charged forward. She moved with the speed of an agile human, much faster than any Protector ever had. She was wielding two swords from the arachon armory, blue steel enchanted with silver runes. She drove one blade into the ogre's chest, straight through the breastbone, and stabbed the other down into its pelvis. She gave a twist and severed that one's spine.

"I have been remade," Uinahd told him, answering the question on Barr's face. She pulled her blades free, letting the ogres collapse.

"What happened to you?" Barr asked. He studied her runes again, staggered by the complexity, then looked out across the battle where hundreds more golems had come through portals.

"We are no longer Protectors," Uinahd said proudly, as an equal. "We are arachon."

Barr dodged a thrown ogre, its body broken before it landed. "You used what I taught you to rewrite your instruction runes?" He recalled Hanar saying she had a difficult decision to make. "That's amazing!"

"I am glad you think so." She cut off a stalker's head in one swing and kicked the headless corpse into an ogre that came too close. "It was not without sacrifice. There is only so much room to work with, and not enough for the Oath. I have given up my place in the protectorate to become a champion."

A champion was an arachon weapons master, Barr remembered, born and bred to the Art of Melee. Shocked by the transformation, he couldn't shake the disbelief at what he was seeing. The golems had done more than evolve. They had taken evolution into their own hands.

"What of the others?" he asked her, still wary of the battle and longing to be after Solastin. He looked out toward the hills, searching for the revenant. "Travelers and what else?"

"Enchanters and eldarath." A massive portal opened in the center of the field, where a dozen travelers had gathered in a circle. "Oh," Uinahd added, "and one other, something entirely new."

A colossal golem stepped through, sending a boom across the land with its first footstep. Made of white and blue granite, it stood a hundred feet tall. Thick limbs stretched out from its rounded center, and its head was the size of a carriage. With giant eyes of golden *furie*, it surveyed the battle before walking slowly forward. The golem had an overall look of a Protector in armor, though its shaped stone was covered in blue steel runes.

"It is designed after the wardens," Uinahd went on to explain. "Its size was necessary to allow room for the Oath and its other instructions. Though it is part of the protectorate, it is not sentient like us. We do not yet know why."

"What is it?" Barr's eyes were still wide at the sight. The golem bent down and lifted ogres like rag dolls. It crushed them with granite hands, raining blood down its arms and legs, and tossed aside the corpses as so much refuse.

"The only one of his kind, we call him a destroyer." Barr ducked an axe, which Uinahd casually blocked at the haft. She sliced off the ogre's hand then cut a leg out from under it. "We thought to let him choose his own name, but he has not yet done so."

"He's still young," Barr said. "None of you began as you are now."

Barr! Idelle scolded. *Enough talk! I found Solastin. He's at the top of the hill with the giant stone and withered tree.*

I see it. "I'm going after the revenant that gathered this army." Barr eyed the spot Idelle had indicated and caught sight of the undead king. "He's got an Emblem, and I can't let him leave here with it."

"We will assist," she said and called others over. No longer part of the protectorate meant never again would she hear the voices of other golems in her mind. "This is my command." To the twelve arachon she said, "We will be assisting friend Barr in an attack on a revenant. Stay close and kill everything in our path."

Barr immediately saw the differences in their runic patterns. Eight were like Uinahd, champions of various colored stone, but the other four were something else. Only two of those were the same, which he assumed were enchanters. The remaining two then would be a traveler and an eldarath. With no time to wonder how their individual personalities had transferred with the new runes, having thought their sentience existed within the protectorate – their collective minds – Barr led them toward Solastin.

He glanced back at the field behind them. Littered with the dead and dying, it was a wasteland of speared, broken bodies, with giant limbs and headless ogre torsos forming brackish mounds. Gray light glinted off of steel, where fallen dwarves had been crushed to death inside their armor. Disemboweled stalkers laid scattered across the field, their entrails and green blood a stark contrast to the murk. Smoking black craters still burned with the intensity of magical fire, despite rain that had continued to fall in a heavy downpour. And in the distance, over two dozen stalker carcasses laid in a pile at the base of a sheer cliff, where they had been smashed against jagged rocks and torn open before falling. The battlefield was slick with comingled rain and dark blood. The miasma clung to legs and armor, leaving those still alive stained by its touch and slowed by its grip.

At the bottom of Solastin's hill, two hundred ogres formed a natural bulwark with their bodies, side by side with massive weapons held to fore. Hellfire rained down upon the dwarves and arachon soldiers struggling to win past. In sheets of swirling flame, like liquid demons on a rampage, the fiery onslaught consumed flesh, armor and living stone. In defiance of the storm, the fire raged with its own maelstrom. A torrent of steam drifted out from the fiery carnage, obscuring the battle on either side.

Disciples and eldarath did what they could to heal the burned and dying, but many had been charred alive where they fought. Shields rose up in half-shells of blue or violet light. Their magic took the brunt of another fiery wave but could not withstand both Solastin and a frenzy of vicious ogres. Boulders dripping magma shot toward the revenant from evokers working in unison. It struck against the undead king, sending earth and stone flying outward in an outburst of angry fire. When the resulting ruin had cleared, Solastin glared back at them, unhurt and eyes ablaze. The firestorm ravaging their front line intensified to a white-hot inferno. It set the very air on fire, blinding those nearby. It burned away their hair and skin, like vibrant flowers wilting beneath a desert sun in the span of a breath.

Barr and Uinahd's command cut a bloody path up toward the hill. Never stopping to engage the ogres in his way, he dodged past their heavy-handed attacks. He only took the time to riposte or strike out for blows that either killed or incapacitated. His ironwood blades easily sliced through the thick hide of ogres and stalkers alike. Leather armor, chainmail and bones all parted with the same ease. Barr chose his attacks in less time than it took to blink, with an unparalleled skill and precision earned from lifetimes on the battlefield. He took a hand at the wrist and darted past its spray of dark blood, was gone before the meaty flesh hit the ground still clutching its weapon. He sliced through tendons and arteries, left the giants to bleed or stand helpless to fight on. Through armor, ribs, layers of dense muscle and fat, he struck at major organs in a straight jab, always moving forward. At times too fast to be seen, his attacks left more than a few standing in wonder at what had just happened. Ogres dropped and died behind him as he ran, like trees being felled in a forest.

The arachon were a force to be reckoned with as well, their champions artful fighters. Fluid movements of body and weapons, graceful and elegant in unison, they fought to a martial dance all their own. Spinning in quick wide circles, ducking low through a twist of living stone and glowing blades, wading through enemy ranks in evasive blows that led one to another, the champions fought like lethal dancers. Their bodies were as much weapons as the enchanted blue steel they carried. From round kicks to swipes, elbow thrusts to pommel strikes, they attacked with the practiced style and expertise of sword masters.

Uinbro's illusory knights joined the fray from the east, cutting down ogres in great swipes of spirit blades.

Champions and juggernauts rushed in from the north, shouldering ogres aside to widen the opening. Barr and Uinahd reached the rocky base of the hill at the same time, slicing and kicking their way through.

The black of an enormous silhouette blotted out all light from above Solastin. Wind beat down in a heavy gust of rushing air, a single blast that sent ogres forward to their fronts and had dwarves struggling to push on. More thumping gales of icy wind, pounding bodies to the ground, and the shadow crashed atop the revenant. It gripped him with a gigantic claw, man-sized talons of mirror black digging deep into earth and rock. The bony prison of Solastin's corpse was pinned beneath the mass of an armored gold dragon.

Dar-Paj! Barr said.

Aren rushed forward. *Is that really him?*

Dar let loose a blast of fiery breath, a stream of gas and viscous liquid ignited to such heat that rocks were reduced to molten slag beneath Solastin. The earth dried of all rain in a cloud of steam, charred and crumbled to flakes of black ash.

"You are *nothing!*" Dar shouted down at the undead king, his voice rumbling like thunder. Solastin's bones were blackened, but the crimson runes etched upon them were still intact. "You and yours have earned the ire of a dragon. Perhaps time has dulled your memory, and you forget what that means."

Solastin struggled to move beneath the claw, but he could sooner bend a mountain to his will. The Emblem Faelsha was in his grasp. He conjured fire to rise up from his body and rain down from above, but no fire, not even magical, could scorch the battle armor of a dragon, let alone mar the scales of a Patron. All across the field, the battle had come to a jarring halt. Every eye was on the dragon. Ogres around the hill looked up at Dar with shocked fascination, a wordless fear that had left them frozen in place.

"You gain nothing with this victory," Solastin rasped in his hollow voice. "Even dragons will fall –"

Dar pulled him up from the ground, grabbed hold of the lower half with his other claw and tore the revenant in half. *Furie* exploded outward with concussive force, a sphere of visible energy that sent ogres and molten rock in all directions. It did nothing to Dar's black and silver armor, nor did it so much as dirty his scales. He let fall Solastin's bones and wiped his claws in disgust.

A luminescent form rose up from the shattered body, a figure of bright cerulean and icy white. Slender and tall compared to a mortal, the spirit looked up with glowing eyes like sapphires. It bowed its head and disappeared upon the wind.

"It's good to see you," Barr said to his friend and climbed the hill. Aren padded up and nuzzled Dar's claw. Barr looked up and strained to see Dar's face. "Though your size is a bit hard on the neck."

Dar trembled the ground with a chuckle. "It is good to see you as well," he replied, bowing his grand saurian head. The heavy battle armor, inches thick, was forged of a metal Barr didn't recognized. It had an inner gleam, like fireflies in a globe. "Fluora, Hanar," Dar said and nodded in greeting. "I trust my arrival was not too late?"

"Not at all," Fluora answered and smiled. "You could not have chosen a better time."

Barr picked up Faelsha. To Hanar, he said, "I think you should have this," and offered her the sword.

"You honor me, Master." Hanar took the Emblem in both hands.

Dar looked down at the frightened ogres with a stern gaze. "I assume you lot were somehow coerced into this idiocy?" Fire dripped from his maw as he spoke. "Leave the field now or perish. I care not either way."

Winged shadows loomed far off in the distant gray skies, tiny figures of black steadily growing. As if a flock of strange creatures, they flew together in wide lines. All became deathly quiet, listening to a distant thrum. The storm clouds around the flock lit up in ghostly colors. A flash here and there outlined the roiling dark. Yellow-gold, scarlet-orange, cobalt-white and black-emerald, the display was both dazzling and horrific. It was difficult to tell how many there were, despite the wide pattern they flew in.

"Must be at least a thousand of 'em," a juggernaut guessed, pulling at the crimson braids of his beard.

"Aye," another said, squinting, "but what are they?"

Dar turned his head to look. "Those," he said in mild amusement, "those would be every dragon in existence."

Ogres dropped their weapons and fled the field.

*   *   *

Asmodan arrived in a swirl of fire beetles, filling the icy cavern with their momentary buzzing. The air beside him stirred in a swarm of flies, as Balizar appeared, and Sonneil joined them to the drone of locusts. The other wrathborn looked as he did, human males alight with *furie*. Their eyes burned with an emerald fire. Pale skin pulled taut over rigid muscles with a preternatural glow. The weregods radiated such power to the extent that its energy blurred the very air around them, as if heat from the inferno inside sought release.

Form no longer held meaning. It was an amusement that served whim, though it had the potential for much more: a weapon, a tool of seduction, a fearful inspiration or living proof of the divine. Asmodan enjoyed the feel of fine silks against his body, in crimson and black. He let ebon hair flow back over his shoulders, dark as night like the slender blades at his belt. An extension of his body, both weapons glinted with starlight. Amintro he wore as a bracer beneath his sleeve, a trinket he had no real use for.

Balizar and Sonneil saw their brother in a human shell and after trying it came to realize its utility. Though Balizar preferred the reptilian scales of a demon, oval in shape, hard as steel and glinting like embers, he only wore them to highlight his chosen features. Beneath the eyes, along the neck and tapered ears, across his chest and abdomen, the scales were a stark contrast to his runic leathers and wicked daggers. Each one made of ice and barbed in a leaf pattern, the blades were enveloped in a mist of hoarfrost. Sonneil chose short-cropped hair like the sun and chitin armor with a mirrored sheen. Thick spines jutted out from his shoulders, knees and elbows. He flicked his wrists, and wide blades of jagged chitin sprung from the top of both forearms over his fists like claws. Each dripped a viscous poison that bubbled and hissed on the cavern floor.

Fezuul and Verran had chosen to starve rather than serve. Both were most likely dead by now. Revyn's plan was drawing to a close. Though none of them were privy to every detail, Asmodan could feel demise approaching the known worlds. Each god Nanindar turned sent a jolt of exhilaration across Asmodan's spirit. Tal, Khosh, Irin, Pharan, the new gods were falling one by one. It was only a matter of time before they all joined together and assaulted the heavens. The other children gods, Revyn's brothers and sisters, would either succumb or return to the father.

Guttural shouting and panicked females rang out all around them. Troll warriors hastily grabbed up weapons and armor, rushed to face the three intruders that had appeared from out of nowhere. Stone clubs, iron axes, even the paltry *furie* their shamans called forth, nothing they could muster would stand against the might of a wrathborn – let alone three.

Asmodan drank in the chaos, felt the rapid beating of hearts from young to grown, sensed blood and *furie* coursing through them. He smelled their fear in sweat beading mottled dirty skin, caught the rancor of fish and uncooked meat upon their breaths. More than a dozen females were with child, tiny hearts thumping out in mismatched rhythm. Some of the children were sick with fevers, and a handful of males were dying to parasites. When their alpha approached with the Emblem in hand, Asmodan considered they were doing the trolls a favor.

He attacked, shredding the troll wielder with godly speed. His blades were like slivers of nighttime sky, cold as death and unforgiving to the touch. The troll fell apart in a bloodied heap, its mithrinum weapon dropping to the stone ground in a *clang* of foreboding. There was doom in the hollow ringing, a dread born of disbelief, an ominous resonance that left either anger or despair in its wake.

The angry died first. The others followed soon after, in a methodical slaughter and frenzied feeding. From the bravest to the most craven, the strongest to the infirm, oldest to young, not a single troll was spared. Even the females and children who had managed to flee in time, to hide themselves away in a stony warren beneath a hut, were betrayed by beating hearts and ragged breath. Asmodan and his brothers set them free from existence, cleansed them of life in preparation for a new world. The plan had no room for those stained by free will...

And the plan was coming to fruition.

*   *   *

The God of Fools was often mistaken for a simpleton, disregarded out of hand by the unwary. The role of a fool in society, be they an entertainer for the public or a king, was to make astute observations and impart those bits of wisdom in the guise of humor or folly. No one but a fool would dare shed light on the faults or blunders of their sovereign. Only a fool could advise the king or edify the public by enduring the barbs of his own jests for all to see. Mockery was an art. In the wrong hands it was a blunt instrument that caused harm and ill regard. In the hands of a master, a true fool, it was power unlike any other.

Aside from the multitude of entertainers, performers and players, clowns and merry jesters, there were others who gave devotion to Nanindar. Many scholars saw the god for what he was. Though few in this day and age saw fit to worship a single deity, reverence of any kind and amount granted *furie*. From a gambler down on his luck to an aged academic, a troupe of actors and acrobats to hopeless wives praying for the safe return of a husband or child, all conferred power unto the god.

And each had died to fuel his transformation.

Rather than fade into the ether with the death of his last devotee, Nanindar had been reborn as a god without the need of worshippers. In surrendering his will, he had become more than himself, now served a higher purpose that he would share with his once brethren. The order in which he turned them was of Revyn's design. His second most challenging quarry was at hand, but who better to send against an assassin than a fool?

He arrived in Tehkon-Rai, the blackwood tree city of the shamarrin. A forest island in Undersea, it stretched through the cavernous world beneath Taellus. Luminous crystals, rocks and algae set the waters alight in soft tones of emerald and violet. Even the fish and trees had a glow about them, a bright cerulean shimmer within the endless dark sea and a silvery luster to the craggy bark of the blackwoods.

The shamarrin elves had no need of light to see, nor did they ever use fire for warmth. Their hearts and lives were the dark. Their strength and resilience was in the *furie* it gave them. Though they worshipped others, their Eneir were all clerics of Zilania – the Dark Queen, the Goddess of Thieves and Assassins. They were a female order of devout healers, skilled in the deadly arts of their matron. It was they who were trying in vain to rid the human Jyotika of Revyn's blessing.

Once leader of the Brethren, elite shadow assassins, she was all that remained of the cadre. The others had been slain by Helate, avatar and embodiment of Zilania's will. Jyotika was a favorite and had been spared in the futile hope of finding a cure.

Nanindar stood in the chamber where Eneir tried to save her. Their magic and potions had done nothing for the chained assassin. Jyotika's once dark skin looked pale as death in the tree's silver glow. Like other elven cities, each room in Tehkon-Rai was carved from the bole of an enormous tree. The blackwood chamber had the bittersweet smell of licorice root, of pungent rains that fell from saturated plants on the cavern ceiling.

They immediately noticed him and reacted. Helate had a dagger at his throat before Zilania could arch an eyebrow at the unexpected visit. *Furie* faded away from the hands of three Eneir, and they returned to tending their prisoner. One other eyed him coolly, with a gaze cold and black as starless night – the High Priestess Adrean, Speaker of the Dark.

"You are not yourself, dear brother," Zilania noted in a cautionary tone. Always shrewd, she was the deadliest of them all. She slipped two black crystal daggers from their sheaths. He had seen them before, knew how they broke within a victim and sought out vital organs with their shards. The blades would grow back in an instant, but it would be weeks before his physical body reformed in the ether. "Perhaps you should leave while you still can."

A puff of smoke, and he was leaning against the far wall. Helate narrowed hateful eyes his way.

"Now, now, no need for that." Nanindar smiled, but it had little effect on the avatar. "I came to help. I know of a cure," he said and approached the table beside Zilania. It was strewn with glass vials and beakers of colored liquids. "All it takes is a bit of –"

Zilania was a blur of motion, a black mist that took hold of his front and slammed him against the wall with an irresistible strength. A crystal blade bit into the flesh of his neck.

"You know of nothing but deceit," the goddess said evenly, marring her delicate beauty with dark intent, "and even in that you fall short."

His eyes flashed a beryl sheen. "I have only your best interest at heart."

She pushed the blade into his neck, spurting blood across her arm and the front of her leathers.

"I think not."

Nanindar would have laughed but for the wound in his throat. He reached up and cut open her forearm with a nail. In another puff of smoke, he was gone from her grasp and standing behind the table. Already disoriented with infection, Zilania swayed and fell to her knees.

"Lord Revyn brooks no failure," he said and leveled a deadly gaze at Jyotika. He flexed his palms outward, and two barbed throwing knives appeared in his hands. "The cure I spoke of."

He let fly the knives, one for her throat and the other for her heart. Neither hit their mark. Helate sped to her aid in an ashen wisp, blocked the knives with his body and stared down in disbelief.

"And they call me the Fool." Nanindar frowned. The other Eneir and the Speaker were summoning *furie*. "A short respite for you then," he said to Jyotika with a smile and vanished into the astral.

The next on his list would not be so easy.

* * *

Every soldier, mercenary, weaver and priest who had ever bled or drew blood on the battlefield, every man, woman and child who had ever offered devotion to the God of War, was visited with a waking dream. Tempas showed them the plague threatening to destroy Taellus, the dark army spawned of its infection. He showed the disease in all its malice, the truth in its corruption of body and spirit, how it bent wills to Revyn and led to nothing but death and despair. Hundreds of thousands had fallen in the wake of its spread, family and friends slain by their own loved ones. Turned parents had fed on their children, while the elderly and infirm were deemed weak and slaughtered for food or mere amusement. No one was spared.

All the disease left were shapelings or corpses.

The vision showed how far the plague had spread. It had infested city governments and royal houses, left villages and towns in utter ruin. It had infiltrated and taken over the Guardians, the Brotherhood, the Crimson Order, the Brethren and dozens of other organizations and guilds across Taellus. Entire cities had already been decimated, while others hovered on the precipice. Those races immune to the disease would soon have shapeling armies at their doorstep – if they did not already.

Tempas called through the vision, summoned each and every one of them to take up arms and join forces against a common enemy. Complacence and mercy were no longer options. Shapelings were a blight that must be eradicated. If even one diseased wretch was left alive, the threat of infection, death and enslavement, would forever shroud Taellus in looming darkness.

A final image of a Taellus overrun by shapelings, a bleak and lifeless world but for the snarls and glowing eyes of the diseased, brought the vision to an end for all but one thousand kheos and daumon minotaurs. Each one a veteran warlord, battle mage or harbinger, they were the elite of their species, the culmination of careful breeding and relentless training down through scores of generations. Tempas summoned them to the hallowed grounds of Halifax, the Battle Sanctum. An arena built to seat a hundred thousand, a fraction of the combined minotaur race, it was a sacred meeting place where daumon and kheos gathered once a year to pit their best against one another in games of combat. Only the finest were chosen to compete, while those invited to attend came from privileged houses and honored clans.

Though they answered the god's call with all speed, it would take time for them to reach the great stadium. Tempas stood at the center of its grounds with Herne and Unther. In a set of hunting leathers and strewn with vibrant leaves, his antlered head and thick legs that of a stag, Herne looked more animal than god.

"Are you sure this is what you truly want?" he asked Tempas, tilting his great antlers to one side. "Once it is done, it cannot be undone. Not even by my hand."

All three stood over a wide circle of intricate wards burned into the earth. Multiple glyphs, Herne had woven a trap the likes of which had never been seen before.

"We have no other choice," Tempas replied. He wore a full set of battle armor, heavy plate over chainmail and forged by Kraug himself.

Unther stood quiet and listened. His brow furrowed beneath hair like spun silver and a coronet of fiery stars. He looked as grave as the matter at hand. His hunting leathers were pale, not of this world, and revealed much of the painted markings across his body. Tall and lithe like an elf, shimmering skin and frosted glow like his celestials had once been, the Archer God of Stars and Sky seemed an amalgam of those who revered him.

"But so many," Herne protested. "It would drain you completely. You would be weeks in the ether reforming."

"That, too, is necessary."

"And if one should be turned?" Unther asked, giving voice to his brother's true fear.

"Death," Tempas answered without hesitation. "They will serve none but the geas. Any lapse must result in a swift end, so another may replace them with all haste."

Herne nodded in agreement. He stepped away and began drawing runes into the air.

"What is my part in this?" Unther asked.

Tempas regarded him for a moment, as if taking pains to choose his words. "Your glimmerkin are archers unmatched, with eyesight like no other. They see farther than dragons, scry by thought alone, and each bears the gift of premonition. They draw strength from the night sky, *furie* from the stars." Unther's expression seemed to say he needed no reminder of his children's abilities, but Tempas wanted to be clear about what he was asking. "I would have the same for these hunters."

"That is much to ask," Unther said and frowned. He rubbed at his bare chin. "It is also a great deal to imbue in any single creature, if they are to possess... similar gifts from the both of you and be ruled by compulsion alone. What is to stop them from ruling Taellus when nothing remains for them to hunt?"

"He does have a point," Herne added, rune crafting so quickly that wards were completed in the time it took to draw breath.

Tempas said, "When the last shapeling dies, the geas will fade and lie dormant."

All three gods agreed. Herne adjusted a few wards in his incomplete glyph, a maelstrom of runes grown wide in a wild sphere. Unther began to craft as well, cutting the air with a slender finger that trailed silver runes in its wake. Wards flowed from his hand like water, spilling into the glyph ahead and weaving themselves about the existing emerald runes.

The God of War had no need of runes. His will would fuel the glyph, merge his essence with the directives they were weaving. A small piece of him would forever reside within the hunters – knowledge, expertise and *furie*. It had been much the same for his Warmasters, but these would not number so few nor be contained by cloisters and a misbegotten oath.

"When you did this last," Unther said, continuing to craft, "the oath had not yet been taken." Descendents of the taur began to arrive through corridors and onto the arena grounds. "Have you considered there may be... consequences?"

"Have you?" Herne's tone indicated that he had, and the contemplation had not been pleasant.

Unther remained silent.

The minotaurs were spreading out along the circular wall, surrounding the three gods. Fully geared for battle, in steel plate and chain, boiled leathers and painted hides, each carried weapons hard won or passed down through generations – axes, swords, pole arms, and each of a weight that would stagger a normal man. When all one thousand had entered, their steps echoing through the arena and shaking the ground, they stood patiently waiting without a word.

The glyph completed with a click, as the final wards interlocked and spun into place. The emerald and silver runes darkened to cobalt, the blue of a clear and starless dusk. The spinning fires grew brighter until it seemed a single flame. Blinding to look upon, it rose high into the air. It continued to expand, radiating intense heat. Those gathered below were set aglow by its ghastly pallor, with shadows thrown against the wall behind them.

"It is ready," Herne said.

The glyph pulsed at his words.

"Will you submit?" Tempas asked his minotaurs in a booming voice that rattled dust from the stone pillars and seats of the stadium. "Will you sacrifice what days you have left? Your freedom? Will you forego all else in the service of Taellus?"

As one, each minotaur bent a knee and bowed their horns.

"Luck to you both," Unther said and vanished into the astral.

The War God's jaw tightened. He looked up, blue fire reflected in his eyes. He turned to Herne and said, "Do it now."

Tempas felt a hand upon his shoulder, and the world exploded into a chaos of pallid light and a scream that shook the heavens. Through the gut-wrenching pain, he realized the scream was his own. A maelstrom of pale fire lit his senses, connected him to the glyph as it consumed every fiber of his being. From within, flesh and bone gave way to the conflagration. An ember blown to full brightness, he became cinder and ash falling away onto the ground, replaced by a body of translucence.

He looked down at his hands and saw through them to the marked earth, where his ashes sparked the glyphs in a circle beneath him. He looked around and was alone but for the children he had summoned. He saw them as flickers of silver light, eyes in the coming dusk with whispers all about them. The scream had faded to a coarse memory. Only the thrum and whirring spins of the geas could be heard, its crackle of sated flames set afloat overhead.

When the last of him touched upon the ground, the sphere shot downward and struck the earth with enough force to stagger every taur. It charred soil and cracked stone, sent a deafening rush of air that tossed bodies to the wall. Its fire splashed and rolled over the ground in a liquid inferno, engulfing them all. It lifted their broken bodies, healed and transformed them in etchings across their bones. Pained cries of rebirth rang out in the cold air, as runes flared across flesh and forever left their mark. The geas had stolen all warmth, left nothing but frosted breath and the chill of a dying firestorm.

Tempas looked out at a thousand pairs of glowing eyes the bright cobalt of a fallen star. Each hunter stood tall, in an aura of holy fire. A familiar puff of gray smoke appeared before him.

"It seems I am too late," Nanindar said and eyed the apparition of his brother. "Ah well, it is only a matter of time –"

The Fool cut short his words, no doubt surprised he could not move or return to the astral. He looked down at the glyphs with narrowed eyes and gave a questioning glance to his ghostly brother.

"I have been expecting you," Tempas said, his voice an echo of a whisper. He smiled and fully faded to the ether.

Nanindar rolled his eyes. "How inconvenient," he said to no one in particular. "It could take hours to undo this silly binding." He looked out at the circle of blue fire and wild eyes all around him. "Interesting."

Every hunter raised a weapon and charged.

– 19 –

hen the dragons finally arrived, so many their wings blotted out the dying storm clouds, few ogres remained upon the field. Of varying hue and size, all adorned in battle armor, some dragons landed in a burst of mud and broken corpses, snatched an ogre up and swallowed the brutes whole. Others swooped down with incredible speed and plucked ogres at a full run from off the ground. The dragons were fearsome creatures, huge and exuding power – both physical and magical.

The scales beneath their enchanted armor were not of one solid color but were an amalgam of shades and tints of a base. The greens had a dark emerald along their outer scales, with swirls of a lighter jade when light struck against them, while the underside was a stark contrast of pale olive to the murky webbing of each wing. It was the same for the others, the silvers and blues, whites and yellows, purples and blacks, reds and browns – there didn't seem to be any other golds but Dhar.

Though Barr knew all of them possessed a powerful breath weapon, most were content to rend the ogres by tooth and claw. Only the reds, their scales glittering like spilled blood, blew fire down upon the fleeing ogres.

One of them was particularly savage.

"That is Khrona," Dhar said in human form beside Barr, Fluora and general Tark.

At least it sounds the same, Aren said of Dar-Paj's true name – Dhar'paogi. *The short of it anyway. Part of me liked him better with gold skin and white hair though. He seems so... ordinary now.*

Idelle said, *He looks much better, healthier. Look how he stands, so sure of himself. I'm happy for him. You should be too*, she told Aren.

He has changed, Barr agreed.

Thankfully, it was for the better. Or so it seemed from all outward appearances. Dhar refused to speak of the Mirror Pool or what had first driven him to forsake his memories. Barr was only glad that the man – or dragon, as the case may be – was just who they thought he was all along: a good friend.

"He seems... eager," Tark noted and blanched at the destruction. Khrona charred great swaths of muddied earth to kill a single ogre. "I'm glad he's on our side."

"Khrona is our Emissary," Dhar said and looked away, "head of the conclave." It looked to Barr as if he were ashamed. Either of the dragon's behavior or maybe something deeper, he couldn't tell for certain. "To your people he is similar to a clan chief, one that advises and oversees conclave decisions."

The general nodded. "Not a king though?"

"We have no ruler."

Dhar has an admirer, Idelle said in a playful tone. Barr could feel her girlish excitement at the prospect. *On the hill to your right, the silver in blue armor. She keeps looking his way but pretends she isn't watching.*

Fluora glanced at the female dragon and smiled for a brief moment, then turned her attention away before Dhar could notice. It still seemed strange to Barr that she turned her head about as if using her eyes, and yet her blindfold remained in place. According to Hanar and many of the juggernauts that had fought beside her, Fluora did amazingly well for her first battle. With but a few bruises and scratches, a single gash on her right arm, she had come through all the carnage for the most part unharmed.

Barr had healed her arm but wondered what sort of damage taking lives might have caused. Fluora slipped her hand into his.

The dragons were all landing, as the last of the ogres were swiftly dealt with. Khrona flew directly towards them with another two reds and a black falling in behind him.

"Can the others change shape?" Fluora asked. "All that looking up will be hard on the neck."

"They can," Dhar replied, "but will not. They see our gift as a weakness and fear being without the protection of their scales."

"We would protect them," Hanar said firmly, leaving Barr wondering if she – or the protectorate – had been offended by the comment.

"It doesn't seem to bother you," Barr said to Dhar. Despite the dragon armor, which had reshaped itself to fit Dhar's human form, Barr had to admit their fears were not unfounded. "Or does it?"

"It has its uses, the least of which is helping me to understand the perspective of others." Dhar looked his friend in the eyes, searching for understanding. "Without it, my people will always look down on other races. As a whole, we would become isolated and stagnant."

His tone betrayed a deeper fear that it had already come to pass.

Hmm, Idelle flew by, surveying the field. *They do seem a bit standoffish, don't they? I mean they're helping, but not one of them has said a word.*

"Well met!" Khrona bellowed in a fierce rumble, his eyes upon Dhar alone. He landed before them with a splash of mud and pooled rainwater.

Hey! Aren shook the muck from his mane and glared up at the giant lizard. Barr could feel him wanting to test his teeth against those scales and armor.

Barr was already covered in the filth of battle. A few more drops of mud made no difference. *He's preening for Dhar's sake. Just let it go.*

"Is this the war you spoke of?" Khrona went on and scoffed, molten fire falling from his maw. "Looks more like a massacre."

"You will see it soon enough," Dhar said loudly, for all to hear. He was not addressing the Emissary. "The enemy we face is the god Revyn. His children have been infecting or slaughtering the other races. Soon, there will be nothing left for them to turn or feed upon. Without our help, all of Taellus will die."

Khrona scoffed again, as if the notion mattered little to him. "What would you have us do?"

"We will fight!" Dhar replied to the gathered dragons. He did not look up at Khrona. "We will drive back this plague and safeguard what life remains." He turned to Barr and said, "I must go ready the others. Are you sure of this plan?"

"As sure as I can be." Barr shrugged. "What better way to meet a trap but with another?"

Dhar stepped away and changed form as he walked, shifting his body like an image rippling across water. He took to the skies in a leap that trembled the ground. The rains had all but ceased, and the fading light of day had broken through the clouds. With sunlight reflecting off his golden scales, Dhar looked majestic in air. The size of him made the others look like children.

Disciples and eldarath were scattered about the field and did what they could for the wounded. Women and the elderly had come out from Drakanon, to help bind wounds or carry back fallen loved ones. Food and ale were brought out in heavy wagons, a sight happier to the tired clansmen than the fallen enemy at their feet.

Barr felt the eyes of those civilians upon him, saw them whispering to one another and could imagine what they were saying.

"I have preparations to make," he said, indicating it was time to leave. He bowed his head in salute to the arachon that had gathered. "Words cannot suffice what you've done here today, your bravery and sacrifice. You selflessly put yourselves in harm's way for the good of others. Your ancestors would be proud, as am I. Thank you. I will see you all back in Dwendorim." To general Tark, he added, "And thank you as well."

The dwarf raised a bushy brow. "For what? You lot saved our hides today!"

Barr laughed. "For trusting us enough to help you. I know what I am and how people see me."

They grasped arms in a friendly shake.

"You've earned our gratitude and respect," Tark said, mirroring the thoughts of every vardikor around them. They nodded in agreement or gave a cheer with raised fists. "If you should ever have need, you've got the blood oath of clan Stonefist."

"And Ireheart!" one shouted.

"Ironbeard as well!"

Dozens of chieftains shouted out their clan's name in pledge of a blood oath to Barr and his friends.

"We'll not soon forget you," Tark said and grinned, "weaver Barr." He looked out at the golems. "Nor you, our new friends, the arachon!" Another cheer went out for the golems. A slight bow of his head to Fluora. "And never will we forget the Matron of Faeronthalsos."

Aren barked, startling the general.

"Aye," Tark said and shook his armor with a chuckle, eyeing the massive war hound that stood taller than he. "You too, friends Aren and Idelle!"

The dwarves all cheered together, raising tankards of ale and spilling foam upon the ground. Portals began to open behind them, panes of silver light like mirrors with no reflection. The arachon saluted farewell and stepped through one at a time. The enormous destroyer headed back to a larger portal, where a circle of travelers wove in unison. Barr conjured the mists, waving goodbye to the dwarves. He was surprised to see so many smile warmly and wave back.

"I wish we could stay longer," he said, as mist rose up about their legs. "The vardikor are renowned for their celebrations."

"Not to worry," Burtok replied. His eyebrows were a bit singed, but his beard was still intact. He winked at Fluora, causing her to giggle. "I'll drink enough for the both of you!"

Hearty laughter followed them into the mists.

*   *   *

It was much later that night when Uinahd stepped through the portal. Travelers, hers included, had already gathered in a circle to the east. Hidden behind a rocky outcropping, they stood upon marshland and could see battles raging across a valley of swamps far below. Orcs and goblins were overrunning the naga, the snakelike race of aquatic hybrids called the rallan.

With the scaled upper body of a humanoid, two arms and a head, nagas possessed the lower half of a giant water snake. They propelled themselves across land and through water with equal speed. Webbed spines ran the length of their backs from head to tail. Thick plates, like flared scales, protected shoulders and chest. While all of them were either of cerulean, coral or a sea green hue, the wide scales across their abdomens were the sandy color of their beaches. Fins, ridges, spines and scales were all highlighted by a myriad of shades, from violet to ruby to citrine to topaz and any number of others that varied by sex and lineage.

Uinahd had been sure to have the archives scoured for every bit of information on all races involved before following through with their plan. It had taken fifteen enchanters almost an entire day to break through the wards protecting Feraesk and find him here at Salianne. Others may have forgotten, if for the moment, that all life was in danger of umbrals from the Dark if Aislin was not returned to the Matron.

The arachon had not.

Lumbering through a gateway, what the travelers had decided to call the larger portals, a destroyer came through to the sound of echoed groaning. Incapable of speech, this was as much as it could manage. Other portals had opened behind Uinahd, and the high marsh was filled with arachon commands.

"We will lead the charge on the revenant," Uinahd said. Her voice was carried to the others in her command through the scry crystal hanging from a silver necklace. "Stay close, but do not interfere with the destroyers."

They had learned much at the battle of Drakanon. Though arachon could not bleed, their stone and runes could be marred or even broken. More than shields and wards were needed for protection. Hundreds of suits of enchanted blue steel plate had been taken from the city armory and refitted. Champions and Protectors alike now wore them, just as arachon wardens had done in the distant past.

No longer part of the protectorate, the arachon had a difficult time relaying orders on the field. It was Eanid, first of their rune crafters, who had come up with the notion of scrying crystals. Somewhat limited for the time being, they could only be used to communicate within one's command. The ultimate goal, however, would be to once again hear and be heard within the protectorate.

"There are many," Kalar noted beside her. He wore the reinforced heavy robes of the ancient enchanters and carried a rune-strewn war staff. "Do we take the Emblem and leave, or do we assist the nagas?"

"That," Qilahd said, "will be up to the nagas." He saw a small gouge in Kalar's neck and healed the bloodstone with a touch of *furie* upon his fingers. "I hope they have more sense than those they face."

Ten destroyers stood ready, as the gateway closed behind them. It looked as if a pane of silver water had evaporated in an instant. Still without names, though a part of the protectorate, each destroyer had a Protector assigned to aid them. Each made of dense granite from the quarries surrounding Dwendorim, they were colorful as they were large. Some were black with cobalt flecks, others pink with gray or dusky white and brown, but each one reflected pale moonlight off their dizzying array of blue steel runes.

The travelers returned to their commands and began to weave. A pallid sphere of light materialized between their hands, as if a miniature of the sun had lost all its color. The light rose up and expanded, reaching out to the other globes. When their edges touched, the spheres joined together. Before long, a single half-shell of light encompassed the arachon army.

"Here we go," Aerahd said to the other eleven in her command, concentrating as she continued to weave.

Uinahd tensed her grip on both swords. "Strength to us all," she said in way of a warrior's prayer.

A whoosh of air silenced the area, a rushing intake that pressed against her body. The sphere of light flared and surrounded her vision in blinding white. When the air and brightness finally settled, she saw they were near the field of battle, on soft and swampy earth behind Feraesk's army.

The arachon immediately charged.

Each command had their orders and the authority to adapt their assault as the situation warranted. Uinahd led hers straight toward the revenant, unmindful of the vegetation and muck that clung to her legs. The swamp did not slow her nor were its noxious gases the slightest of distractions.

Feraesk had the Emblem in hand and was throwing ebon fire with the other. Two battalions of orc heavy infantry on either side of him were being held in reserve, while four companies of archers stood directly in front. Uinahd could see the battle far ahead, where goblin and orc foot soldiers clashed against the frontline of naga vindicators. Goblin cavalry rode upon wolves along the outskirts of each skirmish but as yet had not outflanked their enemy. Naga sorceresses rained violet fire and shards of ice down upon the cavalry, working in tandem with spiritists who conjured creatures of water from the swamp. These elementals formed an impenetrable wall, keeping safe the rallan weavers and priests.

Orcs worked siege engines from the small hills at either side, catapults and ballistae aimed at the rear of the nagas' ranks. Fiery pitch and bolts soared far above the field, over a constant downpour of arrows. The nagas threw spears and used slings to some effect, but their artillery was greatly outmatched. If Feraesk's army was allowed to reach the jade city far off in the distance, it would not withstand a siege.

The arrival of a new army did not go unnoticed. Orcs turned and charged with yells of challenge. The revenant looked back as well, though no emotion could be seen upon his illusory visage. Only a flaring of the two flames that served as his eyes showed any sign of surprise or annoyance.

A dozen orcs cried out and were silenced with a wet and sickening crunch of metal and bone. The destroyer lifted its foot, where orc remains clung to the bottom, and continued its slow march toward Feraesk. Unsure how to stop the colossal statues, orcs struck at the feet to no effect. They were soon met with the cold steel and deadly skill of arachon champions.

Only the revenant's dark magic seemed to harm the destroyers. His black fire and wailing bolts of shadow tore wide gashes in their granite, unmaking wards with the destruction and melting of runes. Enchanters and eldarath fired off magic of their own, scorching orcs in their armor or binding their thick legs with swamp vines come to life.

Two destroyers were still, and a third fell over on its side, crushing orcs and two champions with its bulk. By the time one reached the revenant, Feraesk was backing away. He threw *furie* and swung Aislin in desperation to avoid the massive hand that took hold with unyielding fingers of black granite. Crushing body and heart, with its other hand the giant golem pinched Feraesk's head and pulled. The resulting explosion obliterated both its hands.

Aislin fell to the ground unscathed.

* * *

Barr studied the vision in the fountain outside his home, his eyes tired and brow marred with deep concern for what he saw. The pseudo light of early morn cast the city in a golden haze. Idelle watched from her perch upon the fountain, while Aren stood next to Barr and peered down at the scry.

How's that possible? the hound asked.

Fluora yawned from the doorway and wiped the sleep from her eyes. "How is what possible?"

"Markus," Barr replied, looking even closer at the image as Fluora came over and sat beside him.

Where each death of his revenants had prematurely aged the actor-thief, all signs of withering and wrinkles were now gone. The lustrous sheen of sandy brown had returned to his hair, and no longer did it recede at the temples. His skin was smooth, almost glowing, and his frame exuded the vigor and strength of a young man. In fact, Markus looked even younger than he had when he and Barr first met.

Aside from the newfound youth, he held Luorn in his lap while seated at the council table, leaning his chair against the wall. He wore three other Emblems as plate armor over his leathers, shiny mithrinum pieces that reflected sunlight coming in from the windows. The shin plate was Ghaireuk. How Markus had managed to wrest it from the trolls was beyond Barr's imagining. Caorynor was strapped to his left thigh, and the bracer Amintro adorned his sword arm. A shapeling now, Sera would have given it up freely.

"His spirit... is changed," Fluora said, squinting at the image as if unsure of what she saw. "I think he has been turned, like Asmodan."

Seeing Markus wear the Emblems reminded Barr of his premonition, of the man sheathed in silvery-gold light.

"I should have seen this," Fluora said, reluctantly reaching for her blindfold. Barr stopped her. "What if I am being selfish?"

"You're the least selfish person I know," he said and kissed the back of her hand. "Don't confuse selfish with self-preservation."

He's waiting for you, Idelle noted. *He knows you can see him.*

Barr shifted the scry to show Lorelei, Tuvrin and Seltruin still chained to the tree wall. A shapeling, most likely elven, stood beside each of them, ready to bite at Markus's command.

Aren growled. *Why let us know he has them prisoner like that? Is he hoping we'll just show up and surrender? He's not going to let any of them live.*

"That's the trap," Barr said. "Markus hopes I'll give in, rather than watch my father and friends turned."

"But..." Fluora began, and spoke more softly, "they are already turned. Or at least they are not elven."

"I know. That's my trap within a trap." Barr ended the scry. "This isn't a rescue."

"Are you ready?" Fluora asked gently, all too aware of what might need to be done.

"I have to be."

Fluora nodded, sharing in the sadness he refused to show. "We will be ready as well. Dhar is waiting for me at this very moment."

"Hanar?" Barr asked.

"She is still with the enchanters." Fluora tried to give a smile of reassurance.

Barr stood and secured both kyan. "She's decided then," he said, already feeling the loss of a friend. "I hope it makes her happy." He rubbed Aren behind an ear and smiled up at Idelle. "Be ready when I need you."

Always, Idelle replied.

Mist rose up and engulfed him, carried him through twilight and into the council chamber. He drew a kyan and threw it at Markus. The ironwood blade struck deep into the wall, missing the thief's head by a scant inch. Long strands of sandy hair drifted slowly to the floor.

Markus stood and frowned at the sheared locks. His hair grew back to its former self in an instant. "A simple hello would have sufficed," the thief said and smiled with an air of confidence. He seemed sure he had the upper hand. "Oh, before I forget." He pulled a bag of coins from his belt and tossed it on the table. "The two hundred gold I owe you. Of course, I plan to take it back as soon as I kill you. Again. Do try to stay dead this time, will you?"

"Barr!" Tuvrin called. "This is a trap! You must go!"

Barr ignored his father and pulled the kyan back to his hand by thought alone. The blade nicked Markus on the shoulder on its way back. The thief glared for a brief moment then fell back to his facade of good humor.

Adjusting his vision, Barr studied the divine runes that made Markus who he was. They had definitely been changed. The runes were far more complex than his own and seemed to exist in more than one plane. Barr was certain that if Markus should die, his spirit would be sent to the ether, where it would reform a physical body over time – like a god.

Luckily his plan didn't hinge on Markus dying.

"This isn't going to go how you want," Barr told him plainly and drew the other kyan. He paid no attention to the prisoners or guards. They were a distraction and nothing more. "Leaving yourself open was a mistake."

"Possibly," Markus admitted, "but then again, I am immortal once more. I risk little if by some miracle I cannot kill you. Even the Emblems no longer interest me." He held Luorn at the ready, and a nimbus of black fire surrounded his body. The tree floor beneath his feet began to wither and die. "Still, they have their uses, and it was awfully thoughtful of you to bring me another two. Tell me," he added before Barr could grow angry and attack, "what do *you* risk by being here? This is your last chance... at ascension, at enlightenment. Your string of lives will end here, for there will be no more births upon Taellus or any other world."

A shapeling bit Lorelei on the shoulder, and she cried out in terrible pain. Barr could hear bones crunch beneath its jaws, as she fought in vain to be free of her chains. He turned, and their eyes met. The pleading and accusation he saw in her pained gaze wrenched at his heart.

Markus became a blur, moving across the room in a wispy swarm of black wasps. If Barr hadn't moved at the last moment, Luorn would have skewered his chest.

As it was, he only sustained a shallow cut. Barr swept aside the next attack but immediately felt his body under assault from the black fire around Markus. As if sapping the very life from him, it grayed his skin in splotches that began to open and fester.

Barr kicked him away with enough force to send him sprawling. Markus was up and at him again without pause, shifting back and forth between man and swarm. He heard Lorelei crying as he fought back a blinding series of attacks. Markus was too fast. A dozen cuts ran the length of both Barr's arms and hands, while he had done little more than stab at flesh that became wasps and was whole when it returned.

May I? Uinbro asked beside him.

Before waiting for an answer, the Emblem conjured an image of a woman with dark curls. She was smaller than a human but not so small as a faeron, beautiful beyond compare and had a glow to her skin despite the ghostly form.

Markus paused and backed away. "No! What trickery is this? That is not possible!"

"Vengeance shall be mine," she said to him in illuminairen, her eyes like hard emeralds filled with hate.

"Andara, please! You must listen!" Markus held up a hand to pause her advance. "I had no choice. You do not understand what I have had to sacrifice."

Barr drew *furie* from the shapeling attacking Lorelei and used it to heal his wounds. The wolf fell to its knees, alive but no longer able to move.

Red-hot hands of iron rose up from the tree floor, as if they'd been molded and freshly pulled from the forge. They gripped hold of Markus at each ankle. A hiss of smoke and the scent of burning flesh accompanied his scream. The ghost of Andara moved closer, reaching out a hand to touch him upon a cheek. He slashed at her with Luorn, dissipating the image for a few seconds, but when she returned her face was filled with rage and scorn.

While Markus was distracted, Barr rushed forward and attacked. He scored a cut across a forearm, a stab to the unprotected thigh and a near fatal nick at the throat had it been a finger's breadth to the left. Succumbing to the aura of black fire, Barr was forced to back off and recuperate.

Tuvrin cried out. A shapeling was ravaging his neck and shoulder. "Barr! How could you let this happen to us!" His father struggled against the chains, as dark blood spurted from his wound and gurgled his speech. "How could you let me become one of them..."

Pure light sprang from Markus's bracer and struck Andara, burning away her conjured image like a puddle of water beneath a summer sun. Craggy rocks sprang up from the ground and encased Barr's legs to his knees. Two roots broke free of the tree floor and snared his wrists.

"What is the point of fighting?" Markus asked, his breath again steady. "All of the sylvannis have either been slain or turned. Every elf you ever cared for now wishes you dead."

He walked toward the prisoners, casually stabbing Barr in a shoulder as he passed. He lifted Lorelei's head by the chin and kissed her. Body slumped, she used her chains to pull herself up and kiss him back. With a twist of her wrists, the manacles fell away. She kicked off her foot shackles, kissing Markus more fervently, with feral growls like an animal. She then pushed him away, wiped his blood from her lips and eyed Barr with a hateful grin.

"Did you know," she asked as if talking about events of the day at evening meal, "that I am now First of the Ballar? Poor father had an accident." She pursed her lips in a sorrowful pout then laughed. The sound of it was insidious, a mockery of who she once was. "Seems there have been quite a few accidents since you left. Oh, my apologies. I mean since you were exiled."

Barr's jaw tightened, and *furie* rose within him. A pillar of fire sprang up from his feet and embraced him, like salamanders at play across his body. The rocks fell away from his legs in crumbling char. The roots burst into flames and were incinerated. Lorelei flinched and tried to shield her face from the intense heat. Markus called up shards of ice and a winter gale, but Luorn's magic was overwhelmed before it could even be brought to bear.

"Enough games," Barr said. "It's time we get on with why I'm here."

He crippled Lorelei and the two other shapelings, as well as his father and Seltruin, by wresting *furie* from their bodies by force of will. He took enough to disable them all and heal his wounds, with enough left over to give Markus the shock of his life.

The thief disappeared into a swarm of black. The buzz of his passing ended abruptly, with a kyan through his middle. The fire around Barr had forced Markus to rematerialize or be lost to the flames as so many burned insects. Wasps littered the floor, smoking like embers.

Markus gasped and tried to speak, looked down at the ironwood piercing his insides. Blood fell from his lips, and his own aura seemed to falter. Barr pushed forward with all his might, shoved Markus into the tree wall behind. When he struck, the kyan went firmly in, securing Markus in place. Barr plunged the other kyan just under the left breast and into the tree for good measure.

He missed Markus's heart by half a thumbnail.

Barr pulled a coin-sized step cut sapphire from a pouch inside his belt and held it up between two fingers. He focused upon its surface, seeing deep inside to the glyph he had stored there and set it free with a thought. Runes of gold and silver shot outward, bathing Markus in a shower of intertwining colored light. The runes spun together and formed wards in an instant, clicked and trapped the thief within a holding glyph. Barr pulled free both kyan. They were no longer needed, and the wounds had already been healing around the blades.

He took Luorn from Markus and slipped it into a leather sack at his waist. Though the sack was no longer or wider than two hand spans, the sword disappeared fully inside. Barr took the other three Emblems as well, placed them in the sack and pulled tight its tie strings.

The shapelings began to stir, regaining the strength to move. Barr breathed easier with Markus trapped, but his plan was only half-done.

Bind them, he told Vereu. Iron arms broke through the woven branches and packed earth. They grabbed hold of all six elves at arms, legs and waist. *Barricade the door as well.* Iron spikes as thick as a man shot up from the entryway floor and down from its ceiling, leaving little room to see the corridor beyond. *Bind anyone that reaches that doorway.*

Barr could hear heavy footsteps approaching. Elves soon began to scream, and the distant clash of battle rang out in the hall.

Uinbro chuckled and shrugged at Barr.

"Revyn!" Barr shouted to the heavens, certain the god could hear him and had been watching the entire time. "Face me! Or lose your favorite child and all the Emblems!"

Long moments went by with nothing but snarls and laughter from the bound shapelings, a wry grin from Markus and pounding on the barricaded doorway. Barr let the fire surrounding him fade away.

"I should have expected as much," he said, "from a god so unworthy of devotion that he's forced to steal it from those more deserving."

Markus snickered at that. "Did you hope to goad him out with insults?"

"You have a better idea?"

The thief considered. "You could ask him to step forward." Markus smiled wide, as if this all were part of his trap. He looked over at the six elves bound in iron. "Which one of them do you suppose he is? Maybe you should kill them all, just to be sure."

Lorelei glared at him. "That is *not* what we agreed!"

"Things change," he told her calmly. "You must learn to adapt and improvise, my dear."

Barr already knew it was Seltruin. The old sage had said nothing since Barr arrived. As the only Valar left, he would have fought and died in any uprising against the council. Just as Barr would have. Their eyes locked, and his once mentor gave a cold smile.

"Well done," he said, stood and walked forward. His chains and manacles, the iron hands at his feet, all shattered and fell away like crumbling ash. "You have been a busy little boy." Revyn's body changed in a single step to Barr's mother. She wore a shimmering dress of blue gossamer, her hair tied back with living gems and spiraling water. She looked vibrant, as she had before the umbrals drained her *furie*. "And for what? You failed. Nothing you do now will save your family and friends. Taellus is mine, and the other worlds will soon follow."

Adjusting his vision again, Barr studied the god. The divine runes were so complex that it nearly caused him a headache to look. The wards spun further out than the physical body, revealing a massive shape. The runes too existed on multiple planes, could be seen as transparent wards floating between in faded colors. It left Barr with the notion that Revyn had been created – far more complicated than a mortal but still much the same.

And what had been created could be unmade.

"You're wrong," Barr said calmly and sheathed both his kyan. "There is something I can do that will save everyone." He looked the image of his mother in the face with steadfast resolve. "I can kill you."

Markus and the other shapelings laughed. Revyn merely arched a brow in amusement.

"That is impossible," she said. "I cannot be killed. At best, I can be inconvenienced by the loss of a body, but my spirit is eternal."

"Would I have come alone if I thought otherwise?" It was Barr's turn to smile at the glimpse of uncertainty he spied in the god's visage. "What do you suppose that would be like for you? Do you think you'd be reborn as a mortal? Or would you simply fade away into the ether forever?"

It was clear Revyn was no longer amused. Her eyes burned with a beryl fire behind an angry gaze. With a wave of her left hand, she summoned what revenants remained. They materialized from a buzzing swarm, and the five undead kings of old – Dhalak, Wyllnuor, Caeryk, Khalydaos and Trafaelos – moved towards Barr without hesitation.

It was the moment Barr had been waiting for.

He pulled a handful of gems from his belt pouch, two sapphires, two rubies, three emeralds and a large fire opal. Barr raised his arm and smashed them all against the floor. Colorful shards exploded outward, leaving a trail of *furie* in their wake. A myriad of runes leapt from the fragments in all directions, filling the chamber with sudden light. Runes quickly interlocked, formed wards that raced toward one another and clicked into eight separate glyphs. Those then joined and clicked again, so loud it shook the tree, and a single glyph of unparalleled intricacy took shape. It set the chamber to thrumming with the echoes and vibrations of unbelievable power.

The revenants had stopped in their tracks, frozen in place. Revyn moved about, studying the rune work. She waved a hand, no doubt in an attempt to dissolve the enormous glyph, but nothing happened. She prodded a rune as if to alter its position and was met with a shock that blackened her fingertip. She sucked at the burned digit and considered Barr anew.

Barr grinned in triumph. "And you thought you were laying a trap for me."

"Set me free," Markus pleaded of the god. "Let me be the one to kill him!"

"What happens here is irrelevant." Revyn ignored the bound thief, shifting form to a knight in black plate. His voice rang hollow inside the helm. "In truth, I care little for the Emblems. I only needed one to begin work on a new shapeling – my wrathborn. Even as we speak, the other gods are being turned."

Barr shook his head, trying to comprehend the mad designs of a deity bent on destroying all life.

"You still do not understand," Revyn remarked with a bitter laugh. "It was all a ploy. Your father's death in the woods, your time here with the elves, the running about for useless artifacts... well, almost useless." The god slowly paced the room, studying the glyph further as he spoke. Barr wondered if Revyn had yet surmised its true purpose. "It was all to keep you occupied until the right moment, when entire cities could be turned and overtaken unopposed, when my children could form vast armies across Taellus. They all worship me now. Their devotion grants me power greater than all my brothers and sisters combined." He clenched a gauntleted fist. "Soon they too will bend a knee to my will!"

"Revyn!" Markus snapped, struggling to break free of the glyph. "Quit talking and set me –"

Revyn silence him with a flick of his fingers.

"Since you *are* in such a talkative mood," Barr said and crossed his arms. "Why me?"

"Do you not yet know what you are?" His armor shook with laughter. "Your whole reason for existing, your only purpose in this life, is to *stop me*. But it is too late for that now. I cannot be stopped."

Barr considered but almost immediately tossed aside the idea. Revyn was not to be trusted, not his actions nor his words. Barr was convinced his only lesson in this lifetime was to join together the experiences of his past lives into a single cohesive understanding.

"Why all the scheming?" Barr asked. "Why not just turn or kill me when I was a child?"

"There are rules even I cannot bend."

He was forbidden, Barr realized, *by someone more powerful, someone he fears... the Father God?*

"He knows," was all Barr could say, shocked with disbelief. He began to grow angry. "The Father God, *your* creator, knew what you were doing and did nothing to stop it!"

"Of course he did!" Revyn barked. "He sent *you*! He told me so himself. I was merely not permitted to harm you directly, unless you were to attack me first."

Barr reeled with incredulity. "You've done nothing but harm me my whole life!" He seethed with anger, felt it burning his throat. He wanted to reach out and rend the god limb from limb. "Directly or not, you're to blame for the deaths of nearly every single person I've ever loved or cared for."

Revyn shrugged. "You should thank me. I made you who you are. In any case," he went on, oblivious to the rage overtaking Barr, "Yes, father knows what I intend. It is the downside of free will. Change is inevitable." He stopped his pacing to regard Barr. "And to think I was once concerned over your existence. You cannot begin to imagine the scheming and machinations that centered around you. Pity you proved such a poor adversary." The god clucked his tongue in a *tsk!* "Mortals. You make it all too easy."

Barr narrowed his gaze and drew both kyan. "Well, let's see if I can't make things a little more difficult for you."

The god made no move but waited for Barr to strike, landing a glancing blow across the chest. In that instant, Revyn was free to take Barr's life. Two strange weapons appeared and elongated in his hands. Thin as a staff but longer than a broadsword, they had square double-edged blades on either end a foot long. The weapons looked to be forged of blackened steel, but each blade was a bright and pure emerald. Darker green runes glowed along the surface of either side, casting an eerie haze across the gemstone. Revyn twirled them about his body with such speed and precision that it seemed impossible he didn't injure himself in the process. Barr was hard-pressed to find an opening in the whirl of deadly emerald and was forced to back away.

"Now!" Barr yelled.

Mist erupted behind Revyn, and Fluora attacked the god with both her Emblems. Dhar ran for a window and roared an order in the dragon tongue. Idelle darted in from yet another window, snatched a revenant in her claws and carried the undead king out a window across the way. Aren growled at the immobile shapelings then turned his attention toward Markus. He padded up to the thief and bit deep into a thigh. One pull and the leg was ruined, bleeding out across the floor. The hound left him that way and leapt at Revyn.

The god fought them all off, blocking and evading from all directions. He turned aside Fluora's swords and caught the back of her legs in a twirl, lifting and sending her crashing to the ground. Continuing his spin, he cut Barr across both forearm and thigh, disappeared into a swarm of black as Dhar's blades passed harmlessly by and reappeared behind him with a swipe across his back that cut open the dragon armor and flesh beneath.

Massive claws slipped in and gripped every window of the tree. The heavy beating of wings sent dust flying in eddies, as the chamber was torn apart from both sides. The tree was then exposed, nothing more than splintered wood. Two rounded pieces of wall yet stood, one of which Markus was bound to. The winter sky overhead revealed hundreds of dragons, all circling the tree city. An adult blue swept by and snatched up another revenant. A red soared in from the other direction and did the same. In moments all five were gone.

It was then Barr felt Idelle growing cold. Her breath became ragged, as she fought to take in air too thin to breathe. He felt the feathers of her wings frosting over, stinging the fragile bones underneath. Still she pushed higher. Her vision narrowed to a growing dark. Her heart pounded to near bursting.

That's high enough! Barr shouted at her. *Let him go!*

Revyn kicked Aren across the room, snapping two ribs and forcing air from his lungs. The hound yelped as Idelle passed out and began to fall.

"Dhar!" Barr cried. "Idelle needs help!"

Barr pressed his attack against Revyn, turning the god away from Aren. Fluora struck without relent, using her gift of sight to counter the god's speed. Dhar shouted another roar, this one much different. Barr caught slight variations of inflection and intonation in the prolonged cry.

"Kaolanni will catch her," Dhar promised. He swung both Emblems up and rushed headlong into the fray.

Suddenly Markus was free.

"Finally!" the thief said and threw knives at Barr and Fluora. All were deflected. One even flew back toward him, striking the wall next to his head. "Fine! We do this the hard way!"

Markus drew two knives and walked toward Aren with a deadly intent. His leg was completely healed. The blades grew longer with each step, until they were equal in length to short swords. Aren growled and readied to leap, though his side burned with every breath. Hackles raised, he attacked as Markus brought down both blades at his head.

Buzzing filled the air, and three different swarms of insect took shape as wrathborn. Asmodan, Balizar and Sonneil looked to the skies in unison and leapt after the gathered dragons. They each changed shape the moment their feet left the ground. Massive parodies of the grace and beauty of a dragon, they became winged wraiths of promised destruction. With roars that shook the sky, knocking dragons from their path, the three wrathborn began slaughtering Dhar's kin.

Revyn whirled to face Dhar and became Eoraini. "Are you going to just let them all die?" she demanded. "Help them!"

Dhar was taken aback by the image of his dead mate and hesitated, lowering his guard. He was rewarded with a stab of emerald through his shoulder. It parted armor and bone with ease. When Revyn pulled the blade free, blood spattered across his front. Dhar staggered back and nearly fell from the tree, gripping painfully at the splintered remnants of wall for support.

"And you!" Revyn spun on Fluora, in the guise of Elaedraoni. The Grand Seeress did not look pleased with her daughter. "Drop those swords this instant and act like a Matron!"

Fluora paused, eyes wide behind her blindfold. She almost complied by force of habit. Revyn swarmed to her and bit down on her shoulder. His teeth met unyielding steel beneath her dress. Surprised, he tore away the silken cloth and revealed a plain rounded spaulder. Fluora gave him a sweet smile, as if she had known he would try to bite her at that very spot.

Both Barr's kyan stabbed through Revyn's middle, lifted the god and began slicing upward through flesh and gauzy dress. Barr was careful not to kill the god. He needed Revyn severely weakened but alive for his plan to work.

A crackle of lightning threw all three of them wide. Zilania, Tal, Irin and more than a dozen lesser gods appeared from the astral. They stood between Barr and Revyn. Barr quickly got to his feet, just as Markus was thrown across the chamber. Aren ran after him, a sword stuck in his side.

"OK, I didn't plan for this," Barr said of the lesser gods. *Are you alright?* he asked Aren.

I've been better, the hound replied. *I am having fun with Markus, though.*

I'm back as well, Idelle said, her voice strong in their minds. *I'm trying to help the dragons, but those three... monsters are unstoppable.*

The lesser gods attacked. Two went for Dhar, Tal and three others flew off after dragons, Irin rushed at Fluora and Zilania charged Barr as a wisp of smoke. She swung two black crystal daggers. One he blocked with a kyan, cutting her wrist, but the other bit deep into his side. He felt the crystal break inside him. The goddess smiled at her victory, pulled the dagger free and showed Barr the broken blade. It reformed before his eyes and was whole once again. He felt the piece inside him begin to move, shredding his body from within. It was cutting a path toward his heart.

"Barr!" Fluora shouted, her voice strained with the fear of losing him.

Her fear turned to resolve, hardened into anger in the span of a heartbeat. She sped through the mists, disappeared from where she stood and reappeared with her sword slicing through Zilania's neck. The goddess's head fell away. Her lifeless body fell to its knees and toppled over, releasing her essence back to the ether. Fluora turned on the other gods, seething with the wrath of a protective woman.

Did she just use the mists to attack? Aren asked. Barr was on his knees, fighting to heal the crystal shard out of his body. *Why can't you do that?*

I'm a little busy, Aren!

Fluora became a blur of swirling mist and twirling blades, vanishing into thin air with a burst of cloudy haze and reemerging to strike through smoky vapor. She cut the legs out from one facing Dhar, disappeared in a rising twist of her body and reappeared with a kick across the face of a startled Irin. Dazed, the goddess backpedaled. Fluora vanished and appeared with her sword through Irin's throat. Mist still clung to her arm as she pulled the blade free. Dhar fought off the other god, sustaining a blow to the thigh but delivered a counter that severed the god's hand. Fluora's blades pierced the god's chest, mist falling from their tips, and she returned to Barr's side in an instant.

A silver portal opened near what remained of the council table, where Aren and Markus still circled one another. Hanar stepped through, wielding Faelsha and Aislin. She wore a full suit of blue steel, but the new runes that encompassed her body could still be seen. She moved with incredible speed, took hold of Markus and tossed him across the chamber.

More arachon stepped through, one after another, in a continuous line of living statues. Hanar called over an eldarath to heal Aren. Champions rushed forward to deal with the other gods, while enchanters began to weave a maelstrom of fire.

Barr's hand glowed with the *furie* of a ley line far below. He'd never expended so much energy healing a single wound. He forced the crystal back down toward the opening in his flesh. It fell to the ground and broke apart.

"Are you well?" Fluora asked. She knew what the crystal shard had been doing inside him.

"Yes, I'll be fine." He gave a weak smile. "Thanks to you."

She helped him to his feet. Barr looked at the silver portal, at the arachon coming through and caught sight of Hanar.

She's different, Aren said, *like the others.*

Barr couldn't help but feel a pang of sadness at her transformation. He put those feelings aside and glanced at Revyn. The god was down on all fours, once again a black knight. Sparks of blue lightning ran the length of his body. He raised his head and looked around at the glyph encircling what was left of the chamber. Another jolt knocked him over on his side. Tendrils of smoke rose up from his scorched armor.

Revyn's helm turned toward Barr.

"I think Revyn just figured out he can't leave," Barr said, gauging a path to the god through all the fighting. Revyn placed a hand over the gashes in his armor, and the gauntlet began to glow a bright emerald. "We need to move before he heals."

A red landed and took hold of Revyn, pinning him to his back and leaning down in a crushing grip. Liquid fire fell from the dragon's maw, scorching the tree floor and Revyn's armor. He looked as if he intended to loose his breath upon the god.

"Khrona, don't!" Barr shouted and ran toward them. "We need him alive!"

"How *dare* you address me by my familiar name!" The Emissary's eyes widened at the lack of due respect, and the spines along his neck flared in anger.

"Emissary," Dhai called out weakly but could not be heard over the din of battle. "Khrona, wait..."

"So help me, if you don't let him go," Barr warned, gathering *furie* from the ley line until it glowed about his body like a golden aura, "I will kill you myself."

Khrona reared back to breathe fire at Barr.

Barr reached out and grabbed the air with an open hand, as if clutching the dragon's throat. A giant hand of golden *furie* gripped Khrona by the neck, cutting off any attempt to breathe fire or take in air. Khrona let go his hold upon Revyn and was lifted off the ground. Barr swung his arm to the right, and the golden hand tossed Khrona like a rag doll. The Emissary flew across and through the tops of Geilon-Rai, tearing apart branches and whole trees for a thousand feet.

Revyn leapt up and took Barr from behind in a firm hold around the neck. He held one of Markus's knives poised to strike.

"You should have let the dragon kill me," he said in a gloating tone.

Barr placed a hand on Revyn's arm. "But then how would I have been able to do this?"

He brought them both into the mists, held open the rift to the Dark and slipped free of Revyn's grasp. With a shove to the god's middle, Barr sent him toward the rift. Revyn barely touched against the inky void, but it was enough to preclude any hope of escape. The Dark began pulling him in. Eyes wide in panic, as he disappeared slow inch by inch, the god looked at Barr as if he were insane.

"Do you have any idea what you have just done?!" Revyn struggled against the inexorable pull, flailing his arms in a vain attempt to grasp Barr. Frantic, the god said, "You fool! You damned mortal fool! You just upset the balance!" Little of him was left. Bit by bit the Dark was claiming him whole. "Do you know what this will mean?!"

"Freedom from your disease," Barr replied coolly, "for everyone you've infected with your touch. It means the death of a god is not so impossible after all."

"Death..." Revyn's laughter was cut short, as the Dark engulfed his helm. Nothing of him remained.

Barr closed the rift and returned to Geilon-Rai.

– 20 –

Eldarath were healing dragons on the forest floor. Of those that had survived the fight, their wounds ranged from severe to near fatal. Some would never fly again. Far too many had made the ultimate sacrifice for the freedom of Taellus. By the conclave's accounting, over a hundred had been slain outright. Another fifty would die of their wounds. The damage was just too much for the healers, both dragon and arachon, to manage and still save others more likely to survive. Many ancient and noble houses had been lost forever, gone with the deaths of their last scions.

The sylvannis were in just as bad a state. Many had been crushed or burned alive during battle, from dragon breath and wayward magic raining down upon the city. Those deaths, however, paled in comparison to the loss sustained during the attack from Alixhir. More than a thousand elves had been slain before their dark brethren from Tehkon-Rai, the shamarrin, arrived. Assaulted on all sides, the human army had never stood a chance. Within minutes they had been utterly destroyed. The same had been true of the orc tribe guarding the eastern path.

"A full third of our nation," Tuvrin explained, forcing the words out through his grief. "So many are now gone, Seltruin, Roedric, almost the entire council... I fear we may never recover. Barr," he seemed near to breaking, "all our children, *every* one of them –"

He could not finish the thought.

Barr hugged his father, sharing his pain. Though tears would not come, he felt keenly the loss of any elf, like an empty chasm in his middle. There were few he considered friends, but over his time with the sylvannis, they had all become his family. He knew their names, their faces, their worries and needs. For most of his life, it had been his duty to care for them.

The pens are empty, Aren said from below. He could barely think, let alone move. *They're all gone.*

Aren, Idelle began, but her voice became choked. It didn't matter. No words could undo the loss of so many companions.

"I must go," Tuvrin said, fighting down his sorrow. It was the elven way. "There is much to be done." He took Barr by the shoulders and gave a nod. "Consider your exile lifted. You may come and go as you please. In fact I am counting on it. Your people need you now more than ever, Sage Barr."

His father turned and walked away, waving the other elves to follow. They headed out into the corridor and continued on until Barr could no longer see them.

Lorelei touched his hand. He hadn't noticed until then that she'd been standing beside him. She was still just as beautiful as he remembered. When their eyes met, tears she'd been holding back slipped down her cheeks. She embraced him as if he'd never left.

"The things I said," she sobbed. "The things I did..."

Barr tried to comfort her, but no words would come. How do you console someone who most likely killed her own father?

Fluora cleared her throat.

He gently eased Lorelei away. "I'd like you to meet Fluora, my intended. This is Lorelei. We were... friends, before my exile."

"A pleasure to make your acquaintance," Lorelei said awkwardly. She briefly looked at Fluora and turned her eyes away. "I am glad Barr has found someone to share his life with."

"He has much to do," Fluora said in a critical tone, "before he earns my hand, but things do seem a bit promising." Lorelei caught the faint smile. The two girls shared in a small laugh at Barr's expense. When their merriment ceased, Fluora sighed and her voice grew solemn. "It will be quite some time before those who were infected come to grips with what they were forced to witness and do at Revyn's bidding. Do not torture yourself with recrimination. I can promise you that any blame falls squarely upon the god."

"And him," Dhar said and glared at Markus. Though the revenants had all been slain, the thief yet lived. He still appeared young as well. "Shall we kill him now?"

"My," Markus said, "but you do hold a grudge." He stood between two champions but was not restrained. "I have lost my revenants, my immortality and any power

I had, short-lived as it was. What more would you take from me? What good could come from my death?"

Dhar shrugged. "It would make *me* feel better."

"What of you?" the thief asked Barr. "Would you see me dead now that I am helpless?"

Barr stepped close to him, and Markus backed away ever so slightly. "I still remember what you said to me. *'Never leave an enemy behind.'* It's beginning to sound like good advice." Barr put a hand to the pommel of a kyan. Markus stiffened, as if expecting to die, but visibly relaxed when Barr let out a breath and shook his head. "There's been too much death already. I won't take any more lives today."

"Wonderful!" Markus beamed. "Does this mean I am also free to –"

The tip of a sword poked through his chest, with a tendril of mist clinging to its end. Barr knew immediately the heart had been severed. Markus collapsed to the floor, eyes wide in shock and choking on his own blood. Fluora stood over him with a hard look to her face, her blade stained a bright crimson. She stepped over the dying thief, took Lorelei by the hand and walked away from the spreading nimbus of blood.

"Barr," Markus rasped, growing deathly pale as he bled out. "You could heal me..."

"You're right." Barr nodded. "I could."

Both he and Dhar turned and headed after the girls.

"You were amazing earlier," Lorelei was saying when they caught up. "Do you think you could teach me to fight as you do?"

"You can't do that anymore," Barr said to Fluora. "No one can ever again use the mists. There's no telling if Revyn can come through a rift the way the umbrals do."

Fluora slowly frowned. "You are right, of course. I should have known that." She looked as if still wrestling with the idea that her people would never again traverse the mists. It was a gift they had paid dearly for, Barr's mother especially. Without the mists, life on Faeron would never again be the same. Barr could feel the sadness overtake her, as Fluora shut tight her eyes behind the blindfold. A few moments later she relaxed. "It is done. None but I may enter." She glanced past him to Hanar. "I suppose that means I will not need Aislin after all."

"Speaking of which," Barr said and pulled the sack from his belt, "I'm going to need the Emblems from both of you."

You plan to hide us away again, Uinbro appeared and said. Barr nodded. *I see. At least this time we will have each other for company.* Uinbro smiled and winked. *You have been a most admirable wielder. I hope one day we shall meet again.*

No offense, Barr replied, *but I hope that won't be any time soon.*

Fluora gave Barr an odd look and handed him both Emblems.

Idelle asked, *Are you talking to those swords again? It's very impolite!*

Don't worry. Barr placed each Emblem into the sack. *You won't be seeing them again for a long time.* Dhar handed his over as well. Both went into the sack. Barr then placed Uinbro and Vereu inside and turned around to look for Hanar.

"How did you do that?" Lorelei asked.

"Yes," Dhar said, "I could use a few bags like that myself. If the opening was wider, I could store my armor inside."

Barr caught Hanar's attention. She finished talking to three arachon, an eldarath and two enchanters, then came over to join them. She put a hand to his cheek and smiled.

"I see you are well, Master."

"Master?" Barr blinked. "With all the new runes, I thought you –"

"I could never give up my family," Hanar said. Barr wasn't sure if she meant the protectorate or himself – possibly both. "I will always be your Protector."

That filled Barr with such happiness that it nearly brought him to tears. "I wouldn't have it any other way. But what about the changes? You look like the others, like an arachon."

"Improvements," she said proudly.

Dhar and Fluora chuckled at that and seemed glad their friend had not been changed after all.

"I'm going to need the Emblems," Barr told her. "I think it best if we hide them away again."

Hanar nodded. "They are very powerful," she said and handed over both her swords, "and wise. So much power and knowledge should be carefully guarded."

With both Emblems in the sack, Barr pulled the tie strings and held it out to Fluora.

"What do I do with it?" she asked.

"Hide it somewhere or somewhen, so that no one can ever find them." Barr looked grave. "Not even me."

"I understand." Fluora accepted the leather sack, seemed surprised at how light it was, and added, "I have the perfect place in mind."

"I should be going," Dhar said. "The others will need my guidance for a time. Of all that has happened this day, the memory that will forever be etched in my mind is you throwing Khrona halfway across the city."

Dhar smiled and started to walk away.

"Revyn was wrong," Barr called after. "He said my sole purpose in this life was to stop him. If that was true, I would have ascended when I pushed him into the Dark."

"Maybe you did not stop him," Dhar shrugged and kept walking, talking back over a shoulder, "but only contained him. Then again, it is more likely he simply lied."

Dhar leapt from the tree and rose up as a dragon before flying off into the distance.

"Maybe." Barr didn't seem convinced.

Uinahd approached with another arachon, a jade traveler. Barr thought it odd that he could now tell them all apart at a glance. It seemed the more he adjusted his vision and studied the divine runes all around, the more he understood about a great many things.

"Would you like to use a portal back to Dwendorim?" Uinahd asked. "We have one prepared."

"Thank you," Barr replied, "but I don't think that will be necessary."

He adjusted his vision, reached out and gathered empty runes to form a rift. A touch of *furie* from his own essence, and the runes filled enough to activate a glyph. An opening appeared before them, like a wide doorway with hazy edges. The fountain outside Barr's home in Dwendorim could be seen on the other side. The cobbles leading up to the rift, the sound of water splashing down over the fountain, all of it looked as real as the chamber they stood in.

"It's not a portal," Barr explained. "It's a rift, a tear between planes. You can put one foot down on that cobble and be in both Geilon-Rai and Dwendorim at the same time."

Fluora stepped up and studied it closer. "When did you learn to do this?"

"I don't know." Barr looked at the rift as if trying to understand it himself. "It just sort of came to me as I was watching Revyn disappear into the Dark. The rifts that open in the mists are a lot like this one."

"Is that wise?" Lorelei asked. "Considering what you just said about Revyn coming back through a rift."

Barr stepped through and looked back at them. "As long as I don't open one to the Dark, there shouldn't be any problem."

Lorelei and Fluora exchanged worried glances.

Come on Aren, Barr said. *It's time to go home.* Idelle flew into the rift and landed on the fountain's statue. Barr crossed his arms and looked at Fluora. "Are you going to stand there all day, or are you coming?"

She looked back through her blindfold with a frown.

"I am still considering."

*   *   *

While Protectors had always tended to the farms and fisheries, gardens and groves, none of them possessed the advanced knowledge of their forebears. Agriculture, horticulture, aquaculture and husbandry were specific fields of expertise among the arachon. At best, Protectors served as workers with little understanding as to why or how their tasks proved successful.

That is, until Hanar.

She was the first to be given focus, a set of particular skills and abilities intended to aid her in a new role in arachon society. She had chosen to become an arbiter, one of twenty representatives that would create laws for the betterment of all, adapt those laws as needed and uphold them when one had been broken. The concept of individuality brought with it unforeseen side effects that would not exist in a hive mind like the protectorate.

Others had chosen from a multitude of possibilities, specializing in crafts both exotic and mundane. Eager to take a place among their resurrected culture, Protectors were lined up out the door of every shaper's workshop. Oath intact, equipped with knowledge from the library archives and university, armed with newly forged tools from the smithies, arachon craftsmen had been working tirelessly.

Barr and Fluora sat at their kitchen table, literally enjoying the fruits of that labor. Renahd, one of the first horticulturalists, had discovered a seed cache hidden away on the bottom levels of the university. Overnight, the gardens were flourishing with fruits and vegetables unseen in Dwendorim for centuries. Watermelon, figs, tangerines, bananas and golden apples were just a taste of what was to come. As the only ones in the city able to eat, aside from the five demon hunters brought back from Danarriden by travelers, a constant stream of food was delivered to Barr's door.

Hanar had mentioned earlier a decision made by the assembly, the collective group of arbiters, to invite other races – the faeron, sylvannis and vardikor in particular – to come live in Dwendorim among the arachon. Barr had thought it a wonderful idea, especially now that humans knew elves still existed and where to find the tree city. He had even asked if he might borrow a classroom at the university to train sages for each of the elven nations.

Will they rebuild Geilon-Rai? Aren asked. He was outside lying beneath a tree. He hadn't eaten breakfast and showed no interest in lunch. *Or move somewhere new?*

Barr knew what he was really asking. *I imagine so. I wouldn't be surprised if they asked you to help.*

Help with what?

Umm, well, they're going to need new companions. Barr thought on how young Aren was. War hounds lived three times the lifespan of a human and matured at a slow pace. Neither of them had ever before discussed physical relations, and he wasn't sure if Aren had yet felt the urge. *Despite what you saw, my father said hounds and bears did survive. You're one of the largest the Ballar have ever seen. It makes sense they would want you... to...*

Fluora giggled at his discomfort. "He will figure it out on his own."

Don't be so sure, Idelle remarked playfully. *He may be big, but he wasn't the brightest of his litter.*

Aren snorted, and a pile of leaves scattered before him. *I don't know what you're talking about, but I can tell you're making fun. Cut it out, or I'll eat the both of you.* He looked up at his sister flying overheard. *Starting with you.*

You'd have to catch me first!

"Have you been seeing anything?" Barr asked. It had been some time since Fluora complained of a headache, and the blindfold seemed to rein in her sight. He knew that she took it off now and again, testing her limits or just afraid she might miss something important. "How are people coping with all the loss and destruction?"

Fluora put down her fork and looked grave. "Not very well. Grief has overwhelmed many into moods so dark they do not move for hours, eat or sleep. Others have chosen to take their own lives rather than face what they have done." She shook her head, fighting back emotions remembered from her visions. "There is so much sorrow and despair, with so little hope. I do not know how or if the survivors will ever forgive themselves."

"That is the key, isn't it?" A memory sparked in his mind, of a story his mother had once told. "Forgiveness will set him free." Barr pushed his chair back and stood with a look of resolve. "There's something I need to do. I'll be back before dinner."

He kissed her and went outside. He glanced at the fountain but knew he would never be able to scry out someone he had never met or even seen before. Instead, he went to the park, where the nearest ley line was the strongest. He knelt and placed both hands on the grass, reached down into the river of liquid *furie* with his mind. Deep into the veins of the world, where life was carried back and forth from the Dark, he sent his consciousness outward in search of a living statue.

Unlike the arachon, this one was not shaped from stone and given life but was born flesh and cursed with the wrath of a scorned mother. Recalling the story, Barr realized Nedryn would be awake. It was only by night that he slept as a statue.

Unsure what to look for, with only a brief description from his mother's story, Barr let himself float out among the ley lines across Taellus. Like existing in a hundred places at once, sensations washed over him that were difficult to sort out. At first he could not distinguish the differences between animal or man, bird or insect, tree or plant. The more he opened himself up, the longer he persisted to follow the flowing lines, the easier it became to recognize and understand what he was sensing.

Whenever he reached the Dark, he let go that strand of consciousness and started it anew. At first he had thought it dangerous to stay too long. In the past, his body had come perilously close to being consumed. By focusing his intent, he was able to keep at bay the influx of *furie*, to find a balance, a rhythm, a give and take with the natural flow. He wasn't sure how much time had passed. It was difficult to gauge while the ley lines sustained him. He felt no fatigue, no hunger or thirst, only life in all its facets in every corner of the world.

There.

His spirit halted and rejoined, converged at the spot. It was a rocky outcropping surrounded by the ebb and flow of a forest. Trees rolled over the hillsides, beneath the canopy of night. The stone ledge was worn by years of coarse scales dragged across its surface. Its sides were covered in a layer of dark moss. Yellow mountain grass sprouted up through the cracks between rocks, and the biting scent of mint wafted up from below.

The wyvern did not stir. As if carved of the very stone upon which it stood, every painstaking detail highlighted by silver moonlight, it looked as if born of the mountain. Wings wide and swept back, hooked tail stretched out and poised to strike, it was menacing as it was beautiful. A kindred spirit of dragons, the far smaller wyverns were graceful and feral creatures. Barr could sense nothing more dangerous than a stag for fifty miles. The wyvern would not have allowed such trespass upon its territory.

A stand of trees above the outcropping granted full view. Barr went to gather a few things and opened a rift beside the statue. He placed a package in plain sight and opened another rift to the trees above. Hiding among the bushes and quiet shadows, he looked down at his father.

"I forgive you," he whispered.

Though Nedryn stood a hundred feet away, Barr's words had an immediate effect. The stone cracked in fine lines of spider web fissures, rippling the wyvern's body as if shedding its skin. The stone crumbled into motes of gray pebbles and dust, revealing a man on all fours. He was young with dark hair, fit and well-tanned.

As if waking from a nightmare, naked and confused, Nedryn jumped to his feet and looked around. He felt his chest, his arms, like a man unsure of what he was – or had been. He studied the ledge, looked down at a steep trail leading up to where he stood and turned his eyes toward the stars.

"I'm sorry," he said quietly. He waited, looking about for whoever had set him free. After moments of silence, he threw his head back and shouted at the stars. "I'm sorry!"

Breathing heavy and shaking from the cold, Nedryn caught sight of the package against a rock. He walked over and picked it up, untied the leather straps and unfolded a deerskin coat. Inside were clothes, linen pants and a shirt, a belt and simple shoes. A small sack of coins fell to the ground, breaking the night's silence with a *clink!*

"Daesi?" his father asked, eyes searching in the dark. His voice betrayed the hope she was there.

Barr wasn't sure what else he could do. There was no bringing Nedryn to Dwendorim or even revealing he could weave. His father was so afraid, so mistrusting of other races and magic, he had abandoned his only son in a foolish hope the child would be raised by humans and not faeron.

No, there might be a time in the future when Barr would try to talk with his natural father, but that time was not tonight. There was only so much forgiveness in his heart.

"I'm sorry too," Barr whispered.

"Daesi, please," his father pleaded to the empty air. "Will you just come out and talk to me?"

Barr opened a rift and stepped through.

*   *   *

Saernol waited for the others to arrive. She had felt it the moment her brother Revyn was taken by the Dark. In truth, none of them really knew what it was. Of them all, Laeryk had a better understanding of things, but the Dark was part of a cycle, a magical cycle. Of magic, no one knew more than herself.

She knew the Dark replenished spent magic in this realm, what they had euphemistically called the Light when creation was new. They themselves were but newly born, made of the father. Free to create life, to fashion worlds for it to dwell upon, what the children gods knew they had learned by trial and error.

A great many things already existed when they had first awoken: countless galaxies, stars and planets, all of which they assumed had been created by father; the astral, where they had been born and resided – a plane superimposed on the physical realm; the ether, where life was made anew – a plane between planes; and the spring, so high its source could not be seen or reached – its constant flow of pristine water fell down into the astral and on through to the physical realm.

They had quickly learned there was another...
place, another universe and one opposite to their own.
There had been signs of it all around, in each task
undertaken. They had seen spent runes flow through a
ley line and into the Dark, only to return fully restored
in another line. Creation was taxing, not for the
expense of *furie*, but for the balance they could not see,
only feel. It was a natural equilibrium, an inherent
counterforce to their will. It had pushed against every
effort they made, as if creating was anathema to its
existence.

Though she had no proof, Saernol believed the
Light and Dark were parts of the father, that each
universe was a half of the same whole. While the Dark
kept in check what they were able to fashion, she felt
certain it was they who held at bay what the Dark
represented: the ruin of all creation. It was death,
decay, merciless entropy given substance. It tainted
their creations, was the reason their first children had
been immortal but could die by violence. It granted *furie*
but consumed, like a steady stream eating away at a
mountain. Left to its own devices, it would devour
everything, dismantling the Light until all that
remained was an empty void. It was their combined
will, their very existence, that bolstered the Light and
provided counterbalance to the destructive nature of
the Dark.

That balance was now irrevocably altered.

"Sister," Laeryk said with respect, his cowl dipping
in a bow. He took a seat at the table, adjusted his robes
and patiently waited.

Saernol tapped her polished nails against the wood.

A burst of sunlight, and Balsina was in a chair
beside Laeryk. "I trust I am not late?"

"No," Saernol replied, "but neither are you early."

Curoch, Celene and Wynter arrived, took their seats and said appropriate greetings. A few minutes passed in idle chatter before Kraug and Veralnon showed up, then another before Kierna stepped through a splash of ocean water.

"Has anyone heard from Unther or Herne?" Saernol could not sense them in the astral, nor could she feel them on Taellus.

"Last I heard," Kraug replied, tugging at his beard, "they were assisting Tempas with a, err... task."

"Please!" Wynter scoffed. "Mortal weavers could hear that *task* from halfway across the world! If you ask me, they are in hiding."

Celene chuckled. "From what?"

A cautious glance Saernol's way, he added, "I would rather not say."

Veralnon and Kraug laughed at that, both of them sounding like the tumbling of stones. Balsina rolled her eyes at the nonsense, as if her time were more precious than the same banter they had heard for millennia.

"I cannot sense them," Laeryk said curiously.

"Nor I." Curoch looked concerned.

Saernol leaned forward in her seat. "We will have to speak with them later. Time is pressing. I have called this little meeting to discuss what has transpired."

Kierna arched a brow. "You mean the well-deserved destruction of our brother? He was turning gods! Good riddance, I say."

"My children," Celene began, her voice no longer joyful. "How could we have let that go on for so long?"

"We each took an oath," Laeryk reminded them. "The entire point was to let things go on."

"He saved us," Balsina said with no apology in her tone. It was clear she did not mourn her brother. "That single mortal saved us all."

"Yes," Saernol agreed sardonically, "he saved our home from rats by burning it down. Do you not see what he has done?" She held up a hand to stave off any more caustic remarks. "He has caused an imbalance that we cannot undo!" The goddess looked at each of them, her eyes betraying anxiety. "I fear all may be lost."

"I disagree," Laeryk said with calm. "I believe balance will return of its own accord. Do you think it coincidence mortals can create gods by faith alone, by the mere act of worship?"

"Proof enough that we are needed," Saernol replied evenly. "Our children must be prepared for what will come."

Kraug cleared his throat and asked, "Just what is it you propose, that we forsake our oath?"

Her silence indicated exactly that.

"We cannot!" Curoch was infuriated by the idea.

"Why not?" Kierna shot back. "Should we be bound by it for all eternity, no matter what occurs? We cannot afford to be so inflexible!"

"I must agree," Celene put in. "Our children need us now more than ever. To do nothing would be as cruel as anything Revyn inflicted upon them."

Laeryk said, "Children must be allowed to falter in order to learn. They handled this situation on their own, and they will do so again *if* anything should occur."

"No." Veralnon was often the quiet one. The God of Mountains, he frequently stood back and listened. When he spoke, all eyes were upon him. "I love my children, from the first titan I molded to the beings they have become over time. I cannot, will not, bear more needless death."

"As of this moment," Saernol said with firm resolve, "I forsake my oath. I would ask that you do the same, for the well-being of all our children. Curoch, how many of your dragons died because of Revyn? How many more will perish on his return?"

"Breaking an oath," Curoch replied and shook his head, "goes against my very nature."

"Leave pride behind," Balsina advised. "Think only of what is best for them, not for you."

Kierna was decided. "I forsake my oath."

"I forsake my oath," Celene said shortly after.

A ray of sunlight appeared in Balsina's hand and went out like a snuffed candle as she closed it. "I forsake my oath as well."

"Right then!" Wynter cracked his knuckles. "I refuse to be outdone by a bunch of women. I forsake my oath!" He muttered, "Father have mercy on us."

Veralnon slammed a fist down on the table, sending cracks along the wood. "I forsake my oath. I will face any punishment he deems fit."

"Oi," Kraug muttered. "I knew I should have brought a keg. Right or wrong, I will always stand by the lot of you." He gave Curoch a comforting pat on the shoulder. "I forsake my oath."

"I am sorry," Curoch said and lifted his eyes to the clear and dark blue of the astral. "I forsake my oath."

Laeryk stood and walked away without a word. He vanished as he passed the first column. His decision had been evident from the start.

An ominous rumbling rang out across the astral, a place where no storm had ever formed. It grew louder, closer, shook the table and sent cracks along the tiles and rows of columns. Lightning flashed all around them, crackling through the air in luminescent flashes of blue and white. The scent of ozone overwhelmed all else, and the very air seemed alive with a growing charge.

The hair on Saernol's arm began to rise. She looked up at the others, eyes wide in fear, as lightning struck and engulfed all eight deities.

When the light faded from her eyes and the ringing in her ears subsided enough to allow thought, Saernol found herself in a forest upon Taellus. The others were with her, looking just as confused and disoriented by the strike. She looked ahead and blinked, as if deceived by her own eyes.

Seated at a campfire, roasting two hares on a spit, were Unther and Herne. Both looked worn and tired, their hands and faces stained by earth. She was not sure which was more surprising, that they should find both gods here or that they were actually... dirty.

"Just in time," Herne said pleasantly. He looked like any other human. "These are about done, and we have another four cleaned and ready to be roasted."

"I suggested a second fire," Unther said, turning the spit, "but neither of us felt up to gathering more wood."

An empty, lonely silence crashed down on her mind. There were no voices of prayer. All she could hear were her own thoughts. The quiet was maddening! Her bones began to ache, a dull throbbing from within she could feel with every heartbeat. Each movement strained her muscles, as if they burned and begged for rest. The chill of a winter wind blew through her, prickling skin and causing her to shiver. Worst of all, the most awful sound began to rattle in her stomach. Pain wracked her middle with a hollow twisting.

Saernol looked to the others and saw they fared no better. All of them were shaken by the cold and sudden shock. Realization dawned, forcing its way up from the haze that clouded her mind. Her hands began to shake, and she stared down at them as if they were not her own.

"He made us *mortal*," she said in disbelief.

About the Author

J.A. Giunta has been writing for most of his adult life, in between bouts of serious online gaming. Though self-published, he perseveres in the hope of drawing a wider audience and a publisher. He continues to write fantasy novels, in both adult and young adult genres, in his selfish need to create worlds that amuse him. That others might enjoy the work is a happy coincidence but one that he fully appreciates.

With a Bachelor of Arts in English from the Arizona State University, he is both an avid reader and addicted gamer. He writes novels full-time and longs for the day when those efforts pay some bills – seriously, even just one bill would be nice. For those of you who purchased copies of any of his books, he is eternally in your debt. Note: this is not a legally binding contract.

He lives with his wife, Lori – who is not only a doctor of both internal medicine and psychiatry, she's *also* an avid gamer! His daughter, Ada Rose, is only five years of age at the time of this writing. She hasn't quite broken into online gaming, but she has commandeered his Xbox 360. They all live happily ever after in the perpetual summer that is central Arizona (technically there is a winter, for about three weeks in January).

Joe attributes much of his success in life to good looks, incredible talent, luck, modesty, air conditioning, friends & family and his DVR – though not necessarily all in that order. Oh, and his computer.

He hopes you enjoyed this book immensely and will either share it with a friend or write to your favorite publisher of fantasy and inquire as to why they have not yet taken notice of this man!

Please visit Joe online at www.jagiunta.com.